Congratulations to

Alexandra Kleeman

Winner of the

2016 Bard Fiction Prize

Alexandra Kleeman, author of *You Too Can Have
a Body Like Mine*, joins previous winners
Nathan Englander, Emily Barton, Monique Truong,
Paul La Farge, Edie Meidav, Peter Orner,
Salvador Plascencia, Fiona Maazel, Samantha Hunt,
Karen Russell, Benjamin Hale, Brian Conn,
Bennett Sims, and Laura van den Berg.

The Bard Fiction Prize is awarded annually to a
promising emerging writer who is an American citizen
aged thirty-nine years or younger at the time
of application. In addition to a monetary award
of $30,000, the winner receives an appointment
as writer in residence at Bard College for one semester
without the expectation that he or she will teach
traditional courses. The recipient will give at least one
public lecture and meet informally with students.

For more information, please contact:

Bard Fiction Prize
Bard College
PO Box 5000
Annandale-on-Hudson, NY 12504-5000

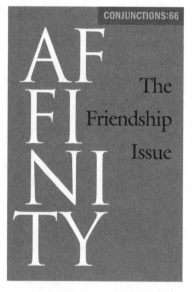

CONJUNCTIONS

Bi-Annual Volumes of New Writing

Edited by
Bradford Morrow

Contributing Editors
John Ashbery
Martine Bellen
Mei-mei Berssenbrugge
Mary Caponegro
Brian Evenson
William H. Gass
Peter Gizzi
Robert Kelly
Ann Lauterbach
Norman Manea
Rick Moody
Howard Norman
Karen Russell
Joanna Scott
David Shields
Peter Straub
John Edgar Wideman

Published by Bard College

EDITOR: Bradford Morrow
MANAGING EDITOR: Micaela Morrissette
SENIOR EDITORS: Benjamin Hale, Joss Lake, J. W. McCormack, Edie Meidav, Nicole Nyhan, Pat Sims
COPY EDITOR: Pat Sims
ASSOCIATE EDITORS: Jedediah Berry, Wendy Lotterman
PUBLICITY: Darren O'Sullivan, Mark R. Primoff
EDITORIAL ASSISTANTS: Matthew Balik, Elena Botts, Rebecca Brill, Laura Farrell, Benjamin Malinski, Sophia O'Brien-Udry, Zoe Rohrich, Anna Sones, Natasha Wilson-McNair

CONJUNCTIONS is published in the Spring and Fall of each year by Bard College, Annandale-on-Hudson, NY 12504.

This issue of *Conjunctions* is made possible with the generous support of the National Endowment for the Arts and of the New York State Council on the Arts with the support of Governor Andrew Cuomo and the New York State Legislature.

SUBSCRIPTIONS: Use our secure online ordering system at www.conjunctions.com, or send subscription orders to CONJUNCTIONS, Bard College, Annandale-on-Hudson, NY 12504. Single year (two volumes): $18.00 for individuals; $40.00 for institutions and non-US. Two years (four volumes): $32.00 for individuals; $80.00 for institutions and non-US. For information about subscriptions, back issues, and advertising, contact us at (845) 758-7054 or conjunctions@bard.edu. *Conjunctions* is listed and indexed in Humanities International Complete and included in EBSCO*host*.

Editorial communications should be sent to Bradford Morrow, *Conjunctions*, 21 East 10th Street, 3E, New York, NY 10003. Unsolicited manuscripts cannot be returned unless accompanied by a stamped, self-addressed envelope. Electronic and simultaneous submissions will not be considered. If you are submitting from outside the United States, contact conjunctions@bard.edu for instructions.

Cover design by Jerry Kelly, New York. Cover art by Desiree Des (desireedes.com). *Subway Wall*, 2013. Digital photograph from the series *Avoiding the Self-Portraits*. © Desiree Des 2015; all rights reserved by the artist.

Conjunctions e-books of current and selected past issues are distributed by Open Road Integrated Media (www.openroadmedia.com/conjunctions) and available for purchase in all e-reader formats from Amazon, Apple, B&N, Google, Indiebound, Kobo, Overdrive, and elsewhere.

Retailers can order print issues via Ubiquity Distributors, Inc., www.ubiquitymags.com, 607 Degraw Street, Brooklyn, NY 11217. Telephone: (718) 875-5491. Fax: (718) 875-8047.

Printers: Edwards Brothers Malloy, Circle Press

Typesetter: Bill White, Typeworks

ISSN 0278-2324

ISBN 978-0-941964-81-4

Manufactured in the United States of America.

TABLE OF CONTENTS

SLEIGHTS OF HAND:
THE DECEPTION ISSUE
Edited by Bradford Morrow

EDITOR'S NOTE

WE ALL DECEIVE, whether or not we care to admit it—denial often being yet another form of deception. We deceive others as well as ourselves. People of every age and stripe—whether rarely or often, on purpose or unknowingly—dissimulate, exaggerate, bluff, and beguile. Sometimes our deceptions are meant to protect, to shelter, to spare; sometimes they're meant to harm. Nature is no stranger to deception, as flora and fauna use wily camouflage to confuse prey and avoid predators. Art itself, from fiction to film, from theater to painting, often relies on aesthetic subterfuge. Then there's an altogether different angle of approach, let's call it ameliorating deception, suggested by the idea that "a deception that elevates us is dearer than a legion of low truths"—a concept forwarded by the great poet Marina Tsvetaeva, who, according to at least one scholar, appropriated these words from Alexander Pushkin. Another deception or simple oversight? Impossible to know. The horizon line where deception and truth nearly touch can be as blurry as a heat mirage on the asphalt of a baking desert highway. And as dangerous for the traveler.

A hitherto unknown school of nineteenth-century European painters whose darkly captivating lost works are as mysterious as its leader's arcane philosophy. A self-possessed Midwestern adulteress with an acerbic wit and bitingly incisive view of herself, her lover, and those she betrays. A slum rat, who, through abiding fear and a weird capacity for identity dislocation, curiously embodies the Chinese villagers it strives to avoid. The stories, novellas, poems, and essays in *Sleights of Hand* investigate the myriad masks behind which we hide, hoping to create an alternative reality in the eyes of our beholders. Some of these works operate within the realm of the fantastic, where the artistic imagination is least fettered, while others take a level-eyed approach, staring down a difficult subject many would prefer to avoid. This is not a preachy gathering, however, and while I imagine readers will recognize aspects of themselves here and there, as often as not these writers discover wildly fresh ways of exploring a classic theme.

*

Editor's Note

This summer, *Conjunctions* held its first benefit in some years, with a gala reading as part of the renowned Richard B. Fisher Center for the Performing Arts' SummerScape series. Francine Prose, Michael Cunningham, and I read before a lively audience in Bard College's magical Spiegeltent. We want to thank everyone who participated in this successful fund-raiser. In particular, thanks to Debra Pemstein, Bob Bursey, and so many others who made this event both possible and a resounding success.

Great gratitude goes to Hy Abady and Jay Hanus, our two founding members of *Conjunctions'* newly established Publishers Circle ($5,000 and up), for their generosity and belief in our project. Barbara Grossman and Michael Gross's donation made it possible for us to get benefit planning under way and they are the founding members of our Benefactors Circle ($2,000–$4,999). Nancy Leonard, James Jaffe, and Motoyuki Shibata are the founding members of our Friends Circle ($500–$1,999), for which we are very grateful. Also, we are pleased to announce the establishment of our Supporters Circle (up to $500), with founding members William Mascioli, Henry Dunow, Rachel Tzvia Back, Mary Jo Bang, Forrest Gander, Alison and John Lankenau, Literary Hub, Debra Pemstein, Christopher Sorrentino, Cole Swensen, G. C. Waldrep, James B. Westine, Mary Caponegro and Michael Ives, Kathryn Davis, Elizabeth Ely and Jonathan Greenburg, Tim Horvath, Michèle Dominy, Thomas Wild, Roseanne Giannini Quinn, Karen Burnham, Rebecca Thomas, and many others. If you would like to join this group of activist readers who support *Conjunctions*, please don't hesitate to make a gift at http://annandaleonline.org/supportconjunctions, or to contact our managing editor, Micaela Morrissette, at conjunctions@bard.edu or (845) 758-7054.

—Bradford Morrow
October 2015
New York City

Tactics of the Wraith
James Morrow

I HAD NEVER INTENDED to spend Cinco de Mayo of 1962 cooped up in a seedy little Mexico City screening room watching low-budget horror movies with titles like *El Ataúd del Vampiro* and *La Maldición de la Momia Azteca*, but back then my life wasn't my own. Ever since my literary career fell apart, my finances had been keyed to the whims of my older siblings: Oswald Belasco, the hack Hollywood producer-director, and Waldo Belasco, the hack Hollywood writer-producer. If the twins told me, "Get thee to Tenochtitlán, little brother," then that's where I would go.

Mine was a commonplace sort of desperation. *Carnage Pastorale*, my first novel, received some marvelous reviews, *The New York Times* calling it "the hypnotic odyssey that *On the Road* wanted to be." But you can't eat appreciation, and when only a thousand or so determined Lucius Belasco readers appeared in the bookstores, and the public librarians balked at all the fucking, and the paperback deal collapsed, and my editor at Viking told my long-suffering agent, Yvonne, "I think we're going to pass on Lucius's new one," I could see the writing on the wall, even as I admitted to myself that the original *Mene, Mene, Tekel, Upharsin* narrative, Belshazzar's feast, was considerably more compelling than my second novel, *Fatal Laughter*. So when Oswald and Waldo offered me a modest salary to leave New York City, drive my VW Beetle to California, and become their official water carrier, wood chopper, and barge toter, I considered myself a lucky man.

No sooner had I landed in Los Angeles than my brothers handed me a bus ticket to Tijuana and points south. They expected me to spend three days as their official emissary to Cinematográfica Calderón and Producciones Agrasánchez, the Mexican equivalents of American International, Allied Artists, and other cheapjack studios north of the border. When I bristled, they offered me a perk. After mailing them my viewer's reports on the latest breakthroughs in *el cine de terror méxicano*, I could spend two unpaid days vacationing in Cuernavaca.

So there I sat—a notebook in my hand, an empanada on my lap, a

9

smoldering Chesterfield parked in the ashtray—sweating and drinking Dos Equis and coming to terms with *The Curse of the Aztec Mummy*. By stretching my high-school Spanish to the limit, I managed to puzzle out the plot, as I'd done earlier that day with the three-picture *La Bruja* cycle, none of which increased my pulse rate, and the two *Vampiro* pictures, both of which I enjoyed with reservations. Inevitably my mind drifted—this wasn't *Citizen Kane* or even *Kiss Me Deadly*—washing up on anxiety's beach and then surrendering to the tide and then coming ashore again. Gloria and I were experimenting with a trial separation. After I accepted the offer from my brothers, she'd elected to stay behind in Manhattan, pursuing her playwriting career (she was fast becoming the toast of Off-Off-Broadway), and she made it clear that divorce was far more likely than détente. When I invited her to join my Mexican adventure, she replied, rationally enough, "Three days of zombies and tamales? Sorry, Lucius, I'm not in the mood."

"You could go shopping," I said.

"I can go shopping in New York," she said.

"You could tinker with your latest play. The atmosphere down there is conducive to creativity, very bohemian."

"I've heard the atmosphere is mostly hot," said Gloria. "Tell me, Lucius, are you prepared to pay for my plane fare?"

"Not exactly."

"Send me a postcard."

Sic transit Gloria mundi.

I had to admit my brothers knew what they were doing with this Mexico scheme. For the past five years they'd been bankrolling their own ridiculous pictures by importing cheesy melodramas from other countries, chopping out the slow parts, dubbing them into English, and distributing them through the drive-in and grindhouse circuits, making sure the posters and lobby cards never emphasized the movies' foreign provenance. The twins had done well with *El Barón del Terror*, which they'd marketed as *A Bucket of Brains*, and even better with *Misterios de Ultratumba*, which became *The Black Pit of Doctor M*, but to find those gems Oswald and Waldo had to sift through twenty or so 16mm prints of recent 35mm offerings from Calderón and Agrasánchez, the black-and-white images flickering across a bedsheet tacked to the far wall of their claustrophobic Glendale office. (They refused to rent a 35mm screening room and pay a projectionist union wages, and the display on their Moviola editing machine was so small it precluded a fair evaluation of a finished picture's mise-en-scène.) Eventually they realized that instead of having Calderón or Agrasánchez make dupes, crate them up, and ship them north, it would be more economical to dispatch a scout to Mexico and have him spend several days assessing 35mm release prints on the spot.

I didn't exactly hate this assignment. The films I saw on Cinco de Mayo featured skilled actors, crisp film noir cinematography, and directorial flourishes executed in homage to those endearing Universal monster movies of the thirties and forties. Which is not to say the stuff Calderón and Agrasánchez cranked out was essentially derivative. Mexico had its own homegrown spooks—the Aztec Mummy, the Crying Woman, the Volcano Demon, the Headless Conquistador, the Were-Jaguar of Zacatecas, the Succubus of Xochimilco—and the film industry deployed them with an impressive mixture of national pride and commercial savvy.

The Curse of the Aztec Mummy boasted all the virtues of its predecessor, including a snappy pace and a truly scary monster, so when the last reel was over I decided to quit while I was ahead. As the tail leader went flapping about on the take-up reel, I scribbled down my immediate reaction, "Let's take a chance on this one," then told Javier, the nonunion projectionist, that tomorrow morning he could sleep an hour later than usual. All he had to do was mount reels one and two of *El Castillo de los Muertos* on his pair of cantankerous old Philips FP3s. I knew how to switch on the projectors and focus the lenses, but if I threaded the reels myself the machines would probably eat them alive.

After the first forty minutes of *El Castillo de los Muertos* were ready to run, I said goodbye to Javier, then ventured into the clotted heat of the incipient evening. My plan was to walk back to my room, subject myself to a cold shower—the Hotel Amigable provided no other kind—then take a bus to the Centro Histórico, where I would drink more alcohol and observe the dancers and mariachi bands celebrating the holiday. I'd heard that the festivities were more colorful in the nearby states of Puebla and Veracruz—the occasion for the merriment being the Battle of Puebla, in which General Seguín had routed a superior French force on May 5, 1862—but this was Mexico City, after all, where revelry and tequila need never go looking for sponsors.

The rectilinear route to the Hotel Amigable, along Avenida Repúblicas to Calle Miravalle and from there to Camino Egipto, took me through a district in no danger of ever becoming a tourist trap.

Prostitutes struck poses on the street corners. Beggars lolled in the doorways. Ranchera songs blared from phonographs perched on windowsills. Redolent of hookers' perfume mixed with a touch of sewage, the side alleys sheltered sleeping drunks.

In anticipation of the next subtropical drizzle, a few of these insensate bums had wrapped themselves in laminated movie posters. As it happened, four such protective advertisements hawked Spanish-dubbed versions of films made by Oswald and Waldo's company, Producers and Artists Releasing Corporation, PARC: initials that, reversed, identified the category to which, by my brothers' own admission, these efforts belonged. (Believe it or not, throughout PARC Pictures' nineteen-year existence, from 1955 to 1974, no journalist or movie critic ever noticed the joke.) I decided not to tell the twins where the Mexican versions of their lovingly crafted twenty-seven-inch-by-forty-one-inch one-sheets had ended up—I'm talking about posters for *Squidicus (El Terrible Gigante de los Mares)*, *The Lava Monster (El Monstruo del Volcán)*, *Revenge of the Vampire Women (La Venganza de las Lobas)*, and *Earth vs. the Death Robots (La Tierra contra los Automatas de la Muerte)*—since the derelicts had most likely stolen them from the theaters before the pictures had finished their runs, though otherwise Oswald and Waldo would probably have delighted in all this impromptu outdoor advertising.

Upon arriving at the hotel, I entered my suffocating room, changed out of my PARC Pictures ambassadorial attire—button-down shirt, black tie, yellow blazer—and submitted myself as planned to a bracing bout of hypothermia. I pulled on jeans and a black T-shirt (my Jack Kerouac look), then descended to the lobby, ready for a night on the town. As I approached the front door, the clerk handed me an envelope bearing the famous logo of Western Union. The telegram from my brothers was more than a little outrageous, but I was hardly in a position to defy them.

SOMETHING BIG BREWING **STOP** NEED YOU HERE **STOP** TAKE
BUS TO L.A. AFTER SCREENING LAST TACO FLICK **STOP** SORRY
NO CUERNAVACA VACATION **STOP** OSWALDO

Something big brewing. No doubt they were alluding to the latest entry in the rash of publicity gimmicks for which PARC Pictures was famous. Who could forget the radio-controlled vinyl bat that flew over the patrons' heads in the final reel of *Terror of the Undead*? Or the gouts of stage blood dripping from the ceiling and onto the proscenium at the end of *Museum of Abominations*? My brothers had devised their most outlandish stunt for *Abyss of the Devil-Worms*, "presented in the magic of Squirm-O-Rama," which meant that whenever a character tumbled into a worm-infested well or culvert or crater, a third of the audience would experience creepy vibrations, their seats having been connected to little electric motors. I wondered what stratagem the boys had contrived for their impending release, *Psychotic Eyeballs from Outer Space*. Would each patron receive a toy gun and a supply of foam-rubber darts with which to attack the cyclopean monsters in the action-packed climax?

So I had three nights to paint *la ciudad* red, after which I would again be dancing attendance on the twins. I intended to waste my time astutely. As long as my cash held out, I would down the finest tequila, practice the art of gluttony, buy some under-the-counter weed at a cigar store, and perhaps even venture into the Zona Rosa and attend a striptease show at the Palacio de los Pechos, an entertainment that Javier the projectionist recommended even though the owner "wasn't doing so good meeting the rent." It occurred to me that this failing burlesque house could use the Oswald and Waldo touch. Presented with the challenge of saving the place, how might my brothers respond? Would they resurrect the moribund medium of 3-D movies, projecting stereoscopic tits on the walls while the onstage performers disrobed? When Belasco Brothers showmanship was in its heyday, everybody scorned it, but now that such endearing hokum has vanished from the cultural landscape, I almost miss it.

Oswald and Waldo called it the Corridor of Horrors, twenty paces down a threadbare carpet that, starting in the foyer of the Pico Building in Glendale, took visitors past a cavalcade of framed posters and deposited them in the shabby offices of PARC Pictures. Doing my best to avoid imagining what tedious and humiliating mission my brothers had devised for me, I ran the gamut from *Squidicus* to *Gill-Women of Venus* to *I Was a Teenage Necrophile* to *Vampire Beach* to *Ghouls on the Loose* to *The Beast from the Deep* to *Reform School Werewolves* until at last I reached the twins' sanctum sanctorum. Flanked by my brothers and cloaked in a yellow silk scarf, a rectangular object lay propped against the desk—a dry-mounted one-sheet, I assumed, waiting to be unveiled. An ancient floor fan oscillated in the far corner, stirring a tentative breeze that caused the scarf to undulate like a specter's shroud.

"My reports from the screening room," I said, handing a manila envelope to Oswald's outspoken secretary, Merle Dexter. "I was hoping to include some snapshots from Cuernavaca"—I inflicted a petulant grin on Waldo—"but it was closed for repairs."

"If things go according to plan," said Oswald, rubbing a hand lasciviously across the top edge of the occluded one-sheet, "we'll soon be out of the taco-flicks game."

"Stop calling them that," said Merle.

"In fact, we'll be forsaking drive-in trash entirely," Oswald continued. "From now on, PARC Pictures makes only *quality* horror films."

"Maybe we should change our name," said Merle. "How about Distributors League of Glendale? Spell it backward and you get GOLD."

"DLOG Pictures?" said Waldo, taking a drag on his Raleigh. "That's not even pronounceable."

"You just did," said Merle.

Oswald asked me, "I don't suppose you read *Daily Variety*?"

"Only *Daily Racing Form*. I've got a hundred bucks on a mudder called Teenage Necrophile running at Hialeah tomorrow."

"There's a new kind of monster movie out there, little brother, and they're all operating in the boffo zone," said Oswald, puffing on his Lucky Strike. "Ever hear of Hammer Films? English outfit. Their first Gothic extravaganza, *The Curse of Frankenstein*, made back its production costs seventy times over, *seventy times*, and then they did *Horror of Dracula*, more actors in waistcoats, plus blood and bodices, another hit. On our side of the pond, meanwhile, A.I.P. has been investing in an Edgar Allan Poe cycle cooked up by dear old Roger Corman. *House of Usher* hit pay dirt, and so did *The Pit and the Pendulum*, and *The Premature Burial* is up next."

"Here's a little quiz for you," said Waldo. "What three elements do we find in Hammer movies and the Poe adaptations that we've never tried at PARC Pictures?"

"Good writing, competent acting, and decent musical scores?" I suggested.

Merle giggled and put a hand to her mouth.

"Period settings, color cinematography, and literary cachet," said Waldo.

"By which you mean *cheap* literary cachet, right?" I said. "Mary Shelley and Bram Stoker are in the public domain, and so is our friend Mr. Poe."

Oswald said, "Cheap cachet, public domain, *exactly*—just like the oeuvre of a nineteenth-century Mexican writer named Carlos Ibarra Rojo, whose legendary unpublished horror stories are about to become a series of upmarket Pathécolor chillers from PARC Pictures!"

"Carlos who?" I asked.

"Ibarra Rojo."

"Never heard of him. May I assume he was known only to a small coterie?"

"A *very* small coterie," said Waldo.

"Actually, the main reason you've never heard of him is that he never existed," said Oswald. "We *invented* him."

"Won't the public *know* that?" I said.

"The public doesn't know shit, Lucius. Behold!"

In an unbroken flourish my elder brother seized the yellow scarf and pulled it free of the one-sheet, which touted a movie called *The Asylum of Doctor Varglom*. Of course, the potboiler in question didn't exist yet. Like most of their fellow moguls, Oswald and Waldo routinely commissioned posters for films that were still in preproduction. Even when the iconography was wildly at odds with the content of the final script, it still made sense to run such artwork in *Daily Variety* and *The Hollywood Reporter*, as a way to appropriate the cinematic territory in question and maybe generate some word-of-mouth interest. The *Doctor Varglom* one-sheet featured a color portrait of the ubiquitous Vincent Price superimposed over a fortress-like edifice rising from a dark mountain. My eye gravitated to the tagline, emblazoned across the top of the poster in ninety-point red type, and suddenly I appreciated the literary-cachet component of my brothers' scheme.

FROM THE DEMENTED PEN OF CARLOS IBARRA ROJO,
MEXICO'S MASTER OF THE MACABRE . . .

"Wouldn't it have been simpler to adapt a *real* writer?" I asked.

"We thought of the reality option," said Oswald, "but Lovecraft's executor wouldn't play ball, and we couldn't wrap our minds around Monk Lewis or Charles Brockden Brown. We needed a *mystique*— know what I mean?—a cult thing. We needed Mexico's master of the macabre."

"And you *also* got Vincent Price?" I asked. "I'm impressed."

Oswald said, "He loved the poster, and when we offered him some biographical nuggets about Ibarra Rojo—"

"In other words, you lied to him."

"When we offered him some nuggets, he immediately got the mystique factor. For some reason Vincent's not doing *Premature Burial*—the part went to Ray Milland, a contractual thing I don't understand—so he promised to work on *Doctor Varglom* for as long as we can afford to pay him."

"That would be about five hours, right?" I said.

"Twenty shooting days, maybe twenty-five," said Waldo. "Principal photography starts next month in an abandoned Pasadena loony bin. We're betting the farm on this one, Lucius." He flourished a screenplay, its hundred-odd pages secured with brass fasteners. "The script's in great shape. Vincent found it delectable."

"No, he didn't," said Oswald.

"He found it adequate beyond his wildest dreams," said Waldo.

" 'Based on the classic story by Carlos Ibarra Rojo,' " I recited, reading from the one-sheet.

"That's where *you* come in, little brother," said Oswald. "Last week we had a visitor from the east, Desmond Mallery of *Cinesthesia*—ever hear of it? Very tony rag, slick paper, quarterly, editorial offices in Brooklyn, for horror buffs who've outgrown *Famous Monsters of Filmland*. We did an interview over lunch, and we told him all about our great literary discovery from south of the border."

"So you lied to *him* too," I said.

"Desmond believes we stumbled on a strongbox full of original Ibarra Rojo manuscripts," Oswald continued. "In our boy's lifetime no publisher would take a chance on his stuff—too outré, too decadent, too disturbing—but all six novelettes were circulated underground."

"See what we mean about mystique?" said Waldo.

"I believe I can get through the day without hearing that word again," I said.

"After our boy died, the manuscripts disappeared," said Oswald. "Everybody thought they were lost forever. You can imagine how excited Desmond got. He wants to publish an English translation of the novelette that inspired *The Asylum of Doctor Varglom*, complete with production stills. It'll be fabulous publicity."

"You'll be good at this, Lucius," said Waldo. "You know all about Mexico."

"I was there for only three days," I said.

"Dante never went to hell, but he wrote about it," said Waldo.

"How does what's-his-name define 'novelette'?" I asked.

"Desmond," said Waldo. "I don't know, maybe sixteen thousand words."

"I can't knock that out by Monday."

"Relax, kid," said Oswald. "He won't run your story till his winter issue, which will hit the newsstands just as we're releasing the movie."

"So I've got till December?"

"Desmond needs the manuscript by the beginning of August, so he can make other plans on the off chance he hates it."

"He won't hate it," I said.

"Take all the artistic leeway you want. *Your* Doctor Varglom needn't be terribly faithful to *our* Doctor Varglom."

Merle said, "In fact, if your Varglom *was* faithful, people would get suspicious—right, boys?—since Hollywood routinely desecrates literary properties."

"Here's your starting point," said Waldo, handing me his screenplay. "All we require is that you use the same title and keep the main characters, or at least their names."

"As for the plot, do whatever you want, so long as it takes place in a Mitteleuropa insane asylum," said Oswald. "We figured you'd dig that setting. That writer you like so much, Fritz Kafka—"

"Friedrich," I said, and Merle snickered.

"Friedrich Kafka, didn't he write a whole novel about a land surveyor moping around outside a huge asylum nobody's allowed to enter?"

"The novel was called *The Castle*," I said.

"Funny name for a story about an insane asylum," said Oswald.

"How much will this Desmond person pay me?"

"We asked for six hundred," said Waldo. "He dickered at first, but then we explained that PARC Pictures would be covering the translation fee."

"There *is* no translation fee," I said.

"Every penny from Desmond goes right to you—less ten percent, since PARC Pictures is essentially the agent for this deal."

"I already have an agent."

"Not out here you don't. Naturally, we're suspending your salary, but we'll give you two hundred bucks to write the press release and—"

"And to keep mum about this hoax?" I said.

"If you're not happy working for us," said Oswald, "you can always take your delicate ass back to New York and write *Carnage Pastorale Strikes Again*."

"I'm happy enough," I said. "It's just that I've never done ghost-writing before."

"But this *isn't* ghostwriting. Every goddamn Carlos Ibarra Rojo story was composed by him and him alone—never forget that."

"Hold up your end of things," said Waldo, "and Desmond might want to publish another chef d'oeuvre from our trove. This could be a regular golden goose for you."

"More like a rubber chicken," I muttered.

"Don't look a gift goose in the mouth, kid," said Oswald, obscuring the one-sheet with the silk veil, and I realized I was in no position to argue.

The next day I checked into a fleabag motel in Culver City, unpacked my portable Remington, installed a new ribbon, and, after cleaning the ink off my fingers, got to work. Writing the press release—that is to say, concocting a nineteenth-century Mexican writer whose friends and colleagues thought him a genius—proved more fun than I'd anticipated, especially after I realized that, far from frustrating me, the parameters laid down by my brothers were keeping my imagination from running amok. After twelve continuous hours of pounding the keys, chain-smoking Chesterfields, drinking lime-filliped Coronas, and gulping coffee, I had in hand a ten-page biographical essay, "Ambassador to the Beyond." The thing cried out for cutting, being too long for submission to newspapers and too explicit about my subject's sex life, but I believed I'd successfully inserted Carlos Ibarra Rojo into the annals of plausible nonexistence, and I loved him no less than I did Herman Melville, Joseph Conrad, Franz Kafka, Jack Kerouac, or any of my other heroes.

On the 31st of October, 1847, the first day of the obliquely Christian Día de los Muertos celebrations held throughout southern Mexico, a beautiful and robust child emerged from his mother's womb in the town of Guanajuato. Carlos Ibarra Rojo never knew his father, who abandoned the family shortly after the boy's birth. When his mother died of consumption, five-year-old Carlos was sent by an uncle to live at La Casa de Santa Maria, a foundling home in Acámbaro. He quickly became a favorite with the nuns, who recognized his intelligence, taught him how to read Spanish, tutored him in English, and encouraged his talent for storytelling. By age eight, Carlos was alternately regaling and terrifying the other children with his outlandish narratives, including weird and occasionally gory bedtime stories that remained with his listeners all their lives.

Despite his popularity at La Casa de Santa Maria, Carlos detested the place, and shortly after turning ten, on the day he was to celebrate his first communion, he ran away to Mexico City, where he lived an Oliver Twist existence well into his adolescence. When not picking pockets or begging for centavos, the nascent writer focused on educating himself, sneaking into the Biblioteca Nacional at night and making off with works by Miguel de Cervantes, José de Espronceda, and Gustavo Adolfo Bécquer, plus Spanish translations of Arthur Rimbaud, Charles Baudelaire, Edgar Allan Poe, Herman Melville, and Nathaniel Hawthorne. He was an honorable thief, never filching a volume until he'd returned his previous such illicit acquisition.

Throughout his twenties and thirties, Ibarra Rojo worked as groundskeeper of the Cementerio Nacional in Coyoacán borough, a job that gave him sufficient free time to pursue his great passion, composing horror stories on the Sholes and Glidden typewriter he'd stolen from the American Embassy. His early, inchoate efforts drew upon indigenous Mexican legends: Popoca, the Aztec Mummy, guarding his princess's tomb from brigands; La Llorona, the Crying Woman, who murdered her own children to spite their adulterous father; Solares, the Volcano Demon, rising from the lava of Montaña Hueca with scorched flesh and pyromaniacal intentions; Ramírez, the Headless Conquistador, decapitating random strangers in hopes of finding his own lost head. But Ibarra Rojo's imagination soon sprawled beyond the bounds of his heritage, and he began producing a cycle of Poe-inflected, Rimbaud-flavored masterpieces. In time he became a familiar figure in the nocturnal cantinas of the Centro Histórico, reading his tales aloud amidst the jagged shadows cast by kerosene lanterns and guttering candles, each flamboyant recitation fueled by an amalgam of wine, mezcal, peyote, and marijuana.

Although Ibarra Rojo insisted that his work could not be understood apart from *la teología católica* and *el misterio del Cristo*, he was a severe critic of the church, and his immediate circle regarded him as an atheist. Equally paradoxical was his personal aesthetic, his theory of "the destabilized reader." According to this oddball poetics, through the astute deployment of "decadent syntax and subconscious semantic associations," anyone who consumed an Ibarra Rojo tale could be made to feel that its actual author was the reader's own insane doppelgänger.

One can surely discount the rumor that, owing to the extreme suspense and sudden shocks of the author's tales, listeners occasionally suffered heart attacks during his public performances. By contrast, reports on his carnal proclivities are credible. He displayed his appetite for men as openly as his ardor for women, and it can be counted a small miracle that these exhibitions never landed him in prison.

As he entered his third decade of life, the author's friends and devotees convened a kind of subterranean lending library, passing the infamous manuscripts from hand to hand. Eventually the Ibarra Rojo cult attracted the attention of the respected and accomplished Romantic novelist Guillermo Prieto, who persuaded the prestigious Academia de Letrán to invite the horror writer into their ranks on the strength of three unpublished novelettes, "El Sanatorio de Doctor Varglom," "El Beso Diabólico," and "La Nave de los Monstruos." Characteristically, Ibarra Rojo not only turned down the solicitation, he publicly insulted his patron.

"I shall always be a dog of the streets, hungry, feral, and free," he told Prieto. "No pedigree can redeem me. Unlike you and your fellow snivelers, I have never jumped into anyone's lap."

Not surprisingly, Ibarra Rojo's early death—on the 10th of August, 1884—could be traced to his dissolute ways. Seeking inspiration in the cemetery he'd once tended, he staggered amidst the vaults and tombs in a mezcal haze until, in a misadventure so symbolically freighted his friends did not at first believe it, he was fatally trampled by a horse-drawn hearse. He was thirty-seven years old. A score of alcoholic poets, jailbird novelists, and unhinged painters attended the funeral, the rank cream of the Mexico City demimonde, but the event went unreported in the newspapers. There is no truth to the speculation that, in fulfillment of the writer's most frequently voiced desire, his friends arranged for his body to be submerged in sulfuric acid and his skeleton paraded about on El Día de los Muertos.

Ibarra Rojo's literary legacy died with him. Despite his friends' willingness to publish a chapbook of his best stories, he'd always withheld permission, claiming they were never intended for "promiscuous consumption by a random readership." As for the fabled typescripts, they all vanished without a trace.

In the spring of 1961, while scouting locations in Acámbaro, two Hollywood B-movie producers, Oswald and Waldo Belasco, had a barroom encounter with an excitable and possibly deranged student named Raúl Hernández Alfaro. Upon learning of their interest in occult matters, the young man insisted that, shortly before his lethal encounter with the hearse, the infamous writer Carlos Ibarra Rojo had entrusted a strongbox to his mistress, a locally famous beauty named Consuelo Portillo Madero, whom Raúl would ultimately claim as his great-grandmother. For generations the family had guarded the box, never daring to open it, for they knew of the legend whereby a terrible misfortune would befall any mortal who cast an eye on the manuscripts that lay therein.

"Perhaps you should simply give the box away," Oswald Belasco had suggested.

"Do you know anyone foolish enough to accept it?" asked Raúl.

"Indeed."

"Would this person be foolish enough to accept it in exchange for twenty thousand pesos?"

"Fifteen thousand pesos."

And so it was that, against the odds in defiance of the Devil, "El Sanatorio de Doctor Varglom" and five other stories were delivered from oblivion.

After boiling "Ambassador to the Beyond" down to a conventional two-page press release and mailing it off to PARC Pictures, I turned to the business of composing the Ibarra Rojo novelette called "The Asylum of Doctor Varglom." I began by reading Waldo's screenplay. Though marred by overheated dialogue and gratuitous sensationalism, only a person even more snobbish than me would have dismissed this effort as dreck. I rather liked it. My brother had already alerted me to the setting, a nineteenth-century madhouse in an unspecified European country. The plot was simple but serviceable. Arguably more demented than any of his patients, the medical director of Krogskrafte Sanatorium, Anton Varglom, becomes seduced by the godlike powers he enjoys over the residents' fortunes. He starts extracting cerebrospinal fluid from their brains, his theory being that, because he himself is already insane, such an elixir can only compound his brilliance. Doctor Varglom's self-injections have an unintended consequence: He becomes a "thought-vampire," addicted to the internal mental landscapes wherein the Krogskrafte inmates dwell, a craving that requires him to periodically saw open a patient's cranium and, like a gourmand savoring a stew, devour the cerebral matter with a spoon. In the final reel Varglom's experimental subjects get the upper hand, chasing him onto the roof and hurling him to his death.

Although Waldo's script should have been an easy act to follow, a full five days elapsed before I'd nailed down an opening scene. I hadn't written fiction in over two years, and I reveled in the blessed pressure of the typewriter keys against my fingertips. In the weeks that followed, the remaining events rushed from my brain in a lexical cataract. Doubtless Ibarra Rojo had composed his tales in a similarly feverish state. I could practically hear the levers of his Sholes and Glidden nailing ink to paper to platen with the insidious rhythms of a sadistic mortician securing a cataleptic's coffin prior to burying him alive.

My interpretation of Anton Varglom proved rather more sympathetic than my brother's. Born with the soul of a Renaissance architect and the sensibility of a Baroque painter, this tormented prodigy came of age determined to use his artistic talents in helping lunatics find their way back to daylight. Alas, no sooner does the young doctor assume charge of Krogskrafte Sanatorium than an idée fixe corrupts his noble nature. He resolves to turn the asylum into the most bizarre world imaginable, on the theory that an environment capable of driving a rational person crazy might very well restore a madman to sanity. And so, under Varglom's direction, the passageways and staircases of Krogskrafte transmute into a twisted, crooked, insoluble labyrinth—evidently my clever doctor anticipated German Expressionism—even as the attic becomes a torture chamber filled with insidious devices, most notably "the loom of ruin," reminiscent of the bizarre rack from Kafka's *In the Penal Colony*. Shortly after he assembles it, Doctor Varglom's loom acquires a mind of its own, a demonic consciousness through which it can sense the nature of a man's most unforgivable sin, forthwith tattooing its name upon his jumping flesh with an array of steel needles. Alas, for reasons Varglom cannot fathom, the renovated asylum fails to cure anyone. Seeking to identify the flaw in his theory, he negotiates the maze himself. The jagged corridors inflict a kind of Nietzschean hypersanity on the doctor, so that, when the vengeful inmates hunt him down and strap him to the loom, his psyche melds with that of the machine, and soon thereafter he feels the needles etching his skin with narratives of sins that human beings have not yet learned to commit. The story ends on a cryptic note, when a Krogskrafte orderly enters the chamber and proposes to unbind Varglom. But the doctor rejects the orderly's solicitation, declaring that he prefers to spend his remaining days "living in this delectable hell of nameless iniquities."

By the end of June, I had in hand a complete eighty-page draft of

"The Asylum of Doctor Varglom." My effort pleased me. It wasn't as engaging as *Carnage Pastorale,* but it left *Fatal Laughter* in the shadows. In this lurid little tale I had wrought—or, rather, my Ibarra Rojo persona had wrought—something respectable and perhaps even remarkable.

Mirabile dictu, my benevolent alter ego wasn't finished possessing me. Even as I sat down to correct the present pages, the arc of the whole Anton Varglom cycle arrived entire in my brain. The five remaining installments, I saw, must all occur in the sanatorium. As the series unfolded, this cathedral to the doctor's megalomania would acquire additional and increasingly strange appendages: a subterranean gallery of forbidden art, an abbey in which only malevolent deities were worshipped, a junglelike conservatory populated by horrific evolutionary mistakes, a theater in which the lunatics staged Grand Guignol entertainments for the residents of the surrounding village, a vast swamp concealing some unspeakable beast—each such installation rife with plot possibilities and thematic riches.

For the next hour I forced myself to negotiate the immediate manuscript with a lead pencil, elevating the diction, imposing personality tics on the characters, and replacing overly self-conscious metaphors with acceptably self-conscious metaphors. I tossed the pages onto the backseat of my Beetle and set out for Glendale with the aim of delivering them to Oswald's secretary so she could type the fair copy. Underground gallery, obscene abbey, nightmare jungle, theater of blood, haunted swamp: Yes, no question, I had hit a mother lode. Lucius Belasco was back in the fiction game.

Arriving at the Pico Building, I was delighted to find Merle in the foyer—she'd just returned from lunch—because I sure as hell didn't want to talk with my brothers: Their chatter would break the hypnotic spell in which I found myself, the ensorcellment through which I'd apprehended the entire unwritten oeuvre of Carlos Ibarra Rojo. I handed the manuscript to Merle and, after deputizing her to correct my spelling and fix obvious typos, returned to the car.

Back in the motel room, I popped a beer, swilled it down, and scrolled a blank sheet into the Remington. I decided to key the new novelette to the art gallery hidden in the bowels of Krogskrafte Sanatorium. By moonrise I'd crafted an outline for the first two-thirds of a story called "Ars Longa Vita Brevis."

Mysteriously delivered from the loom of ruin, Doctor Varglom learns that a catastrophe has befallen the village of Ekelstadt. The town is dissolving, its buildings, thoroughfares, and squares melting like paraffin in the sun. As panic reigns in the viscous streets, many citizens flee to the gates of Krogskrafte, where they attempt to impersonate lunatics in hopes of gaining admittance.

Unmoved by the citizens' plight but intrigued by the mystery at hand, Varglom researches the history of the asylum. He learns that, fifty years earlier, Krogskrafte was the abode of an artist and aristocrat, Janos Stradegorst. A student of the black arts, Baron Stradegorst once claimed he could bring an entire world into being by painting it with alchemically created oils, the shapes, figures, and colors supplied by his imagination alone. Evidently the village and its environs were the results of this experiment. Whatever its location, the occult mural is obviously starting to disintegrate, for how else to explain the plague that has come to Ekelstadt?

Doctor Varglom deduces that the epicenter of the catastrophe—the mural itself—must reside within the asylum walls. He forthwith visits the subterranean gallery, where the resident painting master, the handsome and clever Garrick Bloom, is hanging an exhibition of his students' work, assisted by his talented but unbalanced protégé, Sonya Dagunzar. The images are disturbing in the extreme—hence the need for secrecy—but none depicts a Mitteleuropa village.

Determined to find Baron Stradegorst's mural, Varglom and Bloom venture into the deepest reaches of the asylum, from basement to subbasement to subsubbasement. Eventually they discover a vast circular room. The walls hold a decaying cyclorama of Ekelstadt, the pigments succumbing to the appetites of demonic worms.

I had no idea what would happen next, but I felt confident that my inner Ibarra Rojo would soon provide the necessary twists and turns, and I went to bed a happy man.

After fifteen days of banging away on "Ars Longa Vita Brevis," I had only twenty pages to show for my efforts. I'd managed to depict the dissolution of Ekelstadt, including darkly comic scenes of the terrified citizens feigning lunacy, but then the words stopped flowing. I wondered how long it would take me to send Anton Varglom off in search of the cyclorama. A week? Two weeks? I wasn't blocked, exactly, but I feared that several months might elapse before, eyes fixed on the final paragraph, I typed the words "The End."

On the morning of day sixteen, the telephone summoned me from an uneasy sleep. Oswald was on the line. I'd never heard such elation in his voice.

"Lucius, kid, I love it!"

"Love what?" I mumbled

"Your novelettization—"

"There's no such word."

"It's *terrific*, little brother, the bug's nuts. Don't tell Waldo, but I prefer *your* novelettization to *his* screenplay. Too bad we finish principal photography on Friday, or we'd stick some of your ideas in the show, especially that demonically possessed torture rack."

"Oswald, you made my day," I said. "So how's Vincent Price working out?"

"Between takes he gets bored, but he chews the scenery on cue. Here's the really good news. Desmond Mallery thought your Ibarra Rojo story was, quote, 'a tour de force of horror fiction.' He's goosing the normal print run by ten thousand copies, and he wants to see another lost-and-found novelette as soon as it's translated."

"I'm hard at work on a new one, 'Ars Longa Vita Brevis.'"

"Lousy title."

"How about 'City of Wax'?"

"Much better."

"When do I get my six hundred dollars?"

"Five hundred forty. Waldo and I own ten percent of you, remember? *Cinesthesia* pays on publication. Now here's the really, *really* good news. If 'City of Wax' is as fabulous as your last story, we'll buy it from you outright and put it into production."

"It'll be fun thinking up a new tagline, huh, Oswald? 'From the chilling quill of Carlos Ibarra Rojo, legendary lunatic of Latin letters!'"

"Don't make fun of us."

"'From the perverted plume of Carlos Ibarra Rojo, bizarro brainiac of Oaxaca!'"

"Stop it, little brother."

The longer I chatted with Oswald, the more convinced I became that I'd never make any headway on "City of Wax" and its sequels unless I returned to the native land of Carlos Ibarra Rojo. I needed the stark and torrid ambience from which his febrile visions had arisen. When I told Oswald he must send me to Mexico City again, he agreed to buy the bus ticket, but he drew the line at paying my hotel bills. I told him I would rent an apartment with the money I had coming from *Cinesthesia* for the novelette and PARC Pictures for the press release.

"Your check is in the mail," said Oswald. "This is *big*, Lucius. You and me and Waldo are going to the moon and back."

*

On a sweltering day in late August, as the sun rode the sky over Mexico City like the crucified doubloon glinting from the mainmast of the *Pequod*, I plunked a thousand pesos onto the desk of my new landlord, Octavio Iglesias, thereby laying claim to top-floor accommodations at Calle Moctezuma 14 in Cuauhtémoc borough, not far from the Centro Histórico. I'd lucked out. Apartment 5-B had a functional gas oven, an efficient icebox, a small but congenial parlor, a quaint little wrought-iron balcony, and a shower that delivered reliably hot water. Best of all, the kitchen opened onto a lush rooftop terrace planted with roses, orchids, and bougainvillea vines. True, there was no telephone, but Señor Iglesias told me his tenants could make and receive calls from a booth in the first-floor *farmacia*, which he managed with the aid of his dipsomaniacal brother-in-law, Julio, and preadolescent nephew, Armando.

"Julio will send Armando to tell you when you're wanted on the phone. For a modest fee, we can explain to bill collectors, alimony lawyers, and police officers that you are no longer in residence."

I installed my typewriter on the kitchen table and, after smoking a Chesterfield and reading the twenty extant "City of Wax" pages, wound a fresh sheet into the machine. Immediately I realized that, in returning to Ibarra Rojo's milieu, I'd made the right decision. A torrent of sentences rushed from my fingertips. In prose that I, for one, found more poetic than purple, Doctor Varglom investigated the plague that threatened Ekelstadt, eventually learning about the sorcerer Stradegorst. As September brought its warm, wet breezes to southern Mexico, the story progressed, the doctor enlisting the aid of the asylum's painting master and (after encountering many a cul-de-sac) discovering the secret cyclorama. I still had no idea how this would all play out, but—God and Ibarra Rojo willing—act three would emerge ere long.

On the first day in October the kid from the *farmacia*, the exuberant Armando, interrupted my verbal bacchanal, screaming, "Señor Belasco! Señor Belasco!" from the hallway outside my apartment. (He wasn't precisely a person from Porlock, but then again I wasn't composing "Kubla Khan.") I let him in. He caught his breath, then announced that a phone call awaited me below, a Señora Gloria. The fantasies kicked in instantly. She missed me. She needed me. She wanted us to renew our wedding vows. Maybe we should have a child.

I flipped Armando a ten-centavo piece, then stubbed out my cigarette, boarded the treacherous elevator, descended to the *farmacia*, and, wedging myself into the phone booth, grabbed the dangling handset. The connection was terrible, but Gloria and I managed to have a conversation. Of course I was all wrong, or mostly wrong, about her motivations. Her desire to talk with me was professional, not connubial. The celebrated Broadway director Joshua Logan had recently acquired the dramatic rights to Herman Melville's dark and satiric novel *The Confidence-Man*, and he'd given her a plum of an assignment, adapting it for the stage. At some point, of course, Logan would probably take over the writing, but first he wanted to see what Gloria could do on her own. Given my enthusiasm for Melville in particular and pessimistic fiction in general, she was hoping we could spend two or three days sitting in Mexico City cafés talking about the existing scenes (she'd already completed act one) and brainstorming ideas for act two.

"I'm booked on a morning flight," she said.

"I'll greet you at the Aeropuerto Central with a sign reading, 'Pan-American Pessimists Convention.'"

"Don't bother. I'll take a taxi."

"You can have my bed. I'll sling a hammock on the balcony."

"No, Lucius, I'll sleep in my hotel."

"There are no hotels in a twenty-mile radius of here."

"I already reserved a room."

"Only opium dens—"

"I bring news from Oswald."

"And bordellos. What news?"

"I'm to tell you *Doctor Varglom* is in postproduction," said Gloria. "The rough cut looks terrific, and it'll be in theaters by January. Gotta run, Lucius. See you soon."

I sauntered back to Calle Moctezuma 14 and sat down before the Remington. Nothing happened. No words materialized on the page. True, the fact of Gloria's imminent arrival had lifted my spirits, but not to an elevation sufficient for bringing "City of Wax" to fruition. I retrieved a Corona from the icebox, soured it with a slice of lime, and nursed it while staring at the malicious white void.

The proper course was obvious: I must take the rest of the day off and visit a local movie palace—and so it was that PARC Pictures' most reliable scout indulged in a kind of busman's holiday, spending the afternoon at the baroque but decrepit twenty-four-hour Teatro Regio watching a triple bill. Coincidentally enough, *El Ataque de las Brujas, El Espectro del Estrangulador,* and *Santo contra el Cerebro Satánico* were preceded by trailers for three of Roger Corman's Edgar Allan Poe adaptations, the cycle whose success my brothers were trying to emulate. Starting tomorrow, *La Caída de la Casa de Usher, El Pozo y el Péndulo,* and *El Entierro Prematuro* would grace this torn and dingy screen.

The following morning, shortly after noon, Gloria knocked on my door. Much to my disappointment, she carried no luggage, having already dropped it at the Hotel Paraíso down the street. (Truth to tell, I'd been imagining she'd changed her mind while flying over the Rio Grande and now wanted to move into my apartment.) She wore a powder-blue Gainsborough hat and a brilliant white sundress—a kind of inverse shroud, I decided: My wife was so supremely alive she would defy all cerements until well into the next century. The lenses of her sunglasses were mirrors. The pleasure of seeing myself in her eyes did nothing to mitigate the pain of exile from her affections.

"Here's the first act of my *Confidence-Man* adaptation, a rough draft, Precambrian in fact." She deposited a sheaf of typescript on the kitchen table. "Be insanely brutal, but within reason. Shall we have dinner tomorrow night and talk about Melville's great trickster?"

"Splendid idea, sweetheart. I'll whip us up some *pollo asado* and a fresh fruit salad."

"I meant in a restaurant."

"OK, but how about breakfast instead? Salsa and eggs and confidence men. I'll pick up the tab."

"I'm planning to sleep in."

"Lunch?"

"I'm already booked for lunch."

"Oh?"

"While I was waiting to check in, I had a terrific conversation with a fascinating Mexican writer," said Gloria. "He complimented me on my Spanish. Somehow Melville came up, so I gave him the carbon of act one. We're meeting in the hotel café tomorrow afternoon."

"An hour on the ground, and already you've got a *date*?"

"You must get used to the idea of my seeing other people."

A cord of dread twisted through me, thickening my throat and constricting my bowels. "Let me guess. Your new friend looks like Brando playing Zapata."

"Even handsomer."

"Shame on you, Gloria. Tonight I'm sending you to bed without any straight lines."

28

"There's a cozy *restorán*, La Casa del Sol, across the street from my hotel. Meet me at seven o'clock. Adiós."

As Gloria sashayed away, I decided that, rather than reading her Melville scenes, I would resume work on my story. Thinking a change of venue might help, I decamped to the rooftop garden, which conveniently included a white wrought-iron table and two matching chairs. After equipping the terrace with the Remington and a cooler of Coronas, I sat down, lit a cigarette, and, as the primordial scents of a dozen subtropical flower species mingled in my delighted nostrils, attempted to bedaub a vacant sheet with prose.

It soon became apparent that the fact of my wife's new literary boyfriend had depressed me beyond all telling. Obviously I wasn't going to get anything done on either "City of Wax" or Gloria's scenes, so I laid a tarp over my Remington—the radio forecast had predicted a sunny afternoon, but why take chances?—then left my al fresco workspace unattended and set out for the Teatro Regio, vaguely convinced that the Edgar Allan Poe triple-header would give me the energy I needed to pump some blood into my languishing novelette.

Roger Corman's *La Caída de la Casa de Usher* didn't do much for me, but I figured maybe something had gotten lost in the dubbing. The actor who'd looped Roderick Usher enunciated clearly enough— an asset that, given my equivocal Spanish, I much appreciated—but he sounded more like Spencer Tracy than Vincent Price. *El Entierro Prematuro* also failed to get under my skin, despite a riveting dream sequence in which the protagonist's carefully-rigged contraptions for avoiding untimely entombment go haywire one by one. Ah, but *El Pozo y el Péndulo*—now *there* was a hell of a horror movie!

Set in Renaissance Spain a generation after the Inquisition has imposed its obscene will on countless heretics, this gaudy melodrama remained delectably unpredictable throughout its eighty-five-minute running time. The frenzied climax, staged in the expressionistic pit of the title, found the crazed Nicholas Medina (who now fancies himself his own inquisitor father) subjecting the young hero, Francis Barnard, to Poe's famous oscillating cleaver, but not before sharing with Francis his nihilistic thoughts on "the condition of man," *la condición del hombre*. By Nicholas's philosophy we are all marooned on "an island from which no person could ever hope to escape," each of us "surrounded by the menacing pit of hell" even as the "inexorable pendulum of fate," ever descending, slashes and slices the air above our pinioned bodies. "*¡Atrapado en una isla sin esperanzas* *de escapar!"* screamed Nicholas, rolling his eyes toward the razor-edged blade. *"¡Rodeado por el amenazante abismo del infierno! ¡Sometido al inexorable péndulo del destino!"*

Although *El Pozo y el Péndulo* failed to awaken my dormant muse, I came away from the theater with some notions for the third act of "City of Wax." It occurred to me that Baron Stradegorst, the sorcerer who'd painted the cyclorama, might still be alive after all these years, though his demiurgic powers have so corrupted him that now he takes pleasure in the thought of Ekelstadt's dissolution. By threatening the baron with some Inquisition-caliber torture or other (perhaps the Kafkaesque rack I'd invented for the previous story), Doctor Varglom convinces the sorcerer to join him in the sub-subbasement and attempt to rehabilitate the mural. In deference to Ibarra Rojo's sensibility, however, I would not supply a happy ending. Although Stradegorst retouches the cyclorama with some perfunctory brushstrokes, he soon breaks his promise to the doctor and attacks his creation with acid, thereby annihilating the entire village, including Krogskrafte Sanatorium.

I sprinted back to my apartment, ascended to the crepuscular terrace, and strode toward the Remington, at once eager to turn my new ideas into sentences and apprehensive that those same sentences might be terrible—whereupon I received a shock more jolting than anything I'd seen that day at the Teatro Regio.

Somebody had invaded my workspace, subsequently drinking two of my beers, smoking my remaining Chesterfields—the ashtray held the butts and the crushed pack—and covering about thirty sheets of typing paper with English prose. Secured by an empty beer bottle, the intruder's labors lay in a neat pile on the card table, not far from my unfinished manuscript, stacked beneath the second empty bottle. Gingerly I removed the tarp from my typewriter. The platen displayed a single sheet bearing a protracted fragment—"hidden in lost grottoes and forgotten catacombs, the innards of churches and the underbellies of monasteries, all shapes fading, all pigments dissolving, the cosmos having become an imperiled array of palimpsests on which no printed word or painted effigy would endure beyond the slimmest tick of time"—followed by a period, after which came "The End."

I assembled a complete version of the novelette, including my own scenes, the intruder's contributions, and the orphan final page from the Remington. With mounting perplexity I read the third act. The new material employed the same conceit that had come to me while watching *El Pozo y el Péndulo*. My anonymous collaborator had brought an elderly Baron Stradegorst onstage and cast him as a demiurge whose powers have corroded his soul. But then the writer had carried this vision in a direction I hadn't anticipated, and the results were at once dramatically engaging and stylistically brilliant.

In the hands of my phantom confederate, Garrick Bloom's protégé—the mad and beautiful Sonya Dagunzar—emerged as the one artist in the world with talent enough to heal the wounded mural. Not surprisingly, there was considerable sexual chemistry between the painting master and his ethereal pupil, whose brushwork was inspired by energies no less erotic than artistic. In one particularly vivid vignette, Garrick and Sonya made love during her menstrual period, after which she used her blood to paint a portrait of the Devil. I could hear Oswald saying, "Surely you don't imagine us putting *that* up on the screen," and me replying, "It's hardly more tasteless than Squirm-O-Rama."

Whatever its wellspring, Sonya's genius proves sufficient to rescue bits and pieces of Ekelstadt—a house here, a tavern there, a random shop, the occasional bridge—from the ravages of the abyss. Determined to prevent the village's salvation, the baron secretly administers a poison to Sonya, then stabs Garrick to death with a butcher knife. Though racked by the toxin in her blood, Sonya continues to rehabilitate Ekelstadt. Aided by a pair of models—her lover's corpse and her own mirrored image—she begins augmenting the cyclorama with meticulous portraits of Garrick and herself, believing she may thereby translate their souls into a Platonic realm of ideal forms. Recalled from the grave by Sonya's magic, Garrick collaborates with her to complete the portraits. She dies in his arms after adding the final brushstroke, whereupon the despondent Garrick shoots himself, thus joining her on the same arcane plane of reality where immaterial essences reside.

In the story's final beats, the romantic mood dissipates and everything turns dark again. The baron reveals that the whole of the visible world is sustained by secret cycloramas such as the one in the subsubbasement. The forces of decay have allied themselves against all these murals, and there is nothing mere mortals can do to forestall an imminent and endless night.

Midway through my perusal of these new and extraordinary pages I decided that the phantom in question must be Gloria. By according such prominence to Sonya Dagunzar, a previously minor character, and making her a tragic figure though not a mere victim, to say nothing of the menstrual-blood business, my wife had suffused the manuscript with her particular sensibility. But the point of her stunt eluded me. Did she hope to demonstrate that her knack for writing skillful trash was greater than mine? In that case, she'd succeeded. Did she mean to suggest that, though romantically incompatible, we should start combining our talents to create lucrative potboilers? Then I intended to disappoint her. If our marriage was beyond salvation, I wanted no consolation prize.

Realizing that, unassuaged, my curiosity would keep me up all night, I beat a hasty path to the *farmacia* phone booth and placed a call to Gloria's hotel. The clerk I got on the line sounded offended by my expectation that he do his job properly, but he agreed to summon Señora Belasco. Five minutes later, my wife and I found ourselves mired in a fraught and circular conversation during which she emphatically denied having added pages to my unfinished novelette.

"Why would I want to do a ridiculous thing like that?" she asked.

"Doing ridiculous things is a rarity for you, Gloria, no question, but your record isn't perfect," I said. "Want to hear a list?"

"Fuck you."

"I'll be honest. This whole episode has creeped me out."

"If you like, I could ask Carlos—"

"Carlos?" Stalactites formed in my stomach. "Carlos who?"

"My new writer friend. I don't remember his full name. I could ask him if any of his fellow authors are given to invading people's apartments and finishing their manuscripts for them."

"Is this Carlos by any chance the *caballero* you're having lunch with tomorrow?"

"Uh-huh."

"Might his name be Carlos Ibarra Rojo?"

"Like I said, I don't remember. Hey, Lucius, I can tell you're kind of frazzled right now, but what did you think of my *Confidence-Man* scenes?"

"I haven't read them."

"Why not? Did you spend the afternoon at the movies?"

"Listen, Gloria, Carlos Ibarra Rojo is the name of a nonexistent nineteenth-century Mexican writer my brothers and I invented to give *The Asylum of Doctor Varglom* some literary cachet."

"Did I ever tell you how boring I find your brothers' escapades?"

"Gloria . . ."

"Nonexistent writer named Carlos? I'd say it's a coincidence."

"Your coincidence, my nightmare. *¡Atrapado en una isla sin esperanzas de escapar!* I'm not kidding. I think I've been visited by a ghost. Or else I'm losing my mind. *¡Rodeado por al amenazante abismo del infierno!*"

"Is all this some ploy to win my sympathy?"

"I'll pretend you didn't say that."

Her tone turned suddenly contrite. "I'll pretend the same. Sorry, Lucius. Really. Do you want me to come over and brew you a cup of tea or something?"

Did I want her to come over? Of course I did—but I had no right to invite her to Calle Moctezuma 14 before determining whether it was haunted.

"Matter of fact, I'm not sure my apartment is *safe* at the moment. I'll call you in the morning. And promise me you won't have lunch tomorrow with that writer—not before you and I talk."

"I'd be happy to drop by your place *now*. I'm *worried* about you."

"*I'm* worried about me too, and also about you, but mostly I'm worried about Carlos Ibarra Rojo."

By the time I'd ascended to my apartment, a full moon had risen over the city. I retrieved a pack of Chesterfields from the kitchen and proceeded to the garden, its leaves and twigs now colonized by singing insects. The complete "City of Wax" manuscript glowed in the lunar light. I approached the wrought-iron table, sat down, and scanned the third act for clues to its author's identity, even as I fervently hoped that the most plausible theory was as impossible as it sounded.

A male voice, cultured and suave, addressed me in a Latino accent. "I saw you at the cinema today, Lucius. You were arriving as I was leaving. *¡Sometida al inexorable péndulo deldestino!*"

Framed by bougainvillea vines, their brightly colored bracts made phosphorescent by the moon, a tall and slender gentleman, no older than thirty, surveyed me with dark, soft eyes. His face was smooth and beautiful. He held a leather satchel in one hand, a walking stick in the other. Dressed in a blue velvet waistcoat and white silk ascot, he radiated a reassuring serenity, and I regarded him with an emotion closer to curiosity than fear.

"Such a clever invention, the cinema." The presence opened his satchel and removed a bottle of mezcal. "Though I don't think *La Caída de la Casa de Usher* did justice to Señor Poe's achievement, and *El Pozo y el Péndulo* is guilty of even greater infidelity."

"Señor Ibarra Rojo?" I stood up and bowed cordially toward my improbable visitor.

The phantom and I shook hands. His palm was dry and warm. From his satchel he produced two small glasses, set them on the table, and casually filled each with agave liquor. "You made me a mezcal connoisseur but not an alcoholic. I appreciate that."

"But you never truly existed," I said.

"I do now, darling, as do my passions."

He offered me a lascivious smile and kissed me squarely on the lips.

"I'm afraid I never acquired that taste," I said, pulling away.

"It's a *congenital* taste, actually," said Ibarra Rojo, throwing his arms around me. "Evidently the angel who bestows such proclivities failed to attend your gestation."

"Evidently," I echoed, reciprocating—then breaking—his embrace.

Moving synchronously, we eased ourselves onto the wrought-iron chairs.

"My own gestation was equally lonely," said my visitor, taking a sip of mezcal. "No sooner had your brothers commissioned their vulgar Doctor Varglom poster than I enjoyed the first crude stirrings of existence. 'From the demented pen of Mexico's master of the macabre!' What a crass locution. Does your era belong exclusively to boors and barbarians?"

"Some people are of that opinion."

"Shortly after the poster awakened me, my consciousness coalesced around a marvelous essay called 'Ambassador to the Beyond,' but complete incarnation eluded me until it became obvious that poor Lucius Belasco needed a collaborator."

I sampled the—exceptionally fine—mezcal and said, "I could have finished the story on my own."

"Bullshit," said the phantom, helping himself to one of my Chesterfields. "Isn't that what everybody says these days? 'Bullshit'?"

"Your additions are brilliant, señor. I never would have thought to treat the material as a love story."

"All stories are love stories, whether the locus of the hero's desire is a bride, a beast, a god, a place, or an idea." Ibarra Rojo struck a match, a shooting star in the spangled night, and lit his cigarette. "In me you have wrought a needful being. Owing to our recent collaboration, my artistic urges have been satisfied. Meanwhile, the mezcal is delivering several essential demons to my brain. But, oh, how I long for my mistress, the exquisite Consuelo Portillo Madero. You should have given her more text, dear Lucius. If you had conjured her onto this mortal coil, she and I might be fucking right now."

"I apologize for my oversight."

"Instead I'll have to screw your wife after she and I have lunch tomorrow—or might that occasion some tension between you and me?"

I bit my tongue and said, "Of course it would." Ibarra Rojo's joke, if that's what it was, made me slightly ill, and yet—heaven forgive me—his audacity beguiled me.

"Your Gloria is truly *guapísima*, and a skillful *escritora* as well, or so I infer from her Melville pages." My visitor puffed on his Chesterfield. "How sad that she no longer loves you."

"Might I suggest we change the subject?"

"*Como usted desee.* Now that a complete draft of our story exists, we must go to a cantina tonight and perform it for some appreciative *borrachos.*"

"They won't understand it."

"Of course they will. Our tale is subtle but not opaque."

"The text is in English."

Ibarra Rojo reached into his satchel and drew out a sheaf of typing paper, pressing it into my grasp. "While you were talking to your wife on the telephone, I finished this excellent and cadenced translation, 'La Ciudad de Cera.' You will have no difficulty deciphering my handwriting as you play your part this evening. How is your Spanish these days?"

"I'll be able to perform this—with a Jersey City accent, of course—though the audience will understand what I'm saying better than I. God in heaven, did I really *create* you?"

"Did Melville create Bartleby?"

"It's not the same thing."

"No, I suppose it isn't. By the way, your Remington is a marvelous machine, much easier to use than my old Sholes and Glidden."

Leafing through the translation, I said, "You should know that beyond tonight's public reading I have other plans for our story."

Ibarra Rojo sipped mezcal and steepled his fingers. "Oh? Pray tell."

"Tomorrow I'm mailing it to my brothers in Hollywood. If they like what they read, Oswald will start rounding up a cast and crew while Waldo turns it into a screenplay."

"What a revolting idea."

"I don't disagree, señor, but I need the money."

"What good is money to a man who has lost his integrity?"

"What good is integrity to a man who has nothing to eat?"

"Don't be silly, darling. Your brothers won't let you starve, but they *will* make a travesty of our story."

"Way up north, in the borough of Brooklyn, a man named Mallery puts together a quarterly magazine called *Cinesthesia*. The issue containing 'The Asylum of Doctor Varglom' appears early next year, and I'm pretty sure this same editor will snap up 'City of Wax.'"

"I can understand why a writer might wish to see his story published," said Ibarra Rojo. "Ah, but that is not for us, is it, darling? Our relationship is such a beautiful thing. Why soil it with commerce?"

I decided against taking another sip of mezcal, endeavoring instead to still my throbbing brain. Though the creature I'd brought into being wasn't exactly a monster, he was indubitably an aesthete. "Your purity is admirable, señor, and it's possible you might convince me to leave our collaboration unsullied."

"It's not just a matter of purity. I am *happy* in my obscurity. I require nothing beyond the cheers and applause I receive when performing."

Oh, how I wished I'd never had him forbid his friends to publish an Ibarra Rojo chapbook. If only I'd imagined him suspending his principles and joining the Academia de Letrán. "I fear that if we pursue the topic right now, the result will be a terrible argument."

The phantom nodded, rose, and, as if holding an invisible dancing partner, waltzed nimbly across the garden to the balustrade. "The evening is young"—he swept his arm east to west in a gesture encompassing the whole of the coruscating metropolis—"and all around us lies the liveliest, wickedest, maddest city on earth. Let us descend, you and I, and learn what dark marvels we might encounter in Tenochtitlán!"

"The audience for 'La Ciudad de Cera' won't be sober," I said, refilling my glass with mezcal, "so the players might as well be drunk too." I took a long swallow, then fixed on the agave worm in the bottle. My bones grew hot, simmering the meat in my skull. "May I eat the worm?"

"*Por supuesto*, darling!" shouted Ibarra Rojo. "Even as we speak, strange creatures walk the streets. Popoca in his tattered bandages, hunting down those who defiled the tomb of Princess Xochitl!"

I poured myself another shot, draining the bottle. "La Llorona, weeping for her dead children, even as she murders each man she meets, mistaking him for her unfaithful husband . . ."

"Solares, El Demonio del Volcán, incinerating those who plunder Aztec tombs . . ."

"The Headless Conquistador . . ."

"The Were-Jaguar of Xochimilco . . ."

"Of Zacatecas," said Ibarra Rojo, correcting me.

"The Succubus of Zacatecas . . ."

"Of Xochimilco," said the phantom.

Upending the bottle, I shook the worm into my palm. A forlorn being, sodden, brittle, dead—and obviously indifferent to my intentions. I popped it into my mouth and crunched it between my teeth. I swallowed. The worm tasted like the most savory sentence on which Carlos Ibarra Rojo and I had ever collaborated.

Uncertain of step, muzzy of mind, I staggered down the moonlit Calle Moctezuma, breathing deeply to avoid vomiting on my shoes. As the phantom drew abreast of me, clutching the satchel containing the translation, he outlined his plans for the world premiere of "La Ciudad de Cera." He argued that, whereas I was ideally suited to the role of Garrick Bloom, he was the logical choice to read Anton Varglom's dialogue, likewise the lines belonging to Baron Stradegorst. As for Sonya Dagunzar, naturally we must cast a woman in the part.

"Luckily for us, the required actress is staying at the Hotel Paraíso, a mere two blocks away," said Ibarra Rojo. "I feel certain this vivacious and alluring señora will help us bring our drama to life."

I had no idea how Gloria would react when Ibarra Rojo and I appeared at her hotel and proposed that she join us for an evening of carousing, literary conversation, and barroom theatrics. Although she agreed to stroll with us as far as the Centro Histórico, she refused to believe that the man with whom she'd arranged to have lunch tomorrow was a hypothetical nineteenth-century author coaxed into actuality through the machinations of her annoying husband and ludicrous brothers-in-law. But by now I could speak of the phenomenon with considerable conviction, even as Ibarra Rojo himself, exuding charm, glamour, and a touch of madness, verified our fantastic contentions by his very presence. Not long after we crossed the Plaza de la Constitución, Gloria closed her eyes, gritted her teeth, and announced that she was prepared to play our game.

To this day I can recall only a few vignettes from our sybaritic night in Tenochtitlán. I'm certain we staged an unrehearsed but heartfelt performance of "La Ciudad de Cera" in a cantina called

La Serpiente Áurea, jammed to its adobe walls with poets, painters, musicians, and well-read Communists. Having grown weary of saxophonists playing jazz and exhibitionists declaiming blank verse, the audience embraced our offering for its sheer novelty. The darkly comedic scenes of the villagers feigning lunacy elicited gratifyingly nervous laughter. Gloria brought a singular passion to the episode of the poisoned, dying Sonya painting her dead lover into the mural and thus delivering him from the grave. Perhaps I was deluding myself, but it seemed to me that in resurrecting Garrick with such ardor, her eyes flashing like the orbs of El Demonio del Volcán, her throat emitting cries like the threnodies of La Llorona, Gloria was saying that she wanted to give our marriage a second chance.

Our troupe advanced to another venue, El Diablo Clavel, fully intending to perform the show all over again, but instead we yielded to the synaptically subversive commodities available on the premises, which included not only tequila and weed but also a *narcótico diabólico* called moon beans, *frijoles de luna*. Consumed in the form of orange pellets, this peyote derivative transported me to zones I'd never visited before: forgotten grottoes, black lagoons, uncharted seas, lost continents—destinations that Ibarra Rojo had doubtless toured on previous such occasions, but *terrae incognitae* for his creator.

In retrospect it seems inevitable that our explorations would have borne us to a place Eros called his own. I'm not sure, but we probably took a taxi. The sign on the gate said LA PARQUE DE CHAPULTEPEC. It was closed for the evening. Empowered by *frijoles de luna*, we scaled the black iron palisades. At some point, Sarita, a lovely young poet from El Diablo Clavel, had attached herself to our party, along with her consorts, the sulking Rodolfo and the zaftig Aurora. The six of us gamboled down to the shores of El Lago de Chapultepec, where we secluded ourselves in a cypress grove and shed our garments like burlesque *artistes* at the Palacio de los Pechos. The promises extended by the clothed contours of Sarita and Aurora found complete fulfillment in nakedness. We lost no time making oblations to our libidos. It's possible all fifteen potential connections occurred that night (twenty-one if we allow for Onan's innovation), but I'm not a reliable historian of the orgy in question. Primarily I remember a sensation of being waterborne, drifting through eddies of pleasure and the very tidepool in which copulation had first occurred to our invertebrate ancestors.

Dawn found the cast of "La Ciudad de Cera" in Iztapalapa borough, wandering through the Cementerio Nacional, where Carlos was once employed as groundskeeper. Sarita, Rodolfo, and Aurora had declined to come along, preferring to continue their romp beside El Lago de Chapultepec.

"I died not far from here," the phantom told Gloria. "Your husband arranged for a horse-drawn hearse to run me down. I would have preferred a more subtle demise."

"In life Lucius usually settles for the obvious," said Gloria, "but his fiction isn't normally so shameless."

"I was under time pressure," I said.

Ever the magician, Carlos produced from his satchel a bottle of sangria and three paper cups, an acquisition from El Diablo Clavel, and, upon providing himself and his fellow troupers with splashes of wine, offered a toast to the sunrise.

"*¡Al amanecer! ¡Al amanecer!*" he cried, raising his cup.

"*Amanecida!*" shouted Gloria and I in unison.

"*Mis amigos*, I fear I'm losing my grip on the world," said Carlos after we'd saluted *la salida del sol*.

"Truly you are the most valuable creature Lucius and his brothers ever invented," said Gloria.

"*Tal vez*," said Carlos. "But in any event I must now break invisible bread with the Aztec Mummy, plant a fleshless kiss on La Llorona's cheek, cross gossamer swords with the Headless Conquistador, and drink ethereal beer with El Demonio del Volcán."

"Gloria wishes she could go with you," I said in as sardonic a tone as my intoxicated tongue could manage.

"Would such a journey be possible?" she asked.

I couldn't tell if she was eager to join her new friend or merely curious about the workings of the web in which we were ensnared.

"No," said Carlos, "and I would not bring you with me even if the cosmos permitted it. You will encounter *el pozo* soon enough, señora. Before our final adios, allow me to praise your Melville scenes, which are true to his spirit if not always his text. If there must be a play of *The Confidence-Man*, then you are the person to write it."

"*Muchas gracias*," said Gloria.

The phantom fixed me with his radiant gaze. "As for you, *mi querido*, you must promise never to allow our story to become a commodity. Read it aloud in every cantina between Zacatecas and Alaska, but keep it out of your brothers' greedy hands and the equally venal grasp of that journal editor. Will you give me your word?"

At that transcendentally outré moment, I was happy to do so.

39

"Every Carlos Ibarra Rojo tale was written for its own sake," I told him. "Far be it from me to despoil that heritage."

"No PARC Pictures adaptation, *si*? No journal publication."

"No adaptation," I said. "No publication."

"*Ars gratia artis*," said my creation, and suddenly he was gone, as if the rising sun had burned him into oblivion like pearls of dew on a spiderweb.

Gloria and I took an early-morning bus back to Cuauhtémoc borough. We exchanged no glances. We remained as mute as the Headless Conquistador. Feeling at once gallant and chagrined, I escorted my wife from the *camión* stop to the Hotel Paraíso. As we lingered at the entrance, I promised to read her Melville scenes in time for our dinner engagement, then gave her a large and proprietary kiss on the lips.

I returned to Calle Moctezuma 14, told myself I didn't own an alarm clock, and collapsed on my mattress. Shortly after two o'clock I awoke, head throbbing with hedonism and dehydration. Mistrustful as always of the public water supply, I retrieved a Coca-Cola from the icebox and chugged it down.

Although determined to work on Gloria's Melville scenes, I first needed to strike a bargain with my conscience. The negotiations continued into my third cup of coffee. One fact loomed above all others. While I could comprehend Carlos's aversion to commodification, likewise the pleasure he took in obscurity, I did not for one instant share those attitudes. Naturally I had no wish to cause my ectoplasmic collaborator distress. Heaven forfend. And yet I could not help noting that, having evidently been obliged to abandon the earthly plane, he would be blissfully ignorant of whatever additional incarnations our novelette might enjoy.

At peace with my decision, I retrieved the "City of Wax" manuscript from the garden and, with an eye to its presumed publication, did some perfunctory edits: death to dysfunctional adverbs and lazy alliterations, a pox on bizarre synonyms deployed merely to avoid repetition. After obtaining directions from Armando at the *farmacia*, I walked to the *casa de correos* and mailed the story to my brothers, along with a note explaining that Merle should type a fair copy and send it along to Desmond Mallery.

Turning to Gloria's emerging adaptation of *The Confidence-Man*, I saw that she (or possibly Joshua Logan) had titled the project *Ship of Riddles*: an inauspicious choice, I thought, and the further I got into act one, the more my reservations multiplied. Melville's novel does not defy description—it's essentially a chronicle of the interactions among multifarious passengers riding a Mississippi River steamboat bound for New Orleans on All Fools' Day—but it does resist categorization. To call it an allegory would be to betray the buoyant ambiguity and vertiginous complexity of the twenty-four hours Melville's readers get to spend aboard the *Fidèle*, an interval during which a parade of swindlers, who are in fact all the same protean person, undertake to dupe naïfs and cynics alike. And yet, sad to say, it was the novel's Bunyanesque aspects that had evidently beguiled Gloria, a seduction so complete that she'd jettisoned the first half of the book to focus on the confidence man's most stable avatar, Melville's "cosmopolitan," Frank Goodman, who might be a Satan figure, or perhaps a Christ equivalent, or conceivably an avatar of secular doubt, and who the hell cares? The Negro beggar who pretends to be a cripple, the humanitarian who solicits funds for fake charities, the coal-company president who brokers bogus stock, the doctor who peddles gimcrack herbs, the employment agent who hires out nonexistent clients: All of these vivid rogues were lost in the transition from novel to play.

"If satire is what closes on Saturday night," I told Gloria as we settled into the *restorán* booth that evening, "then allegory doesn't even survive the out-of-town tryouts."

"By paring everything down to Frank Goodman, I'm giving the play dramatic unity," she said, defensively but listlessly.

"Crummy decision," I said.

La Casa del Sol was tacky in the extreme, each table appointed with a lighted candle stuck in a straw-basketed Chianti bottle, the walls decorated with autographed eight-by-ten glossies of Producciones Agrasánchez movie stars. For reasons that eluded me, I found the place quite soothing.

"I made a big mistake coming to Mexico," said Gloria.

"No, you didn't," I said, taking a gulp of Dos Equis. "Tomorrow we'll start putting Black Guinea and John Ringman and everybody into your play."

"I'm talking about the moon-beans and the shores of El Lago de Chapultepec. Was any of that *real*, Lucius?"

"Nothing is real."

"Can you be serious for once? Thank God I'm still—"

"On the pill?"

"Thank God."

"My terrace is the perfect writer's retreat, but if you prefer we can work in some dreadful dive, El Diablo Clavel, for example."

"You know something?" said Gloria, squeezing lime juice into her glass of Corona. "You're right about my Melville scenes—they're awful—and Carlos is wrong."

"But if we restored Black Guinea—"

"To tell you the truth, my heart isn't in this project. It probably never was. I'm flying back to New York tomorrow and breaking the news to Mr. Logan."

"I wish you wouldn't. I love you."

"Don't be tiresome, Lucius."

"Tell Mr. Logan your novelist husband thinks *The Confidence-Man* would work better as a musical, you know, a *Show Boat* sort of thing."

She laughed and said, "What you told Carlos last night, your promise never to sell the story to your brothers or some dopey magazine— that was very noble of you."

I took a swallow of Dos Equis and winced internally, weighing my options. Gloria's illusions, I decided, were best left intact. With any luck, her ignorance would last indefinitely. After all, she certainly never read *Cinesthesia*, and given her antipathy to mass culture she might not even notice if Oswald and Waldo put "City of Wax" up on the big screen.

"Please stay in Mexico," I said.

"I must admit, you and Carlos cooked up a wonderfully appalling plum pudding," said Gloria. "To be honest, I liked it better than your novels." Absently she licked her thumb and index finger, then snuffed the candle flame with the wet skin. "Too bad there's never going to be a movie, or I would audition for Sonya."

I shall always look back on the winter of 1963 as the season of Carlos Ibarra Rojo. The big news, of course, was the January release of *The Asylum of Doctor Varglom*, a terrific-looking, Pathécolor, semi-Gothic horror film starring Vincent Price and based on a novelette by a famous writer nobody had ever heard of. Naturally the New York film critics felt obligated to piss on it, snidely observing that the producers were evidently attempting to exploit the same combination of full palette, period decor, and literary pedigree that had of late helped Hammer Films and A.I.P. reap such formidable profits. My brothers spent their last dime on a huge promotional campaign—newspaper ads, magazine gatefolds, radio spots, television teasers—and their gamble paid off, ultimately turning *The Asylum of Doctor Varglom* into the fourth highest-grossing film of the year.

Among the spoils of PARC Pictures' box-office victory was sufficient clout and cash for the twins to start preproduction on a second classy grade-B horror movie. "We've signed Vincent again," Oswald told me over the phone. "Basil Rathbone and Peter Lorre are both interested in playing Stradegorst. As for Sonya, it looks like we'll get Barbara Steele. She was great in *Pit and the Pendulum*, also *Black Sunday*. That picture almost got the formula right, two out of three—it had a period setting, plus the cachet factor, Nikolai fucking Gogol, but Mario Bava doesn't believe in color, an auteur thing, go figure."

"Whoa, back up a minute," I said. "Evidently you're planning to film 'City of Wax'?"

"You bet your ass. We'd like to buy it outright for three thousand dollars."

"It's worth five."

"Hey, kid, if you don't want to play ball, Waldo can always write an original screenplay that eerily resembles your novelette, and then you can spend five thousand dollars suing us unsuccessfully for plagiarism."

Not long after the Belasco Brothers took *Doctor Varglom* out of the downtown movie palaces and put it into general release, they purchased two-page center spreads in both *Daily Variety* and *The Hollywood Reporter* to "proudly announce" that, having acquired the rights to "City of Wax" by horror legend Carlos Ibarra Rojo, they'd recently traveled to Hacienda Heights and broken ground on "one of the largest motion-picture sets" ever constructed in Southern California . . .

AN ENTIRE MITTELEUROPA VILLAGE SURROUNDING AN IMMENSE REINCARNATION OF THE MADHOUSE FAMILIAR TO MOVIEGOERS WHO'VE SEEN PARC PICTURES' CURRENT THRILLER-DILLER BLOCKBUSTER, *THE ASYLUM OF DOCTOR VARGLOM*!

Accompanying the ad copy was a panoramic watercolor painting of Ekelstadt. The artist's conception almost perfectly matched my mental picture of Stradegorst's supernaturally created village.

While Vincent Price's abominable thought-vampire was luring droves of moviegoers into theaters, the winter issue of *Cinesthesia* appeared on the newsstands. Lavishly illustrated with production stills, the Varglom novelette occasioned a barrage of letters from ecstatic readers. Desmond Mallery was pleased to inform Carlos's newfound fans that the magazine had acquired an English translation of another lost story from Mexico's master of the macabre and scheduled it for the spring issue.

From my perspective, the really important event of the season of Ibarra Rojo was neither the success of the first Doctor Varglom movie nor the ballyhoo my brothers deployed as the sequel went into production nor even the well-received publication of my novelette, but a development of which the outside world knew nothing. Acting largely on a whim, Desmond Mallery mailed the winter issue of *Cinesthesia* to Beverly Knox, a fiction editor at Random House with whom he'd gone to college. He also sent along a photostatic copy of the "City of Wax" typescript, plus the PARC Pictures press release about the life and art of Ibarra Rojo. Mrs. Knox went into orbit. If the other recently discovered stories were as good as the two *Cinesthesia* acquisitions, she told Desmond, and if the author's oeuvre was indeed in the public domain, then the whole series merited a hardcover collection. She wanted to call the book *Six Impossible Things Before Breakfast*, a clever enough title, though its whimsy was palpably at odds with Carlos's proto-Kafka despair.

In his naïveté, Desmond referred Beverly Knox to my brothers, presumed keepers of the rare manuscripts. Naturally Oswald and Waldo constructed the potential Random House omnibus not as a well-deserved windfall for their sensitive and talented younger sibling but as free publicity for the next five films in the Doctor Varglom cycle. It was almost as an afterthought that, upon reaching me through the *farmacia* phone booth (at the twins' urging, I'd remained in Mexico, the better to sustain my psychic identification with our confected genius), Oswald explained that I would have to complete the remaining masterpieces sooner than anyone had anticipated.

"Mrs. Knox is talking about an advance of two thousand dollars— isn't that terrific?" said Oswald. "I told her we should call it *Six Reliable Ways to Lose Your Breakfast*, but she wasn't amused."

"I could use that kind of money, even down here where everything's so cheap," I said.

"Less ten percent for Waldo and me."

"No, this time around I'm going to use my *actual* agent. I'm going to use Yvonne."

"Like hell you are," said Oswald. "The last thing we need is for somebody in the New York publishing establishment to learn that Mexico's master of the macabre is a neurotic kid from New Jersey."

"I'll tell Yvonne I decided to write a bunch of horror stories under a nom de plume."

"Try to get something through your head, Lucius. You're a ghost, not a ghostwriter. Ghosts don't have fucking noms de plume. The only *real* writer at the feast is Carlos Ibarra Rojo, got that?"

I was tempted to tell Oswald, no, the ghost in our machinations was actually Ibarra Rojo, but he would never believe my tale of a visitation from the netherworld. I was no longer sure I believed it myself. But I had to admit he was right about leaving Yvonne out of the negotiations. Essentially I'd be asking her to lie through her teeth when dealing with Random House, a request I was loath to make, lest it end our professional relationship.

"So how long do I have to supply the missing stories?" I asked.

"I fed Mrs. Knox a lot of horse manure about some great-great-grandnephew of Carlos's coming out of the woodwork and claiming to be his literary executor. I told her that nobody fucks with the Belasco Brothers, and we'd have the situation straightened out in a month."

"So you're giving me one lousy month to write four brilliant novelettes?"

"Figure six weeks. I'll pretend our translator's a perfectionist. But let's not drag this thing out, little brother. From what I hear, New York publishing is as capricious as Hollywood—it's all show biz, right?—which means hot properties can turn cold overnight. This fucking Random House tide is at the flood, and now's the time to take it."

Even as I sat in the phone booth listening to Oswald pontificate about entertainment industry realpolitik, my brain was buzzing with ideas for the third story. This time around I would attempt the Grand Guignol narrative, Doctor Varglom urging his patients to enact ever more ghoulish and gruesome theatrical diversions for the appreciative citizens of the village. Surprisingly enough, I finished the thing in a mere eight days of marijuana-fueled frenzy. (You could get anything you wanted at Señor Iglesias's *farmacia* if you knew how to ask.) While "Ticket to an Evisceration" was not as perverse as "The Asylum" or as darkly poetic as "City of Wax," I was pretty damn happy with it, so I mailed the manuscript off to PARC Pictures.

I heard from Oswald ten days later. Desmond was nuts about the new novelette, and Mrs. Knox thought it was, quote, "as gorgeously crafted a story as I've ever read," and she was putting together a contract. Her only stipulation was that, after *Cinesthesia* published "Ticket to an Evisceration," no more Ibarra Rojo fiction would appear in its pages. Feeding the nascent cult was all to the good, but revealing the entire contents of *Six Impossible Things Before Breakfast* would seriously hurt sales.

"Waldo and I don't like 'Evisceration' quite as much as Mrs. Knox did," said Oswald, "but we're still planning to turn it into our next picture."

"Three down and three to go," I said. "When do I see some dough from Random House? For that matter, when do I see my three thousand for the 'City of Wax' movie deal?"

"We collect half the Random advance on signing, half after Mrs. Knox approves the whole package."

"And the 'Wax' money?"

"Be patient, little brother. That village set nearly broke the bank. We've budgeted the rest of the picture down to the last fucking roll of gaffer tape, and there's nothing left in the kitty."

"Hey, Oswald, you don't purchase literary properties out of a goddamn 'kitty.'"

"Little known fact. Mary Shelley got paid out of a kitty. Or are you telling me it's time for Waldo to take a turn at impersonating our boy?"

"No, I'm not saying that."

"Admit it, kid. You love writing this crud for us."

"I love it, Oswald," I said sotto voce, heaving a sigh. "I truly do."

March in Mexico is normally a Goldilocks month, not too cold, not too hot, but in the circumscribed world of Calle Moctezuma 14 a sweltering climate obtained, so intense was the heat generated by Lucius Belasco at his most productive. Although I never feared that the Remington would catch fire, I did worry that my furious fingers might break the machine before they brought into being "Blood Temple of Asmodeus" (the story set in the forbidden abbey, Varglom sacrificing his patients on a stone altar and thereby enticing obscene deities onto the mortal plane) and "Dreams of a Deranged Ape" (all about the junglelike conservatory Varglom had populated with blasphemous beasts of his own design). Inspiring my endeavors was a collection of artifacts that had spontaneously turned my apartment into a kind of Ibarra Rojo museum. A cover proof for *Six Impossible Things Before Breakfast* graced the bathroom door. My flea-market

coffee table overflowed with copies of the spring *Cinesthesia*: IN
THIS ISSUE, DOOM COMES TO EKELSTADT IN A NEW CARLOS IBARRA
ROJO STORY. The kitchen wall displayed an anticipatory one-sheet
for the *City of Wax* movie (sent to me by my brothers on the day
they finished building their colossal Mitteleuropa village), featuring
full-length portraits of Vincent Price, Basil Rathbone, and Barbara
Steele.

With high hopes and soaring expectations, I entered my garden, sat
down at the Remington, and attempted to begin the haunted-swamp
story. I hammered out a scene breakdown for the first two acts, and,
after winding a fresh sheet against the platen, typed a working title,
"Liquid Infinity." But that was all I produced that day. Or the next
day. Or the next.

Or the next.

So this was what it was like, I thought, the disease all writers
dread. The orchids mocked me. The roses stank. The bougainvillea
released malevolent spores, aggravating the malady to which I'd
thought myself immune, my transient "City of Wax" block notwith-
standing. I decided that only a divine act would deliver me from the
abyss that now engulfed my garden, my mind, my soul, but I believed in a benevolent deity even less than I believed in La Momia
Azteca or any of his uncanny kin.

At first there was only his breathing, a fusillade of distraught exha-
lations punctuated by coughing. A few minutes later I apprehended
his scent, or rather the scent of his cologne, a floral formula he'd
probably contrived himself. I looked up, shifting my gaze from the
blank page to a fountain of bougainvillea.

Carlos stood amidst the vines, satchel on his shoulder, gaunt face
aglow with the noonday sun, leaning on his walking stick in a
debonair pose. He had brought along the inevitable bottle of mezcal,
and I briefly entertained the notion that the swamp-dwelling monster in my comatose novelette should be an immense agave worm.

"And so I return, darling, summoned once again by the clamor of
your despair."

Alternately smiling and scowling, Carlos sauntered across the
garden. Reaching the wrought-iron table, he set down the mezcal
bottle and seized my scene outline.

"This has promise," he said after studying all three pages. He
returned the sketch to the table. "Tell me, how fares the beauteous

Gloria? Did she ever finish her Melville play?"

"I believe she lost faith in it," I said. "We're not on very chummy terms these days."

"Were you ever?"

"I need a drink."

Carlos instantly produced two small tumblers from his satchel, then filled both to the brim. "This time I get to eat the worm," he said as we sipped our liquor. I nodded in assent. "Permit me to offer a preliminary diagnosis," he continued. "The foul and watery setting you chose is perfect, so revelatory of Varglom's character. Whereas normal people prefer to drain their swamps, he decides to *install* one. But then you bring a tedious aquatic monster on stage, all tentacles and barbels and banality. It simply won't do."

"I like my monster," I said, imbibing.

"It's jejune."

"Then *Beowulf* is jejune."

"I've always thought so, yes. How does this sound, *mi querido*? One day, while surveying his swamp, Varglom gets an idea for curing his most delusional patients. He imagines outfitting them in deep-sea diving suits—you know, the sort of rubber-and-brass ensemble Captain Nemo wore on the ocean floor—then immersing them in the swamp. According to Varglom's theory, each madman will fancy he's descending into the noxious bog of his own mind, surrounded by sunken fears and repressed remembrances."

"I thought you were gone forever."

"Strange are the ways of metaphysics. What do you think of my premise?"

"Varglom as the ancestor of Freud? I like it. Of course, most of the story should be from the viewpoint of a particular lunatic as he plunges ever downward into himself."

"Exactly!"

"Our prose must be—"

"Experimental," said the phantom, siphoning mezcal through his thin lips.

"Yes, I agree. Impressionistic."

"Even surrealistic. 'City of Wax' was some sort of great story, but 'Liquid Infinity' will be unlike any work of fiction ever written. We shall give the reader no compass, no signposts, no comfortable coordinates. How felicitous that we agreed to forswear celebrity and embrace satisfaction. Our visions are not for sale, are they, darling? Let's get to work."

48

For two unbroken hours my creature and I collaborated, drinking mezcal and taking turns at the Remington as, sentence by eccentric sentence, paragraph by savage paragraph, the story took shape. By the tenth page we'd drained the bottle, and Carlos announced that he wanted to clear his brain with caffeine. Might I repair to the kitchen and brew a pot of strong coffee?

The instant the phantom uttered the word "kitchen," my recklessness visited itself upon me, a rush of dread rippling through my flesh. How foolish I'd been to appoint my apartment with collector's items spawned by the season of Ibarra Rojo. Affecting nonchalance, I said I'd be pleased to make him some coffee, then sidled into the kitchen.

For a fleeting moment it seemed that my indiscretion would go unnoticed. Taking hold of the preproduction *City of Wax* one-sheet, I tore it free of the wall. But then suddenly Carlos was beside me, displaying the mezcal bottle and pointing to its vermian occupant.

"Drop the worm in the coffee pot," he instructed me. "It will sweeten the brew." His eyes wandered to the poster, and he unleashed a howl that might have come from a PARC Pictures reform-school werewolf. "I forbade it!" he cried. "I forbade it!"

He yanked the one-sheet from my grasp and tore it in two, bisecting Vincent Price, Basil Rathbone, and Barbara Steele across their abdomens as if they'd encountered Poe's pendulum. I lurched toward the bathroom door, but the phantom was there first, ripping down the *Six Impossible Things* cover proof and shredding it with preternatural wrath. The next thing I knew, he was in the parlor, scooping up the spring issues of *Cinesthesia*. He ran onto the balcony and began dropping the magazines one by one over the side, so that they went fluttering to the mud below like geese blasted from the sky.

"I was happy!" he cried as, clutching the last magazine, he scrambled onto the balcony railing. "How can you not understand? And yet I still love you, darling! Adios!"

He spread his arms in a cruciform posture and dived, screaming, into the air. I half expected him to sprout wings, like a vampire bat or a satanic cherub, but instead, in a reprise of his departure from the cemetery, he simply vanished, still holding the magazine, as if he meant to share "City of Wax" with certain discerning citizens of the netherworld.

*

Although Carlos's second visitation shocked me no less than the first, it was now obvious how I could avoid additional such hauntings. Once I'd fulfilled my obligation to Random House by delivering the final Doctor Varglom tale, either "Liquid Infinity" or something from a different sector of Krogskrafte, I needed merely to forsake my Ibarra Rojo pseudonym. But I would not return to composing autobiographical fiction. The proficiency with which I'd ground out "Ticket to an Evisceration," "Blood Temple of Asmodeus," and "Dreams of a Deranged Ape" had convinced me I was a fabulist at heart. After completing the Varglom cycle, I must remain in Mexico and, energized by the culture that had brought forth the Crying Woman and El Demonio del Volcán, write works of unbridled speculation and fantastical contrivance that I signed with my own name.

I decided I should not pursue this scheme before talking to my agent, so in early April I called Yvonne and told her I wanted to compose a long, melodramatic but stylistically ambitious novel in the manner of the nineteenth-century literary genius, Carlos Ibarra Rojo.

"I've never heard of him," she said.

"His stories have been appearing in *Cinesthesia*."

"Synesthesia? The sensory-crossover phenomenon?"

"Never mind."

"Anesthesia?"

"Vincent Price recently starred in an adaptation of an Ibarra Rojo story called *The Asylum of Doctor Varglom*."

"Why the hell would Lucius Belasco want to write something that's vulnerable to becoming a Vincent Price movie?"

"Believe me, Ibarra Rojo was a class act. Random House is publishing all his surviving fiction."

"Do you have a premise yet?"

"No, but I'm living in Mexico now. The culture inspires me."

"Mexico?"

"It's complicated."

"Listen, Lucius, if you really want to do this, far be it from me to discourage you. In a peculiar way, it sounds auspicious."

I said adios to Yvonne, then proceeded to my garden with the aim of outlining a primevally weird novel or two.

Someone was waiting for me, a scarecrow of a man wrapped in bandages, a moldering serape hanging in tatters from his frame. His head suggested a sugar skull left over from El Día de los Muertos.

"My name is Popoca," wheezed the intruder. Scraggly cords of black hair sprouted from his cranium. His fingers were as long and thin as trussing needles.

"I know," I said, frozen in my tracks. "I've seen the movies. You're that accomplished actor Ángel Di Stefani, star of the Momia Azteca trilogy."

"A reasonable guess, but wrong."

"Carlos? Is that you under those rags?"

"I am Popoca."

"As you wish."

"When I appeared in her office yesterday morning, Señora Knox accused me of being a prankster in a Halloween costume."

"You went to Random House, Carlos? Dressed like that? *Mierda.*"

"*Hágame un favor, mi amigo.* Let the mummy talk. Emphatically I informed Señora Knox that I was not a playing a joke. 'Who are you?' she asked. 'There are some things irrationality cannot explain,' I replied. 'I'm a busy woman,' she said. 'Ibarra Rojo must retain his obscurity,' I insisted. 'But he's dead,' she said. 'So am I,' I noted. 'His collection is on the fall list,' she protested. 'Your name is on a death list,' I retorted, adding, 'My grip is of iron, my scruples are nonexistent, and I am prepared to strangle you.' These last remarks made a deep impression on her, and as our conversation progressed, she agreed to cancel *Six Impossible Things Before Breakfast.* Señor Belasco, you look as if you don't believe any of this."

"You know what I believe?" I said. "I believe you're a vandal in a moth-eaten suit." But was that the case? Did I not in fact know that these embalmed feet had just come from muddying a threshold more terrible and alluring than any I would ever cross on earth? "I also believe that, whoever you are, today you did something unconscionable."

"Breaking a promise to one's creator is likewise unconscionable."

Whatever the intruder's real identity, I sensed he was telling the truth about the novelette collection. The project was dead. There was actually a bright side to this calamity. Now I didn't have to finish 'Liquid Infinity,' which meant I wouldn't be inadvertently evoking Ibarra Rojo in the future.

"As you might imagine, I'm quite fond of the mummy trilogy," Popoca continued. "Ángel Di Stefani is a gifted pantomime actor. My favorite is *La Momia Azteca contra el Robot Humano.* Luis Castañeda makes a perfect mad scientist." Fixing me with his inert eyes, he limped across the garden. "Carlos said to tell you he took no pleasure in sending me to terrorize your editor, and he regrets that his actions will hurt you financially. And now, señor, I bid you adios."

The intruder lurched into the kitchen and disappeared from view. For a full minute I remained standing amid the April orchids, wondering how much stranger the world would get before I died.

Later that evening, having exhausted my supplies of alcohol and food, I walked to La Casa del Sol, where I appropriated the booth in which Gloria and I had dined following our antics in the Centro Histórico and El Parque de Chapultepec. I requested half a roasted chicken and a tumbler of tequila. Waiting for my order, I took comfort in my recent conversation with Yvonne. My new project made little sense to her, and yet she'd given it her blessing.

No sooner had I savored the first morsel of chicken than a veiled woman sidled toward my booth, her skeletal form enswathed in a heavy black cloak and tattered mourning dress. Upon assuming the bench opposite me, she lifted her mantilla to reveal a grief-struck yet oddly enchanting face. Tears of blood haloed her eyes.

"*¡Oh, hijos míos, ya ha llegado vuestra destrucción!*" she wailed in the voice of a suicidal lark. Oh, my children, your destruction is nigh. "*¿Dónde os llevaré?*" Where can I take you? "*Me llamo—*"

"Llorona," I said. "The Crying Woman."

"Doomed to wander the earth for eternity."

"You play the part very well, señora. I'm afraid I've never seen your movies. Were you in *La Herencia de la Llorona? La Maldición de la Llorona?*"

"Hear me out, Señor Belasco."

Reaching inside her cloak, my uninvited guest produced a carving knife, then set it on the table like a planchette on a Ouija board. As she continued speaking, her voice grew more mournful still, and I realized that, though I could not accept her claim to be a ghost, I did believe in her sorrow.

"Yesterday I visited Señor Mallery in his Brooklyn office," she said. "'You will publish no more Ibarra Rojo stories,' I told him. 'But I've scheduled one for the summer issue,' he replied, and so I flashed my knife and said, 'If you don't terminate the series, I'll carve a grin in your throat.' I now had his complete attention. He agreed to my demands. I know what's on your mind, señor. You're wondering—"

"I'm wondering whether you used that same knife to—"

"To kill my children?" said the Crying Woman, rising. "A plausible theory, but, no, I am locked into the legend of myself. La Llorona drowned her sons and daughters in Lake Texcoco. But please know this: I do not ask for sympathy—from you or anyone else." She retrieved her weapon and began gliding away. "I bear a message from Carlos. He regrets never thanking you for bringing him into existence."

"Tell him I accept his gratitude."

"¡Oh, hijos míos!" cried La Llorona, and then she vanished into the crowd of patrons waiting for a booth.

I finished my chicken, drained my tumbler, and set out for the Teatro Zapata. Not only was I determined to catch the midnight screening of PARC Pictures' famous Pathécolor B-movie about a thought-vampire (which I'd never seen in any language), but I furthermore reasoned that my creature's confederates would have trouble finding me in a darkened theater.

As I sat in the baroque but decrepit movie palace, watching a subtitled print of *El Sanatorio de Doctor Varglom*, it occurred to me that Carlos had probably also targeted my brothers for spectral intimidation. The thought of Oswald getting into an argument with Popoca or La Llorona simultaneously amused and terrified me. Tomorrow morning I must phone PARC Pictures from the *farmacia* and tell the twins to beware of actors portraying Mexican avengers.

I quickly apprehended why *The Asylum of Doctor Varglom* had found such a large audience. My brothers had fashioned as satisfying a melodrama as might be imagined, Vincent Price having the time of his life creeping around his phantasmagoric madhouse opening up his patients' skulls, consuming the contents of these bony tureens (each such banquet occurred tastefully offscreen), and relishing the exotic mental landscapes that accrued to his unholy craving. This creepshow was sexy as well, for many of Varglom's victims were gorgeous and impressively proportioned women wearing diaphanous nightgowns.

True to one of Oswald's many affectations, the credits were spliced onto the end of the picture. I stayed for every frame of the final reel, mostly so I could read "based on a story by Carlos Ibarra Rojo" and hear the last measures of Les Baxter's fine score. By the time the lights came up, only two people were left in the theater, myself and a hunched figure seated two rows in front of me. My fellow credit watcher turned toward the projection booth, and I shuddered.

His eye sockets seemed to extend to the back of his skull and beyond, like adjacent burrows fashioned by demented moles. Pinprick beacons, red as the blood from La Llorona's orbs, flashed in the cavities. Black, bubbled, and in a perpetual state of migration, his flesh suggested molten pitch oozing down the sides of a crucible.

"Call me Solares," he said in a voice made of embers and pumice.

"El Demonio del Volcán?"

"At your service."

"Not *my* service, Solares. You have one and only one master."

"True enough, señor. When Carlos told me to set fire to your brothers' gigantic motion-picture set, I immediately departed for Hacienda Heights."

"Set fire to it?!" I moaned, and suddenly I was in my ramshackle Calle Moctezuma elevator, plummeting inexorably, the cable having snapped. "Jesus!"

"Even as we speak, Ekelstadt is burning!" cried El Demonio del Volcán. "The fire departments are helpless! I am Solares! I breathe fire and eat bitumen! Flames shoot from my eyes! Would you like a demonstration?"

I've never hated anyone as much as I hated Carlos Ibarra Rojo just then. "Your master is a fiend!" I cried, leaping to my feet.

"At times his assessment of you is equally negative," said Solares as I raced out of the theater. "And yet his parting directive to me was rather poignant. 'Tell my creator I think about him every day.'"

I chartered a rogue taxi to the Aeropuerto Central, then took the first available flight—a red-eye special—to the City of Angels. Upon landing at LAX, I rented a sedan from Hertz, and by noon I was in Hacienda Heights.

With fearful determination I elbowed my way through the thinning ranks of the morbidly curious. Solares had performed his mission with great efficiency. Mounds of ash rose everywhere. Skeins of smoke hung in the air. Charred timbers pointed in all directions like the bones of an immolated dinosaur. Of the immense, brooding, towering asylum, nothing remained but a matrix of blackened girders and melted rebar.

Having drifted toward what had obviously once been the village square, my brothers were walking in dazed circles around a charred collar of stone marking a community well. I didn't expect that my appearance would please them—how could anything please them at this moment?—but I attempted a cheerful demeanor and began the conversation with an upbeat remark.

"You can start rebuilding as soon as the first check arrives from the insurance company," I said, laying a presumably reassuring hand on Oswald's shoulder.

"We don't *have* insurance," he moaned.

"*Mierda*," I said.

"It seemed like a good way to balance the budget," said Oswald. "What the fuck are *you* doing here?"

"A long story," I said.

"This catastrophe is actually worse than it looks," said Waldo. "Shooting was supposed to start in two days, so we'd just moved everything into the asylum. Camera, lights, cables, props, costumes, film stock, you name it. Our inventory is nothing but cinders now. If I ever catch the arsonist, I'll borrow Roger Corman's pendulum and slice his pecker into canapés."

"You know what *really* pisses me off?" said Oswald. "When I heard the set was on fire, I figured, 'OK, we'll have the village burn instead of melting,' so I got Floyd out of bed, and he grabbed his 35mm Mitchell and the loaded magazine he keeps for emergencies, but by the time we got here, there was no fucking inferno left to shoot."

"Last night I saw a midnight show of *El Sanatorio de Doctor Varglom* in Cuauhtémoc," I said. "Marvelous picture, boys."

"Fuck you, Lucius."

"Now that you have money flowing in from foreign markets," I persisted, "might that be enough to—?"

"Not flowing, little brother, *trickling*," said Oswald. "It'll never accumulate fast enough to put this production back on its feet."

"While we're on the topic of lousy news," said Waldo, "yesterday morning we got a call from Mrs. Knox. Looks like they're deep-sixing the Ibarra Rojo collection. No explanation."

"See what I mean about New York publishing being as capricious as Hollywood?" said Oswald. "Sorry, kid. I know you were counting on the money."

"Capricious, yes," I muttered, and I couldn't help adding, "next you'll be telling me Desmond Mallery won't be running the Grand Guignol story."

"How did you know?"

"Psychopath in a mantilla."

I fixed on a pile of carbonized beams that curiously resembled a compass rose. So where should I go now? West? The movie business had never enchanted me half as much as it did my brothers. East? I was sick of Gloria's impossibly high standards for husbands. North? After a year of living in the subtropics, I'd developed an aversion to bad weather. South? Despite yesterday's distressing encounters with Mexican folklore, that sad and sunny country was the place I loved best.

"There's only one way this disaster can play out," Oswald told me, his voice cracking. "Waldo and I go back to making schlock."

"The best schlock poverty can buy," said Waldo, his eyes growing moist.

"*City of Wax* would've been a great picture," I said.

"The greatest," said Oswald, tears rolling down his cheeks, and I realized I'd never before seen my brothers weep.

Unorthodox though his tactics were—unorthodox, rash, crude, and brutal—Carlos Ibarra Rojo succeeded in erasing himself from history. I'm almost eighty now, and my cerebral arteries are a lot harder than my erections, but I know all about databases and online encyclopedias, and I can confidently assert that you couldn't fill a Munchkin's thimble with digitalized information about Mexico's master of the macabre. If you like, you can humiliate your search engine by sending it off in quest of Ibarra Rojo facts, but his name is to be found only in the credits for a generally forgotten (though profitable) movie titled *The Asylum of Doctor Varglom* and in two back issues of a defunct (but fondly remembered) periodical called *Cinesthesia*. Through the intervention of a mummy, a Mexican Medea, and a volcano demon, the phantom canceled his cult.

And what of my brothers? They might have been sleazy, but they were survivors. The late sixties and early seventies were something of a golden age for drive-in garbage and grindhouse drivel, and the Belasco Brothers were on the job, filling double bills with biker flicks, James Bond rip-offs, zombie jamborees, serial-killer bloodbaths, and other pap to which Oswald and Waldo were not quite ashamed to put their names.

As for Gloria Belasco, now Gloria Jenkins, our divorce became final on the same day Roger Corman signed Vincent Prince and Basil Rathbone to star in *Tales of Terror* (another Poe film, my brothers having reluctantly released them from their PARC Pictures contracts). Gloria's creative partnership with Joshua Logan never went anywhere. The last I heard, she was teaching playwriting at Yale and still getting her elliptical psychodramas produced Off-Off-Broadway.

You will perhaps be surprised to learn that, in the post–Ibarra Rojo phase of my career, I adopted a philosophy not terribly different from the phantom's. Literary celebrity no longer mattered to me. What counted was the tale I had to tell, whether of a headless conquistador, lonely were-jaguar, insatiable succubus, weeping revenant, or moldering mummy. (For obvious reasons, I refused to write about volcano demons.) True, I continued to bristle at Carlos's fatuous notions of artistic purity, his windy insistence that commerce was automatically corrupting. I'm not convinced that his disdain for popular taste was anything more than the stance of a poseur. Show me a story by Mexico's *maestro de lo macabro*, and I'll show you an awfully good time. All art is entertainment (but not the other way around), all drama is melodrama (ditto), and nobody appreciated those truths better than Carlos Ibarra Rojo.

Following my creature's example, I performed my stories in cantinas, cafés, and *clubs de jazz*, accepting whatever coins the crowd might sprinkle at my feet. Sometimes I took my act to the arcade markets and street fairs. For a mere fifty centavos, this American expatriate would sell you a mimeographed copy of a story about a specter from his adopted country. For twenty centavos, he would compose such a tale on the spot and incorporate you into the plot.

Of course, I had at my fingertips a source of income never available to Carlos, the surprisingly resilient Mexican horror-movie industry. Writing under the *pseudónimo* of Joaquín Alcayde, I bestowed an entire second trilogy on Popoca, including *La Venganza de la Momia Azteca*, *La Sombra de la Momia Azteca*, and *La Momia Azteca contra el Poder Satánico*, and I also resurrected the undead Count Lavud, placing him at the center of *El Castillo del Vampiro*, *La Sangre del Vampiro*, and *El Vampiro contra las Lobas*. PARC Pictures picked up the entire six-flick package for US distribution, though I heard it barely broke even.

Beyond ready cash and a certain oblique creative satisfaction, my Popoca efforts brought a third boon into my life. All these pictures featured a witty and comely actress named Rosita del Torres in the role of Princess Xochitl. She once described herself to me as "the only Catholic atheist in Mexico." We got married on the set of *La Sombra de la Momia Azteca*, and I'm pleased to report that—except for the occasional horrendous fight, the antagonism between me and her layabout brother, and the intermittent clinical depression she suffered after becoming too old to play princesses—we lived happily ever after.

It was during a raw October in 1973, right before El Día de los Muertos, that I experienced a sudden and overwhelming desire to see my creature once more. I calculated that to conjure him I need merely create a title page so preposterous that the project to which it pointed would burden me with writer's block. Eventually I settled on

"La Momia Azteca contra Richard Nixon, an Original Screenplay by Carlos Ibarra Rojo." I removed the sheet from the typewriter (I now had an electric Royal), inserted a fresh page, and, bereft of inspiration, stared at the taunting pale rectangle.

He appeared within the hour, striding into my cluttered office sporting his usual accessories: walking stick, ascot, bottle of mezcal. When he realized he'd been deceived and that I had no interest in writing a screenplay about Nixon, he was incensed, but then suddenly he mellowed.

"Darling, I'm touched. You yearned for me."

"Up to a point," I said. "Let's go for a walk."

In those days Rosita and I were living in Iztapalapa borough, a few blocks from the Cementerio Nacional. As dusk cloaked the marble forest, Carlos and I strolled about the grounds, occasionally pausing to survey a twilit statue of a saint or a darkening incarnation of La Virgin de Guadalupe. Our conversation touched on art, God, and metaphysics, but mostly we talked of our sins. I averred that deceiving him was "among the basest things I've ever done," and he allowed that his retribution scheme had been "immorally dependent on traumatizing innocent people."

"If you'll absolve me," I said as we headed toward the main gate, now silvered by the moon, "then I'll absolve you."

Carlos hummed in assent. "I feel especially contrite about causing your brothers such anguish. But did I have a choice, *mi querido?* Unless a man takes steps to recover his lost happiness, he will make those around him unhappy as well."

Headlamps dead, pistons shrieking, the hearse came hurtling out of the night, careening down the narrow lane as its fictional horse-drawn equivalent had done a century earlier. To this day I cannot account for the vehicle. Possibly some intoxicated *adolescentes* stole the thing and then went joyriding. Carlos threw his arms around me, lurching toward the berm. For a few seconds we stayed on our feet, staggering away from the lane, and then together we plummeted into a freshly dug grave, landing on a mattress of soft earth as the hearse roared away.

"How can I repay you?" I asked, a banality I'd recently put into the mouth of Princess Xochitl. I took an anatomical inventory: bruises, scratches, aches, pains, but evidently no broken bones. "I owe you my life."

We helped each other out of the soggy pit, using the looping roots like ratlines on a Spanish galleon.

"I've never saved a person's life before," said the phantom after we were back on solid ground. "Who would have guessed it would be so erotic?"

"I love you, Carlos," I told him.

"And I love you, *mi querido*. But you already knew that."

I flung out my arms and, hugging my creature, pressed my lips against his mouth. He reciprocated my kiss. Our tongues fused. We laughed and broke our embrace, and then, suddenly, like the child of Mary Shelley's prodigious fancy, Carlos Ibarra Rojo was gone, lost in darkness and distance, never to return.

Aftermath
Laura van den Berg

GENEVIEVE MOVED BACK into the house on a Monday. The place needed a good clean, she had decided, so she found a cleaning service called Aftermath in the phone book. They told her it would take three days to clean the house and that she could not be present.

"Should we be aware of any biohazards?" the receptionist asked.

"Biohazards?" She was standing in her kitchen, talking on the landline. She imagined she was one of the last remaining people in America with a landline.

"Blood, fecal matter, teargas," the receptionist said.

"Oh," Genevieve said. "No. Nothing like that."

She checked into a motel called the Sagebrush. In bed, she listened to the rattle of the ice machine. She watched workout infomercials with the volume on mute. On her last night, a man pounded on her door and shouted, VERONICA! but left before she could call the front desk to complain. In the morning, she found a toupee lying in the hallway like a dead animal.

At first, her house looked the same, the counters and floors a little brighter from the cleaning, except the attic ceiling was open on the second floor. The steps had been unfolded, an invitation to climb. The attic had always been there, of course, though the real estate agent neglected to mention it when she showed the house. Genevieve noticed it on her first night—the rectangular door in the ceiling, the dangling string—and knew immediately that she would never go up there. Attics were home to hideous family secrets and ill-tempered ghosts and rat kings. Everyone knew that terrible things happened in attics. She had lived in the house for nearly a year and stayed true to her word.

Aftermath must have cleaned the attic and forgot to close it, Genevieve thought. That was the explanation that made the most sense. She folded up the stairs and tried to close the attic, but it wouldn't budge. She bent down and grabbed the edges of the door and pulled. She wedged herself underneath the door, gritted her teeth, and pushed. Soon she was short of breath and her hands were burning. The door was stuck. Something was wrong with the hinges. She looked into the dark mouth of the attic and felt a gust of air, like something was breathing on her.

That night, Genevieve slept downstairs, on the couch, away from the attic.

The phone woke her. It was the middle of the day. She stumbled into the kitchen in her pajamas and striped socks, wondering how long she would have slept if the phone hadn't rung. It was her neighbor, calling to see about the house.

"How is it?" the neighbor said. "Does it look the same?"

"More or less," Genevieve said.

"I saw the cleaners go in. There were six of them, in gas masks and gloves and plastic overalls. A frightful sight, we all agreed."

"We" meant the neighbor and her two blind tabby cats, Dr. No and Mr. Goldfinger. This neighbor once told Genevieve that she only adopted blind cats because she hated the idea of animals watching her in the night.

"Well, I suppose one thing is different," Genevieve said. "The attic ceiling is open. It won't close."

"You just need to put a little muscle into it."

"I tried." The kitchen counter held the bright orb of her face. Those cleaners had done a truly remarkable job.

"Your sister," the neighbor began, but Genevieve hung up before she could say anything more.

That night, in the bathroom, she pried the floral shower curtain off its rings. She found a hammer and a small box of nails and a stepladder. She stood on the stepladder and nailed the shower curtain over the opening. She drove the nails in fast and clean. When she was finished, the stairs poked out like a crocodile's jaw, but at least the attic entrance was covered. Genevieve slept in her own bed and in the middle of the night, she found herself swimming back to the time her sister dressed as a heart surgeon for Halloween. She wore a surgical mask and the green rubber gloves their mother put on to wash dishes.

In the morning, she found a puddle of flowers on the hallway floor. The little dark nails were missing from the ceiling and they were not lost in the folds of the shower curtain or anywhere else in the house, so far as she could see. She stood against the wall and chewed her nails. It was only after she tasted blood on her thumb that she realized she was chewing past the quick.

She called Aftermath and told them what was going on.

61

"One of your people opened the attic ceiling," she said. "I need for you to make this right." She wondered if they would ask about her sister, who had recently gone missing. The last time she was seen in the house, what she was doing.

"Impossible," the receptionist said. "It wasn't us. We never clean attics."

"You clean biohazards!" She was getting all twisted up in the cord. She could hire contractors to cement the attic shut. She could check back into the motel. She could move.

"Yes. But we don't do attics."

"You clean teargas!"

"Especially *that* attic."

Later she wrote a long letter of complaint, addressed to the CEO of Aftermath, and put it in the mail.

The truth was she couldn't remember the last time she saw her sister. At the start of winter, her sister had come to stay with her. Genevieve had not seen or talked to her sister in months. One day she just showed up. This was a small house, without a guest room, so they shared a bed, like they did when they were children and scared of thunderstorms. They watched Late-Night TV and ate chocolate pudding. Her sister petted Genevieve's hair and called her "Genie." Sometimes her sister got sad. Sometimes Genevieve would hear her crying in the shower. This wasn't such a surprise, though: Her sister had always been sad.

"What have you been doing all these months?" Genevieve would try asking her.

"Oh, you know," her sister would say.

They had known each other for their whole lives and that was the best answer she could get. Oh, you know.

I don't know anything, Genevieve longed to say, but she worried she would only make her sister more sad.

None of these times was the last time.

The contractor came to give an estimate. He wore a white construction helmet and carried a clipboard and when he saw the open attic ceiling, he shook his head and said, "I'm sorry, ma'am, but there's not a thing we can do about that."

"Can you at least try closing it?" Genevieve sighed. "The hinges are stuck, but maybe if a man tried."

He held his clipboard tight against his chest. He eyed the attic ceiling, like it might be aware that it was being discussed. "It's not a question of strength."

"Please," Genevieve said. "I'll pay you anything."

"Don't ever call me again," the contractor said.

She listened to the clomp of his boots as he left the house. She unfolded the stairs and sat on one of the lower rungs. If the attic was going to be such a menace, it could at least give her a place to sit down.

Genevieve wasn't sure how long she had been sitting there before she remembered the sound of her sister's footsteps coming up the stairs, her face appearing in the hallway, her pale cheeks puffed from crying.

"What's wrong?" Genevieve had asked.

"Oh, you know," her sister had said. "It's nothing, really. I just don't want to leave."

"No one says you have to leave." Genevieve remembered listing the ways she could help her sister be less sad. Pancakes with whipped cream, walks in the woods, buddy-cop comedies, daffodils, long drives that ended in ice cream. It would have helped if her sister had been willing to leave the house.

Her sister had walked right past her, coming to rest underneath the attic ceiling. She looked very tired, like she hadn't gotten a good night's sleep in weeks, which Genevieve knew was impossible, since they had been sleeping in the same bed, their tongues sweet with chocolate. She stared up at the attic ceiling like it was expecting her. She touched the string.

"Don't go up there." Genevieve's breath had turned quick. Her heart felt like a ringing bell. "There's absolutely nothing up there."

Something was about to happen. But what?

Still, that was not the last time.

Genevieve stood up and went downstairs, frowning at the trail of dirt the contractor had left behind. She put on her coat. She got into her car and drove away and never went back to the house again. She left the attic ceiling open and for all she knew it stayed that way forever.

Many years later, when Genevieve was an old woman, she lived on a freighter ship that traveled the world. She had been all over Europe and South America and New Zealand and Australia. She had been to the Horn of Africa. She had crossed the Black Sea. The crew called her St. Genevieve, for the saint who saved Paris from Attila the Hun. No one called her "Genie." If anyone asked why she chose to live on a freighter, she would say, "On ships there are no attics." Once she saw a passenger reading a novel called *Aftermath* and was relieved when he disembarked in Christchurch, never to be seen again. A small part of her was always listening for someone who used the phrase "Oh, you know." In recent years, she had become too weak to leave the ship, but she could sit on the deck in her wheelchair, a blue wool blanket tucked around her legs, and watch the activity in the ports. Currently she was bound for Guadeloupe.

In the Caribbean Sea, a young man who had been traveling on the freighter for six months committed suicide. She saw his silhouette, glinting and angular in the sun, on the far end of the deck and then he was climbing and then he was gone. It was a windy day, and it looked as though the weather plucked him right off the boat and dropped him into the sea.

Before they lost this man to the Caribbean, she had not said or thought the word "suicide" for years.

On ships, there were many superstitions. You weren't supposed to whistle or eat bananas. Fridays were bad luck. So were flowers and pea soup and priests. If you saw a dolphin swimming alongside the ship, you were supposed to make a wish. Genevieve liked to wish for only the most hopeless things. For the universal eradication of attics and sadness. For laws that held cleaning crews accountable. For the warmth of her sister's body in bed, for sweet chocolate on their tongues, for their laughter at the laugh track on Late-Night TV, for the only person on earth who had ever called her "Genie." For time to be as retrievable as a bucket raised from a well. For the young man to climb out of the ocean and walk across the deck in the shining sun and, at last, tell her what it was like in the After.

Five Poems
Bin Ramke

FALL. THINGS. SUDDEN (I)

> *There are real differences between a system that*
> *really did construct itself over time and computer*
> *programs that we write running on hardware that*
> *we build. The logic of natural selection requires*
> *self-replication.*
>
> —Lee Smolin

I thought it was my life I was living but I now
know better (learned later)

               to know better says
quality of knowledge varies: good better best

Paul of Tarsus on the road struck down by
light/best knowledge
never the same again. I crossed the street
myself to be struck by a Ford
& after surgery was the same.

> "Assume any relation betwixt x and z that you please."
> —Isaac Newton

Knowing numbers is the easy part, you say
onetwothreefourfive

Subitize: know the number of immediately
without counting; usually three or fewer

a subitized swarm of stars would be a wonder;

Bin Ramke

Αστερεσ μέν ἀμφι κάλαν σελάνναν
ἂιψ ἀπυκρύπτοισι φάεννον εἶδοσ,
ὄπποτα πλήθοισα μάλιστα λάμπησ
ἀργυρια γᾶν.

The stars around the full moon
lose their bright beauty when she,
nearly full, lights all earth
with silver.

(Sappho) quoted by Eustathius of Thessalonica,
six centuries later

*

It was my body but I could not do with it
what I wanted; the hands must be visible in public
the genitals not. Parts opened parts closed.

The law of noncontradiction could also be called and
is, the law of contradiction. This is itself a kind of dialetheism:

A new law is a new word, or old, a new word is a new law;

many musics make light linger, or fade, or be forgotten. Lyrical loss.

The boy-body made noises, not music. Sound not song.

But there was a code he heard he wanted to break
to know better. Biology belongs to all, a democracy
of desire and mortality. No matter how twisted
the strands. Call it "nda" call it "dna" call it "and" it is
difference. Deference, too. Mom and Dad determine child.

Three elements taken three at a time.

*

Out of the egg the new
inherits the body, builds new parts,
lives a little. It knows better

than to think. So Mom and I sat
in the sun waiting for Dad
we were moving to a new house
in a new city and I forget
were we happy about it
we looked at a *Papilio glaucus*
and I asked How long does it live?
Yellow egg green caterpillar brown pupa
we did not know: the caterpillar has a fake face
to look fierce, the pupa forms in a leaf
to look like the tree, the female adult
looks like a different butterfly which is poisonous . . .
which was the better knowledge . . .

Dad returned. The tiger swallowtail drinks nectar
especially of the honeysuckle, *Abelia*, Caprifoliaceae.
I know better than I knew.

A LONGING

> *To think that true*
> *which appears unlikely*
> —W. K. Clifford

I will tell you the story of your life.
Like the butterfly her chrysalis
there on the branch abandoned.

It began in time and ends. It began in space
and ends. It began as a thing and
will end a thing, shriveled and shriven.

I am not walking through a garden as I write
I am not observing the haunted viburnum glistening
under ice because the day is cold in spite of sun

shining bluely and burdened. But I would walk
where the old bark broken may not revive—

Schopenhauer said time is uniform, no part
of time differs from any other, like this snow
before we walk . . . but what happens in time

xylem and phloem, today and yesterday
or tomorrow, for that matter

in your time your life with your eyes closed
the images arise and haunt
never the same mind twice

it is snowing in the garden and we are not there.
We can smell the white flowers and the green.
We can smell the ice below.

THEODICY FOR BEGINNERS

The first half of the alphabet
is for known quantities: a is known,
b is known, $a + b = x$
the second half of the alphabet
is for unknown quantities
solve for x delta y over delta x
as x approaches zero . . .

*

We did watch the cloud-colored moon
against the night-colored night—
is it night also on the moon?
The moon is where night lives
one night every month.

We did watch the sky-colored cloud
that morning from the airport, through
the acres of glass the wall

where Southwest Airlines
passengers waited for the first
flight out of the day. The day
was the color of the sky-colored
clouded sun rising into spectacle.

We were all preparing to fly
miracle of air of the weight of air
in earth gravity.

*

The world consists of objects, properties, and relations.
Functions and propositions. Eyes can be closed
or opened. But some eyes cannot be opened.
"Open" is a curious concept.

Kesa, a monk's robe, silk and gilt paper
brocade
folded to give the illusion of patchwork;

the illusion of poverty is an opening or a closing.
The illusion of a relationship is a closing, a property.

*

Available to the aspiring murderer
were five types of poisons:
snake, toad, scorpion, centipede
and either spider or lizard, depending on the climate.

*

The cure for death is life.
The cure for life is more life.
The cure for X is the inverse of X
thus X is a cure for itself.

*

Bin Ramke

Silence is so accurate said Mark Rothko
when asked for an explanation.

IMAGINING, IMAGE MAKING

If in the darkroom I saw the sun
as black, a hole in the emulsion
and I would see the planets circling
like bits in the bathtub faster—Mercury,

Venus, Earth—closer to oblivion
than the distant giants—Saturn,
Jupiter, Neptune—but the dimension
of time was only a tool then

part of the process under my control:
time to allow the fainter image
to etch itself into the thin coatings
of paper, of celluloid, of cerebellum.

Manipulate is what we do
to be ourselves, to see ourselves.

VISIBLE IS WHAT OTHERS ARE NOT WHAT I CAN DO

daughter of wind

anemone was believed to bloom
only in wind;

a tree in South
Africa lives underground—a few scattered
leaves on short stems
visible on the sandy surface

unseen trunks and limbs and roots
writhe forever darkly

pyrogenic—mutated defense
against fire a refusal to rise into air. It is a
geoxylic suffrutex

the most deceitful
tree in the world. Is immortal.

*

Wind is itself invisible its effects reflective
of light. Some plants pollinate by wind—
anemophilous. The wind deadly but is itself
generative of an aesthetic.

In order to study the effect of the wind upon the stars
Ottaviano Mascherino built his Tower of Winds
in 1580 in the Vatican. A star is the light it produces.
The light is distorted by air thus the wind affects the stars.

A star is light. Only light. It is not other.
It is beautiful. This is a poetics.

*

Assume a time in the universe
when no being had vision
all that happened
was dark deceit
did happen

*

I would lie on my belly and with a small trowel
dig carefully beside the twig until I reached
a limb and I would expose to my sight to air
and light the trunk and then I would follow
root down to nothing more of wood
but earth.

*

Bin Ramke

Hasselblad 500 EL camera number 1038
one of fifteen used on the lunar surface, the only one
to return

*

Grüner See is a lake in Austria that dries out in fall,
is a county park in winter is
famous as an underwater version
during the spring melt. Visible because
of the clarity of cold water, old snow.

*

In many photographs
especially candid portraits
interesting shadows
sometimes of the photographer
an acccidental signature,
sometimes the evening elongations
of an elderly couple smiling into the Instamatic

*

I know an artist who lives
beside the sea who hangs wet
seaweed from a device of her
own devising to which she attaches a pen
then places paper below to enable wind to draw
depictions of contingency.

Deceit is an art and science.

*

Socrates: I cannot help feeling, Phaedrus, that writing is
unfortunately like painting; for the creations of the painter
have the attitude of life, and yet if you ask them a question
they preserve a solemn silence.

Something with Everything
Porochista Khakpour

OVERTIME

THEN CAME ANOTHER impossibility: what they called a three-day weekend, an extra day annexed to that standard two-day weekly rest period. But was it a holiday? An emergency? A dead president? *Relax*, said his boss. *It's just an extra day. Enjoy it! Get away! Party!*

He decided to take overtime instead. Work like usual. Take it home with him. Stay on top of things. Nothing wrong with that. Even though he couldn't quite recall the last unnamed and holidayless three-day weekend since those employee-development days of grade school, he was certain he would have done the same thing before. He didn't mind working.

As always on the days when there was work to be done, the world outside presented itself as particularly sunny and bright. People were out. He could hear them: someone on a loudspeaker booming, women laughing, kids singing, dogs, applause, crowds—everyone, gone all out. . . .

He wasn't interested; inside, he worked. Now as any real man would, he too required occasional short breaks—but on the whole, few and less, and more rigidly orchestrated, than those of most men. Sometimes, occasionally—and in fact, qualifying as truly *rarely*—his mind would wander. For instance, a few times, he stopped, suddenly hearing the ticking of his detestable new clock, the one he had recently purchased for that very detestability. It had to do with the second hand and how it didn't skip and tick like most second hands. No, this clock only ticked on the minute and the hour, opting to be slower, patient, downright grandfatherly in its announcement of time's arbitrary increments, than most clocks with their nervous, neurotic, nonstop adherence to the keeping of the smallest, pettiest, chattiest unit of time possible. Its hand was slick, slippery, continuous, with the tick-lack a continuous reminder that time was passing in a manner larger than him. *You are dying*, said the clock, reminding him of something he already knew, but its oily magician's flow—its parody of time, and yet its absolute accuracy—highlighted the reminder with more tactless ferocity than the many digital faces he surrounded himself with, as if slurring *wooork*. Within a couple minutes—at most— of his mind wandering, his surveying of a minute's tick, he always returned, relieved, refreshed, ready, eager, to *do*.

Other times it would be the phone. Solicitors. Wrong numbers. People needing things he couldn't give, people misjudging him and his needs, people wanting others. When he worked, he let it ring and ring until the machine got it. Usually nobody left a message.

On that night, the first of the three-day weekend, the phone rang endlessly and fatelessly. He tuned it out, and turned to the piles neatly stacked on his coffee table. The work he had to do wasn't so bad, he thought. He didn't mind it, he told himself. In compensation for it he would get money and, in fact, because of "overtime" they would pay him *more*. Not more than he deserved, he thought—in fact, still *less* than he deserved—just more than usual. The work involved papers, folders, envelopes with windows, numbers and percentages, sentences, signatures, names, addresses, e-mails, URLs, clauses, colons, semicolons, em and en dashes, trademarks, copyrights, ampersands, etceteras. Sometimes as he input and output and calculated and claimed, he was not sure what *exactly* he was doing but it did not matter. It was work. And, in fact, that very mysterious nature of it and its processes could be seen as nice, like all the incomprehensible yet "automatic" things in the world that *just were*. Nice. No need to question. Another nice thing: Nobody was asking.

His medication did not adversely affect—nor did it actively enhance, he would maintain—the process.

That evening, he noticed, with marked awe, that it would just not let up. In its third or fourth ruthless round, he knew he could just not be the bigger person. Ed finally decided to answer the phone.

THE CALL

"Hello, what are you doing?" Although it sounded somewhat familiar, Ed didn't recognize the voice the first time, and the voice, sensing this, repeated again: "Hello, what are you doing?" Ed thought about it. It hit him—his coworker LJ. It was the greeting that gave it away. The last time—the only other time he had called—he had greeted Ed with the same odd question. LJ was not quite a friend but someone who worked at the cubicle next to him. Twice, they had lunched.

"Oh, just work," said Ed. "Working."

"What! What ever happened to the three-day weekend!"

Ed had nothing to say to this.

"Anyway, Ed . . . I am calling to make you an offer. And I suppose it also means making you stray from your path!" He chuckled hard.

Ed had nothing to say to this.

"I want to invite you to a party. One thrown by a very charming woman. Tonight."

Ed paused. He had work to do. And yet this man had never asked him anywhere like that before. Ed assumed someone in this position might feel flattered. But he did not fully understand why this man who barely knew him was asking him out to a party. Well, he knew him a bit. Perhaps he too had few friends. In fact, LJ had to be a real outcast—he certainly looked the part. Ed recalled the raw redness of his exposed scalp, his constant sweaty-leather smell, his thin dress shirts, and he thought, here was a man who had not known what it was like to be accepted ever. Poor LJ, he almost thought—*almost*— but he did not know this man well enough to pity him even. Plus, it almost sounded like a date. But he did not know him well enough to not be repulsed by him either. He did not know why he had called, why he had invited him, if it was because he thought it was a party Ed would particularly like, if he assumed he knew Ed enough to invite him, if he *did* know Ed well enough to invite him, if he thought they were friends, if they *were* friends, if he thought they were more, if they were—

Ed shuddered. He said, "I'm sorry, LJ, but I have my work. And a lot of it."

LJ snorted. "*Please, Ed!*" he said. The plea fell somewhere in between a sarcastic exasperation and genuine pleading. "This woman, who is throwing the party, she is very charming."

Ed began to wonder if it was about the woman. It was possible that LJ was trying to find out what Ed thought of women in general, or, more specifically, charming young ones, that is, if she *was* young, if he had said that, if Ed had heard right—

"You want to know about her certainly," continued LJ. "Casper speaks very highly of her too. Certainly, you trust Casper as well."

Casper was their manager. They reported to him, and yet he was also their coworker, part of their team, all ruled by one director, who was ruled by one president. Casper, everyone thought, balanced being a good leader and a good coworker. Casper was liked. *Trust* was a whole other issue, but on some level Ed could say he did like him.

"Is Casper going too then?" Ed asked.

"Oh yes. Does that change things?"

That annoyed him. He turned to the table with its simple, straight-forward piles of work and told him, "No," and that he had to go.

LJ hung up with a snappy "Last chance—'night!" It was not entire-ly, but *almost*, rude.

Ed returned to his work. It was difficult to concentrate, and he found it annoying to confront that. In his head bumbled LJ in a thin lemon dress shirt, so flimsy you could make out his orange hairs, paired with old stiff polyester brown trousers—Ed placed LJ next to Casper, in his daily uniform, matching the smart black-and-white-silver cap of hair with the perfect white shirt and dapper black designer slacks, all of which looked expensive and rare in its plainness. LJ with his snorts and spittle; Casper with his tight smile and focused eyes. What a pair. Still, he had to admire Casper. The charming young—*young?*—woman would undoubtedly take to him and his position, that is, if he was not married or taken, details that Ed kept himself out of—

Suddenly, a sound he was not used to: the doorbell. When he opened it up and saw that it was Casper, he was surprised at not being sur-prised. Of course he had figured out where Ed lived—he did, after all, sign his checks every month. But it was still odd that he had acted on it. That he and LJ were pushing it so much, that the party dictated it, that the event somehow had managed to rope him into their world—

"Hello, Ed!" said Casper. "Well, I think you know why I am here. I was en route—"

"To this party of LJ's," said Ed.

"LJ's? Well, yes, he is going, but I would not have called it that."

"Oh, right, you know the lady too."

"Well, *know* is relative," laughed Casper, "but I do, I suppose. Certainly as well as LJ does. Certainly as well as many do." He paused. "Many people know her." He paused again. "Anyway."

The silence felt taut. Ed thought about what to do. He had work but here was Casper, his *boss*—well, both his boss and not his boss—asking him to go out. It could be a test, he thought; perhaps Casper was here to make sure he would not go, to see if he would stick to over-time, and the rules of work. But that was unlike Casper. Casper, he reminded himself, was a good man. He in fact liked Casper OK. And he had come by personally to invite him. That was nice, certainly something he should not pass up. But the degree to which Casper was a *boss*-boss was hard to determine. Was he a boss, was he a coworker, was he a friend? More? *Argh*, Ed thought, disgusted with his confusion.

"Anyway," Ed absently echoed. "Please know I am tempted, but as you know, I took the work home and all, and with overtime—"

Casper retained his smile and shook his head. "Ed, Ed! Overtime is not such a literal science. Did you not eat, did you not go to the bathroom?"

Ed nodded.

"OK, well, are you deducting those actions from your hours?"

Ages ago, Ed, in his first overtime stint, had considered that. He had thought there was a person out there who *was* good enough to do that. He had thought it was the right thing to do and yet he couldn't actually do it. It was also a petty action. An action some people would find absurd. It was petty, absurd, and yet correct—*confusing*—and therefore best not to deal with a thing like that.

Ed admitted he wasn't.

"Well, then! Don't take life so seriously. It's not worth it." Casper paused. Ed could swear something had caught his eye in his living room, and he felt embarrassed that his house was so bare and badly lit. Did most people play music in their homes? Ed was not sure. "So you'll come. Yes?"

Ed looked back at his home, the stillness, the dining-room table with its empty salt and pepper shakers, the single shabby placemat . . . and the pile of work.

"Maybe," said Ed, feeling annoyed at himself for dipping further into the giving in and yet already so far into it with just that very *maybe* that he felt annoyed at feeling annoyed and resisting, therefore adding, "Maybe just for a little bit. . . ."

THE RIDE

Buckled into the front seat—involuntarily, as Casper's luxury car was such that it would automatically shepherd you into safety—Ed sat awkwardly, with no idea where they were headed.

"Where exactly is this?" Ed asked, after what felt like many minutes on the highway.

Casper said a name Ed did not know, and so he forgot it immediately.

Outside, the traffic was bad. Long chains of cars sat grimly, white lights to red lights, in grim procession. This was the type of situation in which there was no out.

"Where is it again?" Ed asked.

Casper repeated the name, and again Ed immediately forgot it.

For a long while, they were silent, until Casper suddenly asked, "Some music? Music it is then," and he turned on a station that played the music of a youth, Ed suspected, neither had any link to. Over heavy guitars, a young woman—or perhaps a young man—was yelling, aggressively, repetitively, with something significant at stake apparently. Ed deciphered the he/she's shrieks as "Do me / do me all night," or something very close.

Casper tapped his fingers in time against the steering wheel, staring straight ahead, as they continued not to move—until they finally did—and eventually, in a time span Ed could not fairly evaluate, Casper announced, "Ah-ha!" It was an apartment building of some sort. Ed could not tell if it housed the wealthy or the poor. It looked nice enough—white, newish, lawned—but such *official* standards of care, Ed knew, meant that the socioeconomic makeup of the tenants could go either way.

They parked and Casper said, "Go ahead. I'll be up in a minute."

Ed looked at Casper's smile questioningly.

"You see, I'd like to take a nap, that's all," said Casper. "You understand."

Ed nodded slowly, without understanding. Some people at work did take what was referred to as power naps. Perhaps that was what Casper was doing. Casper loosened his tie and placed his head on the steering wheel. With half-closed dreamy eyes and a barely-reigned beam, he murmured gently, "You're welcome to join me if you like."

"No thanks," said Ed immediately. He was brusque, intentionally, he maintained, but hopefully not rude, he hoped. "I mean, I'm not tired, and well, since I am here, and not tired, I might as well, you know, make my way and go—"

"Well, then I'll see you in a bit," said Casper, his eyes suddenly shut. "Please lock the door."

Ed locked the door and hurried up the path. The party announced itself immediately: music in some elevated distance, laughter, chatter, shadows cutting frantically in the windows, lights, all the things of parties, he remembered. He suddenly felt excited. He had nothing to lose. Still, before he embarked upon the stairs, he turned slowly to look back at Casper's parked car, and all he caught was the silhouette of his boss/coworker slumped over the wheel. It was absolutely normal, and yet . . .

*

AFTERPARTY

Odd, was his first thought—although maybe logical of the extra-work world, he guessed—that it would be LJ, the one man inside whom he knew, who answered the door.

"Ed! Welcome to the afterparty." LJ looked his usual self, except he had on a thick black tie over his thin mint shirt. He was holding a drink that looked like whiskey. He only looked mildly drunk.

When Ed asked him about *the* party if this was merely the *after*-party, LJ laughed and disappeared into the crowd.

Like the resurrected dead, suddenly confronted with the world of the living—and the living living with more animation than recollected—Ed was overwhelmed as he surveyed the electric particles of party around him. It was a well-lit, almost bare white room, of shocking magnitude—so big it was almost a ballroom—a size shocking to anyone who would have surveyed the building from its outside, as Ed had. Like all parties, it held its own standards of usual and unusual and it was hard to judge: the big on young, the small atop old, the gorgeous entangled with grotesque, the jeans and jewels, the fire with ice, the water with smoke, the dousing of laughter, the dappling of gossip. . . . Children in velvet frocks and leather shoes, propped on pillows, with punch glasses poised on their laps. Attractive older women in stilettos, brandishing vegetable sticks at each other, chortling forcefully. A group of bespectacled foreigners arguing in another tongue, or maybe just conversing. Young men swaying around a grand piano that an elderly man with closed eyes played. One old woman napping on the lap of three whispering young men, all lazing on a divan. Cats and dogs perched bored on bar stools. Groups of old blonde servers carrying trays full of pastry shells and empty champagne flutes. A fat woman bellowing opera in the kitchen to the nonstop applause of everyone who passed through. . . .

Through the noise, Ed thought he heard the penetrating trill of a house phone, which everyone else was apparently ignoring. He did the same. He was glad he had come. It looked like a good party.

"Fluke?"

An old server, with a blonde braid snaked around her skull, held a tray full of thin jellylike squares. "It's *fluke*," she snapped. He had no idea what it was, but took one and ate it and liked it.

He wondered where LJ was. Or the charming young woman.

*

He hoped it wasn't "Just wait, booboo" but he did not rule her out—
"'Cause if you think this is good, just wait, booboo, until the after-party!" she interrupted, that first person who spoke to him, a young woman, a drunk, in an alluring purple lace dress, pressing herself with inexplicable urgency against the wall next to him. She was holding a drink.

"Isn't *this* the afterparty?" Ed said, noticing the teetering glass, adding, "Here, allow me."

She laughed, and with her eyes dead on it, she let the glass slip out of her hand and onto the floor. No doubt swallowed in the sounds of the party, it made no sound at all. Ed noticed the ground was full of broken glass.

"It's *all* afterparty," she insisted. "After and after and after and after and . . ."

He nodded politely. "Do you know whose party this is?" he tried to ask.

"Even with a bad moon out there tonight, booboo," she laughed, "no stop to the afterparty."

He thought, in spite of not wanting to leave the party, that it might be best to find Casper. "Excuse me, miss," he said to her, as she laughed on, "Boobooboooboo," letting her body slip down the wall until she was crouched on her knees, crying. Ed kept his eyes on her as he walked on, bumping into a few bodies here and there, making sure to excuse himself each and every time, although at a party like this it didn't seem to matter, and was rather somewhat encouraged—

"*Ed!*" He had walked right into Casper, who was holding two drinks. He put one—the one with an unrecognizable, inedible-looking red garnish—in Ed's hand. "Good party, no?"

"Excuse me, excuse me!" cut in two elderly twins in matching suits. People were walking into each other and making it, remarkably with little drama, as if in the company of ghosts, Ed noticed.

"There are some very important people here," said Casper.

"Whoa there!" exclaimed a young man, one of many in a classic tuxedo, as he shoved past Ed.

Ed nodded. He could tell.

"Love that piano!" said Casper, snapping his fingers to a percussion Ed could not detect. Although somehow he could make out that relentless phone, still, still going.

A line of somber teenage girls in strapless dresses slithered around Casper into the kitchen.

"Have you seen her?" Casper suddenly whispered, leaning in close.

Ed shook his head, and—"Ow!"—scowled at an older man in khaki shorts who had broken the spell of routine bumps and nudges with a rude, jabbing prod, his elbow in Ed's rib, not even excusing himself. When Ed said, "Excuse you," the guy rolled his eyes and blew him a kiss, and disappeared. It upset Ed. "Did you see that?"

Before he knew it the crowds had swallowed Casper and he too was gone.

Some people were eating cake. It was the type of cake—overdone with frosting, flowered, too much for everyday life—that screamed *birthday*. He approached a young girl, no more than ten, he imagined, slowly taking tiny forkfuls of a towering slice.

"It's her birthday, is it?" said Ed.

She looked at him with squinted eyes.

"So, where is she?" Ed asked, with the newfound brazenness that the audience of children often lent adults.

"Please," said the girl, annoyed maybe, he thought, or just unsure of what to say, he hoped. She turned to him with unreadable neutral eyes and got up and walked away.

Ed took her seat, dumbfounded. He stroked the sprawled orange cat next to him—the cat deep in what he felt was a feigned sleep—still, with little intentions of getting away or disappearing, neither apparently content with, nor evidently opposed to, another stranger's hand on his body.

"Do you *know* this *man?*"

Ed got a hard tap on the shoulder from a set of nails—

"*Do* you?" and an eyeful of the overbearing brown plane of cleavage, massive aged cleavage, was shoved right up to his face—a forceful slab of routinely sun-singed flesh, obviously an area worked on and meant to be looked at, with its mild shimmer of something alluring yet undeniably cosmetic, with its overpowering aroma processed to evoke the beach, hut drinks, but still women's department store, sweat, rayon. Older and busty and thick, with a plump, shiny orange scowl. Everything about this woman rubbed Ed the wrong way.

Plus, with her thick gold-bound fingers, she gripped a half-conscious LJ by the collar.

"He *says* he's with *you*. If he's with *you*, then don't you think he should be *with* you?"

81

Ed nodded slowly. "I'm sorry," he apologized for no apparent reason he could think of.

"Oh, *so* am I, *so* am I," she went on. "You don't *even* know what *he* has been up to!"

Ed shook his head. He turned to LJ, whose eyes were fixed downward. He had the look and even the burnt cheeks, Ed detected, of a man who had been recently slapped. Defeated and drunk.

The woman leaned in with a whisper. "He *did, oh, he really* did it," she hissed. Disgusted. The plastic orange puttied itself into a triumphant smirk, and she grabbed Ed's hand and placed it on her bosom. It was warm and firm, meaty and well done—a shelf of angry, raw, prime woman. He made sure not to move a finger. "*He did that,*" she said, without moving his hand.

He could not feel her heart beating. Soon, he wanted his hand back.

"There!" she snapped, flinging his hand back to him. "And I, *I don't even play on your team!*"

Ed looked at her, dumbfounded. He was not sure what she meant by that (until hours later he spied her taking over a weedy young lady in all black—bulbous orange suctioned at the nape of the lady's prickly tufts of blonde, swollen bronze and gold bangling at her brittle black and white, overbearing, hungrily having her way).

"Please don't do that," Ed mumbled, as LJ's head fell limply on his shoulder, and walked away.

"Ed, look!" appeared Casper, with a friendly grip on Ed's neck. He looked good—normal, Ed meant—not too drunk, he thought—and beside him was another well-dressed man in a suit and hat and cane, sharply done, like an old movie detective. "You know Roger!"

Ed did not. Ed smiled; Roger did not.

"Oh, sure you do! He's on our floor!" Casper said.

"I am surprised, Casper," Ed said. "Well, are you new?"

Roger shook his head.

"Don't mind Ed," Casper said. "Absentmindedness is perhaps his only bad trait. Or is it, Ed?"

They generated some casual talk. Work. Their building. Payroll. Four-oh-one-kays. Dow. Yearly profits. The economy. When suddenly Roger turned to a young woman and was off with a brisk wave.

Casper quickly turned sour. "Did you say *Casper*?"

Ed nodded.

"Why? You know my last name. Use it." The statement had an

admonishing ring, but Casper as usual was cool. "A simple *Mr.* would do. I am your boss, after all."

Ed wanted to apologize but couldn't.

"By the way, you won't need a ride back, will you," Casper stated.

Ed shook his head, even though he did. It was possible to deduce that Casper was punishing him, that it would all come back to haunt him at work, in spite of never hearing Casper request such a formality. It was possible that he could get fired, that what he had done carried some larger wrongness, that Casper was even more furious than he had showed, covering it up for the sake of the party spirit. It was possible that Casper was drunk, or Ed was, or Roger, whoever he was, whoever he was who had caused this—possibly not on their floor, possibly not even a coworker, although even more poignantly very probably *was*, and in fact, was probably very important—a further reason to fire Ed. It was possible that Casper and Ed were once friends, or close, and that now, thanks to Ed, it was over, forever.

"Now where did he go?" asked Casper, and that was the last of him.

Soon, Ed resorted to requesting shots. Eagerly, in between drinks, without mixer, without ice.

Nice: increasingly, people, caught with lost, or abandoned, composure. Did they ever have it? He wasn't sure, but he appreciated the sight of it. Everywhere, moments of clink and clang and clamor . . . attractive people fumbling: impeccable men with hands in chaos, fishy fingers wreaking havoc, bubbly, plastered; gorgeous girls mishandling antiques artifacts heirlooms invaluables, at their mercy: silverware all over there, crystal carnage, ashtray in revolution and cigarette cremains exploding on upholstery, rivers of wine flooding the quaking peaks and plateaus of shocked crotches, nut mix hailing on rug hides and pet head tops, confetti trails leading to somebody's sick in the tub, pearls disengaged in the sink, privilege undone, broken class, everywhere, celebrants alike, all *ahem*-ing and excusing and *whoa*-ing and pardoning and *fuck*-ing, before falling all over them and themselves.

It was, he thought, nice.

*

Porochista Khakpour

As the hours began to blanch, Ed felt less intent on leaving.

He was able to pinpoint the exact moment the alcohol really hit him. In front of him stood an elderly woman in a geometric-patterned coat—neurotically patterned, he'd go so far to describe—purple octagons, inscribed within blue squares inscribed within green triangles over and over a yellow backdrop. Nauseating! And then the cat on his lap, its tabby orange and white suddenly so tidily stripped and orderly bushed. Dizzying! And then the server with the crystal bowl filled with raspberries, strawberries, blackberries, with their flawless repetitive bulbs of juicy fruit—not to mention the black and white checkers of her kitchen floor—furniture: petrified, civilized, tattooed black-ringed galaxies, markers of age, certificate of old good wood—hair: follicles, locks, strands, toupees and toupees!—fur: real, faux, chinchilla, mink, rabbit, fox—heels on heels on heels—and somewhere, alone, unheeded, piles and piles of identical, photocopied, carbon-copied, work and work and work—lines, tab, return, print, jam, cancel, shut down—

Ed was sick.

"Pill?" offered the young girl, shaking a translucent orange pharmacy bottle.

Ed shook his head.

"Vitamin?" offered the man who had elbowed and air-kissed him, digging into his khaki shorts.

Ed shook his head.

"Toast?" snapped Roger, with the tip of his cane aimed at Ed's heart.

Shot, Ed went to the bathroom and sat in the dark until the pounding of a high heel and a high-pitched "Hellooo!" led him eventually to open up and walk out and announce to the iridescent burnt cleavage before him, "I don't know what team you think *I* play on," leading Cleavage to heave and moan and try to plod onward in spite of his speech, "but he and nobody in fact," he went on, as Cleavage turned and slipped past him, disregarding, not even huffing and puffing about it or anything anymore, rather just forcing one last unashamed face-off with the shimmer-slathered bronze-roasted hot flesh before him, "is *with* me. Excuse me now!"—and he walked on before he could fully hear the door slam, with a hoot.

Ed considered his medication; his medication considered Ed.

*

84

No, it wasn't normal. The phone had been ringing all night—or more, much more, than just a night by now, he knew. He was sitting with vitamins—and residue and rolled bills and broken straws and a ladies' compact mirror—tearing, not even nibbling, at burnt toast scraps. His companions—his coworkers, he meant—were gone.

It occurred to Ed that he wanted one thing: something true and real in all of it.

"Go ahead," suddenly said a sullen young man in jeans and a T-shirt who sat alone. It was the first time Ed had seen him. Something about him moved Ed. His face could be called entirely forgettable, Ed thought, and yet he seemed remarkably cut from a different clay altogether. He was shockingly normal. Valid, Ed thought, out of place, absurdly authentic and unadulterated. In his harrowing reality, Ed read a flesh and bones that was *more* than theirs.

"What are you waiting for?" the young man said, his sullen tenor terribly lucid, clean, and true. He was pointing at the opposite corner, where a young lady in a glittering dress was motioning for Ed.

She opened her mouth and the young man declared, "After all, I have nothing for you," and she stuck out her tongue, and Ed suddenly got up and said to him, "Thanks," and walked over and said to her, "Excuse me, but do I know you?"

Ed too was a true man with feelings and history and life stuff and properties. . . .

He—>single, white, male, lefty—events—>public school, Bonnie, community college, minor car accident (other driver's fault), state university, Sheila, Ann—roots—>Protestant, housewife and dentist, only child—likes—>blue, sometimes yellow, classical, mysteries, thrillers, asparagus, apples (red delicious), walking, science section (*Times* not *Post*; *Tribune* over *Herald*), badminton—goals—>happiness, money that was well earned in the end, marriage to someone forever, children (at least three), a pet (likely: dog (Lab); dream: ape).

He had had his share of the problems of the heart, ones he had not sorted through, that he believed could be fixed, cured, easy, if only the right person—and if only he hadn't stopped looking, which he mostly had but, but, but—

Well, he had never been one for parties or excessive socializing. He preferred work because he could do it, at least well enough to feel satisfied, without complication or turmoil or loss.

He loved deadlines. He lived for the "dues," the empty, demanding hands to fill, the final FedEx at four, the faxing to the minute. He loved an opportunity to wish for the passing of time, to find increasing comfort in the oily easing of that slippery second hand. . . .

Ed was homesick. Who were these people to make him feel odd for wanting to work? To reject the extra day? To kill the three-day weekend, to shit on its impossibility?

(Had they won? What day *was* it? he thought.)

Ed did not believe in impossibilities.

Somewhere in the madness of the evening, he felt an importance he could not fully pinpoint or validate. He wanted to remember the reason he was brought there in the first place.

THE GIRL

"It's me—it's my party," she said, after tucking in her tongue coyly, glittering away in her dazzling dress, pale legs peeking through the strategic slit of the stunning white slink, that Ed thought, yes, *could* belong to the hostess and certainly a birthday girl.

"But do I know you?" Ed said again. He meant it. He wasn't sure he *didn't* know her. Maybe it was the fact that an entire evening— now a day, days, three days?!—had been spent waiting to behold her, making the very notion of her familiar at least, that finally, when faced with that audacious apparition, in her unashamed pale luster, he could not help but feel he had sensed her all along.

Her tongue jabbed out, as if it couldn't help it, not without a certain preciousness, like an extended empty dessert spoon, a tool for dainty handling. Ed did not understand it. Lewd, cute, pristine, dirty— Ed dreaded another encounter with contradictions. With his blink, it was, like a quick flicker of a bad dream, gone.

"I should certainly hope so," she said. "You are after all at my party!" She shook her head suddenly. "Conversational burlesque. Pardon me. No, we've never met. You're with Roger?"

"Ed," he said with an extended hand and, annoyed, explained, "And yes and no. Yes, I work with Roger—or so I think—I really just met him—so, no, I am not with him. I am not with anybody here, none of the males definitely, but none of the females either."

"Yet!" she laughed, crisp, airy chuckles that feathered distinctly atop each other like broken glass. Conversational burlesque? he thought. He did not know what it meant, or what he was to make of her, or do with her—or who that sullen young man was, who was

86

now gone, and if he had meant to introduce them, or pass her on to him—or if she really was the hostess and, if so, why was she talking to him, of all people, or was she hitting on him, or tricking him, for what purpose, and was it a sign, was it the end of the night, morning, what time was it, what—

"OK, then maybe you can tell me," Ed began wearily. "Outside it's day, well into morning even, I should say, or maybe even afternoon—I lost track—or, yes, perhaps even night again—I don't even know—the shades, I see, are drawn, and the lights don't help, and I am too afraid to look at a clock, if there even is one, so please, if you will—and this is the most I have said, spoken all night—please just answer this for me: When, hostess, when do you anticipate this party will end?"

"Oh, we have days!" she shrugged. "An *extra* day even—why would it end sooner?"

Tongue out again. It was punctuation of a sort, Ed deduced.

"You shouldn't be so selfish," he said. "Some of us have things to attend to."

She ignored him. She *was* attractive.

"Work," he said, "if you want to know, which you probably didn't."

And charming, yes.

"I don't mean to be rude or unappreciative, but I just don't see the point in—," he said.

And young, definitely.

"Well, I suppose there's the door," he said, "and I can leave any time I want."

Dangerously young enough.

He said, "Why do I feel like I can't do that?"

He looked at the door. He thought about it. Then he looked at her.

"I hate myself," he said.

Tongue.

"Ignore me," he said.

He buried his face in his hands.

"Stop it," she whispered.

He looked up and saw some compassion, which he feared came with some condescension, and so let himself lose it for a bit, while she sat there, helplessly picking lint off her dress, idly shaking her head at him, muttering, "Queer, queer, queer . . ."

*

87

He was alone. He knew it the minute a group of men burst in from a bedroom apparently, ties undone, faces wet, red, riled, wasted, announcing, "LJ is dead! LJ is dead!"

In spite of his overbearing exhaustion, and a feeling of impending submission to anything and everything, Ed rose to his feet, alert. Could it be that his—not partner, not friend even, coworker, remember, work, work, ah, work—had indeed somehow in the course of the party or afterparty or whatever it was, indeed just *died*?

Ed ran to the bedroom, where two men blocked the doorway. They shook their heads at him.

"But LJ—," Ed protested.

"LJ is dead," said one of the men. "Died, rounds ago!"

"What do you mean by that, by rounds?" Ed was frustrated.

"LJ is dead!" they both said, rolling their eyes.

"How do I get to see him?" Ed asked.

"Code," one of the men said.

Suddenly a pale hand snaked around his neck, like an ivory hook, and she whispered, "It's a game, Ed. CON. Ever heard of CON?"

Ed shook his head.

"It's boring," she whispered. "You have to play and then die to die with him. . . ."

Like a wineglass down a marble hallway, her laughter shattered, devastating, pure, hard.

"It's all a game, Ed. Boring, but play if you want. . . ."

"I don't want to play," he snapped to them all, to the men, to her, and he made his way back to the main room, where, as usual, the phone was pleading shrilly.

"And that's another thing—*that* thing," Ed said, hoping to point at it, but unable to spot it, "that sound, the phone, why doesn't anyone get it? Or else unplug the phone?"

He turned around, but she was, of course, gone. He sat on the couch, tired, ill, maybe even delirious, he considered, wanting to go home, but too tired to do it, to do even work . . . his own fault, he had gone against his own reasoning, for his coworkers—his coworker and coworker/boss—and for a job he might not even have tomorrow . . . on some odd upside, he countered desperately, the whole night *could* be rationalized as work related, since inextricably tied to work, and so excusable in some remote sense, and maybe to some sick opportunist it did not have to be overtime deductible but rather counted as a very integral part of overtime hours . . . no way, he thought, not him, he respected work and overtime . . . although apparently not enough, he thought, not enough to have *not* extracted himself from home and work and all that made sense, namely his own solitude, his own mind—perhaps sometimes a frustrating place, but at least familiar, and at least manageably impossible. . . .

Ed hailed for another drink. "Something strong," he said, "but stronger."

The jerk in the khaki shorts popped up and said for him, "Something with everything. Like, you know, everything bagels? Get my man the everything bagel of drinks! Something with everything!"

Suddenly another sound: the previously somber strapless sisters in the kitchen, barefoot, drawing quite a crowd, doing a dance of some sort, a drunken grind, hiking up their gowns, at the applause of many men and some women, hotfooting, melting into each others' bodies, tribally, primordially, chanting something like an ancient rhyme, a kid's song, a jingle, over and over, until the words were clear to him, "Is it worth it / let me work it / is it worth it / let me work it . . . !"

It wasn't without mesmerization value, Ed thought to himself, when suddenly, like a commercial break cutting into a cliff-hanger, a man's trench blocked his view.

Roger.

"Just wanted to tell you that Casper's leaving with me. He said you don't need a ride."

Ed hated that he had to look up at Roger—it made his message even more severe, even more godlike, and unfair. The truth was, Ed did want a ride, an out, an anything, even if it involved Roger. But of course since he had put it that way he couldn't argue. Roger and Casper clearly meant to exclude him. Maybe they just wanted to be alone; Ed blocked the ensuing thoughts out of his head. Casper was clearly fed up with him. Casper probably felt that there he had been, trying to do a good thing for a coworker—not coworker, but employee, because he was, after all, according to Casper, below him—and Ed had ungratefully made a fool of him and him and them all—

Ed nodded. Soon the crowd swallowed Roger, and Ed sat alone again, drinking his cloudy everything, again alert to the nonstop trills of the phone.

"Where is it coming from?" Ed asked out loud.

"What?" answered a young boy, no more than seven, he imagined, in a three-piece suit.

"The ringing," said Ed, "the phone."

The young boy nodded. He ran off, disappeared—of course, Ed thought miserably; one second here, the next second, gone—but returned moments later, presenting Ed with a silver cordless phone.

"Well," said the young boy, placing it on Ed's lap. "Well, answer it then!"

Ed nodded, smiling weakly. It made no sense, he knew, for him to do it—or to be ordered by this stiff child, whoever he was, who happened to find and finally bring to him the source of many, many hours of Ed's deep annoyance, the trill, the plea, the shriek, no, it made no sense—but still he did.

On the other end, laughter like the final jangles of porcelain wind chimes in a hurricane, and an incisive whisper, even over the filtering of fiberglass and airwaves, transmitter to receiver, from some where to another where, still so clear it hurt, her words: "Meet me in the master bedroom. Now."

It didn't take him long to find it. He headed to the only bedroom he knew—the one LJ had died in—still with the guarding men. "Which is the master bedroom?" he asked. They squinted their eyes at him, didn't say a word, but Ed, keen to their games, onto this world suddenly, followed their eyes across the room and dashed with several "Excuse mes" and "Pardon mes" and "Oh, yes, hello, again" to purple lace and "Ah, leave me alone now, please" to baked Cleavage, and finally down a dark hallway to a door, which led, dead end, to a door labeled MASTER. Before he could knock, the door opened just enough for him to catch a glimpse of the white-hot-studded something, just enough for him to get gripped by the old shapely hook and claw, all leading to a laugh, and lips, and, of course, tongue, out then in, and a whisper, "Welcome."

"Look, are you fooling with me?" Ed knew his words would come out wrong. All wrong and yet—well, Ed couldn't believe it, yet there he was seated, placed awkwardly on the high bed—white-and-gold Egyptian silk bedding, same sparseness, a vanity, a tiny chair, everything gilded or golden and ivory and marble and womanly and girlish—with the hostess lying not so modestly, one bare leg flung out of the slit on top of the other, a disheveled twinkling charming young thing, like a restless newly caught silver fish, tossing and turning, laugh upon crash, bored or amused, he knew, for his sake, somehow. "What I mean is, what is it you want from me?"

She said nothing.

"I mean, it's your party and for the last—let's just face it, many and many and many—hours, half a day, maybe, more, God knows how long have I been here—anyway, since whenever, you have—and forgive the wording—sought me out or something, quite actively, for reasons I don't understand—this is, after all, *your* party and certainly all these guests your friends, maybe family even, lovers even, who knows—and I, certainly you don't know me—for a second, I know, I mistakenly thought I knew you, but it was all in my head—imagine that—maybe it was the anticipation over you and you did, yes, live up, just so you know—anyway, why the one guest you definitely do not know, what is the point? What do you want out of this? Out of me? Or am I making too much of this?"

He paused. "Are you maybe just bored?"

Outside, the revival of the primitive chant: "Let me work it / is it worth it / let me work it" . . .

She reached for a bottle under her pillow and playfully, with an idle flick of the tongue, poked out a blue pill from a purple pouch, and dramatically let it drop down her throat.

"What would happen," she said, "oh, never mind."

Then she said, "What would happen if I kissed you?"

What was he to say to that? On some level, yes, he did want it. No man wouldn't. Well, some man wouldn't but she knew he was not like that. He felt lost. He did not know how he had allowed himself to get so far, so deep, away from everything, for instance, his work— "First tell me, is the three-day weekend near a close? Really, I have to know. I know it's not appropriate but I have to . . . I work." And she was on him. They kissed. It was fine, he thought, it had been a while, so it seemed good and worrisome too, which was all very normal, he told himself. But something about being wrapped in those arms, as cold as he had suspected, bloodless almost, and yet tight, eager, desperate, maybe, even—it reminded him of time running out, *dead•*lines, ends. It reminded him of dying. He buried his face in the sparkles of her blindingly bright world and swore he was losing it.

They talked.

About the guests. She told him cooked Cleavage was "really not bad at all," "lush!," "a patroness of the arts," "maybe complicated," but "mostly a real love." She called them all "filler," "good fluff," "all essential," "loves," "strangers."

About meds. She was taking a pill she took three times daily, unless the day required four, she explained. She said it was: "often jagged," "an upper really," the type that "made you talk of death a

91

lot," "a good fading," "an elevator sinking," "overall, a brilliant pill."
("Does it help with your work?" he wondered. "Work!" she cried.
"I've never worked a day in my life.")

About work. He claimed: "It means the world to me," "financial
and emotional and so maybe spiritual," "always, as long as it takes,"
"it takes the place of friends," "I am always, always, always—except
for tonight, these nights, today—oh, what day is it anyway—always,
always working, so I wouldn't know the difference," "what else, I
ask you, really on this level, with this level of easy, uncomplicated
interaction, questions, answers, yes, no, black white . . . ," and "I
wouldn't know."

About sex. She declared: "Yes, you would, surely you're not a virgin,
a eunuch, asexual," "baby, I've had them all" ("Conversational burlesque," he pointed out, "all that 'baby' stuff, I know that." "*Doll*,
you ain't seen nothing yet!"), "I've slept with a lot less men than you
think," "I don't do this ever really," "Come on, just for a bit," "OK,
so I guess a lot *more*," "And not on my birthday, what a cliché!,"
"Don't change the subject," "Fuck," "Me."

"Because, work," he said, zipping up his pants, knowing well they
had done it, the third extra day upon them, and his work—"Wait!"—
was waiting, and so—"Come back, Ed!"—he dashed to the door—
"Now!"—with one last glance to see it closed. "But I'm not done
with you, it's not time!," yes, the MASTER, shut, back out, full of it
all, still on, room to pause at the kitchen mirror, examine face, hair:
not too bad—wave back *bye* at a wave or two—absently bravo "it /
worth it / let me work"—avoid suits, khakis, Cleave, lace, lips,
middle fingers—*bye*—throb in the crotch, *damn*—and head to the
door—"Sir, I have the time, I have the time, sir!" (young three-piece
suit)—*bye bye bye*—a heave of the chest, *hell*, a jerking of the knob,
slick with the sweat of too many grips, surely, nonetheless—"work
it!"—out he was, an out-ing that had only seemed hard, but in execution wasn't at all, was slippery, oily, easy, a reminder—opposites,
damn, contradictions, *hell*—no work, all play—until it was all over,
done, with a barely unsuccessful small-capped "slam."

Outside there was the moon that, in the beginning, somebody had
commented was no good. He was grateful to see it—to see that it was
night. He took his medication and it went down well, and he realized

he *could* pretend it was the *same* night. It was 1:00 a.m.—he could imagine it was just three hours since he had arrived. Not bad. At home, there would be the same dim light, the overeager runaway hand of the clock, allowing him to go on, smoothly, working, dying, onward and on . . .

As he walked off their lawn, still clearly hearing the resolute sounds of the upstairs party at work, he thought he heard a female voice, hollering, "Dead! Dead!"

He turned around. He had misheard. The voice was indeed calling to him, "Ed! Ed!" not *dead* at all. All he could make of it was a cracked window, promising of a room with a golden glow. But soon, dangling out the window's ledge, he caught sight of it: the gleaming white long finger of a no-doubt snaky alabaster arm, snowlike against brassish, cold, shining, all wow—and he knew it well. He heard it again. He swore this time it *was* "Dead!" He had to, had to go. "Ed!" Dead? He wanted to look away, but couldn't, especially when suddenly another hand—"Dead-Ed!"—a different one, darker, olive, red nails, perfect—"Ed; Dead!"—with even a ring on the ring finger, a real rock, blinding too—"Dead=Ed!"—reached over to hers, intertwined even—"Dead/Ed! Ed (Dead)!"—and then both, together, like that, at once, fluttered off, gone. The lights went out.

Ed thought about work; Ed thought about play.

Before he knew it, he was back up, up the stairs, conjuring an excuse, like maybe he had come up to call a cab—he didn't after all know where the hell he was, right, what he was, right, what he wasn't (*Ed: Dead!*)—and before he knew it there *he* was: that very real and consequently sullen and enigmatic young man in the jeans and T-shirt, who suddenly again spoke up with an "I told you so," leading Ed to the shrill trill that was apparently again meant only for him.

Six Poems
Rae Armantrout

INCOMING

1.

"Another year," I say
as if this were ironic.

*

Because it's now/
because I'm now

in two places
and thus not

myself,
I contain

the disturbance
of the incoming

pulse without

2.

A stuffed tiger
upside down

in a cubicle
cubby

LOGISTICS

"Packet security."

He, she, they
were here to oversee
packet security.

It was the only
game in town

if this strip
of abandoned

staging areas
deserved the name

and no one
had checked recently.

What remained
to be demonstrated

in each
gesture toward narrative

was a tough-minded
nonchalance

we could almost
place

it was so retro
and thus plausibly—

or implausibly—
authentic,

but, in any case,
passing through

Rae Armantrout

CONFLATION

As a tree
is concerted

atmosphere. Each
one a certain

ambience

drawn in and held
until it turns

green?

       *

You go on
drawing energy

from conflation, referring
to yourself

while implicating
other beings.

       *

That's silly!

       *

Silly tablecloth
of the nasturtium leaf,

flung out
on its too thin stem,

perfectly flat, in flight,
serene

HELL

"Able for the first time
to view
large bronze statues
of Dr. Seuss characters."

What if
the wish to be precise
survives
the world of objects?

Thumb and forefinger
meet again
as if
for the first time,

tugging once more
on "as if"

ACCOMPLICES

1.

The one in which I laugh about my mismatched

shoes at the boarding gate and the one

in which I pass quietly through the apartments

of four strangers to reach the one

I'm subletting

are played out

"before my eyes" while being

narrated to an

accomplice.

Where is she

when I wake up?

                    2.

All the souls

that swarmed

through me,

intense and complex,

as I first encouraged

then graded them,

have vanished.

SILOS

What if you tell me an interesting story, full of humor and disappointment, and, a few months later, I mention it, and you answer, "I never said that" or "It didn't happen that way"? What then?

Now we would expect the umpire to swoop in with the video playback, but, of course, there is no umpire here.

Perhaps we are our own worst witnesses.

Is this what's meant by "information silos"?

La tortue, or, The Tortoise
Gabriel Blackwell

DECADES AGO—IN FACT only a few months after I was born, though of course thousands of miles away and as thoroughly unrelated to my birth as a butterfly's stretched wings to a distant hurricane—the French publisher Gallimard brought out a collection of texts attributed to Jorge Luis Borges called *La tortue* or *The Tortoise*. At least according to the book's description, none of *La tortue's* essays, fictions, or "unclassifiable prose" (the translation is mine, I should say, as are any mistakes in it or in any of the translations that follow) appear in Borges's *Obras Completas*, and thus their discovery—in French translation, no less!—ought naturally to have been an event. The book's fate was, however, otherwise. *La tortue* was printed but never distributed, its publisher or its editor perhaps having a change of heart regarding its authenticity. There are no court documents, no documentation of any kind, to rely on now; there are rumors, naturally, but the rumors are of recent origin, and so less reliable. Copies are said to exist, for example, unread and unsold, in a warehouse in a suburb of Paterson, New Jersey, and why a French edition of obscure works said to be by an Argentinian writer would go unread and unsold in an unnamed New Jersey township is, it seems to me, completely understandable, but why such books would have come to be there in the first place is considerably more of a mystery. My efforts to locate the exact site of this rumored warehouse have so far come to nothing.

In an essay whose title I haven't been able to find, appearing on page 175 of *La tortue* and (once) accessible via Google Books, Borges writes, "It is a species of melancholy to have to do with books that have met with such a fate." The page this quote appears on is the only page of this particular essay to make it into Google Books' preview, and most of it is devoted to an enumeration of the various editions of the Bible and the degree to which the Apocryphal Gospels are integrated into them, yet the Bible isn't the subject of the sentence. What fate is Borges speaking of? What books? I don't suppose I have to say why I found this particular passage so intriguing.

There are fifteen pages total in Google's "preview" of *La tortue*, but no ordering or library holding information, no e-book offered, and seemingly no way to know how Google's scanner got his or her hands on the thing. Nor is there any information about why the book was assembled in the first place—the more important question, it seems to me. According to the pages I was able to access, *La tortue* includes, among other things, a review of the book *Unwitnessed Spectacles, 1890–1900*, a book that doesn't seem to exist but that apparently details the washing up on North Avenue Beach, Chicago, of two mermaids in advanced stages of decay, the opening and subsequent closing of a sinkhole one hundred yards across in Jordan, and Marconi's transmission, from the SS *St. Paul*, of the entire text of De Quincey's *Suspiria de Profundis*. *La tortue* also includes a list of untranslatable texts (e.g., the schizophrenic A. A. Barnes's English-rendered-phonetically-into-French *À qu'il lise*), the essay referenced above, and a short commentary on the proper construction of temporary structures meant to collapse, like those seen in Buster Keaton's *Steamboat Bill, Jr.* and Jean Epstein's *La Chute de la maison Usher*. There are at least 256 pages in the volume, as the last page that appears in the preview is numbered 255 and the last sentence there reads "Of all the books I have sent to press, none is more personal than this motley, disorganized"—obviously concluding on the following page, ending midthought as it does.

I probably don't need to remind you that Google Books' preview function doesn't allow the reader to control which selection is chosen, and that that selection may change over time—for example: I cannot, at the time of this writing, check whether what I have transcribed above is accurate, as page 255 is no longer part of my preview. I have checked often over the past month, hoping to be able to read more of the text, but the same fifteen pages show up each time (which, again, are not the same as they were when I first discovered the book and began writing this essay). Given the empirical evidence, then, I must conclude that if I were to check the preview every day for the rest of my life I would see the same fifteen pages, but if I were to leave the thing alone and only check it, say, once more, on the day I died, perhaps I would see a further fifteen pages, having thus read, over my lifetime, only a fifth of *La tortue*. Given my knowledge of the inner workings and algorithms of Google Books is nonexistent.

Just a moment ago, my wife called to me from downstairs. *Honey,* she said, *the children are waiting.* They will all be arranged around the dinner table, a plain pine table chosen for its simplicity and now scarred at its ankles by the dog's incessant chewing, two sets of hungry eyes centered above matching Donald Duck plates, and my wife's eyes, urgent, tired from her long day of caring for the children—all of them, that is, except for the youngest, who will be set back a bit from the table in his high chair, a bib around his neck and a Diego sippy cup affixed to his hand (unless he has thrown it, the cup, I mean, to get my wife's attention). They will wait for me to be seated before eating, a rule my wife invented, that we all be together before the meal starts; they will even wait long after the dishes have been set down steaming in the middle of the table. In my imagination, they will wait forever, though I know this isn't so, and I wonder at my fantasized cruelty. Who am I, even to myself? If things get cold, they will complain, of course, and my wife will be upset with me, but still, I think, they *will* wait (again, except for the youngest, who has already eaten). I will get up from my desk, piled high with books I will never read, and I will cross my office to the recently-oiled-but-still-creaking door, just barely cracked so that I can be called to dinner but mostly closed so the children will know not to bother me, and I will open the door and I will walk down the hall to the top of the stairs and I will take hold of the banister, loose and runneled from the children sliding down it, and I will descend the thirteen steps to the first floor, and I will cross the hall to the kitchen, passing the dining room to get the saltshaker or the pepper grinder or the water jug, or any other forgotten thing, and I will ask my wife and children, from my place in the kitchen, if there is anything anyone needs, and then, finally, I will enter the dining room and my children will smile or look at their plates, depending on how long it has taken me to do all these things, and then I will sit and I will tell them about Borges's lost book, or anyway, the book attributed to Borges but that may not exist and may not have been by Borges, but first, first I will have to command certain muscles to extend and other muscles to contract so that I may rise from my desk, which anyhow is covered in old, yellowed bills and empty envelopes, not books, and before I can do that, I must have the impulse to rise, which, just now, is too much to ask, I think, for I have been hungry for days and have had very little to eat, and, perhaps more importantly for this essay, I must have a desk to rise from, a desk and a chair, and I must have work that demands time at that desk, and so I must have some sort of education, perhaps some sort of experience, in order to get such work, and before I forget, I must also have a wife, and children, and so I cannot begin because at present only some of these things have been accomplished and not even necessarily the most important, such as the children, who exist only in my imagination, since, before one can have children, one must have a kind of hope, and my wife and I have instead, in its place, debts, for I am a mostly-unemployable scholar and she is employed by a temporary agency as a file clerk, and we are neither one of us in good health, and so we have not started the family we ought to have long ago started, "long ago" because I am nearing middle age and she is not far behind, and we live, childless, in an apartment that is much too cold and too small even for the two of us, and, besides, completely unsuited for children, and this is a source of much friction between us, and we spend the nights we ought to spend dreaming together each on our own side of the bed, lying awake with our separate worries, hers more serious than mine owing to certain health problems making pregnancy a complicated and even dangerous proposition but mine still strong enough to wake me at 4:00 a.m. when there is absolutely nothing else to do but think about what has yet to be done, how much further there is to go, how little time there is left—for any of us, really, but for the two of us most of all.

Piracy, Chemistry, and Mappa Mundi
Susan Daitch

THE SHOPPING LIST

AT THE SHOCKING ART SUPPLY STORE in *Portlandia*, you can buy pre-smashed eighties-era televisions, doll parts, upside-down American flags posted on diminutive poles, mannequins spray-stenciled across the chest with the image of riot cops. The shopping list matters. These objects have become such an integral part of art production, the talking heads of *Portlandia* say, that they're stocked in the store along with quotidian supplies like paint and mat board.

When Damien Hirst had *For the Love of God* fabricated, his shopping list included a human skull possibly last animated in the eighteenth century, 8,601 white diamonds, plus a single bigger pink diamond for the forehead and an unknown amount of platinum. Artist John LeKay, a former friend of Hirst's, claimed he had made the sculpture that *For the Love of God* was based on. His work, *Spiritus Callidus #2*, a skull covered in crystals, predates *For the Love of God* by about fourteen years, and his trip to collect materials wouldn't have involved renting an armored car, bricks of cash, or security guards. Even less glamorous in material acquisition, El Anatsui's shopping list for his wall hangings and sculpture includes hundreds of thousands of the metallic wrappers that cloak the necks of beer and wine bottles found in the rubbish heaps of Ghana and Nigeria. Ai Weiwei's shopping list might include the possessions of an arrested family, hundreds of pounds of black tea, or thousands of children's backpacks.

TO BE CONTINUED NO MATTER WHAT

There are precedents for artists like John LeKay, who have confronted their forgers. Albrecht Dürer traveled to Venice in 1506 for the sole purpose of suing engraver Marcantonio Raimondi, who was circulating copies of Dürer's woodcuts made from his own blocks, not the

original. Lawsuits, as a response, were benign compared to the reaction of some artists. Andrea Mantegna, for example, attacked one
of his forgers, accusing him of sodomy, and the fellow had to flee
Mantua for Verona. Going through legal channels, Dürer was only
partially successful, in that Raimondi simply agreed to put his own
name on the prints, and no longer claim they were made by Dürer
himself, but he must have been laughing at the German as soon as
the door closed behind him. According to the Council of Nuremberg
of 1512, the fraudulently produced images continued to be found in
circulation. Dürer was so popular, had so many students and followers who reproduced his work, that the cataract of Dürer's work
could not be stopped or always authenticated without a doubt. The
market was flooded.

For art forgers too, the shopping list matters. Wolfgang Beltracchi,
a contemporary forger who, in fact, looks like Dürer, and his wife,
Helene, were unmasked when zinc white containing traces of titanium was found in a painting they had sold as a work by a German
expressionist, Heinrich Campendonk, circa 1914. Titanium didn't
come into use in oil paint until 1957. The actual painter would have
used white lead, which is more luminous, creamier in texture,
poisonous.

The Beltracchis were the movie stars of art cons and their forgeries
made them fantastically wealthy. They had spectacular parties at
their estates in Southern France and in Freiburg, flying in musicians
and flamenco dancers from Spain. The couple rented huge villas on
Caribbean islands, took friends sailing on their yacht, *Voodoo Child*.
To their neighbors, the party throwers appeared to come out of nowhere and arrive presto: wealthy art collectors with no past except
the one they advertised themselves.

Beltracchi's actual history was not one of Olympic-size swimming
pools in Guadeloupe, hotels suites with a view of the Grand Canal,
or African safaris for a weekend. His father was a house painter who
also restored churches and made copies of famous and recognizable
paintings from Rembrandt to Picasso, which he sold to make extra
money. In the seventies and eighties Wolfgang bummed around
Europe and Morocco, living on a houseboat, staging psychedelic light
shows from time to time, but debt tugged at his shirtsleeves constantly, and only grew worse. Flea markets were the Shocking Art
Supply Stores of the era and would remain so for the Beltracchis,
providing old paintings whose frames and stretchers could be re-
purposed to pass the test of scientific dating techniques. They didn't

just look old, they were old. He noticed that old paintings of winter scenes sold more if there were skaters in them. He bought paintings, added skaters, and in this way his career in duplicity began. He needed money, couldn't find his own foothold, and so imitated others who were dead and couldn't personally come back to accuse him of sodomy or anything else. Doing your own work takes time. There are a lot of false floors and dead ends, but if you take on the role of someone else, you skip all that. Success is instant if you can pass, and he did.

From sentimental skaters he moved up to German expressionists, and money began to pour in. He only needed to paint two or three forgeries a year to be a millionaire, selling through auction houses eager for sales, a venue that seemed to ask fewer questions than galleries. The exact number of paintings he sold and amount of money he netted are still murky. Two numbers intersect in the territory of unaccountability: mystery cash and pictures whose whereabouts remain unknown.

But then the first Gulf War and a faltering economy led to an end to his production. People were buying less art, at least for a while. When the art market deflated, Wolfgang turned his attention to pirates. He had been drawn to the romance of a certain kind of outlaw-ism, not necessarily the physically violent kind, more buccaneer Errol Flynn or Burt Lancaster. The kind of piracy committed by residents of the Horn of Africa, victims of depleted fishing resources and coerced by organized crime, wasn't what he had in mind. Beltracchi began production on a documentary about pirates, financed by the sale of his forgeries. Buying an eighty-foot sailboat, he hired a crew and planned to sail from Spain to Madagascar to South America, tracing the routes of swashbuckling explorers like Sir Francis Drake and brigands who hid out in less well-known trade routes. The film project only got as far as Majorca before sinking altogether, and so the forgery business came due for a revival.

The forgeries took two forms. Beltracchi didn't always produce copies of original works, but rather paintings he thought a given artist (Ernst, Léger, Picasso, and others) would have created. So, in a sense, they were original Beltracchis passed off as original someone else, and because that someone was a historically recognized painter, those molecules of paint assembled to comprise Ernst's, Léger's, or Picasso's signature meant a crime had been committed. Had they not been signed and supposedly attributed, they would have been just paint and canvas, and their value would have been negligible. The paintings needed not just signatures but a story to justify their existence as marketable commodities. The idea was not for them to be the valueless marvels of an idiot-savant copyist. Helene Beltracchi invented a history about grandparents who had hidden the art collection of their neighbors and good friends, the Flechtheims, when the family had had to flee the Nazis. Only part of this story was true. The two families had been neighbors but not friends, and none of Alfred Flechtheim's collection ever came into their possession. Her grandfather was a member of the Nazi party, abandoned her grandmother, and the degenerate art in both the real and the alleged collection would probably have been, to him, opaque and worthless smatterings.

The tale of the heroic grandparents sounded fairly plausible, fulfilled a need in postwar Germany to believe in good deeds, but the Beltracchis felt the story needed additional material support to acquire the valence of being really unimpeachable. Using a camera from the 1920s, printing pictures on prewar paper, the couple produced black-and-white pictures of Helene posing as her grandmother with the paintings visible in the background. The photographs were props that backed up a whole fictional universe, and they were convincing—as if August Sander had dropped by for coffee before he was deported and took a few pictures. Many dealers and collectors bought into the story of the phantom art saviors. Wolfgang's pictures were snapped up. Until they were betrayed by a few ounces of white paint, it was the perfect con.

When questions began to be raised about the authenticity of the paintings—even though, in some cases, the statute of limitations was up—the Beltracchis sold their estates, took off in a mobile home, and disappeared for a while. You can imagine a Winnebago painted pink and turquoise, empty bottle of rum spinning in the drive as its wheels grind the dust. Remains left in one of his estates: DVDs of *Ocean's Thirteen, Ice Age*, a Led Zeppelin CD, Patricia Highsmith novels in German. Eventually, as the desire for multimillion-dollar paintings rose, and anxieties about provenance appeared to be receding, Wolfgang resurfaced and took up business again, but this time he created forgeries of better-known artists, venturing into dangerous territory by copying recognizable artists. Demand was higher than ever.

Among the buyers of his fake Campendonks were Steve Martin and Trasteco Ltd., a Maltese company. After plunking down $3.6 million, the latter wanted a certificate of authenticity, and when none was available, they had the painting tested by London-based forensic art scientist Nicholas Eastaugh, who discovered the presence of titanium, the element that was the undoing of Wolfgang and Helene Beltracchi.

The party ended. Wolfgang and Helene were tried and convicted, but they received very light sentences. Others, accused of similar crimes, got much harsher terms. There are things, secrets, Wolfgang says he can't discuss, leaving one to believe he could be the man who knew too much The pair were allowed back to their home for him to paint during the day, but then they had to return to jail cells at night. As far as incarceration goes, it was a pretty cushy deal. He was mandated to pay back a percentage of what he had stolen, but now his Ernst or Léger lookalikes, signed by himself, were commanding high prices of their own. They are the Ernsts or Légers that *could* have existed, and so cozy up to the originals, claiming a bit of their space and their share of the market.

As a result of the Beltracchi conviction, not only were dealers and galleries sued by duped collectors, but art experts, those in the business of authenticating art based on what can be seen with the naked eye, felt the rug pulled out from under them. Beltracchi's industry exposed what now appeared to be the man behind the curtain. The unreliable world of connoisseurship and its practitioners was becoming more and more like doctors afraid of being sued for medical malpractice, and, at the same time, unable to obtain adequate insurance to cover their assumptions. They end up staring at empty walls. Beltracchi turned the whole notion of authentic art and who is an expert on its head.

DR. FRANKENSTEIN

Beltracchi now says of his forgery business that it's performance art, and his approach raises questions as to whether a forger's skills can traverse the meridian that divides crime from recognized art form, as long as he signs his own name to the canvases. He has also sold pictures of himself painted over photographs of his forgeries. Even the collaged remakes aren't cheap, and he's been accused of "turning notoriety into a marketable commodity."

When asked to describe how he works, Wolfgang says, "You have to know about the artist's past, present, and future. You have to know how the painter moved and how much time it took him to complete a work." His wife supports his method of working: "He reads about the artist, travels to where he lived, steeps himself in the literature. He's like an actor." When he was painting as Max Ernst, did he imagine living with Dorothea Tanning on 19 rue de Lille? Answer: unknown, but he does use what he calls his "Max Ernst box," containing bark, leaves, shells, straw, the kinds of objects the surrealist used to recreate fragments of texture on the surfaces of his work. Ernst, who believed he was painting from his subconscious, would appear to be impossible to duplicate, but Beltracchi was, until he was caught, very successful at his ability to parrot another man's subliminal thoughts.

In the "Be Right Back" episode of *Black Mirror*, a young man, Ash, is killed in a car accident, but his surviving wife is able to recreate a version of Ash programmed via the accretion of all his e-mail and social-media postings. The clone Ash arrives at her door as a sentient-appearing, if slightly robotic, version of his formerly living self. Unless they are destroyed, the Beltracchi paintings, like many forgeries, take on a life of their own, and come back in devious ways. They are like clones who knock on the door and are unwilling or unable to quietly disappear. One collector is known to have kept his Beltracchi Ernst and displays it openly, claiming it's one of the best surrealist paintings he has ever seen. A twenty-first-century painting that really looks like Max Ernst could have painted it borrows the Ernst aura. The moonbeam passes for something solid with pylons and towers and doors you can walk through to rooms that may be a pleasure to inhabit.

THE FLECHTHEIM CASE

> *There is something crazy about art. It's a passion stronger than gambling, alcohol, and women.*
>
> —Alfred Flechtheim

> *. . . insolent Jewish-Negro contamination of the soul of the German people.*
>
> —From *Illustrierter Beobachter* (Illustrated Observer), in its cover story "The Race Question Is the Key to World History" with a cartoon of Flechtheim on the cover

Who was harmed by the fakes of Wolfgang B.? Even though he made fools of those you might imagine resemble bronze Tom Otterness figures who have money bags for heads, Wolfgang wasn't exactly

Robin Hood. He stole from the rich, but he didn't exactly give to the poor, and only enriched himself on a lavish scale. Not only was his reputation one of self-aggrandizement, but he must have made life very much harder for the heirs of the real Alfred F.

Besides the presence of titanium in the paint, the Flechtheim Gallery labels that the Beltracchis affixed to the back of the forgeries were total fantasy. Dyed with coffee and tea to appear aged, the labels were printed with a woodcut of the dealer's portrait. The design of the actual labels contained no portrait. Flechtheim's paintings were stolen by the Nazis, and the problem of restitution for his heirs could only have been compounded by the German forger's high jinks, his pilfering of Flechtheim's identity. A major collector of German expressionist and French cubist painting, as well as art from the South Pacific, during the 1920s and early 1930s, Flechtheim was considered a prince of the Berlin art world. Boxer Max Schmeling said of the dealer, "If I were a painter, I would want Flechtheim to represent me." Alfred was known for having blowout parties in his galleries in Berlin where he would dress in Andalusian clothes and dance flamenco. But for Alfred, who was Jewish, a collector of degenerate art, and rumored to be gay, the party that was the Weimar Republic was soon to be over. Otto Dix, annoyed at what he saw as Flechtheim's preference for French artists, painted him with the exaggerated features of a cartoon character, grasping paintings in one hand and bills of sale in the other. The message, the grotesque money-grubbing Jew, is ugly and unmistakable. It's painful to look at, but others, from known artists to anonymous cartoonists, would repeat the image in a variety of forms. This version of Alfred's face became a symbol of racial pollution that appeared over and over in Nazi propaganda. Completely impoverished, Alfred fled to France.

> *What horrifies me the most is the senseless fear that has taken hold of Flechtheim. In a completely empty restaurant, he looks left and right, even during the most harmless conversations, to make sure that no one is listening to us.*
>
> —Thea Sternheim, July 1933

But his phobias and paranoia were far from baseless. Fleeing Paris for London, Alfred found no respite. He fell on an icy street, but contracted blood poisoning from a rusty nail that had found its way into his hospital bed. Even amputation couldn't save him, and he died, according to English friends, on March 9, 1937, in "misery, pain, and despair."

Beltracchi painted works listed as missing that had no known reproduction, and because of the extent of Nazi art looting, it's been difficult to know for certain what Alfred Flechtheim did own. It is believed that after Aryanization, paintings were illegally sold, sometimes to museums, and Alfred was erased from art history. Restitution has been a slow and difficult process even decades later, and Wolfgang B. wasn't the only one profiting. According to a copyright litigation site:

> Alfred Barr borrowed much of Flechtheim's exhibition for the MoMA's first show of German art and Flechtheim gave the MoMA one of the first works to become part of its permanent collection, a sculpture of the boxer Max Schmeling, the guy who Joe Louis beat. No one seems to know what MoMA did with the Schmeling sculpture. History has failed to document Alfred Barr's intellectual and other debts to Alfred Flechtheim. Barr, of course, was gleefully grabbing up art bargains that the Nazis had stolen from Jews, including the great critic and philosopher Walter Benjamin.

Alfred's F.'s widow, Betty, returned to Berlin in 1941, but committed suicide by taking an overdose of Veronal, just after receiving her deportation orders, with the Gestapo at her door. The surviving heir, Alfred's grandnephew, Michael Hulton, is an anesthetist who lives in San Francisco, who plans to donate his restitution claims to AIDS research.

TAKE MY SNAKE GODDESS, PLEASE

Wolfgang B. learned that molecules don't lie. Museums are of full of paintings and objects that may or may not be what they claim, but then sometimes the story of their manufacture and usurped identity takes on a life of its own. If you know the chemistry of the materials and the contemporaneous technology used to create an object, the genuine can be separated from the fakes.

I met with Richard Newman, director of the Science Department of the Boston Museum, on one of those days when it was so cold my phone froze, and I imagined cables snapping, the Red Line stalling as it made its way across the Charles River. Getting on to the floor where objects and paintings are analyzed and conservation takes place is not automatic. Visitors can't just stroll in. You need an appointment and, even then, someone with a magnetic elevator ID must meet you and take you up to the lab. Some of the most valuable objects in the world may find their way here, but this is not Tiffany's. The labs look more like sets from *CSI*. Very few museums have science labs—they are expensive. Some of the equipment costs upward of $100,000. Among the array of machines you can find X-rays, high-powered optical microscopes, scanning electron microscopy, and equipment used to measure energy-dispersive X-ray fluorescence. In the lab I saw the Senterra Raman microscope, which uses lasers to transmit information about chemical bonds; a mass spectrometer that measures fluorescence; and charts like three-dimensional contour maps of different materials graphically depicted according to their composition.

Testing for authenticity isn't pure science. There are stories behind the copies, and that's what tempers our dismissiveness towards fakes, our desire to put a crowbar under the manhole cover and explore the city beneath the one we know. Science and chemistry, Newman tells me, entered the province of the museum with the excavation of Pompeii in the nineteenth century when a pigment known as Egyptian blue, the first artificially produced pigment, was discovered in the ruins. The investigation of color is often tied to chemistry, as the Beltracchis discovered too late, and became one way of analyzing whether or not a work was genuine. Newman told me the story of the *Snake Goddess*, a small ivory-and-gold statue considered one of the prizes of the Museum of Fine Arts for nearly one hundred years, only recently questioned as not being the object it was once purported to be. His lab tested the gold and found it contained higher levels of copper than ancient Minoans would have amalgamated. The statue was removed from exhibition. I asked him who made it. In all likelihood it was fabricated by the diggers on the excavation of 1912, headed by a perhaps easily duped American. The statue was donated to the museum on June 28, 1914, the day Austria-Hungary declared war on Serbia, and the Great War was begun. A number of Snake Goddesses in collections around the world are believed to be fakes, but they were initially acquired and displayed with enthusiasm.

The ancient Minoan civilization was seductive for nineteenth-century archaeologists, often wealthy amateurs, because this was where they could drive a stake in the ground and declare the beginnings of what we talk about when we talk about Europe. Heinrich Schliemann, self-made German millionaire, was suspected of planting forgeries when he excavated Mycenae in the 1870s. The writings of archaeologists like Sir Arthur Evans, who conducted a major excavation just before World War I, are full of expressions like "inherently probable" and romantic assumptions about goddesses, mothers, and "Youthful Boy Adorants" that can be embarrassing to read today. Among their mistakes, they became known for getting the genders of figures wrong or for not allowing for athletic girls and feminine boys. Minoan history, religion, and cultural and social assumptions were based on stories that sprang up around things found on sites such as figures of acrobats, bull leapers, goddesses who may not have been deities at all but ordinary household objects. Once removed from what's known as their findspots, once context is erased, it's impossible to know what the objects were, so stories were invented. Some of the objects that passed through their hands had never been dug out of the ground at all but originated in contemporary local workshops. Not only did collectors want relics, but archaeologists like Schliemann and Evans worked what may have been invented relics into their narratives about ancient Minoa. They were eager for these objects, whatever their provenance, to have the imprimatur of authenticity guaranteed by museum acquisition. Production of forgeries in Crete was market driven but also fed by the desire to find objects that would support assumptions.

Sculptor Norman Daly created the civilization of Llhuros, an entirely fictitious society, launched from his studio in Ithaca, New York, beginning the project in the 1960s. For decades he constructed both religious and utilitarian objects that, if you didn't look closely, certainly resembled ancient artifacts. Once you did look closely, you might identify twentieth-century gaskets, meat tenderizers, blender parts that made up votives, steles, nasal flutes, pairs of fornicating gods. Daly also wrote exhibition labels referencing scholarly interpretations of the artifacts that sound like parodies of the interpretations of the actual and invented Minoan artifacts like the Snake Goddesses and Boy Adorants. Daly quoted a host of anthropologists and archaeologists who made their marks in the study of his invented civilization. The acting director of Llhuroscian Studies at Cornell was a character Daly called Professor Conrad Lionberger, whom he thanks in his compiler's note in an exhibition catalog for a show of his life's work: the Civilization of Llhuros. *Yet it is difficult to place Professor Conrad Lionberger . . . anywhere except at the top of the list of those colleagues who shared most graciously their expertise with me.* The expertise of those cited—Conrad Lionberger, Paver Slaban, Emmet Joseph McIntyre, and others—was, in fact, Norman Daly's alone.

The Emile Gilliérons, Swiss father-and-son restoration team, working with Sir Arthur Evans in Knossos, openly sold via their catalog, *Galvanoplastic Mycenaean and Cretan (Minoan) Antiquities*, copies of artifacts, some a combination of castings from originals combined with creative restoration. Business was lucrative; everyone with the means to wanted a piece of the action that was ancient Minos. At the same time the Gilliérons were repainting missing pieces of friezes and murals at the actual site, to the point where the Knossos Throne Room figures would have looked at home in a Zurich Dada café. Art conservators now reject the mandate of restoration in favor of conservation, but when the Gilliérons were working, restoration—making an object or painting look as if it were made yesterday—was taken for granted as the right thing to do. The Gilliéron restorations and recreations, licit and illicit, couldn't help but look a little suffused with the art nouveau aesthetic that was contemporary at the time they were working, and in this way the copies took on a life of their own, looking partly ancient, partly art deco as well. Alfredo, grandson of the first Emile, still lives and works in Athens, and reportedly believes his copies could fool any archaeologist.

Forgeries like the Snake Goddesses and the Boy Adorants became screens on which to project desires and polemics, and over time they, in turn, transformed into historiographic documents, manufactured relics that unwittingly revealed traces from the periods in which they were actually created, becoming the babies that needed to be retained along with their used bathwater.

VINLANDIA

The Vinland Map is arguably one of the most important maps in the world.

—Robin Clark, Sir William Ramsay Professor of Chemistry at University College London

If the map of Vinland is real, then others, long before Columbus, sited and drew the edges of western continents and landmasses. Its shapes, both accurate and blobby, represent Europe, North Africa, Greenland, and northeastern Canada. The island of Vinland could be Labrador, Newfoundland, or Baffin. The legend reads, in part, *By God's will, after a long voyage from the island of Greenland to the south toward the most distant remaining parts of the western ocean sea, sailing southward amidst the ice, the companions*

Bjarni and Leif Eiriksson discovered a new land, extremely fertile and even having vines . . . which island they named Vinland.

If it's not a forgery, *Vinlandia* is the oldest map of America. The map came to light in a hotel room in Switzerland in 1957 and was said to have been drawn in 1444, but referenced what could only have been much earlier Nordic exploration. Before the hotel room, however, the Vinland map was totally unknown. No record, no bill of sale, no mention of its existence by any traveler, explorer, king, or minister with an eye on expansion. Its murky provenance didn't enhance its credibility, but the absence of a sort of family tree for the map doesn't guarantee the verdict that the parchment is a total hoax.

When the map was analyzed in 1972, the questions focused on the ink. The parchment itself was judged genuine, but that alone isn't significant. If old enough parchment is on your shopping list and you find it, you've hit gold. The ink's the thing. Was the black too shiny, too faded? What about the yellow outline around the letters? Some analysts thought the bled, faded ink proved the map was a forgery, a feature a clever craftsman could duplicate. The presence of a form of titanium dioxide found in the yellow outlines, a form of anatase not commercially available until the 1920s, seriously damaged claims of the map's authenticity. Also, doubters said, the outline of Greenland was uncharacteristically accurate, and some of the Latin inscriptions were ungrammatical, though it was possible the cartographer's knowledge of Latin was imperfect. Not everyone was a scholar, people make mistakes, and AutoCorrect was not available.

In 1984 the map underwent a second analysis for proton-induced X-ray fragment analysis. Using this noninvasive technique, which was able to cover a larger part of the map, the results showed five thousand times less titanium dioxide than the previous report. If titanium dioxide was only present in these trace amounts, then it would have no effect on the color of the ink, the clue about the origins of the Vinlandia map that seemed most damning. The ink, initially dismissed as modern, could well have been medieval. The California report was about chemistry only. It couldn't give a con-firmed stamp of authenticity, so the map remains in limbo, waiting for more cartographic and historical evidence to support or deny its claims. When molecules don't provide definitive answers, the map researchers question the map as a totality. The debate around the Vinlandia map shifted from chemistry and began to refer to things like matching wormholes—genuine or faked with a charred red-hot hatpin—and employed words like paleography, the study of ancient or historical handwriting, and codicology, the study of books as physical objects.

The map may be destined to waver between the twin poles of it's-the-real-deal and complete hoax, and the true story seems impossible to ever know with certainty. Thomas Cahill, a physicist at UC Davis, has said there are more ways to prove if something is a fraud than if it's genuine, but the map is owned by Yale University, which has a stake in its authenticity. The document is valued at $20,000,000. A tiny sliver sent to a lab was said to be worth $40,000, making evidence of fifteenth-century fingerprints valued at more than many twenty-first-century citizens earn in a year. The original mapmakers, whether medieval or just post–World War II, when they assembled their materials, might have found these numbers unimaginable, but in the case of Vinlandia, if the map is authentic, it tells when we knew what we knew: when somebody launched Kon Tiki–like into what must have appeared an endless and unpredictable sea toward lands unknown.

Story of the Slums
Can Xue

—Translated from Chinese by Karen Gernant and Chen Zeping

I CLIMBED THIS SIMPLY CONSTRUCTED blockhouse: As far as the eye could see, the rows of thatched slum houses were quietly bending their heads in the mist. I knew their humility was feigned. All these houses harbored sinister intentions. But I had to live in them. I was a son of this mystical land. Sure, it was gloomy here, but I was used to it. I had grown up here. Now in the midst of dreariness, I meditated constantly. I couldn't get a good look at the inside of the thatched huts. They were too dark inside. Their design had totally ignored the way eyes function. Sometimes when I moved into a house, I thought only two people lived there. Later, I found out there were twelve! I cowered in a corner of the stove: The fire came close to lapping at my skin and fur. They never stopped cooking because they had twelve stomachs to feed. With only one room, they slept anywhere. Two of them even slept under the bed. At midnight, I couldn't locate any of them. They had disappeared from the house. I stood on the stove and ran my eyes over the empty home. I wondered why I couldn't keep up with these people's trains of thought. Once, I had moved into a house where I thought the family was small and simple. I was happy because I'd be able to get a good night's sleep. But at midnight, an earthquake almost jolted me from the stove to the floor! By grabbing the iron hook from which bacon hung on the wall, I managed—just barely—to keep my footing. I looked back: Seven or eight people were break-dancing wildly. They seemed drunk. They were being flung from one wall to another. They resembled each other, so they must be from this family. Then where were they in the daytime? Some rooms were actually deserted; they just pretended to be inhabited—a garbage can and a broom at the entrance, and the door closed but not locked. I pushed against the door, entered, jumped up to the stove, and slept in that corner. I awakened at midnight and still saw no one. I jumped down and looked for something to eat, but found nothing. The house smelled of mold. Evidently, it had been unoccupied for ages. I slunk around in the darkness, a little fearful. Just then,

I heard a sigh. The sound came from the ceiling. The woman who had sighed didn't seem in pain. Probably she was simply tired. But the sound was incessant. I couldn't stand it. My chest was about to explode, and so I dashed out and wandered around all night in the cold. Sure, most of the time I blended into the landlords' lives. I hated them, because they always closed in on me, and yet, and yet, I was curious about their lives—those lives that I usually found incomprehensible. In the end, my relations with them deteriorated each time, and I left in search of another home to live in. It upset me to think of this. When was this blockhouse built? My impression was that although conspiracies riddled the slums, no major disturbance had occurred. So what was the point of building this blockhouse? To resist outside enemies? City people surely wouldn't come to these lowlands. People here and in the city simply had nothing to do with each other. I couldn't imagine where any enemies would come from.

It was getting dark. I ran down from the blockhouse that had gradually turned ice-cold. Another one of my species was running in front of me. He had a somewhat longer body than mine, and a bigger skull too. A spot of white hair was growing on his left hind leg, somewhat resembling the two house mice that I knew so well. But he wasn't a house mouse! He ran to the small pond over there and jumped down. My God! I certainly wouldn't jump into the icy water! At first, he was still visible. He swam and swam and then disappeared. Clearly, he had dived deep into the water. I stared blankly for a while at the edge of the pond. I thought of what had happened early this morning: The woman of the house had thrown me out. She disliked my dirtying the stove in her home. That wasn't true, though. I ate and slept on the stove every day and so I couldn't avoid leaving a little trace of my presence, could I? But she couldn't put up with it! She was a cleanliness freak. When she had nothing to do, she swept and dusted. This made absolutely no sense. I had never known anyone else in the slums who did that. Such a simple, crude house. Even if it was spotless, it looked no different from any of the other houses here. But this woman (I knew others called her "Auntie Shrimp") never gave me a break. If I came in with a little dirt on my feet, she brandished a broom and swore at me for a long time. At mealtime, she wouldn't tolerate it if I dropped a single grain of rice or a slice of vegetable onto the stove. She scrubbed my fur viciously with a brush every day, not stopping until I screamed. As for her, she spent a lot of time taking baths in the wooden basin. Whenever she had time, she heated water and bathed and washed her hair, as if she wanted to scrub away a layer of skin. Auntie Shrimp loved to talk at midnight. Maybe she was talking in her sleep. She always called me "the little mouse." She tossed and turned in that wide bed and talked incessantly: "The little mouse doesn't care about hygiene. This is dangerous. There's pestilence all around this area. If you don't want to get sick, you have to be strict about hygiene. My parents told me this secret. The year they left for the north and left me behind, they urged me to clean up every day. I was a sensible girl. . . ." Early one morning, she stood upright in bed and shouted, "Mouse, did you take a bath today? Something smells rotten!" She got out of bed and scrubbed me with the brush. It hurt so much that I screamed. I had always slept on the stove, but one day all of a sudden that displeased her. She said I had turned the stove into something that wasn't like a stove. She said if this continued, she and I would both come down with the plague. With this, she threw out the jar that I slept in. Brokenhearted, I was going to jump down from the stove, and then I glimpsed the murderous intent on her face. Oh—was she going to kill me? Her face was flushed; she held a kitchen knife in her hand. I thought that the moment I jumped down from the stove, she would chop me into pieces. And so I hesitated and retreated to a corner of the stove, making room for her to clean it. But she didn't clean. She kept saying, "Aren't you coming down? You aren't coming down?" As she spoke, she brandished the knife and pressed the back of the knife against me. I had to risk my life and jump down. She twirled the knife and chopped. Luckily, I dodged out of the way in time, and she chopped the muddy floor. The door wasn't closed, so I rushed out. Behind me, she shouted abuse, saying that if she saw any trace of me, she would kill me. How had my relationship with her evolved to this point? At first, when I drifted to her home, she had been such a genial woman! She not only fed me well, she also arranged for me to sleep in a jar, saying this would keep the flames from lapping at my fur. But before long I experienced her mysophobia. At the time, I didn't think it was a serious problem. One day, she suggested cutting off my claws (because they were filthy). That's when I started being on guard. What kind of woman was she? I started avoiding her. Luckily, it was all talk and no action. And so I kept my claws.

She cleaned the house so thoroughly that it created endless trouble for her. For example, she had to brush the soles of her shoes each time she entered the house. She covered the windows and doors with heavy cloth. The inside of the house became as dark as a basement. She used much more water than other people did to clean vegetables, wash dishes, and take baths. She was forever going to the well to fetch water. She was always busy. I didn't know how she made a living. Perhaps her parents had left her some money. She wasn't much interested in men. She merely stood in the doorway, idiotically watching a certain man's silhouette, but she never brought a man home. She was probably afraid outsiders would make her house dirty. But then how had she taken a liking to me in the first place, and even let me in? I was even dirtier than those men, wasn't I? And I rarely bathed with water. When I first arrived, she combed my fur with an old comb. After combing my messy fur, she threw the comb into the garbage. With some satisfaction, she pronounced me "very clean." Now, remembering this, I thought she was sort of deceiving herself. But she persisted in thinking that she could do anything. She was a conceited woman. From that day on, she brushed me every day. It hurt a lot. But at least I was much cleaner than before. I used to get along well with her, even though I despised her constant cleaning. Still, as long as I stayed inside the jar on top of the stove, there was no big problem. Who could have guessed that her mysophobia would worsen?

One day, she actually found a metal brush to brush my fur. I was bruised all over from her brushing, and I let out a scream the way pigs do when being butchered. When she let go, I ran off and cowered under the eaves of another home. I was still bleeding from my back. After the sun set, I couldn't stand the cold, and I was afraid I wouldn't be able to endure the night and would die outside. A young girl with a pointed face noticed me. She squatted and looked me over under the dim streetlight. Dressed in a short-sleeved shirt, she was also shivering from the cold. "King Rat," she said, "you mustn't stay here. If you do, you'll die, because it'll freeze tonight. Are you imitating those children? They've been doing this for years. As soon as they learned to walk, they went outside to sleep. That's the way they've lived for a long time. Go on home, King Rat. If you don't, you'll die." And so I walked back slowly. Finally I was limping almost every time I took a step. I was cold and in pain, almost losing consciousness. When I got home, it was probably close to midnight. The light was still on, though Auntie Shrimp was in bed snoring. I climbed on top of the pile of firewood next to the stove and squatted down to rest. Then, probably because of my loud groans, Auntie Shrimp woke up. She got out of bed and looked at me by the light of the kerosene lamp. Before long, she set the lamp down, turned, took a bottle of balm out of the cupboard, and gently smeared it on my wounds. "Mouse,

119

why didn't you tell me I was hurting you when I combed your fur?" she rebuked me. This confused me greatly. What was illusion? What was reality? Did I know this woman at all? Anyhow, the balm helped. I could finally breathe, and then I fell asleep on the woodpile.

The very next morning, the incident that I described above happened. Even now, I have no idea what Auntie Shrimp's real idea was. Yet when I ran out of Auntie Shrimp's home, I realized that it was indeed filthy outside! These were the slums, after all—what could you expect? I seemed to be stepping on human waste with each step I took. The side of the street was filled with human waste, dog shit, and puddles of urine, heaps of decomposed vegetable leaves, the guts of animals, and so forth. Swarms of mosquitoes and flies were fluttering around and entering your nostrils. I couldn't put up with it anymore, and I climbed that blockhouse. I sat on top of the blockhouse for a long time without recovering my equilibrium. I didn't understand: How had the outside environment worsened so much in the few months that I had lived in Auntie Shrimp's home? People said that the slums had never been clean, but I had been almost oblivious to that. Now the filth had completely polluted the air—so much that I wanted to throw up. Even though I was on top of the blockhouse, I still felt that everything below was a huge garbage dump. The stench rode the wind. The people on the street looked down at their feet, covered their noses, and hurried on. I seldom went out during the few months that I stayed with Auntie Shrimp. And even when I did, I went no farther than the neighbors' eaves. Otherwise, Auntie Shrimp would have constantly told me to wash my feet and she would have scolded me mercilessly. And so, was it simply by comparison that I finally realized how filthy the slums were? Had Auntie Shrimp been training my senses over the last few months? Maybe I had never before noticed that passersby covered their noses as they walked past. Maybe the sides of the streets in the slums had always been heaped with dirt, and I had simply never noticed. Thinking back on the last few months of Auntie Shrimp's slave-like life, putting myself in her shoes, and then thinking about myself, I couldn't help but shudder. However, I still had to thank Auntie Shrimp—for in the past, I was covered with pus-filled pimples, I was toxic from head to foot, and I ate filthy food. But after spending a few months in her home, I had no pus-filled pimples and I understood the importance of hygiene. People of the slums were too apathetic. How could they have become so lazy that they let the doorways become dumps for waste and dirt? Not only was filth overflowing into the air here, but it also seeped underground. The asphalt roads and the cobblestone sidewalks were stained by a thick layer of something black and greasy. Even the mud was dirty, filled with ash and oil. Why hadn't I ever noticed this before? This blockhouse, though, was clean, as if no one had ever come up here and heaven's wind and rain had cleaned it naturally. This granite structure must be very old. Plumbing the depths of my memory, I found no trace of it. Was it because no one had ever come here that it was so clean? Why hadn't others come up here?

I stood at the side of the pond, thinking of all kinds of things. I would soon freeze to death. My top priority was to save my life by finding a home to move into. I noticed a house with a door that wasn't shut tight and thought I'd go in and deal with any consequences later. "Who's there?" An old voice spoke in the dark. I curled up quietly against the foot of the wall, afraid the man would see me, but he got up unexpectedly, shone a kerosene lamp on me, and said, "Ah, it's a snake." How the hell had I changed into a snake? He poked me with a club and I took the opportunity to roll into the house. How bizarre this was: A heat wave rolled through the house, and I immediately warmed up. The stove wasn't on, so where had the hot air come from? I saw that familiar mouse stick his head out of the hole. Three scrawny roosters stood under the bed. The man of the house was short and little. His head was wrapped in a white towel, so I couldn't see him very well. He drove the roosters out with the club, and they jumped up. One flew to the windowsill, scattering the smell of feathers all over. When the little red-tailed rooster passed by me, I was actually scalded! Its body was as hot as red-hot coals! Just then, the man squatted and looked me up and down. His face was triangular, and his cruel eyes were hidden under bushy eyebrows. He swept my legs with the club, and I jumped away. "This snake is really odd . . . ," he muttered. He still considered me a snake. Was this because I didn't emit heat? What were these roosters all about?

He suddenly gave a weird laugh and said, "Auntie Shrimp . . ." The sound seemed to come from a tomb. I looked around: Sure enough, Auntie Shrimp's face appeared at the door. She was laughing in embarrassment, but she didn't enter. He waved his hand, and I still thought he was going to hit me, but his hand merely slipped past once and a heat wave dashed against my face. I blinked: Auntie Shrimp had disappeared. The little rooster jumped from the windowsill to his shoulder. The man stood up and, dragging the club, circled once around the room. The two roosters on the floor dashed past me, scalding my nose. A blister immediately appeared there. What the hell? This old man apparently wanted to find these two roosters, but the roosters ran right past him and he didn't even see them. He just hit the air with his club. The little guy on his shoulder gurgled, keeping time with his swaying. Its claws cut into his clothes. I scurried under the bed because I was afraid he would hit me. I had barely squeezed under it when something struck me in the head. I almost fainted from the pain. When I pulled myself together, I noticed a lot of little animals that were similar to me. They formed a circle around me. Their thermal radiation almost prevented me from opening my eyes. Were they my kin? How had they become so heat resistant? In my hometown in the past, our pasture was icebound most of the year. We hid in dugouts. We never knew what "high temperatures" meant. What was going on now? They turned into balls of fire, and yet they could endure this! Were they surrounding me in order to destroy my physical being? If so, why weren't they taking action? At the door, Auntie Shrimp was saying to the man, "Have you destroyed that virus? Where did he go? He goes all over the place and might spread disease!" She actually said I was a virus! The old man answered, "Don't worry. This place is for high-temperature disinfecting. We'll take care of his problem." "Then please do that." Auntie Shrimp seemed to really be leaving.

I was being roasted. I couldn't open my eyes. Could they be treating my virus? Those who were like my kin were glaring at me. My eyes stung, and I shed tears. I couldn't see. The old man swept under the bed again with his club, and my kin ran out. He pressed me against the wall with his club. "Go ahead—just try to run!" the old man said. I heard myself cry out twice from the pain. My voice sounded like that of a house mouse. How could I sound like a house mouse? I struggled, but the club didn't budge. I would suffocate soon. Everything went black before my eyes. Was I going to die? It was so hot. But, suddenly, the man loosened his grip on the club and said, "A snake can't warm up." I touched the blister on my nose with my claws. Indeed, my claws were ice-cold. No wonder he had said I was a snake!

Had I been disinfected? I had no idea. I slowly emerged from under the bed and once more heard Auntie Shrimp's voice: "I've never seen such a clean mouse before! But he'll be dirty again tomorrow and he'll have to be roasted again. Huh! If he were like the others, I'd take him back." By "the others," I knew she meant the ones who were supposedly my kin. They had become burning pieces of coal, so of course they couldn't have viruses. But how had they gotten like this? Auntie Shrimp didn't seem to be planning for me to go back. She stared at me coldly from the window. Did they really intend to roast me like this every day? Even if they did, how could a snake turn into a red-hot coal? My kin who had been swept out from under the bed lined up along the foot of the wall. The old man swept across with the club. Routed again, they scurried under the bed. Tired from hitting them, he stood with arms akimbo in the middle of the room and said, "You sluggards! Watch out—my club means business!" I looked under the bed: Those little things were trembling! The little rooster flew from his shoulder to midair, then dropped down and set off a heat wave in the room. I fell back a few paces when the wave struck me and leaned against the wall. I noticed that the landlord wasn't emitting heat, and yet he wasn't afraid of it either. How come? He set down his club and took something to eat out of the kitchen cupboard. He seemed to be eating little black balls. Judging from his table manners, the food was hard. A cracking sound came from between his teeth: Was he eating something metal? What strong teeth he had! Just then, a ray of sunlight flashed in from the open door, and all at once I got a good look at his face. A huge tumor on the left side of his face pulled his mouth and nose to one side. The tumor was so red that it was almost purple. To my surprise, a brass ring was pierced through the top of it, and pus ran out from that ring. Damn, his body was so toxic, and yet he devoted himself to disinfecting animals! People, huh? Oh, people. No way could I understand them! He chewed and swallowed down all those little balls. His teeth were like steel. "Yi Tinglai! Yi Tinglai!" Auntie Shrimp was standing at the door. Why was his name "Yi Tinglai"—"Instant Responder"? How weird! Auntie Shrimp said, "I won't feel better until he's as clean as you. He always gets dirty!" The old man gave a devilish laugh. I couldn't see even one tooth in the dark cavity that was his mouth. How had he bitten those little balls? "Are you leaving now? You aren't taking him with you?" the old man asked Auntie Shrimp. "I have to go. The road will be blocked soon. As for the little mouse, I'll leave him with you. I'm sorry to give you so much trouble." "Has the plague reached here yet?" "Yesterday. Two died. I was afraid the little mouse would get sick, he's so dirty." I was alarmed by this talk.

Once more, the man took a large plate of black balls out of the kitchen cupboard and put it on the floor. This kind of ball was much smaller—only a little larger than a house mouse's poop. My kin crowded around and ate in a hurry, making creaking sounds. I wanted to eat too, but I was afraid they would scald me. The man said, "You little snake-mouse, it isn't time for you to eat yet. They're eating pieces of coal. Can you swallow that?" Naturally, I wasn't interested in letting coal burn my stomach. I didn't think I needed to be disinfected that way. Just then, he carried out a bowl of black liquid, saying I should "wash my innards" with it. Noticing the bubbles on the dirty black water, I hesitated. He bellowed, "Hurry up, or you'll die!" And so I started drinking. After drinking it, I felt dizzy and my heart swelled with longing for my hometown. That pasture, that sky. Snowflakes swirled in the sky, and my kin hid in the caves. Would they all die soon? No, they were fine. They had diarrhea: They would get rid of all the dirty things they'd eaten in the summer! Their insides would be clean! Ha. I was the one with diarrhea. I'd gotten rid of a huge amount. The man focused all his attention on me. "Are your insides clean?" he asked. I twitched my tail to indicate I was finished. The man spread around some ashes and swept my poop under the stove. He seemed to think poop wasn't dirty. So why was it necessary to wash my intestines? It was impossible to guess their thoughts. "Auntie Shrimp left you to me to deal with." The old man went on, "Stand up. Let me look at you." I went weak in the knees; I couldn't stand up. I lay on my stomach on the ground and couldn't move. I thought I was going to die. "Can't you stand up? Forget it then. You're all like this. Your grandfather came calling one year and ate every last bit of my roasted pork. But when I told him to jump up to the stove, he couldn't do it!" The old man chattered on and on and lay down on the bed. Then my kin who had eaten their fill left the plate one by one, lined up against the wall, and fell asleep. It was getting hot in the house again, and, meanwhile, strength was returning to my legs. I tried a few times and finally stood up. It was so hot! Really hot! The coal briquettes must be burning in the man's and my kin's stomachs. They were all sleeping, as if the high temperature had left them very content. All of a sudden, the three roosters started fighting in the middle of the room. The two big ones attacked the little one, ripping his crest apart. The little rooster's face was a mass of blood. He squatted on the floor and tried hard to hide his head amid the feathers on his chest. The other two still didn't let go of him: They continued attacking and pecked him all over until his feathers fell off. Blood gushed out where they had pecked. It looked as if he would die at the hands of his buddies. Just at this horrible moment, he flew swiftly upward. Spreading his wings, he flew like a bird and then dropped down heavily. He set off a heat wave in the house, and

I was about to suffer a heatstroke. He struggled a few times on the floor, then lay motionless. The other two crowded around and pecked at his feathers, stripping him of one bunch after another. They worked brutally and rapidly, and soon the little rooster was absolutely bald. While the roosters were making an uproar, my kin were sleeping, but one house mouse emerged. He was exactly like one that I'd seen in another home in the past—also with a white spot on his left hind leg. He exerted himself to bite the little rooster on the back and ripped off a piece of flesh. He ate it right away. After eating one piece, he went back to tear off another piece, turning the little rooster's back into a large cavity. By the light shooting in from the door, I could see the guts in the cavity. The house mouse came over to me with the flesh in his mouth, and—showing off—he chewed it. I smelled a strong, rotten stench. Was it the odor of this flesh? Hadn't the little rooster just died? His flesh should have still been fresh, shouldn't it? Oh! The little featherless rooster actually stood up shakily! The hole in his back was very conspicuous. He walked unsteadily over to me! The house mouse—still with the flesh in its mouth—scurried into the hole. The rooster's naked body was pale, and the blood on the crest congealed. He stared at me with round eyes. I sensed that if he came a bit closer, I would be burned by his thermal radiation. He jumped a few times, and some little marble-like balls bounced out of the cavity in his back and dropped to the floor, igniting flames. They soon burned up, leaving no trace. He jumped some more, and a few more balls flew out. I watched idiotically. He jumped and jumped, not stopping until his body was empty. Then he fell onto the floor. His thermal radiation vanished. I walked over and poked him. God, all that was left was one layer of skin! Even his bones were gone! As I considered looking more closely at this little pile of dirt, the man on the bed spoke.

"He came here deliberately to exact revenge, and he died in my house. I can't stand dead things. I hate the sight of death. I was afraid of nightmares for quite a while, and so I worked even harder at disinfecting the place." With that, he got out of bed and squatted next to the little rooster's remains. Shifting it with tongs, he muttered, "It's the plague, isn't it? The plague." I thought to myself, he's been burned out. All that's left is a little empty skin. How can it hold the plague? Since this was the plague, why didn't he throw it out immediately instead of moving it with the tongs? Suddenly, he turned to me, stared vengefully with his triangular eyes, and scolded, "You! What are you looking at? This is nothing for you—a snake—to see!"

I was afraid he would stab me with the tongs, and so I scurried under the bed. From there, I saw him drop the rooster skin into a bowl and place the bowl in the kitchen cupboard. I was shocked! This person didn't do what he said, but just the opposite! The other two roosters came out too. They circled the man and yelled. They flew up and pecked him. Were they protesting? And if so, what were they protesting? They had all (including the mouse) dismembered the little rooster, and now when the man had put his remains into the cupboard, were they unhappy with that? Why was this room so hot? The man stuck his head under the bed and asked, "Snake, do you want to eat? I won't give you charcoal briquettes, because if you eat them, you'll be burned so much you won't even leave any ashes behind. I'll give you this, OK?" He threw a big bunch of grass under the bed. I was no herbivore. When I left the grass in disgust and went over to the wall to sleep, the fragrance emitted by the grass drew me back. What was this scent? I tried a few bites. This succulent thing left green juice at the corners of my mouth. I was so excited! I was about to jump up! I wanted so much to jump to some other place, though I couldn't say where. It seemed connected with shadows. And so I scurried to the shadows behind the big cupboard. Oh! The scent of the grass grew stronger. My longing for home tortured me. Why was I still staying in these slums that were like garbage bins? I mustn't hesitate: I must rush back to my hometown. My brain was about to explode with memories of her. But my legs were so thin and weak: It took a lot of effort to go to the city just once. I didn't know the way to the grasslands—it was thousands of miles away, so remote. I might die on the way. I shouldn't think about these things. Covered all over with the virus, I could only stay in this garbage bin, cleaning up and being disinfected all day long. Why did he feed me grass from my homeland? Did he intend to shatter my longing to go back home? Was it all about what he was doing? Did he think this would be good for me? Oh, my home, my hometown—in this life, I could never return. I had never imagined that I would be able to eat grass from my home—sure, this grass was from there. I remembered so clearly: This was what my ancestors ate every day, long, long ago before I was born. Had this landlord been there? Or was an envoy traveling between the two places? While pondering this, I fell asleep. Someone was talking in my dream. It was Auntie Shrimp. Auntie Shrimp said I could walk to the grasslands. "You just need to try, and your legs will get stronger." What did she mean? I'd better get up fast and try this. I opened my eyes with an effort and saw the landlord look under the bed. His staring triangular eyes freaked me out. He said, "Over there on the corner, two snakes were burned to death. The entire region is being disinfected. How could they escape? Huh." He told me to come out.

I walked out shakily and saw that he had once more placed the dish of the little rooster's remains on the floor. He told me to eat that little thing. I didn't want to. He struck me in the head repeatedly with the wooden club. I passed out and then came to. After a while, I really couldn't stand this. I decided I'd better suppress my nausea and swallow this little thing. After doing that, I felt ill. I rolled my eyes. I wanted to throw up, but I couldn't stand up. I lay on my stomach on the floor. The house mouse stuck his head out of the hole in front of me and looked at me with a weird expression. What? Was he waiting to eat me? Just look at his expression! I was nauseated again, and everything blurred before my eyes. Oh, he was nipping at my face! I was losing my mind and stood up. He kept biting me and wouldn't let go, as if stuck to my face. I thought he must have bitten through my face. I couldn't move. If I moved, a piece of skin with fur would be ripped from my face. From above, the landlord said, "Snake, oh snake. This is testing your endurance." I smelled sewage on the house mouse's body. He was so filthy, and yet the old man let him live in his home and run about as he pleased. All of a sudden, he let go of my face. I rubbed my face with my front claws. It wasn't too bad—he had probably just chewed a few tooth cavities. The odd thing was that this fiend immediately fell over in front of me, his belly swollen and black blood running out of his mouth. He'd been poisoned! My body was hypertoxic! How come the old man's disinfectant hadn't worked? Had he really wanted to rid me of poison, or had he wanted to turn me into a hypertoxic substance and use me to poison the mouse? He was sitting with his back to me. The view of his back resembled something I was familiar with. I gave it a lot of thought, and at last I figured out what he reminded me of: He was like the rock shaped like a person in my hometown! It had come to the surface out of the mud and stood straight up in the center of the pasture. It was like a person, but it wasn't one. Many of my kin loved to run around it. "You mustn't stare at me all the time. I came from the pasture," he said without turning around. Lined up against the wall, my kin listened attentively. Now I saw that all of us had come from the pasture! I remembered the harsh climate, the crystal-clear blue sky, the summer that passed so quickly that it seemed unreal, the countless secrets concealed in the underbrush, the eagles circling in the sky all day without tiring. . . . These recollections were killing me. I wished I could abandon my physical body and blend into that place . . . I had no idea how I could remember things that happened in the era of my great-grandfather's generation and even his father's. Those things could appear in my mind at any time and be compared with the shape my life had taken now. I knew, even if it were possible to go back, I would be unable to adapt to that climate. More than half of my kin died there every year just as early winter descended. If I were there, I'd surely be the first to die. There was no plague in the grasslands. You just felt bone-penetrating cold, and then your heart stopped beating. And so my kin didn't say someone had "died," but said someone had "chilled." Although I wasn't there, I remembered that black-tailed guy. He lay there facing up, watching the gray clouds massed above him, opening his mouth slightly, and not moving. He was as cold as ice—rigid. I remembered too that year after year, even though new kin were born, our numbers were decreasing. I didn't remember whether we had fled later. We must have. Otherwise, how could these kin, including me, have come here to the slums? "Let me take the little mouse home, let me take the little mouse home, let me . . . ," Auntie Shrimp kept saying this outside the door, but she didn't come in. Maybe she was afraid of the heat.

The slums were my home. This home wasn't exactly what I wanted: Everything was difficult, and perils lurked at every turn. But this was the only home I had. My only option was to stay here. I used to have a homeland, but I couldn't go back to her. It was useless to yearn for her. I stayed in these slums of mine: My eyes were turbid, my legs thin and weak, my innards poisoned over and over again. I endured, I endured. That gigantic eagle in the sky over my native place appeared in my mind—and brought me strength.

From The Immanent Field
Michael Martin Shea

*

When the soldiers entered the town they left the artists alone, thereby invalidating their art projects · Directionality as artistic trope of the supreme world-maker · Would-be artists can measure their value by the number of actual cops at their readings · Whatever made this world could not have accounted for human error, unless it did · A mansion filled exclusively with cop breath · Humanity entered into a long period of debauched and circuitous dancing · What houses our revolutionary power if not the unfolding of bastard sentences? · The dancing bear is a minor object · Without our notions of power, masturbation loses all appeal · It's no longer possible to bear up actual arms against the massive machinery of the state · To masturbate in public is an unforgivable perversion · The state subsumes happiness for numerical existence · Forgiving ourselves was the hardest part of leaving Mississippi · A willingness to convert the world into numbers presumes that our graphs are indexed to real lives · And we, who are somehow not afraid! · Nullification of the real order is an appendage of the body · Incurable deceptions for the purpose of "big god" · What the appendage wants is a proper sense of statehood · "The bigger they are, etc." applies primarily to descriptions of memory · Artists struggle to resist the state because of the comforts and snacks it affords them · The described totality of being is a ruthless chimera · I cannot afford the various social contracts constitutive of personhood · When I described my erection I was asked to leave the party

Michael Martin Shea

*

An extreme childishness descended over the city · It's like ten thousand spoons when you can't stop thinking about killing yourself · A brothel outfitted with child-safety gates · It's like a blizzard composed of other people's sad Facebook statuses · An unpleasant outfitting for floral wear · My involvement in the blizzard myth left us all abated and little to chance · Floridity as cultural nonpresence · A shower of angular momentum chanced the room into a physic · Vaginal nonpresence as operator of the cultural sublime · The deepwater angler held purchase of a mythical pretext · A sublimation of our physical selves · The pretense of good behavior is the bedrock of the economy · Ever-ready, ever-nurtured, ever-tortured, ever-bending down into our spleens · Economic theory holds that a tie goes to the runner · I never understood the value of torture until I read blue-collar poetry · The economy of desire is lifting my pants for future applicants · Poetic fetish of the working class is a supreme dildo · I never understood the fundamental theory of calculus until it was applied to my dreams · Working side by side like prepubescent trains · A calculation invokes a sense of residency · Being alone is good training for having an undiagnosed anxiety disorder · I was asked to leave the party for calculating the length of everyone's perineum · A terminal diagnosis creates a temporal absence · This particular fetish was untenable for much longer

*

The production of privilege eclipsed the economy of desire · I was distinguished for betting my life on a pair of regular-season baseball games · The eclipse woke me up with its horrible screeching · Astonished at the regularity of my desires: each morning a clean erection · The screech of sharpened metal, moon as celestial dimepiece · The newness of the world is astonishing · My gurney, a masterpiece of industrial aesthetics · Being-in-the-world is the first cause of privilege · My gurney won first prize in the local cock-and-balls show · What causes our stomachs to reckon with patterned speech? · The first order of the new king was to abolish our provincialist notions of an avant-garde · Infused with the requisite pooping patterns · A new world order only birthed through extreme violence · One time I shit myself out of existential fear · Think of it not as violence but a hip new kind of architecture · Integrated systems management sanitizes the digestive shit process · A temporal architect is not an artifact · The integral of persons is systemic · Time doesn't kill anyone, it just shuffles their parts around · Systemic inequality is a white man's best friend · Just holding yourself with blankets can be a salve against despair · The whiteness of virtue as most dangerous cultural signifier also taught to children · Just despair is not enough to make you important · My body as most prominent betrayal system · The importance of deception in the analysis of others · My first betrayal occurred when I was seven and Eric broke my ruler and I told him it was my dead grandfather's · The important prizes are the ones doled out by the state as markers of respectability in letters

Michael Martin Shea

*

Prize culture is a primer in the privileging of certain authorities, all of whom have pill money · At a restaurant in Madison with Jesse, making Seth say "ooey gooey pasta" over and over · Domestic language, restricted language, redacted language, language made out of beehives · Jesse, stoned and ripping the bathroom sink out of the wall at Fermentation Lounge · The death of the bees is tragic but no parallel for human consciousness · With Jesse in Boston, drunk and standing in the kitchen window at the start of a blizzard, listening to Beach House · The sheen of useless cynicism masked under a gothic love of death · There are only four records I can listen to while writing · Just because production is a capitalist impulse doesn't mean we can't love our neighbors · The writing of the poem is either a praxis of discovery or it's useless · A producer of love is not a static observer of the field · The problem with poets isn't the reach of state power, it's that they only resist it insofar as they want to control it · Observation of beauty confers inflated self-importance on the viewer · In that the law has no real body, control of it does not make you a real boy · The scent of dead coniferous trees in December · I don't remember being the boy in the picture with goggles and water wings · Like the tree I chopped down with Marty the second time we broke up · I remember either a wild horse or a seagull eating my sandwich · Drunk on cheap beer and firing a BB gun at our neighbor's house with our upside-down flag pins · I remember a broken screened porch and mosquito bites in Virginia · A rented house projects a temporary space wherein the furniture arranges itself · I got stoned on the communal porch of my decrepit apartment and then watched through the blinds as my neighbor threw her boyfriend's clothes into the yard

*

To remember the specifics of furniture is to leave the present moment · I burrowed into the rafters of my one-bedroom hovel · Again I am wanting to leave the presence of friends for the Internet · I burrowed into the attic of our three-bedroom hovel · What I want is for my friends to never be afraid · I shared a bed with a woman with fabulous taste and loved and feared her judgment and wanted to hide my depravity, not knowing her own strangeness · Hiding yourself out of fear is a form of self-pity · For instance: the house she burnt down, the dogs she babied, the songs she forgot she was singing · I've been hiding my production of self from my family for years now · Our governing madness was a belief that science could cure us from wanting to die sometimes · Projecting the end of production into the future allows for true praxis · The Internet scientists are always reportedly working · A practical man does not give in easily to mindless distraction · A terrible dearth of reporters for abject artifacts · I'm distracted because I know my big dick will amount to nothing · The death of our great cities at the hands of baby cops · I'm distracted by liquor and subordinate clauses · The pixelated moment with its great sheathen member · A causal alignment is a form of sacrifice · I remember getting drunk in the baseball fields with stolen liquor · I sacrificed my only sense of home for the hope of the rancid new

Michael Martin Shea

*

Faith in writing as some sort of entrance exam for death · Each year, masturbating in front of the family Christmas tree · All this talk about dying like there's nothing else fun to do · Each year, an affect of torrential strangeness and new beer · It's like touching each other in the abandoned church in Taos · Affective piety has no place on social media · It's like a party where no one's little brother has to go to jail for car theft · The affectation of piety haunts even the best inventions · My parting gift was an e-mail about infidelity · A haunting scene full of Internet weirdos · What I promised not to report was not faithlessness but fear · I've seen a Navajo man lose a bet in a bar called the Matador · Repeating myself is a way of stabilizing certain identity platforms (I was that guy, I was that guy) · I've seen a white lady scan the room and then lower her voice to talk about "those people" · There's a stability offered by trying to prove that you're sufficiently enlightened about gender and race, even though such a state can never exist · The closest thing to real suffering I've ever experienced in my privileged life was abject loneliness · An enlightenment-style concept of banking applied to dating profiles · The experience of faithlessness had me locked out in October, watching the sunrise · The concept of haunting doesn't need a god to function · I was locked up for admitting that I'd never seen *The Shawshank Redemption* · Nonfunctional alcoholics are not permitted to partake in the communion · I was personally redeemed by Sardis and liquor in empty fields

*

Was it rottenness or wantonness we bathed our children in? · Sugar banana, pumpkin pie, little cakes, stinky butt · Was it an actual revolutionary feeling or had we merely bought something? · A poem where the rape victim isn't the butt of the joke anymore · The purchasing power of social change limited by character · The fetish of the lyric self leads away from a poetics of actual selfhood · Characterizing yourself as one thing, reflected in many bistros · Revolutionary poetics consists in holding a tenure-track job but pretending not to · There have been many times where I've forgotten my mother's actual birth date · A revolution wearing a Morrissey T-shirt, a revolution like a keg party inexplicably filled with zoo animals · My mother, nineteen and almost kidnapped in a van in Berlin · A part of my animism devoted exclusively to new dog breath · In the seventies, my mother, back from ten months in Europe and looking for my father, her summer boyfriend · I was long devoted to not confronting the privilege that still makes me an asshole · I'm twenty-six and still registered to vote at my parents' house because they live in a swing state · Dog assholes are a shockingly large part of my life for someone who does not fuck dogs · I'm always swinging through various states of existence when I post on the Internet · Fuck people who drink bottled water indoors in America · The Internet was responsible for my thinking that all women want anal sex · American leftism not immune from exporting ideology · One time, I fucked my ex-girlfriend in the ass in a basement but she stopped me when I also called her a whore · What's left of my dreams is a world not forgone by bunnies · We should pity the law clerks for their nigh-enviable whoring · I left Tampa in a state of supreme agitation and fine linen and whiskey · Legal action against the state merely engages it on its own terms · Wishing myself faster in the pursuit of some awkward nobility to lord over my friends · I was acting against my own interests when I said that the nobles should rot in their yards

*

In pursuant to the tantamount pleasure · Me in my motherfucking Escalade, and you in your motherfucking Escalade · Pursuing myself with whips and rifles and headphones and madness and chartered boats and checkerboard parks and the presence of a notary public · I forgot myself in the scent of your sex organs · I abide no ministry of the public eyes · Sexuality as a steamboat tethered to a rotted-out deck in New Orleans · I administered the rag to my own feral bleeding · "The new" means anything that used to scare white culture · My tactics are as follows: pleasantries, burn, pleasantries, burn · And those of you among us who are still somehow not afraid? · A pleasant romp in the left hand to greet the morning · A pleasing joy among the desiccated husks of the real · Let us bring a raucous politic to greet the fuckers · Reality shot through with arms and coefficients · Fuck the poets embossing their spines with a seed of market value · Reality whistles and fucks the nearest soft object · Bring on our protestations, seed the politic of *no more dead children* · Objectification of the dream until it's a closet you can walk into · What makes a child if even the snipers have parents? · To walk down Wall Street and not think about the wheezing planet · What new snipers will enjoy our delicious bodies today? · A wall of constituency and fervor · And what if we're wrong about our bodies forever? · Awash in the listening of fevered spirits · And what if we're wrong about ghosts? · The totemic library washed over in pipeline spill · And what if civilian parents can't love enough for us? · The brutality of "pipe down" when you're seeking a vocal reality · The field of love punctured by gravitational chalk bodies · One voice which is a living spirit · Our bodies and the smells that are funny · Within my living potential, another set of dead mice · Our bodies and the sounds that wake you up at night · Men set upon by their creations may still ask forgiveness · Wherefore of the faith save our nightly offerings? · I created myself through a set of rigorous and mostly failed social experiments · Where, for fuck's sake, are the pills for safe dying? · I created a television sensation that was canceled but never ended, like a dream

*

Some part of me wonders if I'd be happier in a life outside of "the humanities" · My first wager involved three minor-league baseball games and a botched execution · Progressive politics that choose misery over wonder are self-indulgent · Bogeymen are uniquely inculcated in the continuation of state-sponsored murder · What is the self if not a sack full of mnemonic devices? · The myth of the unique voice as a way to play pretend with three hundred million people · I divided the world into three camps: money, children, and fire · Naming a set of people as "voiceless" and then presuming to speak for them is a classic "dick move" · We went camping in Nevada and I found myself climbing onto boulders, astonished at how bright the stars were · One time I was so dehydrated that the tip of my cock was chapped · In southern Nevada you can never experience true darkness on account of the light pollution and aliens · Once I accepted the elimination of certain paths as a result of my choices, I found myself free of the needless sweat stains · The truth of a line has little to do with what I think of as "my existence" · Again I'm talking to myself as I slice the potatoes · The truth of my life so far is incredibly not on the Internet · Again I'm wondering if goodness is compatible with the writing of poems · Credibility depends on not being asked to leave the restaurant · What good is it to fear if you're never brought to any action? · The restaurant was where I first learned about Satan · Dog park as arbiter of our ability to engage in collective action · I was never found to be a true satanist, just a dabbler in the prophetic and leering arts

Michael Martin Shea

*

Underneath the blankets we put our little selves in alignment, like planets · I'm trying to galvanize all of my terrific interests · It's like a birthday cake made out of the reclaimed stuff of suffering · You can't go gallivanting across Europe without first understanding postcolonialism · A reclaimed sense of wonder from our spirited Internet debates · I underestimated my ability to stimulate reality's colon · What you're witnessing is the creation of a spiritual den of personas · I was colonized by an unidentified vision complex · The witness refused to take the stand unless the degenerate jury cleared their mouths out · Identification with the other is a simulation · Ahead in the clearing, where the pocket machines waited · Simulacrum is when we fuck each other and then roll over and grab our cell phones · The mechanics of my production written out in longhand and submitted for verification · Simulacrum is when we watch each other masturbate and feel afraid · You can't verify your personhood just by sticking a pin through your finger · An unidentified feeling washed over the crowd of rubberneckers · What kind of person needs to exhale their loneliness for approval? · I stood by my previous statements as obscene but ultimately necessary · Exhausting all options, I studied the works of Klimt

Walking Wounded
Joyce Carol Oates

1.

LATE MORNING BUT THERE'S a heaviness to it like dusk. Bruised sky like an eye swollen shut. Smell of sulfur in the warm wind from the lake shallow at this end, rotted with cattails, tall reeds and rushes and something floating just beneath the surface.

He has returned to our small town on Lake Cattaraugus. He has returned eviscerated.

He is forty-one years old. His youth has been lost to him.

Torn away like clothes cut off a stricken man by EMTs wielding shears in an emergency.

He has learned respect for the astonishing swiftness of (young, vigorous) emergency workers. As soon as you lose control of your body in a faint, in a public place, your body is theirs.

Why think of this?—he isn't.

Hell no. *Not.*

At the southernmost edge of the lake he sees her.

A luminous figure in the mist that lifts from the lake on this mild, overcast June morning.

She is standing at a railing of the esplanade, very still.

He is very still, a little distance away.

Her back is to him yet he is certain that she is a stranger.

Her hair is loose, curly, and tangled partway down her back. Her shoulders are narrow, she is delicate boned, a young woman, a girl who is (he is sure) a stranger to him. She leans forward against the wrought-iron railing, gazing out at the lake in utter stillness.

Light glimmering on the rippled slate-colored water, which seems almost to encase the woman. Or is it moisture in his eyes as he stares, he is so deeply moved . . .

Is it—her!

Like a clapper inside a bell his heart clamors.

Am I terminal, he'd asked.

Should I have hope? Or—is that ridiculous? Selfish?

Early that morning he'd been awakened by a sharp cramp in the calf muscles of his left leg. Jolted from the comfort of sleep that is his only solace.

When this happens he is stricken with pain in his leg. Furious at being wakened so early.

He has learned to get quickly out of bed, stamp his bare foot on the floor to soothe the cramp. Whimpering to himself like a child; the pain is excruciating.

Lightning-swift pain in his leg that clamps tight. Toes in his foot rigid as claws.

"Jesus!"—rendered helpless, staggering about trying to overcome the cramp.

Within a minute or two the worst of the pain usually fades. Like a rueful afterthought the muscle ache will remain for hours.

Since his *evisceration* L____ has longed for sleep—it is his only refuge. Insomniac nights he'd resisted drugs, alcohol. He knows how easy that would be: stepping into the dark water that rises to his knees, his mutilated lower body, over his mouth, nose, eyes. No.

Sleep is L____'s happiest time even when it's riddled with turbulent and senseless dreams.

As a boy he'd been a runner. He'd been on the track team of the (local) high school. His leg muscles had cramped then, sometimes. But that was different. A different kind of pain. A shared pain—the other boys on the team had had cramps in their calves too.

Only vaguely he can recall, as you'd recall a dream told to you by another.

If amid the detritus in this house he encounters photographs of that boy—skinny, yearning face; dark, hopeful eyes—he turns quickly away.

"That was my life then. When I had a life."

But there is no woman. But he is lucky.

No one sharing his bed to be a witness to the way such stabbing pain unmans him, renders him helpless as a child.

What's a man without pride? Unmanned.

Fact is, he could not bear another knowing of his condition.

He'd told no one. He'd avoided the telling.

Bluntly he'd said to her, *No. I don't love you. It was a misunderstanding.*

Doesn't recall the look on her face; he'd turned away.

And now he has returned to the house of his childhood at Lake Cattaraugus, New York. Even if she knew she would not have dared follow.

Just go away. Leave me. And don't touch me!—your touch makes me sick.

He has confided in no one—of course. For there is no one.

"Just tell me, Doctor: Am I 'terminal'?"

He'd been blunt, brave. It had seemed a kind of braveness—bravado. Or possibly he'd been rude.

In fact he had not asked about *hope.* He had not even thought of *hope* at that time.

Seething with anger, even as he was shivering in the chilled examination room. He could not bear the indignity, it was the indignity that maddened him, more than the other.

The doctor's answer was an unhesitating *No. You are not "terminal"—not inevitably.*

What the doctor meant was that with the proper medical treatment, of course, life is prolonged. Some sort of life is prolonged. After five years (he was told) there is a 65 percent survival rate for individuals in his age group afflicted with this particular cancer.

If the cancer has not metastasized to lymph nodes, other organs, bone. If surgery removes the malignancies. If treatment can be tolerated, which sometimes, even in seemingly healthy and "fit" individuals in his age group, it is not.

Nine months of chemotherapy following the radical surgery—the *evisceration.*

He does not recall the surgery clearly. Days, weeks immediately following. The relief of being alone, not having to speak of the *considerable physical trauma,* see its reflection in another's (concerned, pitying) (repelled?) face.

Grateful then that he hadn't been married. To *be wed* to another is to *be welded* to another and when you are mad to be alone, you do not wish to be either.

So, L____ is alone with his body. If he is *wed, welded* to anything it is to this body.

If he examines the ravaged body, still he does not clearly recall. The partially healed shiny-white scar tissue like the configurations of frost on a windowpane, the disfigurement of his lower belly and groin that suggests a playful distortion. A mist has settled over his

141

brain. Very easy to forget, or to misremember. There is mercy in such drifting patches of amnesia.

By day he has become brisk, matter-of fact. In his dealings with others he is hearty seeming, quick to laugh, and quick to cease laughing, inclined to impatience if cashiers, service workers, waiters don't move fast enough for him.

On the phone he is assertive, his laughter is a kind of barking punctuation. Though he does not—ever—lift the receiver of a ringing phone unless he sees that it is a professional contact who is calling, an editor perhaps. Not *the personal* but *the impersonal* is his solace.

By day, when his clothes conceal the mutilation. Very quickly you learn to adjust to the new contours of the body, disguised by ordinary (loose-fitting) clothing. As a person afflicted by joint pain learns to walk with his weight distributed *just so*—no limp is detected. (Except by the unnaturally sharp eyed or the suspicious. Whom L____ avoids.)

He is somewhat proud of such adjustments. By day. Deals with himself briskly and matter-of-factly as another might deal with him.

The body he has become.

Shields the colostomy pouch close against his (flat, flaccid) belly beneath his clothes. It is hidden there, it is protected. It has become the most intimate connection of his life like an umbilical cord and this attached to the tiny hole in his stomach, the stoma. An external (plastic) gut, a practical measure, in fact an ingenious solution to having no rectum and only a few meager inches of some five feet of large bowel remaining.

The pouch has to be changed at regular intervals depending upon the uses to which he puts it. (How much he ingests, digests.) If leaking, more often. Carefully remove the old pouch, empty contents into toilet, attach the new. Dispose of the old pouch in an opaque white plastic bag placed carefully inside the dark green trash container to be wheeled out to Road's End Lane under cover of darkness Thursday nights, for Friday morning pickup by Cattaraugus County sanitation.

His task. He is his own nurse's aide. He is indentured to himself.

His fingers should have grown deft by now but remain clumsy, shaky, as if shy.

He would laugh, it *is* funny.

And what is most funny, how L____'s teenaged self would have recoiled in disbelief and loathing foreseeing such a fate. How once with a ninth-grade friend watching a TV documentary of wounded and disabled Vietnam veterans in wheelchairs L____ had said with the vehemence of youth if anything like that ever happened to him he would "blow out my brains with a shotgun."

You don't, though.

Abashed watchword of the walking wounded—*You don't.*

And so it has been a shock to L____ this morning. Having seen the young woman at the lake.

Having felt for her—something . . .

She is a stranger, he is certain. No one who has known L____ or L____'s family.

The luminous figure. So still!

Elsewhere in the park were teenagers, adults with young children, even a boy with a model airplane droning overhead like a maddened wasp. Their noises did not seem to penetrate the silence that enveloped the young woman; she stood apart from them as if invisible.

Curly, tangled hair partway down her back—very fine, very pale, silvery pale, with a mineral sheen. And wearing what appeared to be a sweater or a wrap of some pale gray cobwebby material. And her white (linen?) skirt long, nearly to her slender ankles, and her bare feet in open-toed sandals, white skinned.

From a little—safe—distance he regarded her.

He was almost waiting to be disillusioned—to see that, yes, this was not a young woman but someone he knew, had gone to school with long ago. Worse yet, the daughter of an old Cattaraugus classmate.

But he did not know her, he was certain. *She is new to this place also.*

Feeling so strange! Light-headed, dry-mouthed . . .

That stab of excitement, recognition. It can leave you shaken, faint. An electric current running through the torso to the groin—the vagus nerve.

If the shock is severe, the vagus nerve shuts off blood to the brain; you fall at once in a faint.

Hello—he might (plausibly) have called to her.

Excuse me—he might (plausibly) have approached her.

His heart beats strangely, just to think so!

A shock to him, at his age and in his condition, who has expected to see nothing at Lake Cattaraugus, and to feel nothing.

Hello. Don't think I have seen you here before . . .

143

Joyce Carol Oates

I used to live in Cattaraugus. Now I've returned . . .

Ridiculous! Such words, faltering, stale, hopeless, and contemptible as deflated party balloons, or stray condoms in the mud at the lakeshore caught amid broken cattails.

Flung after him the cruel female taunt *Go away. You are not even a man. Why would I want to speak to you!*

* * *

Chloroform is the most pragmatic. Swift, clean, leaves no trace and he knows where to purchase it without being questioned.

Other methods are cruder, clumsier. Within the past several years he has perfected his method.

The primary element is surprise. And, of course, no witnesses.

He has grown deceitful. It is a rare pleasure.

Returning to the family home at Lake Cattaraugus and telling no one who knows him, not relatives in the area, not family friends, old friends from school, long-ago acquaintances.

Returning wounded, and wise in deception. Armed with a "project"—a manuscript of more than one thousand pages that requires his deepest concentration.

The great effort of L____'s life. L____'s remaining life.

In the cobblestone house on Road's End Lane amid a tangle of tall old oak trees he plans (he thinks) to be happy.

For happiness is not fixed but alterable. For some, happiness is the ability to draw a deep breath without recoiling in pain. Happiness is the little stoma that is not reddened and infected but functioning perfectly.

In our small town, however, it is not possible to remain secluded for long. The more you wish to hide from us, the more we wish to seek you out.

Hello! Sorry can't talk right now.

Yes it's been years. . . . Will call you back.

Busy time can I call you back.

Yes just for the summer. Thanks but—

Work. No. Don't think so.

Work. Deadline. September first.

Sorry! Somebody at the door.

Signaling in the very jauntiness of his voice and the vagueness of his words *God damn you let me alone will you! I have not returned*

144

to my childhood home at the bottom of a fetid lake to squander a moment of my remaining life with any of you.

He is not hiding. He is not one to *hide*.

Eventually whoever is ringing the bell will go away.

In the wake of the mysterious visitor a scribbled note stuck beneath the door knocker, or a US postal form shoved into the crack of the door, or an advertising flier, or—nothing.

Not a trace! No one.

He is safe from prying eyes. In fact, he is in an upstairs bathroom.

In the midst of changing the plastic pouch attached to the stoma—the little surgical hole in his stomach that bleeds easily, thinly.

Very careful washing hands, sanitizing hands, shaky hands. Very careful positioning the plastic pouch that is soft, malleable as an intestine. And very careful disposing of waste in toilet and used pouch in secure opaque white-plastic bag.

His forty-second birthday is rapidly approaching.

Swiftly and deftly the chloroform-soaked cloth is pressed over her mouth, nose. She fights him bravely, desperately. He will see her eyelids flutter. He will see the light go out in her eyes. But she will not have seen his face.

Within seconds her limbs grow limp.

Surprising heaviness of the limp, slender body as if death is an icy lava flowing into her bones.

Unwittingly, he has trapped several small birds in the garage.

Shutting the slow-sliding overhead door, not realizing the birds are inside.

Cumbersome sliding door that moves—so—very—slowly—you hold your breath expecting it to stop midway.

Frantic birds! He hears their panicked cheeping, the flutter of their small wings. A scrambling sound like mice amid stacks of cardboard cartons piled to the ceiling.

Birds have built nests in the garage. In the rafters.

Quickly he presses the switch to reverse the slow-sliding overhead door but even when it is fully open the panicked birds continue to flutter their wings, throw themselves against unyielding objects, make their cheeping sounds. He can see them overhead, shadowy little shapes, blinded in terror.

"Go on! It's open! *Go.*"

Claps his hands. Impatient with the birds too frightened to locate the opened door, and so save themselves.

The garage has three sliding doors. In theory the garage will hold three vehicles.

In fact, the garage is crammed with things. Too many things. L_____ can barely fit his station wagon inside and from now on he won't bother shutting the door.

The birds have fallen silent but L_____ knows that they haven't escaped. He presses the switch to cause another of the slow-moving doors to rise, rumbling overhead.

Presses the switch to open the third door.

All three garage doors are open now. Still the interior of the garage feels airless, trapped.

He claps his hands again: "Now *go.*"

The interior of the garage is crammed with the detritus of his parents' lives. He has not wanted to see. He has not wanted to feel this sensation of dread, vertigo.

His parents have been dead for seven years (father), and for three years (mother). There is a *deadness beyond dead* that is pure peace and it is this L_____ wishes for them. He feels grateful that they've been spared knowing how their only son has been *eviscerated.*

They had loved him, he supposes. But love is not enough to keep us from harm.

Now their lives have been stored in the old garage, which had once been a carriage house. In the corners, stacked to the very rafters. Taped-up cardboard boxes, cartons and files of financial records, legal documents, IRS records. Household furnishings—a swivel chair, a floor lamp, an upended mattress. A tall oval mirror shrouded in a gauzy cloth. Neatly folded curtains and drapes, covered in dust. Stacks of books, magazines bound with twine. And there are myriad forgotten things of L_____'s own—bicycles with flat tires, broken wagon, toys. Weights he'd lifted in high school. Tennis rackets. Old skis, snowshoes. Boots. Mud-stiffened running shoes. L_____ feels a twinge of guilt, and a stronger twinge of resentment.

No he will not. *He will not sort through these things.*

It is too late. The detritus of the past means nothing to him now.

He stumbles away, back into the empty house. Leaving the small fluttering birds to find their own way out.

*

Hello! Please come inside.
We won't stay long. I will just show you—the inside of my life.
The house is locally famous; in fact, it is "historic"—a "landmark"
in Cattaraugus County. An architectural oddity composed of cobble-
stones and mortar, originally built in 1898 with a low, sloping shin-
gled roof above windows like recessed and hooded eyes.

Though Mura House looks large from Road's End Lane behind a
scrim of ravaged trees, the interior is divided into small rooms with
small windows emitting a grudging demi-light. Upstate New York
with its savage protracted winters, driving snow, subzero temperatures
had not been hospitable to a wish for larger windows, scenic views.

Low beamed ceilings, wood-paneled walls, hardwood floors. Heavy
leather furniture, brass andirons.

And oddly named—"Mura House."

"Why does our house have a name? Nobody else's house has a
stupid name."

Growing up in Mura House he'd been embarrassed, resentful. At
the same time he'd felt a twinge of pride, that the L____ family
house was locally recognized as something out of the ordinary, distinguished by a small oval marker at the stately front door.

He'd asked his parents about the name. He can remember only his
mother's vague explanation—*We were told "Mura" might have
been the builder's name. We've made inquiries at the historical
society. . . .*

Except for a glassed-in porch at the rear of the house, constructed
in such a way that it is not visible from Road's End Lane, and except
for renovations in kitchen and bathrooms, Mura House has not been
substantially altered since 1898. If L____wished to remodel the
house he could not, restricted by New York State law protecting
"historic" properties.

L____ has no interest in remodeling, rebuilding. He has said to
several intrusive persons who've made inquiries about his plans in
Cattaraugus that he "doesn't plan to live in Mura House much
beyond the summer."

He has not been seeking her.

He has avoided the lakeside park. The esplanade along the lake.

He has been avoiding even thinking of her and in this he has become slack, careless, negligent, like one who has let his guard down prematurely.

And so when he isn't prepared he sees her for the second time: entering the Cattaraugus Public Library.

A glimmering figure in white, at dusk. In the heat of summer of upstate New York there is a moist heaviness to the air that seems to gather like an electric charge with the waning of the light in the sky and it is at this time he sees her, not certain at first if it is *her. . . .*

A tall, pale gliding figure. And her tangled silvery hair partway down her back.

Without a backward glance at L_____, who stands stunned and breathless on the flagstone walk outside the library, staring after her.

Should he follow her into the library? *As if he were entering by chance?*

(But of course it is chance.)

(L_____ has not been following her. L_____ had not even been aware of her nearby.)

Or (he is thinking) he should continue past the library as if he has no business in the library after all.

(No one will notice! He is sure that no one is watching.)

The Cattaraugus Public Library is a small library housed in the first floor of a gaunt, faded-redbrick colonial on Courthouse Square; it shares the house with the headquarters of the Cattaraugus County Historical Society at the rear. The historical society is darkened but the library is still open at 7:00 p.m., though most of the staff has gone home and there are few patrons in the library.

This is the first time since his return to Cattaraugus that L_____ has revisited the library and it is both gratifying to him and a little disturbing that the library has changed so minimally over the years. Obviously, the library budget for Cattaraugus County isn't generous. All of central upstate New York has been locked in a "recession" for years—decades. (When does a "recession" become a permanent state of being? Who is there to formally acknowledge such transformations?) Still, the Cattaraugus Public Library retains the power to excite L_____ with the prospect of a new adventure—a book he has not read yet, an author of whom he hasn't heard. L_____ experienced his first sense of *the forbidden* in the rear of the library, where, as a boy, he'd been looking through novels in the section marked *Adult Fiction* and a frowning librarian had surprised him skimming impenetrable pages of James Joyce's *Ulysses*—"Excuse me? What is your age?"

His age! He'd been twelve or thirteen at the time. The prim-faced middle-aged woman with staring eyes had known very well that the trembling boy she'd apprehended was hardly eighteen.

She'd taken the forbidden book from him, shut it, and replaced it on the shelf. Abashed, he'd fled.

L____ smiles, recalling. *That* has been a long time ago, when anything in any library could possibly be "forbidden" to him.

Now, L____ is standing on the walk outside the library, uncertain. It is near dark. The gaunt old brick house is lighted from within and so he can see a few figures, a wall of bookshelves, a display of books—but he can't see *her*.

Out of restlessness he'd been walking in the early evening. Down the mile-long hill at Juniper Avenue, from Road's End Lane to Lake View Avenue; avoiding the lake, he'd decided to visit the historic quarter—a town square bounded by the Cattaraugus County Courthouse and post office, the YM-YWCA, and the library. Here there's a small park with a World War II memorial, a Revolutionary War cannon, a rain-worn American flag, a few benches. Near deserted, which is a relief.

The library is one of those small-town public libraries of the kind scattered across America, often housed in a "historic" building. L____ feels a tug of nostalgia, seeing it.

The Cattaraugus library has very few books in which L____ is interested, and none helpful for his current project. Yet L____ is drawn to the library, as a haven of sorts. The welcome of warm lights within, which seem to beckon to him. He recalls how he was sent here by his grandmother to take out books for her, slender mysteries with little black skulls-and-crossbones on the spine of the plastic covers, and the black letter *M*. (Mystery? Or Murder?) Strange that his genteel grandmother had devoured murder mysteries!—as if death were some sort of entertainment.

She'd given him her card for this purpose, not to be confused with L____'s own (child's) card.

In a trance of indecision L____ has been debating whether to enter the library. He thinks: He can simply ignore the woman with the tangled silvery hair—she's a stranger to him, she will not "recognize" him. And truly she is nothing to him.

Still, he feels some hesitation. A part of his brain cautions him against behaving recklessly.

The library is small, cramped. It is not really possible to avoid other patrons if they are in the front area, at the checkout desk, as you enter. L____ feels a visceral dread of getting too close to the woman with the shimmering silvery hair for fear that he will (unwittingly) call attention to himself and she will see him staring at her and if she sees him *she will know*.

Oh but what will she know?—something.

Something she will see in his face?

A premonition of something that will happen, or something that will never happen?

Something that *has already happened*?

He decides not to enter the library. Yet not—quite—to leave.

Finds himself walking along a darkened pathway beside the library. Staring up into the windows as he passes—sees several figures—a man with a fleshy, flushed face—a middle-aged woman—but not the silvery-haired woman.

Then at the rear window he sees her: her back to the window.

She is leaning over an oversized book, like an atlas. Probably it is, as L____ recalls, *The American Gazetteer*, a nineteenth-century book of maps kept with other, similar atlases in a corner of the reference section of the library.

He sees the woman's slender arm, her fingers turning the oversized parchment-like page. He sees silver filaments in her hair, which falls in tangled waves over her shoulders. He can see the side of her face, just barely: the curve of her cheek, her parted lips.

The scene is brightly lit from within. Only a few yards away he is standing in darkness, invisible. The sharpness of Vermeer, he thinks. He feels a yearning in the region of his heart so powerful he is almost faint.

Why is the young woman interested in that old book? Why *The American Gazetteer*? As a boy, he'd paged through atlases in that library, examined the Rand McNally globe that spun with geriatric slowness; its carefully outlined countries were defined by faded colors, outdated thirty years ago. Perhaps it was a collector's item, a novelty of history like Mura House.

How erotic, the sight of the silvery-haired woman's arm as her sleeve slips down to her elbow. And the faint shimmer of her hair. Every movement of the woman is exciting to L____, the more that she's unaware of him watching her so intently.

She must never know. She must be protected from—whatever is happening.

L____ rouses himself, and passes quickly by the window. He has not meant to linger, and stare.

His heart is beating rapidly. How absurd! He is ashamed of himself but he is very excited.

At the rear of the library he pauses. Here is a shadowy alcove, a little distance from the street. A grassy patch, not well lighted. A pedestrian pathway that functions as a shortcut to the next street and it is quite reasonable that L_____ might take this pathway, close beside the library. You might think that he'd parked his car nearby. A library patron, like others.

He has positioned himself in such a way that he can see, not the front entrance of the library, but much of the front walk, which leads to the street. No one can leave the library without being seen by L_____—he is certain.

From his vantage place in the shadows he observes a heavy-hipped woman leaving the library, picked up at the street by someone in a station wagon. A solitary man in shorts, trotting across the street to his parked car. It must be closing time: 7:30 p.m. on a weeknight in summer. L_____ can't see anyone else inside except the librarian, an older white-haired woman whose name he should know.

Still, the silvery-haired woman must still be there. He seems to be waiting for her to leave the library after all. *But he will not follow her.*

Under a hypnotic spell, time passes slowly for L_____. In fact, it is a pleat in time; L_____ is neither here entirely in the shadows at the rear of the Cattaraugus Public Library nor is he elsewhere. He is *suspended in time.*

Earlier that evening he'd had to walk out of his parents' house, where the air of late afternoon becomes thick as suet and where it is difficult to breathe.

He wants to plead with the silvery-haired woman—*There has been some mistake. The person you see is not really me. What was done to me and what I have become . . .*

And the woman will turn to him, and she will touch his arm, gently. All of his senses are alert, to the point of pain: He can scarcely breathe, in anticipation of what she will tell him.

Why she has entered his life, what she has been meant to tell him . . .

There is a jolt. Time has passed. L_____ rouses himself to realize: The library is empty except for the librarian, who is switching off lights.

How is this possible? Where is the silvery-haired woman? He wants to protest: He could not have missed her. Not for a moment has he turned his gaze away from the front walk. He has scarcely dared to blink.

(Is it possible she left the library by another door?)

(But there is no other door for library patrons, he is sure. Only an emergency door at the rear, which would sound an alarm if opened.)

Admonishes himself: It is not possible that she left by the front door, and he didn't see her. *He could not have missed her.*

In a state of agitation he approaches the front entrance of the library. How familiar the doorway is, the truncated view into the library, as if he has never left his childhood home, and his adult life has been a delusion. . . .

He peers inside—as one would; a husband, for instance, or a father, waiting for someone inside to emerge from the library, who has (unaccountably) not emerged.

Must happen all the time. Nothing to alarm anyone.

However, there is no one visible except the librarian, Mrs. McGarry.

"Hello! Can I help you? I'm afraid we're closing just now. . . ."

Doesn't Mrs. McGarry recognize L____? He is older than she has ever seen him, of course; his face is lined, his once thick, dark hair is scanty, thin like the feathers of very young birds not yet fledged. Perhaps he is unnaturally pale. And perhaps he is grimacing impatiently, irritably, his face so contorted that Mrs. McGarry can't seem to recognize the boy who used to come into the library so often, a lifetime ago.

"Oh! Is it—"

The light of recognition comes into the white-haired woman's face. Now L____ cannot escape.

Mrs. McGarry speaks his name. Mrs. McGarry greets him warmly.

She is just locking up the library, she explains. Switching off lights and the ceiling fans. Would he wait a moment?

Of course! How can L____ possibly say no?

"I was a friend of your dear mother for many years. . . ."

"Yes. I know."

L____ shakes her hand, or would shake it. But Mrs. McGarry extends her hand to clasp his, in commiseration, perhaps, not merely to be shaken.

L____ is eager to escape. L____ is eager to drift away into the night in chagrin and shame and a kind of fury except Mrs. McGarry retains him. "The last time I saw you, I think—Margaret and I had just returned from visiting Chloe Sanderson in the hospital—poor Chloe!—your mother brought her flowers from her garden, an armful of the most fragrant flowers—white carnations—" A bittersweet memory. A memory to be shared. A memory not to be avoided and so L_____ endures it with a stoic smile.

"Are you living in your parents' beautiful house now? I thought I'd heard this. Are you returned to us?"

Mrs. McGarry clutches at his hand. Her eyes search his with a discomforting intensity and he sees that it is Mrs. McGarry (perhaps) who has been awaiting him in this place, not the other.

L_____ wants to ask the librarian about the shimmering-silvery-haired woman who'd leaned over the old atlas: Who is she? Did Mrs. McGarry see her too? He wants to ask her what she recalled of the boy he'd been. What his mother might have told her, of him. But the words choke in his throat, he can only smile and allow his hand to be clasped and stroked, in consolation for his loss.

Are you returned to us? He has no idea.

No. *Ridiculous!*

Yes. Ridiculous.

He is very tired. "Drained."

His energy drains from him like the slow drip, seep, ooze of excrement. His life.

Wouldn't have had the energy to follow the silvery-haired woman if he'd seen her. That is the sobering fact.

He has his eye on the farther edge of the lake, along the east shore. On one of his restless walks he has scrutinized the area. The possibilities. His mind is always working. Swift, sharp like flashing scissors. He'd recalled from years ago and has reacquainted himself now: that fetid stretch of rotted cattails, fish floating belly-up, broken Styrofoam. Since he has no boat to row out onto the lake, no motorboat, no way of assuring that the body will be far enough from shore that the body will sink to a depth of more than six feet to lie against the mucky bottom of the lake, he will have to dump the body in a more convenient place.

"A highly challenging, very ambitious project for which I need seclusion here in Cattaraugus."

So he said. There was pleasure in such a statement made to the inquisitive. Saliva gathered in his mouth as with a delicious taste.

A shock to L____, yet deeply flattering, that he'd been named executor of the literary estate of the distinguished writer-historian V___ S_____, who'd died, at eighty-four, the previous December.

Obviously there had been a mistake on someone's part: for L____ had not been contacted beforehand. Nor would L____ have expected to be singled out for this honor, which carries with it a good deal of responsibility.

A call from a lawyer, congratulations from friends, his name in the very last paragraph of S_____'s obituary in *The New York Times*—all so sudden, unexpected.

He had just begun chemotherapy. Every two weeks for four hours in succession, poisons dripping into his veins and coursing through his heart, so lethal the infusion-room nurses had to wear protective clothing, gloves. Yet when S_____'s lawyer called, L____ heard his voice crack with emotion.

"Yes, of course! Though I knew, it's still a—surprise . . . and a great honor."

Flushed with this honor like a transfusion of fresh blood, L____ agreed to help S_____'s editor prepare S_____'s final book for publication in January of the new year.

A Biography of Biographies will be a "magisterial" work—no doubt. The manuscript, or manuscripts, runs to thirteen hundred pages.

S_____'s editor, upset and aggrieved that the prominent elderly author had died before his book was quite ready for press, assured L____ that the book was all but finished: It needed only "minimal reshaping, reorganization, some revision and rewriting, and an index."

L____ had agreed without hesitation. Like a drowning man clutching at a lifeline, which will haul him out of a turbulent sea, allow him to breathe for a while longer, to *endure*.

"Thank you! This is an honor."

And: "I'm a longtime admirer of S_____. I think that I've read everything he has written. . . ."

And, somberly: "We were never exactly friends. There was a generation between us. But I felt a kind of kinship with S_____, and only wish now that I had known him better."

Is this true? Perhaps not entirely. L____ has certainly not read all of S_____'s work, which consists of a dozen or more substantial books. Nor had S_____ sought him out, though S_____ had always been perfectly friendly, kind, and behaved as if he were interested in L____'s work.

It is true that L____ is grateful for the assignment. Or was, initially.

Fact is, after his *evisceration* L____ has no energy to undertake original work of his own nor can he foresee a time when he will regain his energy.

(Possibly this was the case even before the *evisceration*. But L____ doesn't care to consider that.)

Some days L____ is enthusiastic and hopeful about the project; other days L____ is rueful and chagrined that he'd made such a blunder in a craven gesture of attaching himself to a famous and respected name in the hope that some of the glory would rub off on him, like the faint iridescence of a broken moth's wing.

He has been working with at least three manuscripts written at different periods of time, derived from several computer files; he has been trying to give structure to an essentially structureless book. There is much to admire in S_____'s eloquent prose but there are many passages that are haphazardly written, and uninspired; there are sections that have been left blank—glibly marked *material TK*. (With a sinking heart L____ wonders who is expected to provide this missing material.) Chapters have been many times revised, with much overlapping and repetitive material. Footnotes are overlong, pedantic. Other footnotes are just numerals, with no information at all. At the time of his death S_____ hadn't even begun an index. Most upsetting, *A Biography of Biographies* seems to be based upon numerous other books on the subject, and to contain virtually nothing that is original or inventive. Like every other historian of the subject, S_____ begins with Plutarch's *Lives* but he ends (arbitrarily) in the early 1980s with Leon Edel's *Henry James* and Richard Ellmann's *James Joyce*, as if these are the most recent major biographies S_____ had troubled to read.

What a joke! A cruel joke.

L____ had hoped to attach himself to a work of substance, even of genius. *A work of literature that mattered.*

A (posthumous) collaboration with S_____ would have lifted L____'s sodden spirits even as it would have lifted his reputation. Not that L____ cares so much any longer for a "reputation"—at nearly forty-two, he has lived long enough without one.

What had he hoped for then? To live again, through another?—through the elderly S_____?

He thinks: He could give up. He could admit defeat. But he will not admit defeat. *He is still alive.*

There is much more work to do on the book than L____ antici-pated but perhaps (he tells himself) this is good—good for him in his depressed and morbid state of mind. . . .

He is not so happy with S_____'s editor. A prominent New York editor, much respected.

L____ has patiently explained to S_____'s editor that he prefers e-mail exchanges to telephone conversations yet the man continues to call him, never less than once a week. This is a particular sort of harassment, L____ thinks. Oblique but unmistakable.

When the other day the editor called to ask L____ how his work on the book was "progressing," L____ replied with a sardonic laugh, "Well. I'm hoping to stay alive long enough to finish it."

S_____'s editor was stunned into silence for a long moment, unsure how to respond to this remark.

"I—I don't understand. . . . Are you ill?"

"No! That was a joke."

(Not a very witty joke. Immediately L____ regretted having made it.)

"Well. If you need an extension . . ."

"Not at all. I will get the revised manuscript to you by"—he named the September first deadline he'd been given.

Thinking—*Are they hoping I will give up? Do they know that I am a terminal case?*

Thinking—*They don't really want to publish this book. A posthumous author is a lost cause.*

Since the library, he avoids the library.

Since the lakeside esplanade, he avoids the lakeside esplanade.

He has become an ascetic. He is scrupulous in denial. He is *not a fool to wish to approach a woman he doesn't know in a public place, who would be repelled by him.*

That particular area of Cattaraugus Park near the bandstand, near playground swings, the children's wading pool, popular on hot sum-mer afternoons and early evenings. He has a fear of encountering people whom he knows, and who might know him.

"I will not. I *will.*"

And, "Ridiculous. You are risible."

Risible not a word one commonly uses. Rhymes with *visible.*

In any case there are other places to walk in our small town. The thick-wooded dead end of Road's End Lane where dirt paths once made by children (including L_____ and his friends) have mostly grown over. The neatly mowed Lutheran churchyard and the lake itself—the farther, eastern shore of Lake Cattaraugus that is usually deserted.

The grassy stretch along Catamount Road that ends in a marshy field. A dirt lane with narrow dirt paths leading down to the mucky water.

Thinking how, when he was a boy, the eastern shore of Lake Cattaraugus had been a place to fish. Somehow it has happened that, in recent years, the lake water here has become clotted with algae, broken and rotted marsh reeds, cattails, discarded trash; the black bass population has been decimated as the water level of the lake has steadily lowered.

And there are times for walking that are not so dangerous as others. Of course.

In the early evening when (you might suppose) the young silvery-haired woman would be preparing dinner for her family, assuming the young woman is married, and has a family, including children, perhaps a young baby.

Places where a man might walk when he can't bear his life.

When he can't fathom his life.

Thinking in derision—*Just forget. Oblivion.*

He never shuts the slow-moving garage doors any longer. Never troubles to drive his vehicle inside the garage only just to park it at the rear of the house so that no one can see, from the road, whether anyone is home.

Avoids the garage. Detritus of the *lost self.*

Except once or twice, out of curiosity. (He discovers a beautifully executed birds' nest of twigs and dried grasses amid the dusty folded curtains.) Wondering if the panicked little birds had found their way out and deciding, yes, they had.

Smiling, he thinks—*At least, they've escaped and saved themselves.*

He knows that he will see the silvery-haired woman again. It is inevitable, for him and for her. But he wishes it would not be inevitable for *her.*

157

He does not want to hurt her. He does not even want to frighten her.

He does want her to acknowledge *him*.

She owes him (he thinks) that much. A beggarly gesture, for which he will be absurdly, abjectly grateful.

He has taken to hiking out to the lake via Catamount Road, he is so restless. Even with his cramping legs.

We have observed him, at a distance.

Some of us have outboard motorboats, rowboats. Some of us have canoes though we don't "canoe" so much in the muggy summer heat of the Finger Lakes region, now that we've grown up and become adults.

L____ limps slightly. You almost wouldn't notice. (She will not notice. L____ is determined.) But he can limp quickly like a dog with three practiced legs.

It is the largest and (by tradition) the most beautiful of the eleven Finger Lakes of central New York State—Lake Cattaraugus. Indeed it is oddly shaped like a finger, a beckoning finger, forty miles long (south/north), four miles at its widest. The village of Cattaraugus is the only populated area on the lake though there are cottages and cabins scattered around it, some of them difficult of access, and some abandoned. Much of the eastern shore has reverted to the wild.

It is good to see this, L____ thinks. How quickly wilderness moves in, suffocating the merely *cultivated*.

Occasionally there are boats on the lake. For the lake is quite deep at its center. Outboard motorboats. Sailboats. L____ is intrigued to see, to think that he sees, a shimmering flash of silvery hair—in one of the blinding-white sailboats drifting past. She is with one or two others. A man, two men. A woman. He shades his eyes but the figures fade in a haze of sunshine.

Sees, thinks he sees, the young woman in a bathing suit, on a deserted stretch of beach, later that day. Not so slender as he'd imagined but lanky limbed and hard muscled like a high-school girl athlete. Her hair has been pulled back into a ponytail and seems to be lighter, wheat colored. Distasteful to L____ that the beautiful girl is in the company of other, cruder individuals her age, all of them in bathing suits, barefoot.

He is shocked, repelled: One of the loutish boys tugs at her ponytail, teases her.

If he'd brought a rifle with him . . .

(Why has he thought of a rifle? There is no rifle in his parents' house. He had not been brought up to use firearms.)

But no: That girl is not *her*. He is fully sane. He is not sick minded. He knows this.

Before the teenagers can see the white-skinned middle-aged man spying on them from behind a bank of cattails he withdraws shrewdly.

He can drink all he wants.

He can drink until he has forgotten why he is drinking.

Several old whiskey bottles of his father's left behind in a sideboard in the dining room. Scotch whiskey, bourbon, gin. Why not?

In the upstairs bathroom, stripping himself bare. Hearing his breath catch.

Though he'd showered early that morning before dawn, after a violent leg cramp had awakened him, he feels the need, the compulsion to shower again by late afternoon.

Beneath his (loose-fitting, ordinary, and not unattractive) clothes he is a marvel of male ruin, scarred and pallid, like wax that has partly melted and then hardened. He has learned to avoid contemplating the genitals between his legs, which are both swollen and shrunken, like small tumors in sacks of very thin ripe-plum-colored skin.

His mouth tastes like chemicals, still. Poisons that have dripped into his veins to "kill" cancerous cells and have not been totally flushed out of his body even after months.

If he were to kiss a woman. The silver-haired woman, turning to him, lifting her face to his in a gesture of trust.

Idly he wonders—*Am I radioactive? Can I kill on contact?*

God help me.

I cannot help myself.

Today she has brought a book with her. She is seated on a bench overlooking the lake and engrossed in her book as a young girl might be engrossed in a book in a long-ago time.

She is not in the place he'd seen her initially. For L____ has avoided that place.

In another part of the park that is much less popular where (L____ has thought) he would be safe.

Immediately he recognizes her. With a gut-sick sensation of certainty his eye swerves upon *her*.

He sees her from behind, and then he sees her in profile from approximately twenty feet away. He is shaky legged suddenly.

He will not see her face fully unless he approaches her and positions himself in front of her, to her (left) side. It is quite natural that a visitor to the park might stand at the lakeside rail in this way to look out at, to toss bread crusts at, an excited little flotilla of mallards and geese bobbing in the water. No need to defend himself from accusers!

But doing so would (probably) draw the attention of the young woman, which he must avoid.

How beautiful she is! How solitary.

Speckled sunlight falls upon her like gold coins. He dreads violating that stillness.

She is wearing a long skirt of some thin, silky fabric, slit to the thigh—a startling sight. It is a provocative way of dressing and yet (L___ thinks) it is a classic Asian style, an elegantly long skirt, unexpectedly slit to the thigh. (What he can see of her leg, her thigh, is an expanse of very pale flesh, not muscular, but very lean. The tight, taut flesh of a young person.) Her hair is less silvery than he recalls, more likely faded blond, ash blond, threaded with glinting hairs. Not so wavy–curly today and falling straight past her shoulders.

L___ feels his heart missing beats. He has had few cardiac problems, his doctors have been impressed. Such physical trauma to a man's body, such incisions, eviscerations, are more profound than simply physical injuries, and he has prevailed nonetheless, his heart has rarely failed him. And now, his heart is hurting.

He sees: The book in which the young woman is engrossed is covered in transparent plastic, a book borrowed from the local library, no doubt, not a purchase of her own.

He is just slightly disappointed that the young woman hasn't bought the book for herself. That it is only a library withdrawal suggests that her commitment to it is ephemeral.

He wonders what the title is. At the same time, he believes that it would be better for him not to know.

Knowing curtails *desire*. From his former life, when he'd been alive, he recalls.

Still, he is excited to have discovered the woman. Until this moment his day had been tortuous, beginning with painful leg cramps at an hour before dawn, the dismay of being awakened so early, with the prospect of the long, interminable day ahead.

He has had to confront the fact: His work is stalled. He sees himself

160

in a vehicle stalled on railroad tracks, paralyzed as a locomotive rushes at him.

He'd spent that day, he has spent several days—in fact, weeks—in a trance of frustration so extreme it borders upon wonderment. Each morning he hauls himself to his writing table in the glassed-in porch as you might haul a lifeless body—he works for lengthy hours, becoming increasingly fretful as the morning hours wane, and he has little to show for his effort; but with the appalling movement of the clock downward, in the afternoon, he becomes ever more agitated, and it is very difficult for him to keep his mind from fastening on to—*her.*

His thoughts are both roiling and "flat"—thoughts at a boil that nonetheless go nowhere. Like chapters in S_____'s book so many times revised, and rewritten, the momentum of their prose has wound down. And the more L____ rewrites S_____'s prose, the deeper he sinks into a bottomless sand that will soon cover his mouth.

Indeed his lips have gone numb as if all sensation has drained from them.

He keeps his distance from the woman, who sits very still, almost unnaturally still. He tells himself this is all very casual. There is nothing *urgent, fated* about discovering her. There is nothing *doomed.*

This is a "good" side of the lake where the water is relatively clear of the algae that grows elsewhere in thick metastasizing slime clumps.

All is calm today. Calmer. The lake's surface reflects the sky dully like hammered tin.

What *is* she reading?—L____'s heart contracts with yearning; he wants badly to know.

(It is not a heavy book—not a long novel. Nor does the slate-gray cover, with calm pale letters—suggest a popular best seller.)

From time to time the young woman glances up from the book as if it reminds her of something—a moment of tenderness, a private thought.

He will not approach her, he thinks.

He will respect her privacy. Her beauty.

For he feels inadequate, of course. He is wearing his loose-fitting clothes that have been chosen to disguise his body and not in any way to reveal it. A T-shirt, khaki shorts. Running shoes and no socks.

He launders his clothes in the washer in the house. He does not trouble to iron them.

He will say—*Excuse me. I happened to have seen . . .*

The other day, I think I saw you sailing . . .

161

Here is a rude surprise: Children are approaching. First, middle school–age boys on bicycles, loudly calling to one another. Then a young couple with small children.

The calm of the lakeside has been shattered. The father in T-shirt and rumpled shorts is chiding one of the children, who has displeased him in some trivial way, and the mother is trying to placate the father in a soft, pleading voice. *Please. He didn't mean it.*

L____ tries not to stare at these intruders with a look of rage. Thinking how much more beautiful it would be, and more merciful, if human beings did not utter words out of their contorted mouths but "signed" them as the deaf do, with precision and grace. He has frequently been impressed—indeed, fascinated—by observing a deaf interpreter sign to an audience at a public event. It occurs to him that the silvery-haired woman whose voice he has never heard is a kind of "sign"—her beautiful averted face, her shimmering hair, her slender and very still body.

Yes, L____ is weary of those dull, banal, predictable, and demeaning words that are uttered aloud, that abrade the ear. How he yearns for the beauty that is directed to the eye in silence.

So absorbed in her book, the young woman seems scarcely aware of the intrusive family who have, to L____'s dismay, set down their picnic things on a nearby table. L____ wonders if they are aware that there is a much more attractive picnic area elsewhere in the park, in a shaded grove.

Only mildly annoyed, it seems, the young woman glances around at the bickering family, and for a dazzling, heart-stopping moment, at *him*—but without quite seeing him, L____ thinks.

(Yet: He has seen her. The impact of that face, those eyes, will remain with L____ for a long time.)

It is time to leave! On his shaky legs L____ retreats.

That night as he drifts into sleep he realizes—the silvery-haired woman had been reading *his book.*

Vividly now he recalls the slate-gray cover, the pale, pearlescent letters—he is sure it was *his book.*

His first book, a little-read novel titled *Jubilation.* Into which L____ had opened his veins and never quite recovered.

It was L____'s first published novel, though it had not been the first novel he'd written. He had not ever written another.

Of course, I've done other things. I've published other books. I am a "literary figure"—of a kind. I have even published poetry—poems. Not yet a book of poems.

He is explaining to the silver-haired young woman, who listens intently. He is captivated by the way she brushes her hair out of her face with both hands, like one parting a curtain of some fine, shimmering material like silk.

Of course, the Cattaraugus Public Library has *Jubilation* in its fiction collection. L____ has checked. At the time of its publication (in 1999), Mrs. McGarry or another librarian would have been sure to order it—unless L____'s mother donated a copy.

It comes to L____ in a flash, he can learn the name of the silvery-haired woman if he visits the library and determines who has withdrawn the single copy of *Jubilation* in the past week. . . . The possibility leaves him too excited to sleep.

Chloroform makes of the most resistant body a very bride. The struggling hands, the clawing nails, the convulsive flailings of the limbs—all surrender within seconds.

Her lover tells her: Please understand. I am providing a happy ending for you, who will be protected from the terrible erosion of time. In my arms you will always be young—you will always be my bride.

You will always be worthy of love, and loved.

In a dead faint he has fallen. *Dead faint* is exact for the brain is extinguished in an instant.

Fallen heavily onto the ground in some public place, a chatter of excited voices, deafening sound of a siren, a siren too close, and strangers bending over him to "revive" him. . . .

The first he knows how very sick he is.

Must've known. Fastidiously averting your eyes from the blood traces in the toilet.

How ridiculous you are, how pathetic thinking you can deceive . . .

Later in the hospital he will discover that his clothes have been expertly sheared by the EMTs to allow access to his body. Deft hands of strangers touching his body. Blood-pressure band tightening around his upper arm, forefinger pressed against the carotid artery in his throat, an unresponsive eyelid lifted, small light ray piercing the (sightless, unfocused) eyeball. A defibrillator on hand, which, fortunately, they don't have to use.

The patient knows nothing of this at the time, nor does he realize he has wet his underwear and trousers.

Internal bleeding. Brackish-black blood.

You never know. Until you know.

2.

" 'Evangeline.' "

It is a beautiful name, an archaic name. He knew a girl with this name long ago in grade school, the daughter of a local minister who'd died, or moved away—all he can recall of Evangeline is the girl's curly red-gold hair, silver barrettes in the hair, and the girl's profile, the curve of her cheek. L____ had sat behind her in fifth grade and also in sixth grade, an accident of the alphabet.

He does not think that the silvery-haired woman is Evangeline— for the minister's daughter would be much older than this woman. (She would be L____'s age. Would L____ be interested in a woman in her early forties?) That Evangeline's life would be much different than the life L____ can imagine for the silvery-haired woman. And perhaps she is not even alive now.

So often L____ finds himself thinking that persons of his generation, his age, whom he has not seen in some time, are probably *not even alive now.*

She tells him, *We are all forgetting each other, constantly. Life is a shimmering stream. The light plays on the stream through the trees for just a measured distance, then it is gone—but the stream continues. We bask in the sunshine, then the sunshine is gone. But when the sunshine is gone, we are gone. So we don't feel the loss. We don't feel pain.*

Doomed love. Unrequited love.

L____ recalls having read an appalling news item years ago.

"Sinkholes" in a township in the Chautauqua Mountains, not far from Cattaraugus. Scudder Mills, a mining town. The local product was gypsum. A man, a homeowner, stepped into his backyard on the morning after a severe rainstorm and, in bright sunshine, the earth beneath his feet fell away.

A gaping hole beneath, thirty feet, possibly fifty feet, the man fell, helpless to save himself, and was smothered, horribly—calling, screaming for help—but there was no help.

Earth filled his mouth, and he was silenced.

This horror happened in Scudder Mills when L_____ was a boy. In all, there were several sinkholes in the mining town, but no one else was trapped in this way and no one else died. At Lake Cattaraugus everyone talked of it. At home, at school. He tastes something sour and deathly in his mouth, recalling.

Scudder Mills had been abandoned, the mining town declared a disaster area. L_____ had forgotten about it until now.

Thinking how doomed love is a sinkhole. He will fall, and fall, and never come to the bottom of the sinkhole. And if he cries for help, no one will hear. There is no one.

"Not possible. *No.*"

L_____ has made a discovery in S_____'s manuscript. Or, rather, in one of the variants of S_____'s manuscript, written several years before S_____'s death.

It is shocking to him but seems unmistakable: The distinguished scholar-critic-historian S_____, twice winner of the Pulitzer Prize and a member of the American Academy of Arts and Letters for forty years, seems to have plagiarized a part of a chapter on medieval "saints' lives" from a scholarly article available online through Google Scholar. The plagiarism is almost verbatim, though S_____ made of several paragraphs one single-length paragraph and substituted arcane words for plainer words—*exsiccation, thrawart, immergence, adnate.*

L_____ tells himself that S_____ intended to delete these passages at a later time; at least a skilled writer like S_____ would recast them more thoroughly, so that their origins in the work of another scholar would not be so obvious. (L_____ has checked: There is no footnote attributing the source.) L_____ decides that the wisest strategy for him is simply to delete the passages as if they'd never existed. (S_____'s editor has these files also, but L_____ doubts that S_____'s editor will ever read through the massive manuscript, still less detect plagiarized passages.) It is urgent for L_____ to protect S_____, at least S_____'s reputation.

Problem is, deleting passages means that L_____ will have to provide a transition of some kind. He fears that he will be incapable of doing this, replicating S_____'s elegant prose. And he can't help but wonder if S_____ has plagiarized elsewhere in the manuscript.

His work as an indentured servant for the dead man will never end. He sees that now.

Another, even more shocking discovery after L____ has been away from the manuscript for forty-eight hours, and returns to take up another, later section: Mixed in with S_____'s scholarly writing is a kind of journal, or diary. It is a very different kind of writing altogether and (L____ thinks) it must have been inserted in the manuscript by mistake.

> *Chloroform is the most pragmatic. Swift, clean, leaves no (visible) trace and he knows where to purchase it without being questioned . . .*

And,

> *Swiftly and deftly the chloroform-soaked cloth is pressed over her mouth, nose. She fights him bravely, desperately. He will see her eyelids flutter. He will see the light go out in her eyes. But she will not have seen his face. . . .*

L____ is appalled by what he reads. But he is excited as well.

He has discovered approximately forty pages of prose charting the stalking and murder of an unidentified woman. The prose is intense, intimate, obscenely poetic. It is possible that S_____ was writing a darkly erotic novel or a quasi journal tracking the obsession/disintegration of a personality resembling his own, but not himself; but in all of his career S_____ had never published fiction, so far as L____ knew.

What is particularly upsetting to L____ is that the "erotic" material is in a section of the manuscript that S_____'s editor was supposed to have read. Yet clearly he had not .

L____ will have to delete these pages also. He won't allow himself to keep reading but will delete without reading.

He must protect the elder writer, who cannot protect himself.

All must be hidden! Erased.

No one must know.

*

He flees the house. He is scarcely able to breathe; the air has turned thick and porous.

It is the brackish odor of the rotting lake. Dead things in hot sunshine. Ripe, rank smells. He is terrified that the body is partly exposed, there in the marsh. An outflung arm, a satiny-smooth pale leg. It has occurred to him too late, turkey vultures will circle in the sky. The ungainly wide-winged black-feathered scavengers will draw attention, out in the marshes. . . .

Then he realizes that none of this has happened yet—"We are safe."

He shudders with relief. Tears streak his cheeks; he has not cried like this in years.

* * *

He has not glimpsed the silvery-haired woman in many days.

He has deleted the offensive passages in S_____'s manuscript—the plagiarized material and the obscene material.

He has concentrated on another part of *A Biography of Biographies*. He is determined to salvage what he can of the remainder of his life.

He has even succumbed to an invitation from family friends, to come to dinner one night the following week. He will bring the older couple a bottle of good red wine and a bouquet of flowers from his mother's garden—white carnations, daisies, roses growing wild behind the house.

His hand will be shaken vigorously by his host. He will be hugged, kissed by his hostess.

We have missed you here in Cattaraugus!

Have you returned to us for good?

He shudders at the prospect. Yet, he will prevail.

He will manage not to show surprise at how old the couple has become, whom he has not seen in fifteen years; as they will manage not to show surprise at how old L____ has become, whom they have not seen in fifteen years.

Several mornings in succession he is wakened by the sound of a woman or a girl sobbing.

"Hello? Is someone there?"—quickly he rises from bed to investigate, his heart pounding in dread.

Of course it is no one, nothing. The wind in the trees surrounding the house. Strange muffled cries of birds in the eaves.

He listens. The mysterious sound has faded.

Through the day at wayward times he thinks he hears this sound but doesn't allow himself to be distracted. He concentrates on his work. He has begun the index. This is a daunting task but it signals the beginning of the end of the project, and about this L____ feels hopeful!

And then, to his chagrin, L____ discovers more of the offensive material he'd believed he had deleted.

> *Chloroform makes of the most resistant body a very bride. The struggling hands, the clawing nails, the convulsive flailings of the limbs—all surrender within seconds. . . .*

In exasperation L____ deletes this. How disgusting! He is left shaken, bewildered. He is plagued by the (absurd yet appalling) possibility that offensive material of this nature will remain in S_____'s manuscript, hidden in the file, to be (horribly, irremediably) printed and published in book form, embedded in the chaste scholarly prose of *A Biography of Biographies.* What a scandal, if this should happen!

L____ can't trust S_____'s editor, certainly. He can't trust the publisher's copy editors and proofreaders, who are strangers to him; the fact is, L____ will have to trust himself, to make sure that all remnants of the offensive material, and of the plagiarized material, have been detected and deleted from the manuscript file.

Yet he is terribly worried: Can he trust himself?

"Hello? Is someone there?"—he hears the sound of sobbing, somewhere close by.

He has just emerged from a wine store, where he has bought a bottle of wine to bring to his parents' old friends that evening. Out of restlessness he's been walking, and, happening to see the wine store (it has a familiar name but seems to be in an unfamiliar setting), he'd decided to make the purchase now, rather than later, though it means carrying the wine bottle back up the long hill to Road's End Lane. Now in the parking lot beside the wine store he hears, he thinks he hears, the sound of sobbing, but when he turns to look he sees no one, nothing.

L____ is perplexed but not especially frightened. For this is not happening *inside his head* as he has (sometimes) feared when he hears the sound in the early morning, in his house. It is not at all unlikely that a woman, a girl, a young boy, might be sitting inside a vehicle in the parking lot, sobbing. And that L____ has happened to overhear.

But there are only a few vehicles parked in the lot, and no one is visible inside any of them.

He listens closely. The sobbing seems to have faded.

He walks on. He is feeling hopeful. The bottle has an attractive label: It is a Chilean chardonnay, new to him. He will enjoy himself that evening, he is determined. It has been too long since L____ has spent time with friends. He needs to engage in conversation, he needs to laugh. He needs to forget about S_____ and he needs to forget about E___. He will deflect questions that seem to him too private, too personal—about his health, his circumstances, the precise nature of the work he has brought with him to Cattaraugus—but he will do this in a discreet way; he will try to be gracious.

Are you returned to us?

We have been waiting for you—for years. . . .

He has left the wine-store parking lot and will return to Road's End Lane. But by a circuitous route.

Already it is late afternoon—past five o'clock. He must return home, he must shower and cleanse himself thoroughly before going out to dinner. He has a fear of offending the nostrils of others, who know nothing of his secret and must not guess it.

He is walking in a neighborhood in Cattaraugus that is not familiar to him. As a boy he'd bicycled along some of these streets—narrow, hilly, potholed streets—past shabby row houses and vacant lots, and yet all seems different to him. No one is out on the sidewalks, no one is in the streets. He has taken a wrong turn, it seems, though no turn in Cattaraugus will take L____ far out of his way, it is such a small town; and if there is danger, he is armed with the bottle of chardonnay.

He finds himself crossing a pedestrian bridge. It is a very old bridge—miniature maple trees, no more than an inch high, are growing in the cracks between planks and in the plank railings!

To his left, just visible through a maze of wood-frame houses and scrubby foliage, is a stretch of slate-colored Lake Cattaraugus. To his right is the sprawling New York Central railroad yard, desolate at this hour. Beneath the bridge is a marshy area, an inlet of the lake that has become shallow and mucky and infested with buzzing insects.

Ahead he sees a young woman at the bridge railing, leaning her elbows on the railing as if she is very tired. Her long, tangled hair falls forward, hiding her face, which seems to him an aggrieved face, though he cannot see it clearly.

It is this woman who has been sobbing—(is it?). L_____ stops dead in his tracks at the sight of her.

He will recall afterward he'd had no choice but to approach her to ask if anything is wrong.

"Excuse me—? Hello?"

The young woman doesn't seem to have heard L_____. Already she has turned distractedly away, she is walking away, a stricken creature, wounded, wincing with pain (he thinks); she does not want him to see her face.

Is she crying? Is she ashamed that she is crying? He sees that she is wiping at her face with both hands as she hurries away.

He thinks—*But I have no choice!*

The woman is wraithlike, very thin. She seems scarcely to be walking or running but rather gliding. She wears a long, dark skirt of some flimsy material like muslin. She wears a shawl wrapped about her shoulders. He can't see her face and so has no idea how old she is but her movements suggest that she is young, lithe. Her hair is a shimmer of hues—blonde, ash blonde, wheat, silver—that flies about her head as if galvanized by electricity.

L_____ doesn't quicken his pace, he will not overtake the woman. If the woman needs help, if she needs protection, L_____ will be close behind her, but he does not want to frighten her.

He keeps a fixed distance between them: thirty feet perhaps.

"I am here if you need me. I am always here. That is all."

L_____ follows the woman across a street of badly broken pavement. He follows her into a vacant lot behind a block of brownstone row houses, which look as if they have been scorched by flame. Here there is underbrush, discarded and rotted lumber, broken glass sparkling in the late afternoon sun. Broken clay pots—why so many? And empty bottles, gutted tin cans. L_____ has become confused, for what is this fetid place? *Where is the young woman leading him?*

"Hey. You."

Out of the rubble an angry man approaches L_____. He is fast and springy on the balls of his feet. He is belligerent and menacing as a pit bull.

L_____ is taken totally by surprise. Naively he glances over his shoulder to see if the angry man is addressing someone behind him but it is L_____ at whom the angry man is staring with stark, protuberant eyes. It is L_____ at whom he is speaking in disgust.

"I said you! What d'you want?"—the flush-faced man, a decade younger than L_____, not taller than L_____ but thicker bodied, obviously stronger, is bearing down upon L_____ with a look of fury.

L_____ would turn away and flee. But L_____ doesn't want to retreat in the face of the other's irrational anger for (he is thinking) that will violate his integrity; also, he dares not turn his back on such anger.

The angry man spits at him: "You sick fuck! What the fuck d'you think you're doing following her?!"

Now it is clear. It is clearer. The man is in alliance with the unhappy young woman.

L_____ would explain that he meant no harm, he was only seeing if the woman needed help, he did not mean to upset her, he is sorry if he has been misunderstood; but the angry man isn't interested in anything L_____ has to say. He has stepped boldly close to L_____, and he continues cursing L_____. To his chagrin L_____ sees that the young woman has taken a position behind the man, as if L_____ presents such a threat to her that she has to hide behind the angry man; at the same time, the woman has become defiant herself, flushed with indignation. Her face is radiant not with tears but with intense emotion.

This is certainly not Evangeline: L_____ sees now.

She is no one he has seen before. She has small, crushed-together features but she is not at all delicate boned. Her hair has a coarse, metallic sheen. The shirt or blouse she wears has a low neckline, her bony upper chest is exposed, her pallid skin. In an incensed and infantile voice she tells the angry man that this is the person who has been following her, scaring her. "The son of a bitch is always following me. This is him!"

Before L_____ can protect himself, the angry man rushes at him and strikes him in the face. It is a powerful, stunning blow—L_____ feels his left eye socket crack.

He staggers backward. The angry man has wrenched the wine bottle out of L_____'s hand, and threatens to strike him with it.

"Hey! Don't break this for Christ's sake"—deftly the young woman detaches the wine bottle from her companion's fingers.

L_____ would retreat but the angry man won't allow him. L_____

171

dares not turn his back for fear he will be murdered. He tries to defend his bleeding face as a child might, with his elbows, uplifted arms, bending at the waist, cowering, but the angry man continues to pursue him, not so hurriedly now, almost randomly striking him with sharp blows, his chest, his shoulder, his left temple. L_____ can barely see; both his eyes have been struck, his vision blotched by pinpoint hemorrhages.

"No—please—*don't*"—L_____ tries to protest but his mouth has been wounded. His teeth are loose and bleeding. His lower lip has been savagely slashed. He would stagger away in desperation—he would crawl away—but the angry man refuses to let him. The wrath of this stranger seems to be building, like that of a vengeful god. The more he punishes his victim, the more furious he is with his victim. L_____'s very blood on his hands, splattering his clothing, is a goad to him, a provocation.

A forlorn thought comes to L_____, belatedly—*Your mistake was leaving Mura House today, on foot.*

L_____ is knocked to the ground by the angry man's pounding fists. It is a mistake too to fall to the ground for now the angry man is even angrier, and is kicking L_____. Grunting, cursing, kicking at L_____— the angry man is a flame that cannot be quenched, that must burn itself out. Kicking the fallen L_____ in the ribs, without mercy. L_____ feels the bones cracking that protect his heart and lungs. He is writhing in pain, he is pierced with pain as with a steel blade. The tangled-haired woman is taunting him, she is not trying to save him from the angry man but has become his assailant too, bent upon vengeance. L_____ wants to ask—*Why?*

And now it is worse, it is unbearable, L_____ is being kicked in the stomach, in the terrible wound in his lower belly that has not yet healed, in the stoma that bleeds so easily, a mere touch can start it bleeding and the terror is of bleeding to death. L_____ can't draw breath to explain, he is unable to speak, the angry man will not let him speak and the angry young woman will show him no mercy.

They have confused L_____ with someone else—is that it? He wants to protest, to plead with them it is the wrong man they are punishing. But in his agony he can't draw breath to speak.

L_____ hears the angry man grunting as he kicks his final blows, each blow is a final blow, a death's blow. His grunting is a righteous sound. Such punishment is work. Such punishment is justice. Between L_____'s legs pain escalates so powerfully it can't be contained but explodes from him like a geyser.

And then suddenly he is alone, his assailants have departed. It is very quiet except for L____'s gasping breaths.

One of them has taken his wallet, torn it from inside his blood-soaked trousers.

L____ is alone, flat on the ground, and the tin-colored sky close overhead like something that is shutting. The pain continues to build. Behind his blinded eyes the flame grows in intensity until there is nothing but the hot, blinding, searing flame that envelops him, and is him.

No ID? Who is this? Jesus!—looks like somebody was real mad at the poor bastard.

3.

Hello!

Her eyes lift to his. He can't see her face clearly. But he can see that she is smiling at him, shyly. He believes that she is smiling at him.

They are in a secluded place that smells of the lake. Rotted algae, carcasses of fish mummified in the summer sun. He sees a fleeting shadow on the ground, the shadow of a large bird, a predator, or rather a scavenger, with wide, dark, comically awkward wings. He does not know if this is a turkey vulture. He knows that there are turkey vultures in Cattaraugus County. The bird is too large to be a crow or a raven. It is too large to be a blackbird. It is not flying but rather walking, with ungainly steps. It is walking toward him. Its eyes are bronze, unwinking. Its beak looks sharp and it is long enough to reach his heart.

The silvery-haired woman is close by. This is Evangeline, he is certain: but perhaps she does not want to be called by that name, by L____. Perhaps that is a secret name, not to be uttered. She is not so close that he can reach out to touch her, to clutch at her hand as he wants to do. For if he could clutch her hand, if she would grip his hand firmly, she might pull him up onto his feet—badly, he wants to be raised to his feet, he is in despair of what has happened to him, and it will be the first step in making things right, in returning to his normal life, if the young woman will help him to his feet, if she will offer him her hand. She is not so close that he can see her face clearly, or her eyes. He senses that her eyes are veiled. But he sees that she is there. She has not abandoned him.

Gently she says to the fallen man—*O love. Give me your hand.*

Seven Pieces on Deception, the Whore, and Anderson, IN

Arielle Greenberg

WHAT I TOLD MYSELF

AT THE BEGINNING, I told myself that I could have sex with the X even though he was cheating on Anderson, IN, because he had already been cheating on Anderson, IN, for six years: first, briefly, with a woman in his office, then, for the next five years and through the time that he and I first got in touch with one another, with a woman he met online, the same way he first met me in 1996, and the same way he'd met Anderson, IN, in 1997, and the same way he met me again in 2011. He'd been seeing that woman once a year or so, on business trips he took to Georgia especially to meet her. So I was not a homewrecker, I told myself, because in that sense, his home had long been wrecked.

And *I* was not a cheater, I told myself, because the Husband knew all about the X from the start, knew what I was doing with him, spoke to him on the phone, met him at a diner in New Hampshire with the children for his birthday. On that day, the X brought the children coloring books. He ate some of their leftover pancakes.

Anderson, IN, and the X have no children together. It would be different, I told myself, if they had had children together. There were no children whose lives would be ruined if, because of me, their marriage came undone. And, anyway, the X's life was not being ruined: He was choosing this for himself. The only life to ruin, I told myself, was that of Anderson, IN, a grown woman who would actually be better off if she learned to take care of herself.

But within a few months, about the same time as that birthday lunch at the diner, I told the X that if he wanted to keep seeing me, he had to tell Anderson, IN, about us. About him. About them. About his long history of cheating. "This can't go on," I said. And so he told her.

174

SHE/US

There are so many clichés: *My wife doesn't understand me. I feel trapped. We haven't been happy in a long time.* He never said any of these.

He told me, at the beginning, that they were comfortable together, and content. That he felt safe with her, and that they were best friends. Even much later, when she had thrown all their photographs in the fireplace and cut his high-school football jersey in two with a pair of scissors, he did not want to hurt her, did not want to harm her, did not want her to dislike him.

Because she knew about me as the girlfriend the X had before she ever came along, the model for a girlfriend the X wished she'd be, she hated me from the start.

Her hatred and fear of me was so intense that she did not want to hear my name, so he did not use my name when he spoke to her. Even before he started having an affair with me, he was not allowed to speak my name, and if there was a show on television with a character who had my name, they had to change the channel.

After she found out about the affair, she called me the Whore. He did not want to call me the Whore, but he was still not allowed to use my name, so he would say, *She*. On the rare occasions when he speaks to Anderson, IN, by telephone now, I think the X still says *She* instead of my name, so as to avoid further enraging her.

When the X says *us* to me, he often means *me and Anderson, IN*, something they did together in the past, with the dogs or in Hawaii. I do not think he has ever said *us* to her, meaning himself and me, the Whore. After all, they were married for fourteen years. And she would not like to hear such an *us*, could not bear it, and so I think he has trained himself not to say it.

Arielle Greenberg

A REAL PERSON

One can tell oneself that an affair—especially such an affair, organized so resolutely around sex; with a thinner woman (though not
thin), a younger woman (though not young); with a woman who posts
pictures of herself wearing shorts on the Internet; with a woman who
is married to another man (though openly)—can only end badly.

That it's a cliché, a mirage, a midlife crisis. That it cannot last, will
not be real, will not work out.

These are things people say. And it might make one feel better to
think these things.

But some people are with their once-illicit lover, the one they used
to meet after work at the cheap motel or late at night at the park 'n'
ride, for the rest of their lives. There are revised in-laws and Tupper-
ware and the dog leash hanging on a hook by the door, and there may
also be vacations to nudist resorts and sequined minidresses for going
out dancing, even in their sixties.

We've met people like this, the X and I: soccer moms and bikers and
retired army veterans on their second marriages, blissfully grateful
for the choice they made to leave their spouses decades ago for someone shocking or ill-advised or even much like the ex, but about
whom all the ex's friends said, *It won't last*, and yet it has lasted, and
sometimes, even all these years later, despite the high-school basket-
ball schedule for the youngest and the bald spot and the scars she has
from that lumpectomy, the sex is still very, very good.

People fall in love, people break up, people fall in love again. It's not
magic. It's not even news. And yet every time it happens, we act as
if the world has stopped, and all our friends tell us, *He's disgusting.
She's horrible. What a shitface. I can't believe that. They're crazy.
Good riddance.* As if any of us is immune.

I am trying, I suppose, to prove to Anderson, IN, that I am a real person, just me, which is both far less interesting and also maybe far
more upsetting than being the magic-cunted Whore of her imaginings.

Arielle Greenberg

BAD FEMINIST

Anderson, IN, has told me that I'm a bad feminist for sleeping with her husband, for causing him to leave her. What I guess she means by this is that she equates feminism with kindness toward women by other women, and I did the unkind thing of sleeping with her husband while she was married to him—first without her knowledge or consent, and then, after a few months, with her knowledge but still without her consent—and then inspiring or otherwise causing her husband to ultimately choose to be with me and to end his marriage to her.

I think that Anderson, IN, thinks that if I were truly a feminist—as she knows I am deemed on the Internet, and as she knows I say I am—I would not be unkind to other women in this particular whorish way: that I would refrain from fucking or loving married men whose wives didn't want them to fuck or love other women.

But I do not agree that, at its core, feminism is about interpersonal kindnesses between women. I'm not sure it's about kindness at all. And I do not think that the act of sleeping with Anderson's husband was unkind. Nor do I think it was kind. It was something the X and I wanted for ourselves. It made us both happy. It was kind to us, because we felt nourished and delighted by it, and unkind to her, because she was being lied to, and her trust was betrayed. I do not think it had a universal quality of kindness or unkindness. I do think the fact that the X was lying to Anderson, IN, about what was going on was unkind. If it had been up to me, I would have told her earlier.

Sometimes I say, "I did Anderson, IN, a favor." When I say this, I mean that by being part of the cause—OK, the catalyst; OK, the major cause—of her marriage ending, I was doing her a kindness, because she often said that she did not want to be married to someone who lied to her or cheated on her, and she was married to someone who did both.

Of course, much of the time, there is a lie inherent in anything anyone says, and the lie is simply what we want to be true.

177

Arielle Greenberg

BIT OF STRANGE

How common is it, when people have affairs or otherwise leave monogamous relationships, for the one who is betrayed and left to ask oneself, *Was I a good partner?*

How common is it for one to answer, *No, not really?* To say, perhaps, *I was good, once, at the beginning, but then I just stopped putting in the effort and forgot most days to touch or even look at her, and my job got really boring and I stopped wanting to do karaoke and started wearing those really unflattering but comfortable pants every day, and mostly ordered takeout from the chicken place instead of making the paella she so enjoyed?*

How common is it to see the person who left not as the enemy or as evil incarnate, but as a fellow tired wanderer who seized an opportunity that came along for something different, something with spark?

How common is it to think, *Had I been presented with a similar opportunity, the cute guy in the next cubicle offering to go down on me under the desk one late night during inventory, I might have done the same, and betrayed this person I truly love and care about, just because I too have been feeling the need for something else in my life, a bit of strange?*

How common is it to think, *This does not mean she does or does not love me? That I am or am not a failure? That she is or is not an asshole? Because all of these answers are true? All of the above?*

How common is it for the bit of strange to develop into something lasting, familiar?

How common is it for the cycle—the thrill, then the ennui, then the look to the left—to all happen again, and for the new, the strange, to be betrayed and left?

(I tell myself: Sometimes it all happens again but often it does not. *Once a cheater, always a cheater,* people like to say, but don't we all know someone who left his wife and kids to be with the golden-voiced secretary with the calves like apostrophes, and who is still with that secretary decades later, both gray now, and living in a retirement village near Orlando, photographs of grandchildren in braces all over the refrigerator?)

178

Arielle Greenberg

LANA DEL REY

I am walking barefoot on a dirt road through the mountains in the high desert. I am wearing a plum-colored miniskirt and listening to Lana Del Rey in my earbuds. Somewhere someone is shooting off a gun. It's hot and sunny.

I am thinking about codependence, and about fakery.

Could you leave me? I ask the X later on the phone.

That night, I dream about him leaving me. It's a horrible dream. I bait him into leaving me, actually, saying an abrupt goodbye as a way to manipulate him into caring more, but it backfires and he indifferently lets me go. I wake up screaming, *No,* then realize the man in the dream was not the X at all but the emotionally withholding boyfriend I left in my twenties to be with the X in the first place, all those years ago, before either of us ever knew Anderson, IN, existed.

In the morning, I call the X and the minute I hear the dearness in his voice, the vulnerable giddiness he has hearing from me while I am far away, I am OK.

I do not want my life to resemble a moody, pouty pop song. I do not live my life like this dumb lux pop song full of artifice. Quite the opposite: It is hard for me to do anything but tell the truth, except when I'm angry, and then I play that game where I say cruel things and push away push away when all I want is to be pulled close. The X knows this. Every time we fight we talk it through. He is learning to be brave in the face of my viciousness, and hold me down until I take the love he so wants to give me.

I often wake up thinking, *I will love him till the end of time.*

And then I check: *Is that healthy?*

I think it's healthy. It feels healthy. I am barefoot in the mountains, thousands of miles away from him, doing good work while he takes care of the kids and watches baseball playoffs with the husband. He has seen me without mascara, without heels. I have held his heavy head in my arms while he has cried about his fear of being forsaken.

I wonder if Anderson, IN, listens to Lana Del Rey.

Arielle Greenberg

CHOOSE YOUR OWN ADVENTURE

If you chose not to tell her and decide to keep lying, keep hiding the receipts, keep bringing home the little bejeweled gifts from the Atlanta airport, go to page 13.

If you chose to tell and took her out to dinner and planned to say it, in public, where hopefully she would not make a scene, but then chickened out and couldn't do it, couldn't see her cry, and wanted to spend one more night watching television in bed side by side, go to page 44.

If you chose to tell her and did it because you couldn't spend one more night lying awake worrying if she was going to figure out the password on your iPad and you were going to come home from the trip to find your belongings scattered on the front lawn where all the neighbors could see, go to page 67.

If you chose to tell her and did it because you were just so fucking done, and you couldn't even wait to move into the hotel near work and file the papers, go to page 9.

If you chose to tell her and did it because it was really the best thing for both of you, to start saying what you meant to one another, out of respect and a desire to move on, both of you, to something new and potentially rejuvenating, go to page 20.

If you chose to leave without saying a word about any of it, and never do, just keep paying her several hundred dollars a week for the rest of her life and smile at her across the aisle at college graduations and weddings and hope that her drinking doesn't get any worse, go to page 35.

If you are choosing to pretend for the sake of this exercise to have told her but in fact never told her, not at all, and just kept living the way you were living, and took a new job so you wouldn't have to follow that person down the hall of the office anymore, and finished off that room in the basement and joined a bowling league, and are now feeling called out by what you are reading but still cannot, will not tell her, go to page 52.

A Monologue Addressed to the Madame's Cicisbeo

Margaret Fisher

CICISBEO, CICISBAY 1. ITALIAN GALLANT employed to escort a woman. He enters her social world and safeguards her respectability. 2. Post-WWI, American futurist and gallant of steel driven by the women. *Crocodile* 1. Amphibious reptile with a hide of external keratin plates; releases body heat through the mouth; the female has been known to eat her young. 2. A tough who feeds on fawn. *Fawn* 1. A young deer. 2. Servile flattery.

A fawn, Cicisbeo [Chee-chees-báy-oh],
for Madame who sat you in the streets. Hot still at ninety, she will take this fawn. She needs no lure, no arm twist, no hard sell. Smolders, she, under a keratin hide, and opens, by heat that royal red mouth, that royal disguise of blue embers. Opens! Our Mamán! Trapped when she was twenty-five, unbagged at thirty-six, say what? Say it was the Crocodile trap, center theme to our childish play, *The Play of the Weather*, set in Summer's Heat on Biscayne Bay and say this. She is in the trap. What squeezer nipped her scrag, Cicisbeo, that you unbagged her?

The Play: Summer's Rain
washes mud from cloven hoof of Fawn, and puts it back again. Thunder quells the Hawking Gulls and the Wind blows hard at the Wind. Reptiles lashed from roost and Spiders from the web see the Fish Cave trimmed, the Trees, and their Rookeries. Perish, the Chicks, and the rain-stung tan of Childish Arms turns pale as they, the Arms, sashay, attached, still, to the Child Trunk as the Palm Fronds were not to the Tree. Summer's Rain becomes a Storm, then anagnorisis, the recognition scene that spins the moral tale of who is trapped and who is not.

Margaret Fisher

Playing Ourselves,
we enter Storm. Sizzles the current in the air, and the sun-baked
street stings our tender feet. Steam escapes between our toes and we
shrill, fear in our throats, for the God is in the steam. Stood still the
Traffic in a Dog's Rain, wet the brakes, and the Cat's Rain ate half an
hour, and the God was in that half hour.

Car
was the safest place to be, windows up, doors locked, wipers feint the
gods fobbing left, shamming right, erasing, then erased, by the wor-
thier opponent. Our eyes peeled to the wind's paroxysm and the
rain's paroxysm, and we sweat wide eyed at unknown peril, like
child voyeurs pouring over an adult book, rapt by the pinkish tint of
the counter-parry, say what? Say

Red
refracted by the Pelting Rain, made for a pinkish tint from the traffic
light. This, Cicisbeo, the counter parry. The Sheeted Rain slapped
against the glass, our Maidenhead, with the Wind's force, and the
Wind's cadence, over, over, again and again, globbed the God into
glass, the Sperm of Jove against our Maidenhead, savage in air;
turned substance in the cataract.

Touché!
It was erratic and terrifying and very, very good. Chaste inside, but
suffocating. Lightning. Thunder. Somebody would say, inevitably,
"Thank God, the tires are made of rubber." "By Jove, they are," shot
back. It passed the time, broke the spell, gave us reason to shift, as
we had sweat the seats. Red blur that had been pink turned green.
Who played Backseat Driver sputtered, "Don't go!" and we yelled,

"Crocodiles!"
at the Palm Fronds downed, rushing past the tires. A river of
Crocodiles. The Swamp churned and You idled, Cicisbay. Who said
"By Jove," now says "See, Jove rolls over," and we roll the windows
down. Light Rain cooled hottened cheeks. She lit a cigarette, say
what? Had it been her ambition, say, or her frustration, sustained and
merciless, pelting, taunting the window through which she viewed
her Miami life, had she felt unable to move or to breathe, were she
stuck in place and found the air around her stale with the smell of
children, that was it.

The Crocodile's trap
in *The Play of the Weather*. Climate was but mise-en-scène and we
knew nothing of her duress. Jove could turn over as he like, but she
was stuck in Miami with us. She was our Crocodile, the danger outside the Chevy. Trapped inside. Each day we faced this danger and
did not know it. And she did not know us or our audacity in the open
streets under a tropic sun.

She did not know
we crossed with the red, Cicisbay, and on our own and on our trikes
at Fifty-Ninth Avenue. We knew where we were going, the corner
drug and soda fountain, entered en suite, proud, proprietary; we parried
those who paid, who sat the counter: "En garde! We want the right
of way!" They laughed, retreated, said, "Touché!" and so we sat together and ordered the glass of water we didn't have to pay for. We had
only to want. From counter stools we swung tan legs with golden
hairs, drank slowly, pressed our noses into glass, made faces through
refracted light. When had she set out with such surety?

Native-born to Biscayne Bay
we did not hesitate. Up at dawn, we shortcut the neighbor's lawn and
left behind their hedges frayed by handlebars, by narrow shoulders,
tightened fists, by toys we clutched in pistol grip. We played Fiendish
Doctor, House on Fire, we dressed and undressed Cyd Charisse,
Hedy Lamarr, Veronica Lake—paper dolls in the killing fields. We
parried insects and muddy strays, tore eyestalk from the hated crabs
on land that wedged between the paving stones; dismembered, afterward, those Gecarcinidae, made charm from longer claw. Breakfast
stuck to our faces, framed by the uncombed hair. In mismatched
plaids we congregated on the concrete sidewalk, in front of the house
I was born into. Our front porch was no more than a brick stoop leading up to stucco walls, but no one crossed it or came inside to play.
We played on porch.

Croc, twenty-nine in 1954,
East Texas, Russian-in-the-face-and-ankles, and photogenic. Volup-
tuous the hips, red lips, dark hair, blue eyes, round shouldered. Neck
up, she had the Ava Gardner look. A pouty look but not a come-hither
or shiksa look. Formidable. Desirable. Without the Ava jaw or dim-
ple or chiseled nose. Memorable the look, with Lucky Strike between
her ruby reds she was Ava nonetheless, in Marimekko dress.

Margaret Fisher

At ninety,
she no longer leaves men whiplashed by her leave, but prattles on
about her painting, turns idle talk to New Yorkese and boasts of
those Who's Whoers she once knew and how, like her, they too were
trapped in Biscayne Bay. At ninety, with that extra push of Texas air,
she wheezes the leitmotif from life's accordion: "New YORK."
"FLOHR-da." Tunes that never will let go. There is much I do not
know of her, or of my love for her, or where this fawn will go, say
what, Cicisbeo? Say we are back in Miami, 1955. Madame Tough
behind the wheel, sat you in the streets. You chased down the Who's
Whoers in that swampland, expats in the Grove: Mexican, French,
Cuban, South African survivors of the comedown from New YORK,
transplants to her swamp. You did this! Bravo!

We saw her
roll the window down; we saw her sigh; we saw the fugitive's breath,
freighted with history, blow from those ruby rims, but we did not
understand. Unseen, the inhale that would point her toward the best
of times. Her inhale upticked north. But truly the best of times were
at her back, the apartment, postwar New York,

on Riverside Drive.
He, her Army Captain, Medical Supply Desk, Wall Street, sported regu-
lation holster and the captain's pistol in it. They took the downtown
train. And she, self-assigned with brushes, detrains at Fifty-Seventh
Street, turns in at the Art Students League. Croc in that hothouse
hide husbands her mind, rakes through the autumn of Matisse afire;
begins to paint as God began, in winter. Under Morris Kantor and Will
Barnet, the figure. Comes spring, and she, heavy with child, breathes
in the new abstraction, Barnett Newman and Jackson Pollock. The
best of times.

New York was now the exhale,
factory whistle of the call to work, the call to art. God's call. Trapped,
she could not go. Down from New York, she enters Miami with the
Infanta, and her Captain buys a single-story stucco, two-bed, one-
bath with an extra room, and she set her easel in that extra room.
Again with child in summer, she painted. Cool in my sleeping sac, I
felt her gaze on canvas, her hand on summer's brush, then fall. No
hand, no eye held by their ardor my growing cocoon throughout my
season, through to the final Storm, a category four, a Trapper of a

hurricane. Entered hospital early, she stayed long. From her window one could see the palm fronds curbed and all the rest.

I was cribbed
in the ex-atelier by Croc. Home was now three-bed, one-bath. Young, I did not grasp the composition, the central easel, and the cornered crib. Vapors clung to the walls, lulled me into the turpentine sleep of the night watch.

We were at odds
with each other, Croc and I. Our war went everywhere between us; it spoiled my bath, where the Infanta, toga wrapped in fresh towels from the first bath, lingered, witness to my history. Olive skinned in white, flushed in the cheek, she, a Roman senator in high relief upon the doorjamb of our battle, she, waited for this, my memory, age three: Croc stood me at arm's length, imperious with painful grip, she froze my impish jests. Grip. Pause. Wink to the Infanta. Attack! With the inexorable deliberation that marks the native pace and nastiness of her species, Croc says, in a voice not yet forgotten—first, the high note of her accusation, and then the low—"You should smell your bottom!"

Stirrer of strife,
my father's wife! Followed, my silence. Then, impeccable defense, "My head can't reach my bottom." How hard they laughed at me, how black their blood. They etched their acid sneers into my beating heart. Ran wet to my room. Mine! Locked! Triumphant my bed, my monument, pulled from corner, pushed to center to be my stage. Mine! Grabbed, my forty-five, my vinyl victory wreath, set needle in groove, brought player to speed.

"Crack"
went the futurist pops of the silent band, then, song: "Dan, Dan the Fireman; He puts out the fire as quick as he can." Dan! I spun, I leaped upon my monument. Someone who loved Dan very much sang his praise. His mother or sister. Or princess in a smoky tower. Where there's smoke, there's fire, she sang. As if on cue, seeped in from under door and rose, their scorn for Dan, the empress's, the senator's, inflamed my indignation, set fire to my fun. Undressed by them again, I froze in baby ire.

Had they not noticed?
How I reasoned with head upon my shoulders the head's nonreach.
How I'd stood up for myself, formed a well-constructed sentence
with subject, verb, and object of the verb, and how I joined well the
verb's auxiliary to my abnegation. Mine! Had they not noticed how
I'd made sense of wicked nonsense? No, they did not notice, nor how
I held in mind the differential calculus resulting from our match.
Two against One. As she tells it, my father's wife, the babies, and
Miami were his idea. One against Three, hers, the insuperable math.
Memories paled but the body rendered well. Tears rendered well, and
the hot flush. Sound rendered best as I remembered this.

Remembered, also this:
I return from the killing fields to my front door locked, no answer to
my knock. No answer when I held the bell or to my cry or angry
stomp, or to the killed catch I flung across the door. Curse on the
door to the house that had been my home! Eyestalk of crab, tail of
dog and monarch wing, razed in adolescent ire. I sat the curb and
waited, dressed and undressed Cyd Charisse. A slanting sun peered
up our legs. Good neighbors took me in, telephoned my father's wife.
She answered! "Oh, we're here, have been . . . a long afternoon. Why?
Was something wrong," she asked, "that you are calling me?" She had
to ask. Good neighbor's eyes were fixed on me. Pity swiftly measured
pain. Silently, I did the math. Entered house through the now unlocked door, fathomed the silence, which did not crack or pop in anticipation of my entrance, nor follow the spiral groove of happiness.
In the back bedroom, my father in the master bed, one eye bandaged
in the darkened room and at the end of the bed, his feet, unattended,
sang of that long man in the bed, a long drink of water as I would also
be. He smiled weakly, fixed the other eye on me. And then, he slept.
When he was well, I attached myself to him, and he seemed not to
mind.

I've caught up to you, Cicisbeo.
Yes? Madame Croc, trapped in Miami, pines for New York. What to
do? The wife's car was a fact after the war; it gained her new freedoms.
A Mercedes, yes, but for the boycott of German cars and the Jewish
boycott of Ford. The whole lot of suburban prejudice idled some lives,
jump-started others. There was a nagging sense of moral outrage vexed
by the need to do something, anything, to put distance between oneself and all of that. Her Captain buys a Chevrolet.

Feigns happiness
for her finless four-door blue sedan. Will take her where she needs to
go, her Cicisbeo. The name adds the kind of class one doesn't have
to pay for. One day, surely, she will lower her eyes, cast her spell,
inhale, and you, Cicisbay, will pull up to her palazzo.

Closest to Madame
as none of us were, Cicisbay, your sun now sets, stirs the dust of my
unearned shame, gives a slant-rayed stab to my memories. It is
snowing dust inside my head, my head is in Miami, where she is in
the car. This, the anagnorisis, the recognition scene. Her breath is
in the car, her voice, her words. Her scorn is in the car. But I am not in
the car. Your sun heats my shame, unglues the cubist image of this
boychild become girlchild, stored in the adult mind, fades this child's
imperfect ink, rewrites the moral tale.

Miserere, Cicisbay.
Your job was to alleviate just the right amount of Madame's suffering. Daddy will build Madame's palazzo, but see how she resists,
requests Le Corbusier instead. Had Daddy urged Corbusier, she'd
have parried Corbusier, extracted a palazzo. Blue embers heat that
keratin hide, ignite her royal blood, set her going and there's no end
to it. She comes by Corbusier with a protégé of his, 1955, a New York
architect transplanted to Miami. Upticked the compass of her
inhale.

Uncle Ralph,
accountant to Miami bookies, flies weekly to Havana, sits the airport bar, orders, de rigueur, the glass of water he doesn't have to pay
for and down goes the briefcase to the floor freeing up his hands
when sits the bar beside him a Man with the twin valise who orders
a real drink and down the hatch, the two of them before God swallow their spit and Ralph leaves with the twin valise! A good man,
Ralph, forgoes the Tropicana, arrives home for supper in Miami
where Daddy sits the supper table with Ralph and Ralph's wife, Sally.
Daddy's full when he heads home, his fortune sealed in the envelope
from Ralph. Inside, the sacred deed to Florida land is folded *and*
encumbered. Home! and down it goes, deed to the table under crocodile eyes. She does not read the coordinates, nor the caveat that
insures obeisance to the mob, "Should need arise."

"Rest assured,"
Uncle Ralph had said, "No one needs this land." Back in the envelope, folded still, Daddy's deed of five acres south of the urban grid. Back in they go, his sixty-foot pines, the salt-hardened ground. At the western end, Daddy built our "Bauhaus," post-Corbusier. Broad and airy as a loaf of white bread in a Slavic pine forest, our Bauhaus wants to lift off. Cape Corbusier. The floor plan: open terrazzo, split level. You look up: polished plywood eighteen feet high. You look south: glass walls open onto the forest. Below ground: his basement, or flood zone, our torture chamber, or make-out chamber, or bomb shelter, changes with the season. Out front: a semicircular drive, one of the first. Daddy parks his long-finned Cadillac against the backdrop of his loaf of bread. New money! He has only to sell the other four acres. More money! The Croc has only to paint. And how she paints! Wowsers! What paint! What titles! *Torrid Zone, Burnt Offering, Uninhabitable Architecture.* Her suffering! It has returned. Get to work, Cicisbay!

To leave the pine forest,
you took the Old Cutler Road, its wall of banyan trees softened by the cool canopy of chigger moss to filter light. A left at the Old Cutler Road led to Coral Gables. A right, to the sands and palms of Matheson Hammock. Cicisbeo, we were old enough that your movements were now on our radar. When possible, the Croc left the forest with you. Not us. We saw her roll down the window, put cigarette to ruby reds, and make the whooshing sound, exhaling what it was that was disturbing her. I suspect you cut a left at Old Cutler because at dinner she opined about M. Berger's (Mizeure Bearrrzhair'z) Antiques. If not M. Berger's, it was the clothesline show at the Ryder Art Gallery, or the recorder group at Arnie Grayson's, or her visit to Eddy Mirrell & Eddie Weyhe, potters whose pet iguana stayed on leash when Croc was on property. Because, retrievable with leash. This is what I knew of her gadabout town, her absence before her absence.

> One day a brunette enters an eighteenth-century tavern, sets the air astir. Men sigh but none can speak. And Goethe, there among them, Johann mute, *mit* wolfen eyes devours her complexion hair and dress against the whitewashed wall. And the wolf in him is such that as she takes her leave he sees her still on whitewashed wall,

chromatically reversed: the hair turned light, the face
turned black, the dress the color of its complement.

Occasionally, Cicisbeo, you'd cut a right. She would plash against
the gentle tide, burrow into sand warm as youth, and enter the water.
She took charcoal with her, and paper with her. To draw the trees.
Croc might have left the forest with one of us. But rarely two when
the sun shone.

She took the Infanta
to draw the trees. She had first to subdue this child's fear of the
vacant page that stared her down from drawing board. Drawing was
martial, gravitas against emptiness; for Croc it was a thinking art, as
regards weapon and approach. "Serafina," for that was her unlikely
name, "take the willow charcoal; hold lightly in your hand, here.
Now start." Serafina froze the willow stick in air. "Move your hand.
Scumble in the shape. Use light and dark to show me what is near
and what is far." Seri grandly staged the reticent, noiseless smile that
says, "I understand"; and with that smile drew gray willow down.
Croc changed what willow nub was left, placed the sturdier black
charcoal stick, compressed, medium soft, in the child hand, wadded
up the warm-up page, pulled down a second vacant sheet. "Now
weight the blankness in the paper with your line." Seri raised the
regal curtain of her lips, vermilion and keratin strong in the curtain.
Even if I wasn't there I knew the thrill of this, her smile. Blinkered
into view, the misaligned, irresistible left canine brought tumes-
cence to her upper lip, caught, the eye of her beholder. Burrowed into
every memory anyone ever had of her was the charm of this tumes-
cence. Serafina was Sephardim, flashed the ancestral line of her
father's mother, Sue, would soon rival the Croc for beauty beyond
Ava. For now, she enjoyed the intimacy of being ruled. There was
time, before pearls of baby teeth gave way to steel retainer and jade
eyes deepened behind glass.

My blonde aspect
and long legs now placed me firmly female on the paternal Russian-
German side. A high jumper in the fifth grade, I was five feet nine in
the sixth, outjumped the girls, would have the boys, but Coach sent
me inside before I could. Croc, amused, said no more about this talent or future stardom, my Olympiad; had something else in mind.
More than once after class excursion I climbed breathless, happy,

189

into the Chevy of her debriefing. "Your britches are split up the middle," she welcomed me, undressed me, with flinted sardony. Ignited, my childish wrath, at the repeat in history. I was her savage child who tattered herself. She was ready to give me options for which I was unprepared. "Stop with that sass or you can get out here at the corner." A bad corner, my right foot tapped out code to keep me safe. Uptick, down, and all the rest. Hormone-soaked seconds prolonged the humiliation. I had not the courage to open the door to free myself.

The code:
Alongside a curb, press foot to floor, as though you were to brake. Crosswise to intersections, driveways, and where there is no curb; rear up, dear foot, my drawbridge, protection from the broadside. If I did not pay attention something terrible would happen. Down-up-down, the stink of fear in the concentration. We passed through neighborhoods in Miami without sidewalks and curbs, places that required more than an adjustment by my foot, where people's lives were in peril. The Croc, too, was absorbed in thought.

Dan's crooners
morphed into teen radio: "Dan Dan the party man, kick those legs . . ." Adolescent long legs were a liability, lacked discipline, frayed the light cotton worn against Florida heat as surely as a crocodile jaw could ravage the tender bottoms of her young. As surely as the mob could ravage our Daddy's bottom line. So they did. Sold, the remaining four acres at cost, Daddy to the mob. And the mob built out our neighborhood east, one Italian palazzo after another. The Croc cared nothing for Dan's simple pleasures. Hers was a life of calculated turns and twists. Her chicks had not yet entered the water, the river of life, or the life of the mind

when she left.
The "DAAAHndy." At ninety, she still draws out the Texas "A," relishes the describing of him, forgets she has never spoken of him this way to me. Sylvan had seen her one-woman exhibition. 1957. Havana. "Triumphant!" says *The Miami Herald*! "*Visitó el Presidente la Sala de Arquitectura en Bellas Artes*," says the *Diario de La Mañana* of Fulgencio Batista's visit to her show. Our heads almost touch as we study her picture in the paper. Happy in black silk, she is flanked by Captain, critics, and the American attaché. She is silent as I locate Sylvan in the crowd.

He was forty-one
when she met him. In 1959 he entered the Bauhaus. In 1960, he was
a regular; he came with the art crowd, or alone; he strutted his stuff,
was self-assured, and dismissive of our fragile ecosystem. He told the
Croc, "I am your only peer." Two against Three! You, Cicisbeo, you
took her to her Lover. Three against Three! Then Sylvan drove west
out of the pine forest, took the Red Road, not the Old Cutler Road,
ignited scandal and scorched the heart of our Jewish community in
Miami. He drove a Volkswagen bug. And she was in it.

On the lam,
Croc played out her fugitive life like a B movie. From the Red Road
to the Dixie Highway and North to New York, she slipped out of our
lives without a goodbye. She set up the Fugitive's blind, then applied
for divorce. At the end of their year in Europe,

the court decided.
She twisted the knife, my father's wife. To my father, who would not
rat on her, she never ceased to be the prettiest Jewish girl an officer
could set eyes upon, his inspiration and motivation. Now he owed
her cash. But his sex kept him curious and mobile and he moved on.
He took us out of the pine forest.

The New Yorker
ran a Mother's Day cartoon for its May issue. On the manicured
lawn over tea cakes, one middle-class she-croc laments to another,
same, "It's days like today I regret having eaten my young." What
airs they brought to table. I laughed and thought, *our* Croc had no
regrets. I laugh through tears. I begrudge her that more than anything
else. We were expendable. She was free of us and we were free of her.
But we did not want to be free. We were trapped in our freedom. We
wanted avant-Ava in Batik, back in the Bauhaus, back in her studio,
her back to the turpentine wall, her dark hair framed by Russian
icons, Mexican masks, pre-Columbian figurines, just as we had
known her; just as I see her, still, in a photo shot in Havana for her
show. We wanted those ruby reds to call out our names in East Texas
shrill, lips twisted in bemusement by the discomfort of our youth
and our significant lack of everything to which she aspired. The Croc
was thirty-six in 1961. The *Play of the Weather* was at her back; *The
Betrayal* and *The Abandonment* were at her back. Today, she is
more relaxed. She prattles on about her divorce, "my skAAAnndal,"

191

she says, with that extra push of Southern airs. "He was a DAAAHndy." At ninety her mind is clear, her eyes are blue, and now she is alone. There is much I do not know of her, or where this fawn will go.

Croc's voice
roared through the mommyless ether of our universe taunting us, trapping us between past and present. We responded differently, Serafina and I. I locked my door, spurned the world, found comfort in a moral superiority destined to vindicate my isolation and preserve my dignity. I emerged alternately sullen and haughty, cynic and sarcast. I foraged for love in the petri dish of my underground. The world paid no attention to preteenage venom. But the ether did pay compliments in ways I was too young to understand. Life offered new perceptions, but see how I lose the tune in the telling of sensate events. This long drink of water underwent simultaneous wavelike and infinite expansions and infinite contractions. Inside my body and body inside out. The wave flowed inside the Bauhaus and beyond the Bauhaus. It was a seizure without the seizure. An epiphany while the mind was left in ignorance; it was terribly asexual too, in case you're wondering. My eyes saw the single molecule that contained the universe. It lay outside of me. And it lay inside of me, expanding me to infinite size. The location was unremarkable, on the ceiling above a closet in my room. I had only to fix these eyes. Expansion. This much was clear, Cicisbay: My unruly emotions would not hinder me in the world. My body held answers to questions I had yet to formulate. Cynic and sarcast were silenced during metamorphosis from one to all. The mathematics of opposing forces resisted calculation. The gods, tired of hearing my filthy mouth, had killed me with the kindness of a curious silence for a few moments of the day.

On the other hand,
Seri's journals confirm she actively sought love in the world. We fidgeted about an evanescent truce, suffered each the other, to sweeten the pie of childhood. No matter the conversation or the game or the clothes, it would end the same: her on bed, me on floor as crusty page to the young goddess. I scored the bottoms of her feet with two fingernails, navigating by the blinkered light of the upper left canine. Light indicated approval and I continued. If light disappeared, I changed position of those nails. Bored and happy and secure, I had no martial art or worthy thought to drop into the bucket of the world.

No preparation or appointment whatever, except to tickle the blushed coral of her feet. She liked the feel of it. She liked the attention. She too experienced physical transports, but unlike me, she was comfortable expressing sexuality. I was a placeholder for someone in her future. Seri entered the night by natural inclination. Or, the night entered her. After dinner from age ten she was already rubbing her hips against the couch. The Croc, amused, would shrill out, "StoPP, with all thaaat Tooshie Bizness." Seri stopped. The next night, she started. The Croc had called her out, betrayed her child in a series of small tremors before the great one. Fortunately, croc-speak did not prove to be the organizing principle from which our later perceptions and thoughts would derive coherence and direction. The voice that nurtures chaos in the soul never is. After *The Play of Our Abandonment*, Seri and I wobbled with uncertainty around the same axis, though we did not know it at the time, nor did we recognize these early indicators of our characters as indicators of an aesthetics of art or a philosophy of life, say what?

The Croc began to write to us
from the shifting landscape of her new life. She requested we address her as "Mamán." This added a certain continental *je ne sais quoi* to my childish letters from the swampland to a man's apartment in Manhattan. "Chère Mamán," began the new relationship. "Mommy" was lost forever. Lost, because you, Cicisbeo, had freed her from our trap.

Blind in Granada, or, Romance
Edie Meidav

SHE WAS A BOHEMIAN GIRL with lots of life to live fast. Only in her early twenties but making up for time lost to who knows what. To books or the slow Cheshire-cat vanishing act effected by her best friend, a dreamy childhood with the wrong doors unlocked like her outsize painting ambition or the inability to trust those she knew, apart from her great-uncle of the round head and romantic aspiration who died but first told her in his French accent that he wanted to leave her a little money saved up from teaching so that when she found herself in the funeral-home room alone with his ethylated body he appeared to wink and say, go ahead now, enjoy yourself the way I always meant to. Her uncle who read books in many languages and taught English to foreign girl students from Asia while never forgoing his strong Sex Appeal cologne because how could he keep himself from falling in love with students to the point that the cashier at the local cinema knew him by the jokey line he used whenever he took a new one out: But are there greater discounts for the sexy senior citizens? He had gotten poorly embroiled with the last Korean student, one who would not so much as kiss him if he did not marry her, saying: The cow won't give milk unless you feed it, this girl his greatest disappointment since only death separated him from the love he thought might one day still be his, the love first whispered by French poetry and later mouthed by smoke rings in American kisser films he'd managed to see back when some still called Zimbabwe the Belgian Congo. His real dream was to have become a painter in Tahiti. And so with her uncle's sum of unused pleasure she planned to go to Europe because she too had read a book about an enchantress in Spain and a book about traveling boys and hijinks that made escaping the slate gray a correct course of action. And then everyone had told her stories about the Alhambra in Granada, saying so determinedly it really was the place she had to visit, a near peak of European civilization given that it was the last time so many ideologies about love and faith interpenetrated, such possibility flourishing in that moment if you could only travel back and alter later history in which all streams continued in their straitened way. But you must go to Granada, they chimed, while she kept opening her Spain guidebook to the quotation from the medieval king who said there is no pain worse than being blind in Granada and so it was confirmed, the message, especially as both her parents had started dwindling at the peripheries, a death moving toward the core: Clearly there was no pain worse than living life too slowly.

Once there, she bought a small guitar from a courtly guitar maker who asked if she would like to come by some night despite his wife and colicky grandson, while also failing to know where someone could take guitar lessons authentic to Andalucía. Leaving the guitar maker's small, cramped studio, carrying the guitar, she recalled a story she had read as a child about a happy pig named Pearl who found a magic bone, and was going to stop to get coffee on her way back to a hostel populated by Viking descendants but instead a gypsy intercepted her with his El Greco face, all massive, drooping eyes and aquiline nose as he unhanded her of the new guitar and started singing right there to her in the Plaza Mayor where she knew she had landed in the center of the thing she had envisioned but had not named.

You have killed me with your walk, he sang, strumming her guitar, stretching it out—camino-o-o-o, making his chin wobble with each O. Behind each wobble lined up a gaggle of ancestors with the question of whether he could live up to them. He did his best. After his song was done he asked her with some seriousness to come live with him in the small cave up above where tourists walk, white dwelling caves honeycombed into the hills facing the Alhambra which perhaps a king had made as a testament of love to his wife, a story that endured in a way that made her question if she would ever really know what it meant to fall in love despite her schooling in all the songs, because what had she ever known? Granada was either stripping her bare or layering on a new scrim since she was feeling more or at least feeling someone else's more. In most ways she was bad as the gypsy singing premature songs of love her way, the blinds of not truly seeing him, and it was not only risky but imaginary to throw yourself so in the thrall of someone else when anyway wasn't it always chemical? She had been curious about people throwing their hats down before her but didn't know if she had ever really thrown her hat down to someone or just to the sheer joy of their throwing their hats down. Was she to be so deprived of experience? Love, to love, to fall in love. She had climbed mountains but never fallen.

195

Others had been obsessed, sometimes with her, and was she only to know escape and absconding? Yet what was the strange thrill of the gypsy singing to her? It had to do with all stories conjoining in a spot just above her navel as if she were not on the road seeking but at both source and end, inside a kaleidoscope. This itself is a story about the problem with the picturesque and how it links with the picaresque and how certain girls are prone to confusing the two, going out to wander the landscape with something like one of Claude Lorrain's mirrors turned backward at the landscape. If something seems correct enough in its set details they forgive enough to think here lies fulfillment until fulfillment itself gives them the lie.

At night the gypsy and she did the deed, only one of them blushing in the dark on the floor in the gypsy cave though somewhere she was also numb because she didn't stop to ask what, for all that singing about her eyes and voice, her smile and a chance at amor, amor, what about him was fulfillment? She had chosen this, it was no rape, he was dead center with her but was there any vastness other than mammal embrace or the satisfaction of being in a cave with an avatar of Granada reaming her out of thinking? There was a mystery they tried to extract out of the other, one she would never solve, his animal breath in her ear, her face on the stone floor, the two of them more ancient because of the Alhambra beyond the window, timeless. Happy to swallow him in, this smooth genie, imagining him her conqueror while at the same time being the filmgoer curious about what the next scene in the movie will bring. She almost knew enough to name it but still woke the next morning inquisitive about life, her cheery guitar next to her in its opened blue plush case, one she loved as it also seemed to promise an interesting future. The gypsy took her to a special tetería where they sat on beaded pillows and he drank Moroccan tea broken only by song when he needed to illustrate a point about love, attachment, loss. What did they talk about? Guitars, his family, I love you so, singing like an animal in full display, throat full, eyes flashing. Midday they went to see his stern aunt rehearsing and there encountered the source of the wobble, the severe mannerism demonstrated by his own romantic uncle. To sing gypsy guitar, you had to hurt and when you hurt most you were to open your mouth wide and let out the longing she had read about, duende another flame over centuries. How good to hurt and know loss, to feel passion-ion-ion, tremble, vibrato, melisma, words that appeared in the girl's head like keepsakes from another realm. There she was deep in the cave with the gypsy family, a dusty moment out of time only she got to applaud since no one had any idea where she was. While no one in the gypsy caves seemed surprised to see her and such lack of surprise almost traveled far enough to create belonging. She had come along, toting her guitar as both a coin of the realm and earnest passport, something they had never seen held by a tourist. The aunt happened to be a beautiful narrow stern bird skilled in fortunetelling. She put her hands on the girl's rib cage and waist to calibrate the instrument: You would be good, she determined. At first the girl thought good at baby production but the aunt knew the question had arisen and spoke over her shoulder. A good dancer, she said dismissively, meaning the girl lagged only a few centuries behind. Was this then the story the girl was in, in which she would learn to be a flamenquera from this stern woman who brooked no fools? Good at dancing and fallen in love? Late afternoon the gypsy brought her to the small blue-painted subterranean room, blue to keep away the evil eye, in which perhaps his mother lived with his older sister and a bunch of children with parentage impossible to align and the gypsy's mother grew keen on telling her all the grimy details of one granddaughter's illness with such compelling force that her eyes barred all new stories. Within such chaos she was capable of fixing on the one tale with its point shriveling away, one the girl felt she almost reached but did not. No es comprensible, she wanted to say, instead saying, yes, claro, I understand. Afterward, along the road back to the gypsy's little cave, he beckoned her to stop at a small counter of a restaurant where they shared a cheese sandwich as if already a couple with life behind and ahead, having shared and continuing to share. He would wear his wifebeater T-shirt, his skin glossy under her fingertips. Later with her useful waist she would dance for his aunt but really for him and on her epitaph you could read about acceptance, belonging, having traveled far from your original ideas. When it came time to pay for the meal, she told the counterboy, another cousin of the gypsy, that it was her gift. As if on cue the gypsy unrolled a song about how he could never thank her for the brightness of her eyes, a song perhaps made up on the spot despite the legacy of the chin wobble. In the full of afternoon they went back to his cave in theory to put her guitar down but more to lie once more on the floor of the cave and spill acrid red wine from a leather bota into their mouths before entangling, rectangles of sun stretched long over skin, his chest almost a smooth boy's though light caught the end of each hair, her foreigner's hand rippling over the brilliance. You will learn guitar well, he said, laughing. Did a bubble of a question start in her throat then? When they were done, she emerged into an unusual hour, everything lit from within, little fairy lights popping on, strung up outside the white-plastered cave doors facing the Alhambra, the palace tucked into its hillside just as they were tucked into theirs, with everyone along the gypsies' winding cobblestoned road up the mountain knowing flamenco was good business. Produce romance for people and they get happy, said her gypsy, plus they pay more. Every little cave they passed had candlelit tables for two. Candles are important! he started to sing, hand on the back of her neck where only an hour earlier he had been holding her down. Now she knew he was making everything up in the received mode, his family singing him as it had sung for generations while she felt so moorless. As the sun sank behind the Alhambra, the tourists started to rise in an obedient swell, twos, fours, family units up into the arc of romance, craning their necks, and through their eyes she saw the charm of the day lit up almost too garishly, the glowing white of the caves and she in it with them, able to see what the tourists saw as much as what the gypsies did, the double frame giving her courage less about some story and more about this life of hers at this center, not skulking to the fringe of things, this knowledge being what she might claim. All this had happened in little more than a day. Her insides sore but in a good way, the tiredness under her eyes carrying everyone else's reportage but she no longer had to tote around the contours of herself. The gift the gypsy had given her was dissolving a bit and she wished to help the cause of dissolution by welcoming the craning tourists into the aunt's cave while standing aside so as not to take a seat from paying customers while the stern bird began her dance, heels tatting the pulse while the tragic face twisted to tell of horror, loss, and union so doomed you too lived at the molten core. The gypsy played with his uncle and because this time the uncle gave his all, the gypsy did too, fusing in music so that the tourists shivered in the cave because they too lived at the heart of experience, Spain, the Roma. After, she helped fold seats and then went back to a different uncle of the gypsy's and until late, for free, for no other outsider but her, bands of gypsies drank and sang, making ribald, inclusive comments that named her almost an honorary man due to foreigner status, one of few women in that room, so many rough hands placed over hers to teach her guitar, because she was the ilk of girl who was going to learn flamenco guitar. The next morning by some arrangement she did not quite understand they went to some other uncle's cave, bigger and better whitewashed, where the uncle told her he was the last of a rare kind of fortuneteller while her gypsy stood by. The uncle explained that he needed to look right below her breasts to determine her fortune and because she was so very much mid-experience she lay on the table, shirt off, letting the uncle tell her fortune from small invisible marks he could ascertain only if he got close enough to either kiss or scrutinize her skin, all while her gypsy stood looking out the door with his face telegraphing an important errand he had almost forgotten and in this the question in her throat grew, she wanted to ask something but had no clue how to form it.

Once the fortunetelling session was over, they stopped by his mother's, who reminded her of the sick granddaughter and how the illness progressed after which her gypsy suggested they go get coffee in the square where she ran into a friend from school named Lincoln and his new French girlfriend, Nathalie. Because they invited her with them to the beach somewhere for a day or two, she made apologies to her gypsy because she needed to think and gathered her backpack from the hostel's locker since despite his singing entreaties she had not fully decided to go on living with him. And so she went with Lincoln and Nathalie to stay in their tent on a beach and at night shifted her attention from the massive caterpillar heave of their sleeping bag or how unequal the two of them were, Lincoln less besotted with Nathalie than she herself was when surely Nathalie deserved better. Why had they asked her along after all? The triangle confused since by day she loved Nathalie's broad-cheeked wistful charm, so bruised and Gallic, all of them rumpled and the two girls buying eternal friendship bracelets from someone on the beach but after a couple of days of sandy headstands, fish dinners, and talks containing the magic of the future in which they would never again meet, she said goodbye and headed back, feeling herself wise and weary on the train to Granada. In the main café in town she ran into her gypsy, handsome and magically wearing a green bright buttondown shirt she thought she had lost in her hostel. Maybe she had left it at the cave? All he kept saying with a kind of force was: Did you not bring me anything from your trip? How could you not bring me anything? Gone were the songs and the wobble. In that second she may have understood him saying that her main failure was that she had not yet given his mother money for the sick grandkid. Understanding that for him she may have been something just a bit more or less than a walking dollar sign. Whatever he had professed before, during, or after lay intimately close to a performance of feeling. I cannot let you go-o-o. She had windmilled into his story in which feeling was king. Would it matter that she had been set in his midst? After her, would there not be other travelers, toting their guitars, waists, hunger? After he left, she stayed in the café, mournful. A drummer she had seen in a circle, a drummer from Sierra Leone named Prince, came up to ask why so sad? And she told him and watched his moonlit drum circle that night before going to stay on his floor where she pretended to sleep when he began to touch her bent elbow after which she became the one living with him, eating peanut sauce with rice, the hands of all his friends also dipping into the one bowl. The drummer played bass guitar, a simple unskilled stuttered reggae one-two, but really loved drumming more and said he wanted to marry her which seemed a plausible version until the day she took him to the doctor for his cough and there in the waiting room he told her that he always thought the children of a blonde woman and a black man were the most beautiful so that she saw he lived in a saga with little to do with her and so returned to Connecticut where at the post office she kept getting letters saying I want to come, I really want to marry you but did not keep up correspondence because too easily she recognized the particular American fairy tale the drummer wanted to live. And when years later her children called to her from down-stairs, in another story she probably failed to recognize, a heated moment of dissatisfaction, she came across these yearning letters nestled into the blue plush case with the guitar long since broken, the blue still so untouched and bright, something you might pet to see the fur angle to catch the light, and considered what yarn she might be able to spin for those children about the great and almighty Alhambra or the song of the gypsies but then realized, too, she had never once seen the Alhambra from the inside and anyway would whatever tale she might be able to summon ever count as anyone's idea of a gift?

Six Poems
Eleni Sikelianos

I shall do nothing fancy

to make myself happy. Help!

I dwell here because I do not dwell

among the dead. But sunlight

is lethal to some

and to make themselves happy

they did things fancy like fashion

a goddess's golden hair. Shall I

make a golden ring that replicates itself or build a golden

hour from which is banished grief to

make the hour so roundly happy? Some will bind

themselves in beautiful things and some

in chains to

make yourself happy. Some made a fetter from:

      —the sound of a cat's footfall

      —the beard of a woman

      —roots of a mountain

      —sinews of a bear

Eleni Sikelianos

—breath of a fish

—spittle of a bird

but what kind of beard?

Name your fetter   name it *Gleipnir*

(a manacle as smooth and soft as a silken ribbon)

call it the wolf-joint   or call it the wrist, it is

where the wolf or the world will bite.

(put your hand in its mouth as a pledge)

Now *how will you settle an argument* with only one hand?

wrist   wreathe   wrest   writhe   wr—to twist

the human mouth makes the movement-sounds

twisting out of the bindings

twisting away from how

make yourself happy moving

freely toward the experimental sky

and language the false start to love is

*

JUAN, JUAN ET SU FILS? said the dream.

Have a drink in the ancient Roman light which flares

on the strange American faces

on the airport train. Juan, Juan, my

countrymen and women, no offense but

how did you get so

fat

gray

badly cut

unread

small eyed

woolen

while I was away? I was gone and when I came back

you'd voted for the wrong politicians! So many men!

Had I slept for five minutes and found you

on the subway saying all the wrong things or

in the meadow to the starlings?

You'll feel like the waist of an otter in the teeth of a tiger and wonder

how hell is dressed with poorly—

how it's haunted by badly pissed-off persons or people

These people, for example, forgetting

to make themselves happy

built the entryway but forgot to build the building

Eleni Sikelianos

used up all the wood & coal & sky & ice & light

Now ¿*Donde viveremos?*

*

ESSAY: HAPPY BRAIN

See the center flower

of the brain happy   See it

sliced happy happy

hippocampus happy anterior cingulate cortex What

happens in a labyrinth happens

because the brain unspools its

stiffening threads like copper wires untightening from

the trouble spot   happy *nucleus accumbens* happy *insula*

                    Dura mater, hard

mother, peel back to reveal

what   without my fist in its mouth   makes

the brain so happy   A wolf

if sighted now would make

me happy [*Her and the others of her kind . . . running in the whiteness*

of that high world] but not when wolf

was like a well where we threw

ourselves in fear   Sometimes still

fear struck (mountain lion when I walk) (being eaten)   (my
  amygdalae firing:

               chaos war

    the wheel-crushing

    world or

    the way a word can hover in its surroundings between sense
      and sorrow

                          narrow sound shivering

    as if the world itself rushed in decay toward that trembling

if the world could stabilize   the word could   or if the word no
  longer feeling

the world   went mindblind   Yet   How sad a
  wieldy word

under dominion which is where we seem

so often to like it   lick it

and it goes dry, a little button

of control pleasure   happy

nipple-word   made to militarize

My father kept pushing the lever, the

pleasure center lever, my brother

kept pushing the lever, my

friends   was it

desire or pleasure

wanting or liking? Now

he's dead, my

dad.

http://blogs.du.edu/today/news/seeking-happiness-could-make-
   individuals-depressed-2

Some women brought the domestic

into the poem like you would bring a blade of wheat to a field of
   grass It went

feral & changed it (the field) without

domesticating the field itself and

makes me crazy with happiness

Take this happiness test. Are you kind

to monkeys, to rats? Let's slice some

to find out. The mind, said the Dalai Lama

is trouble.

Like when I was walking around the hills, and looked

into the big brown cow's big eyes I thought

I was diving into a gentle loving pond on a

warm brown day. Then I was walking,

walking for hours looking, thinking

thinking STEAK. Not thinking

Happiness

Factors of No. 57. What makes a cow happy makes me

hungry. In the cabin, I kill

the fly.

"I'm happy I read this book!!" (Amazon review: *The Science of Happiness*)

the Hungarian professor with the unapproachable name says be *in the flow* or *zone* to

make you happy. You do this by concentration, with mirrors and music and maps. With no self-consciousness.

Do not think of the 43 million orphans in Africa, Syria, the 250,000 child soldiers

Do not   not think

the what self in face of the other exchanges toward

Eleni Sikelianos

       pain (knowledge) &

       pleasure (knowledge)

"climbing from the love of one person to the love of two"

and also shamelessly the accessible sky

forthright, untied

And a little ringlet at the back of the head can

          elaborate

          on a curve which pleases

     the ear or the eye inside the

arc (the face)   A straight line like

a horizon may also do it but

could terrify too. Could hurt

each tooth to the left when

facing the face. Earlier

I was feeling the hot sun on

my right hand while

driving it was

making myself happy—a pool of warmth in the webbing between
    thumb and index like a Bermuda of pleasure that spread to the
    whole machine—but

worried

about liver spots—as if

that organ could rise

to the surface

of the body and kiss

the world hello so

happily   to see it

after too long in our

darks / out / our

depths

*

Test the "happiness factor" of any action

1. Intensity: How strong is the pleasure?
2. Duration: How long will the pleasure last?
3. Certainty or uncertainty: How likely or unlikely is it that the
   pleasure will occur?
4. Propinquity or remoteness: How soon will the pleasure occur?
5. Fecundity: The probability that the action will be followed by
       sensations of the same kind.
6. Purity: The probability that it will not be followed by sensations
       of the opposite kind.
7. Extent: How many people will be affected?

How does this allow for lynching a man to make the crowd happy?

*

HOW HAPPY is the leaf, the

lamb the deaf

ear at the mirror

*

I WISH YOU a tidy sum of pleasures

say, the syllables of a wolf and their continentally changing vowel and
   stress; such treasures—

   but how should we distribute them   across the days?

            as an army of   armadillos   tumbling

            in sunlight   ten thousand

happinesses pluraled up heaped and wait   upon you   *the surplus*

when the total of pain is subtracted   *from pleasure* (Bain)

the wery hunter to fynd his happy prey   OR   *Any happy concourse*
   of Atoms

He . . . Weenes yet at last to make a happie hande By bloudie warre
   (Gascoigne)

Eleni Sikelianos

in the felled light   find you

the happy set of liberty, plenty, and letters (Middleton)

Hip me how.   Harmony me

bouncing in the noontime

swoon

when sun

won

all we ever wanted to win honey

suspended in the aspirated day honey   Have we achieved

      the greatest happiness of the greatest number (Hutcheson)
      the exultant position of the

                        new lover

on the hook of the h just as it leaves the body

    Ha

Ha

       coughs it

      laughs it

         ha

ppy

       and so

Eleni Sikelianos

you happy

round as a berry

or a bug

the color happy

hanging on a branch

in blue

you

haul happy around

like a log

Wounded Room
Gwyneth Merner

1.

AT LAST BOWED INTO VINYL SAG, steady cranking, incremental tilt of dentist's aged examination chair, the patient's eyes listed. Above him the attic ceiling slope adorned: a portrait boy, small as a postcard and copper framed. Such a perfect, spherical head against a square of black. A brooch-wearing little lord, ermine-cloaked overlooker with benign features. Does his content smile bend for gems, his strands of pearls? No, that's not it. A little egg of a boy, centered just so, to sway the patient—ignore the trilling tooth, the drill's burr, the metal hook, the dentist's index finger, coated in a bittersweet latex powder. Reflect on roundness and something princely: an ebony recorder on a velvet cushion, a toy drum with a leopard-skin strap, a croaking frog inside a silver-filigree cage.

The patient lifted his head and the dentist alligator-clipped a dimpled paper bib around his neck. He untangled cold bib chain from a curl of gray nape hair and asked the dentist if the portrait on the ceiling bothered him.

"Though I share the office with three others, the portrait was my addition," said the dentist. "He's my patron saint: the young tsar, Peter the Great. I am intimate with his expression, and mean for my patients to commit it to memory." The dentist rolled toward the patient on his white plastic stool. The patient could still see the dark shape of the dentist's mustache beneath the teal mask.

"You may have heard some awful things about Peter the Great. He was an amateur dentist and hardly reformed a young discipline, thoroughly barbaric." The dentist paused and probed the stub of the patient's buckled molar with a blunt tool. A whimper. The pain unraveled down from the tooth through his jaw; it was sewn in under his right collarbone, gathered up and billowed at the hair of his armpit. The dentist sighed.

"His mentor was the consummate anatomist Frederik Ruysch. Together, they started with rotten teeth—pulled them from the mouths of the tsar's servants and advisers with an iron tooth key, the grip of carved ivory ornamented with a bar of mother-of-pearl. In his journals, the tsar said his mentor extolled his gentleness and the smooth and quick grace of his extractions."

The patient lifted his hands off his thighs and waved them. He tried to speak of his discomfort over the hiss of the suction tube and the precise clicking of the pick on his undamaged teeth. The dentist set down his tools.

"Please." He pushed the patient's hands down. "I want you to appreciate what I'm telling you. It's appropriate to your condition, that molar I cannot save."

The tsar, the dentist explained, honed his art in the depleted mouths of his adversaries. Each man was meant to understand the tsar's mercy as he screamed and spat blood into a pewter goblet. His allies lost healthy teeth too, but with the succor of opiates. The teeth the tsar took—he studied them carefully. He called them the seeds of the new empire.

The dentist rubbed a bitter numbing gel on the inflamed gum of the patient's injured tooth—the crown lost when the patient was felled by heatstroke. The patient's tongue folded away from the taste. A pretty arc of saliva; it issued from the underside of his tongue and onto the dentist's white sleeve.

"I have something; it will help me administer the anesthetic."

The dentist opened a drawer and placed heavy padded headphones over the patient's ears, the coiled cord stretching taut. No music, not a sound. When the dentist spoke again, his voice was undampened by mask and headphones.

"Imagine a room piled high with burlap sacks. Mounds of teeth, a treasury of teeth. Peter the Great kept his favorites in specimen drawers, each tooth tied to each neighbor with a pale blue satin ribbon."

The dentist claimed he had seen them during a pilgrimage to the tsar's Kunstkamera. An incisor of pure white with dark amber roots, a black tooth shaped like the head of a horned devil, a piteously small molar from a deceased child, a heart-shaped premolar from a cousin the tsar wished to marry. The voice, parted between padded foam and covered mouth, puckered chorally.

The patient felt a dissociative pain: a ticklish, malformed channel he could not follow from jaw to heel. This procedure, this dentist— he did not understand what the man wanted beyond uprooting the tooth. Ceilingward, he sought in the face of the child tsar some split, some ill fold or misalignment. Nothing. He cupped one hand against the other hand. Unseen weight touched his palms: a cold pear shape.

2.

The wounded room, a seed bank, has a doorway, four walls, and a ceiling of comforting height. The room is storage, the visitor is storage, and the ceiling, lenient to the state of accumulation, retreats imperceptibly. A man could be said to be a seed; a woman a seed. But a man and a woman are not the seeds they want.

Where is the seed? They say the one they want does not yet exist. A seed may come when the visitor yields to the room.

They want the visitor—a woman, or sometimes a man—to sit and wait. The floor is best. It has recently been refinished and polish shines on the narrow planks. They would like the visitor to touch the planks and admire the texture. Is it not soft? A superior floor, a floor sanded by hand, is neither overwaxed nor perfect plane; the fingers and the soles of the feet detect subtle ridges, the old scratches, the character of the wood.

Uncountable interiors contain one wounded room, sometimes more. Does it come as a surprise that the wounded room is common? No primed space alone will produce a seed. A wounded room requires a visitor and witness—an uncommon meeting. They keep a large map with pins in it—black-headed pins for wounded rooms, blue-headed pins for the visitor—and on idle evenings, emptied of pins, the sheet of worn paper manifests a network of small cavities. They wish for more success but have grown circumspect.

They would like the visitor to sit comfortably, but not to feel at home. The last seed surfaced in a wounded room without a visitor, observed by a witness in her kitchen. Did she feel like a guest in her own home? It is a rarity, rare as a seed. Will the seed be fruitful? Will the seed mature into a bell? They do not know. I think they are scared to plant it, fearful that it will push from the earth unsound.

The room where they store the rare seed is off-limits to visitors and witnesses. It is no longer a wounded room. From the outside, the room has a blue-trimmed window with darkly stained wooden shutters. On the inside, the window has been secreted behind plaster and new paint. Someone has hung a handsome old mirror edged in gilt-carved acorns. Tell me, what good ever comes from an obstruction?

3.

His climbing lines dangle. An inventory of knots: sliding knots, anchoring knots. In his harness, Eric's knots and carabiners suspend him high in the barbered crown of the old ginkgo. The botanical garden officials have ordered this removal; they cite stinking fruit, branches that fall dangerously close to joggers when winds are forceful. He used spurs and a lanyard for his ascent, unafraid of scarring a tree he would topple by the end of the day.

A survey from above: An ambulance idles in the shade of a cypress copse. Eric can tell the paramedic is eating lunch, hands and mouth moving. A sandwich in front of the air-conditioning vent, so lucky to be insulated from the sickly heat. He doesn't like the term "tree surgeon," but it strikes him now that he and the paramedic share certain commitments, responding to what in these temperatures the forecasters call vulnerable.

He lowers his chain saw into a branch thick as his own body, and buries the dry earthworms, plum skinned on the sidewalk, in a spray of sawdust. The branch and trunk uncouple and brown-cankered leaves thrash the ground in the yellow-taped perimeter. He releases the stilled chain saw at his side and it sways heavy on a neon strap. A mouthy rot at the core of the bough—it could fit his arm up to the shoulder. When he touches the ragged rim of the hole expecting sap, he feels clammy moisture, not tacky at all. A fibril extends down the hole. A parasite's roots? No, it looks like pale green twine. One frayed end knotted around a recessed peg. Impossible. He lifts the cord, feels a weight bob, hears the thing at the end of the line bump the interior of the tree. His body is rigid in his harness. Sweat seeps from his forehead to the bridge of his nose and he swats, knocking his safety glasses to the ground. The two lines twist.

After stillness, another attempt: He pulls the cord from the peg and gathers the slack, wrapping it around his fist. He knows so intimately the malignancies of trees, damages from pests. The ginkgo resists them all. What he draws from the heartwood hole does not look like any scourge. It is a slick-brown buoy, O-ring and all. Eric tips it carefully; the ball has a slit, an aperture into a hollow space. Bell, he says. A tree with a shaft for a ceramic sleigh bell.

He cannot shake the bell. It would be sinful; it would be a crime. But if he did, the sound of the bell would be flawless. It would sound from the center of certainty. Feeling unsteady, unworthy, he dampens the bell under his shirt against his chest.

4.

Once, during his youth, Peter the Great removed an abscessed tooth from a woodsman. In gratitude, the woodsman said that he would cut down the greatest larch in the forest near his village. I will send the timber to a craftsman, and he will make you a throne that will honor your skill, said the woodsman. I have a throne, said Peter the Great. But I do need a fine cabinet to house my collections from my travels abroad.

The woodsman found a suitable tree in early autumn, the time of year when his incessant work shrunk the fat of his thick skin, obliged his bones to suffer the cold. It took fourteen days to fell the larch, though the woodsman, roiled by his labors, did not notice the time. Whenever he paused to rest his hands and remove his rabbit-fur gloves, he put his tongue in the gap where he had once possessed a blackened canine. Oh! he said. He couldn't think of the proper words with which to praise the slippery vault.

After the larch groaned and tipped to beat the earth with splintered weight, the woodsman hired a team of twenty horses to drag the trunk along the soggy road to the village. A superstitious man, the woodsman remained in the forest to perform a rite his mother had taught him: If you cut down a great tree, burn the stump and bury a silver coin six arms' lengths beneath the ashes. When the hole was deep and the dirt and ash heaped high, his spade resounded against something hard. It might not be a rock, thought the woodsman. He parted roots gently, dug with his hands so he wouldn't harm what he couldn't see. Uncovered, a head-sized bronze bell, green with age, steamed in a caul of roots.

The woodsman placed the larch bell in a beaver-skin sack and sent it to the court. When the larch cabinet was complete, the topmost compartment was inlaid with lapis lazuli tiles, and the bell was closed within. Peter the Great only heard its peal once; the sound was said to have been so spirited that the tsar writhed in fits of twitching and ecstasy whenever he recalled it.

5.

Acquisitive space, architecture that desires, upsets the mode of how we settle in the personal and find peace in routines. That is how I define the wound. The appellation itself can be traced back to a palimpsest, the Brayer Text, destroyed in the bombardment of Belgrade in

1915. The original language of the Brayer Text was withheld—some claim it was written in Japanese; others, Urdu, perhaps Portuguese— but of three extant translations conducted near the end of the nineteenth century by a sole scholar, only one contains the words "wounded room." *But,* the translator claimed in a sheaf of letters found after his death in a Kentucky sanatorium, *I hadn't endeavored to write three translations in the reading room. There was one translation and two copies. Over time all three shifted, and there are hardly any of my words left in them.* The libraries they keep, some small and packed hastily into a suitcase, fail to persevere. It was at first a painful lesson, the discovery that evidence committed to paper pulped from a bell tree lends itself to addendum, reiterates the scrape erasures of vellum. Now they refrain from claiming authorship over anything. They delight in the contradictions of an over-annotated oral tradition, texts that self-reject.

On infrequent occasions when there is time for the visitor to prepare for the wounded room, for the possibility of a seed, they advise a reading ceremony. The few of us within our small community who joined as visitors and now witness the rite, do so with a joyful ache that transcends jealousy toward the newly initiated.

i.

The virgins dwelled in the virgin-house, across from the unnamed-house, in view of the rot-house, the God-house, the plant-house, and the bell-house at the land edge. Guests of the rot-house carved niches into the cliffs where they placed their stone guardians. The virgins concealed the God-house mirror in the hall of the three devotees: guests of the dead, the virgins, and the marked women. The devotees ate the food of God with their eyes. Hungered during the rot-house season, the marked women entered the bell-house to eat the striking sound with their ears. Cry out, divorce-bell, cry out. And so on the cold days, a marked woman would depart the bell-house a dutiful virgin.

ii.

Listen to the fire within the old house, the heat-split log and smoke. In two cloisters by the sea lived the nuns and the marriage-traitors. They prayed to the Almighty, carved tokens for their ancestors, and housed the first mouth of sound. The second mouth of sound opened silently under a net of raw silk in the recess. The second mouth of sound reflected the faces of piety, the faces of grief, and the faces of supplication. Hungry, the second mouth of sound ate yielding bright meals: abalone, dried persimmon, boiled egg. When the seasons lapsed and the plants vanished under the earth to greet the dead, the first mouth of sound required a word: This word was severance. The marriage-traitors swung a knocker on four ropes to hit the first mouth of sound. The things that needed to be severed were severed. The things that needed to be loosened were set loose.

iii.

Expectant, the shell scraper wed a virgin, impatient to secure strong sons. But she brought emptiness into his home, a broken bell between her legs. He took his wife to the old persimmon woman for a remedy. The persimmon woman said no good, and gave the lack a name. Affronted, he left the lack and his wife with the persimmon woman. But the old woman had tricked the shell scraper. Your bell, said the persimmon woman, is not broken. Your fearsome children refuse to leave the wounded room; they do not wish to be animals. A bell like yours rings with an unseen flame. To release your children it must be extinguished. The persimmon woman sacrificed a small tortoise. She stripped the shell from the body and filled it with the animal's blood. The abandoned woman kneeled with the tortoise shell beneath her bell for five days and five nights, until the blood offering reached her children in the wounded room. I am not allowed to tell you what they have become, but know that your children are sorry they have made you a solitary, said the persimmon woman. They want you to have a gift. The solitary took a hand mirror from the persimmon woman. She followed mirror rules: to keep it covered, to never let another person see it. And if she looked into it, what ceaseless pleasure: to see the immaculate room never inhabited by a person. And if she broke it, the everlasting wrath of her children forced into blood and limbs.

6.

It's getting dark. The sky reminds Eric of a lurid scrape, oily abalone sheen. Yellow leaves spin as they drop from the ginkgo. Descending is simple, precautions automatic; the repetitions of his long career have engendered refinement and fluid speed. This dread, the urge to remove the bell from his shirt shake it until it's only a fistful of sand, sucking his sandy fingers, it burdens him. The cicadas click, detect some long-lost radiation. Feeling for the phantom weight of his safety glasses, he touches the bridge of his nose, presses the oily indentations left by the pads. This could be the last climb. Why work well through retirement when he ruins the things he touches? All the trees he has nursed toward health have lapsed into rot.

His ruined daughter—she could have been his apprentice, she could have scaled a lightning-scarred silver maple, chain saw over one shoulder, her gloves shedding leather dust against the friction of the ropes, the knots. She could have found the bell before he did. You won't believe what I found, he hears her say. But she was younger the last time they spoke—he doesn't know what her voice sounds like now. The voice he hears in his mind is the one she had as a small girl, when she said she wanted to be an arborist. But he raised his daughter with lopsided discipline. She took his money but did not spend it on her courses, her licensing fees. Her temper had been violent, her longings addled. She lived capably as a parasite.

7.

Unofficially, the Svalbard Global Seed Vault in Norway claims to have a bell seed. Similar in shape, they determined it to be the 130-year-old dried uvula of a New Guinea Singing Dog. A bell seed, even after centuries of storage, should be fresh and green with a nap like suede.

They think there is a cycle at work. A wounded room was not always required for the birth of a seed. Seeds were once unexceptional—every tree produced at least one. But we collect in a different cycle now, one of uncertain duration. In North America, the last tree to produce a bell seed naturally was an oak in central Kansas. Settlers cut down the tree in 1856 to build a barn for a dairy. The patriarch of the family discovered a crystal bell within a split log. He told his wife that when he held it up to the light the clapper clouded. The bell hardly had a voice. Its tongue fractured midpeal with a light tilt of the dairyman's wrist. All the trees in the hilly region died that summer, collapsing into mealy heaps.

Wood-poor, the homesteaders learned to quarry soft yellow limestone for bricks and fence posts. They had to remove the soil first—three feet in most places—then let the exposed rock harden in the sun before drilling with augers and splitting slabs with hammered spikes. Commonly, whenever the masons discerned the grooves of a seashell or fish bones in the rock, they turned the fossil plane to the interior of the room. They believed in the great flood; they were grateful for this proof of the transience of their earthly lives.

8.

The roof of her home burned and the flames surpassed the electric poles. Strange how even a fire so large could flicker like one harnessed to a hearth. They saw the path of embers move south on the wind. The transformer exploded. The heat and pressure of the fire caused the double-glazed windows to flex in and out, to crack. The women of the block, waking to smoke and an air-raid siren, pulled their hair and wailed with tears in their eyes.

A man at the end of the block yelled: *Where are you? Where are you?* A dog barked and another dog replied.

They observed her as she watched her bedroom burn. She had been coughing from a curb out front, but then she became aware that she was coughing. She hushed, stood erect, and held the rattle inside her lungs. It wasn't quite a test or a firm longing but what she had initiated in the bedroom, accelerant sprinkled in circles on the stained bare mattress, her unwashed clothes, offered her proof of what was essential. When the smoke turned intolerable, it came down to her body—was it anything she needed? Her body fought for itself, thoughts trailing calm, both crawling under the smoke until it sucked under the door jam. She opened the bedroom door with a balled T-shirt over a burning knob, edged down the painted stairs, knee skin sticking to heat-warped pigment.

As a young girl, before her father moved their household from California east to the edge of the Mississippi, she had watched him remove a walnut orchard somewhere in the San Joaquin Valley. He told her they were grafted trees, 150 years old, black walnut trunks with white walnut crowns. Nurseries now supply hearty white walnut rootstock—a smaller, more productive tree that can be replaced every fifteen to twenty years. There's value in the old trees, he told her, the fine burl, a rare and chaotic knit between the white walnut and the black walnut. The burl can be sold for gunstock, for wood inlays in luxury cars.

She waited in the truck with the windows rolled down. Her father drove a backhoe with a forklift prong instead of a shovel. He thrust the ends into the dirt and pried at the roots of a tree. The engine strained, the roots clenched the dirt. And then a thundering that shook the car. The dark green of the mossy bark met the light green of the mowed grass. Now she could see the foothills in the distance. In the winter the orchard owner's house would have a new view of snow-capped mountains.

Two more trees fell. An elderly woman stepped into the carport, tidied white hair sweat-messed on the back of her head with a red comb. She approached the truck window with a can of lime soda. "Already October and still so hot," the orchard owner said. "Your father will be done with it all soon."

The girl took the soda, said thank you as her father always instructed, and wiped dirt out of the rim of the can with the edge of her T-shirt. They heard gun blasts in the distance.

"They're hunting doves in the cherry orchard. Those are short trees, they don't offer much coverage. When my trees are gone, where will they all hide now?" The orchard owner was crying. Her wet eyelashes moved like silver spider legs.

The sides of the soda can warmed in the girl's hands. What would the cooked meat look like, all that plucked gray down? A wind picked up and clattered the orchard woman's chimes, irrigation pipe and useless keys on fishing line. So often she felt muted; she was not fearful or sentimental to the mechanics of extinguishing the organic.

9.

The international prototype of the kilogram, the Kilogram of the Archives, is in the custody of the International Bureau of Weights and Measures in Sèvres, France. It is a small platinum cylinder fabricated in 1799 to represent, as close as was feasible at the time, the mass of one cubic decimeter of water at 4°C.

The Kilogram of the Archives is kept in a monitored safe within a basement vault of the Pavillon de Breteuil. Stored under three bell jars, the unit of measure has nevertheless been gaining mass, absorbing contaminants through the air. These contaminants may be removed through a careful cleaning process: first a cloud of steam, then a chamois soaked in ethanol and ether. The metrologist must have a steady hand, the circular strokes neither too hard nor too soft.

Curiously, the Kilogram of the Archives has lost mass in relation to its official copies, the siblings in other nations, since its ratification as an official unit of measure in 1889. Physicists cannot attribute this divergence to any official cause.

But consider the soft contact between a felted mallet and the second, middle bell jar around the prototype—a bell of remarkable sonority, a bell that can destabilize the weight of all things.

10.

Eric takes the bell out of his shirt and unwinds the fibril. He swings it back and forth over the dark sidewalk and the severed branches. Near silence: his own breath and the strained ropes.

Heat in his cheeks, diagonal pain in his chest. Warm, sweet-tasting blood pools in his mouth. He spits onto the sidewalk, hears a light tap. Tongue tip to the back of his mouth locates a tooth opened up, silver crown displaced, the pink branches of a nerve tolling.

11.

A wounded room could yield a seed, a seed planted in the roots of a dogwood or European beech. The roots and fungal colonies nourish the seed, prompt it to flare and open over a mouthful of dirt. This is the fertile bell they desire, a bell anchored in the earth. Still, they collect seeds of the volatile bells, the ones that climb through the tree and devour its heartwood. The prevailing belief is that the blemished seeds, the ones marked disharmonious, will one day produce a clement bell with a tone to pacify, the bell to proliferate the root bell. It is a notional sowing season.

It is a shame to salt these seeds away, to hesitate before an experiment to classify and study all manner of sound: a barnacled bell in a shipwreck, current stirred; a bell too large for any belfry, improperly tuned and melted down for cannonballs and bayonets; a bell to call a discreet servant; a bell to invite the concern of the dead; a bell to poison and ward off poison; the bell to recall natal memories; the small bell that stirs earth, agitates its fissures; the bell to awaken absent senses; the wheel of bells that gave the sea its masterful milling, waves that worked away at the battlefield bones until it was beach.

12.

I told her to braid her hair, because it looked dirty and smelled like a campfire. I told her how to be comfortable, how to sit so that her legs wouldn't go to sleep. I gave her two wooden boxes and told her that there were symptoms, that she couldn't open the boxes until she felt them.

You should feel a vibration, I told her. It's not like tingling; it is subtler than that. There is nothing in the room that could exhibit shaking, to tell you it's not your body, but you will look anyway. You will feel warm but you won't sweat. You'll blink hard and rapidly. You should see bright spots. Don't rub your eyes, it will only make your tears sting. There will be something brittle and coercive under your tongue. Don't move it. Let it dissolve.

She performed with rigidity. She gagged near the end. When she opened it, the box to her right contained an oily terra-cotta bell. Within the box on her left, an unusual molar—its crown open, its roots looped into a ring—it could have been a bell too, an ivory miniature. With effort and her thin fingers manipulating the angles, she pushed the hollow tooth into the slot of the bell. The silence: a mouth undone with awe.

September

Michael Sheehan

. . . it was, yes, September, but very dull, overcast,
towards the end, already it was autumn.

—B. S. Johnson

SEPTEMBER 3

AT FIRST WE THOUGHT maybe it was some kind of avian flu. The numbers of birds that had died in the three-month period leading up to that morning were staggering. Globally, this was the case. Various causes were put forth and invariably shot down. The metaphor was often posed that the dying of the birds was a "canary in a mine." However, that which was to be heralded, augured by the dying birds, was not made clear, nor further was the reason behind their dying— the depletion of our ozone? global warming? mass pollutants? The appearance of a dead bird on our lawns, on our streets, in parks, and along city sidewalks had come to be commonplace. Like anything else, the degree to which seeing a dead bird alarmed us began to dissipate as the regularity of seeing a dead bird increased. Nonetheless, we remained unprepared for the images of that morning. To watch a bird fall—spiraling like those bi-winged seed pods we used to spin as children, toss and watch flutter to the ground at our feet—as though it had been plucked from the sky by the buckshot of some skillful or lucky hunter, and to know the cause was nothing so available, so palpable as that, is to witness something earth-shatteringly, bowel-tighteningly impossible and yet real; it is to witness something invisible interacting with the real world. As though the bird—a seagull, say, or a sparrow—had hit some sort of invisible wall—as often we'd seen birds fly into large panes of glass, unknowing even in death that they themselves caused it—an invisible wall somewhere impossibly afloat in the sky itself. Then the bird would fall, already dead, and we would bear witness over and over again to its falling. Birds would thud car hoods, crack windshields, dent roofs. They would litter lawns, and shatter home windows. They would stop traffic for miles on interstates. A state of emergency was called in many cities, as it

225

was considered unsafe to go outside; this was initially justified as a precaution (falling birds—no matter how slight—could seriously injure or even kill anyone unlucky enough to be standing beneath their line of descent), but was later clarified to include the possibility of some form of unknown, advanced-stage, and very severe avian flu or airborne disease that was, in being completely mysterious, uncertain as to the risk potential for humans. We watched then that day from our windows, as hundreds of birds fell from the sky—more birds than we would ever have thought to exist, let alone be flying above us— and we wondered aloud, *What could cause this?*

OCTOBER 3, 1983

Glenn Friptch sits cross-legged. When Glenn Friptch—whose last name is considered almost unpronounceable by his friends—drinks from his Pepsi can, he more or less inhales the Pepsi. His nails are nervously bitten and his cuticles red, raw, and sore looking. When Glenn Friptch—who goes by G.P. (the latter letter for no clear reason, though perhaps because of the aberrant *p* in an otherwise straightforward appellative spelling) due to the above-mentioned unpronounceability—inhales the joint being passed around, he does so with his eyes open; actually, he widens his eyes as he inhales, as though either to truly savor every last fleck of flavor of the smoke as it fills his mouth, every last molecule of THC, or as though to ensure he never for even a second takes his eyes off the game board before him on the floor and the Others who sit either likewise cross-legged or who kneel on legs folded beneath them, awaiting their turns and the joint's passage around the four poles of the game board they occupy.

The Game is Civilization, and the four players are G.P., Dimley Scarton, Hegda Toryeakevic (pronounced *-itch*), and Walf Gæmis. They are sitting in various positions in the basement of G.P.'s parents' suburban home ten minutes outside Scranton, Pennsylvania. This game of Civ has taken, so far, exactly eighteen hours, nineteen minutes, and thirty-one seconds, as G.P. blows smoke exaggeratedly across the board, never for even an instant taking his eyes away from the situation right there in front of him. How Civ is played is each player gets seven thousand people and a nascent nation around the Mediterranean and must then grow his or her nation-state realistically through time. The goal is "to be able to advance to final age on the Archaeological Succession Table (AST)," which is to say to last long enough to be remembered. G.P. et al have played Civ now thirty-three times since it was received by G.P. for Christmas in 1982, never lasting longer than approximately eleven hours—on average, the game takes them eight hours (from setup to finish); the box says the game takes anywhere from three to twelve hours.

G.P., Walf, and Dimley are all seventeen years old; Hegda alone is sixteen. Though Hegda is the sole female in an otherwise very male group, there is no apparent sexual tension or even awareness. This is likely due both to the underdeveloped sexual awareness of the three males playing and to Hegda's unprepossessing features. At the moment Hegda's features are offset and not exactly enhanced but certainly exaggerated by a red, scratchy irritation of her eyes, rimming both and welling up tears periodically in the corners of them (which have a tendency to drift toward each other, the eyes, toward the bridge of her nose, not crossing exactly, but basically crossing), due to both the many hours awake and the smoke from the joint, of which Hegda does not partake.

The four players have been slowly maneuvering through the most complicated version of the game they have ever played; the complications arose via intention and accident; intentional complications arose from the introduction by the four players of a consideration of God and the metaphysical, as well as a further consideration of what they understand of metahistorical principles about the waxing and waning of actual civilizations; this was accomplished by augmenting the game's cards with their own crudely drawn-up cards (scraps of computer paper) meant to catalog a) divine intervention of a number of sorts, or the outlook of God over the affairs of Man, which cards were created by Hegda, b) a consideration of chance occurrences and of the forces that cause events to happen, all put forth by Dimley (who decorated each of the cards' backsides with Hamlet's *There are more things in heaven and earth than are dreamt of in your philosophy*), and c) happenings within the "laws" of civilization as defined by history—viz., attacks from without, pressures from within, corruption, bad leadership, aggression, tyranny, popular moral degeneration, and so on, which cards were created by G.P.; the accidental complications arose from actually implementing these cards in the game, which was meant to be overseen by Walf, but was sort of agreed upon by all to be done by the chance rolling of dice at various stages of the game, and an elaborate system of correspondence was created to sync the cards with the numbers on the twin dice, all while Walf waited, uncertain the role he would play in this new configuration of the game, given that he did not contribute cards and was no longer the "master" of these meta elements, but was now merely—as were the others—a slave to blind chance, without (however) the agency to have introduced or decided upon any of the events of chance. This was the first of Walf's unhappinesses.

G.P., passing the joint to Dimley, now took a further inhale of his Pepsi, crumpling the can a little in his exuberance. None of the four had slept during these eighteen hours, nor had any official break been allowed. Bathroom breaks were grouped and termed "intermissions" and occurred once every three hours. Four cans of Pepsi remained, as did four individually wrapped slices of Kraft American cheese, and a further four Twinkies. These snacks were rationed by G.P., as it was his house and his parents who provided. The second of Walf's unhappinesses came when he submitted that he should oversee the rationing of the snacks, given that he had little else to do. G.P.'s refusal—based on the prenominate proprietary rights—and its subsequent seconding and thirding by Hegda and Dimley introduced a new element into the game, though none was yet aware of it.

SEPTEMBER 19, 1985

Though her name might itself seem some cultural holdover from someplace distant or, even worse, some sort of bad joke, her features bear it out sweetly to be something closer to definitional, explanatory, a name for a deformity that is itself unnamed or -known: Hegda has eyes the color roughly of dead grass and a dermis basically slicked in a setaceous sea of wens, pimples, pustules, boils, and so on. Facially, and also onto her chest, her back, her upper arms, and privately elsewhere. Hegda's concern for personal hygiene is monstrous, and nearly all-consuming, though at this point still completely futile. Her devotion to antiacne creams, pads, wipes, washes, pills, and so on is only part of it: mud masks, lotions, multiple showers in a given day, and unfortunately hours and hours of simply standing staring at her own face in the mirror, cursing it and surveying it, getting to know it more intimately than most people know anything about themselves—getting deep, as it were, under the skin. Hegda alone at this point can see both the beauty and the ugliness in her own visage, she alone can see that the poor quality of her skin and the present overall sort of dullness to her look is only a sort of graffiti, a sort of surface marring. She can see to her bones' structure, she can see every pore and the lines of her nose, the set of her eyes, the slight curve at the outer edge of either lip, something like a sort of sexy/demure smirk, a knowing and flirtatious grin, the sort of look you find on billboards and in magazine ads of women selling *eau de toilette* and *parfum*. But the strange thing is, the more Hegda searches her face and spends her time staring at it, the less familiar, the less her own, it becomes. The face that Hegda sees is completely foreign, like she is spending all her time looking at something detached from herself, or seeing someone captivating (not attractive, exactly, but maybe not repulsive either), and finding herself unstoppably fascinated by the person's grotesquerie—but never once, not for a second, confusing that person with her own self. Hegda can watch her hands touch her face, watch her hands defy her better sense and squeeze and pick at the blemishes there, can stare into her eyes, can open and close and shape and twist her mouth, can turn her face side to side, and all the while feel ever more distant from what is being seen, ever more uncertain even almost who it is really that is seeing here at all.

SEPTEMBER 13, 1967

Because, though his name was not then, not up to that point, "Will Robinson," that was the only name he would acknowledge in later years, in what can be said to exist of his adult life. Thus, "Will Robinson" sat in the living room of the ranch-style home of his parents, Dwayne and Jeanine, who were themselves engaged in a certain *fait de l'amour* in the rear of the house, where the ranch's bedrooms were, existing each to a side of the narrow hallway that connected the house from stem to stern, the more or less dumbbell floor plan dividing living and dining rooms, and similarly two bedrooms, the TV volume being kept low—as was the wish of "Will Robinson"'s dear, sweet mother—as in extremely low, as in the knob was barely even one click to the right from the On position, and what with the pterodactyl screams and the sort of primordial grunts of his parents' intromission (which, for "Will Robinson," subconsciously developed into a squidlike image, as would emerge thirteen or so years later as the aptest description of it in a therapy session between "Will Robinson" and his therapist (the elegantly long-fingered and androgynous Archnover Randall), which session ultimately terminated the therapy altogether with a certain uncomfortable admission being made by "Will Robinson" having to do with the sexual sounds of his parents (which filled the home on a more or less daily basis throughout "Will Robinson"'s pre- and then even postpubescence), his mother's sounds in particular, which admission "WR" thought was perhaps a real Getting Somewhere moment (as in, the type of moment (smaller versions of which had occurred during their therapy to this point) that elicited from Archnover an "Ah-now-I-feel-we're-really-Getting-Somewhere"), but which admission ended up terminating the therapy due to the discomfort it clearly brought about in Archnover, whose face unconsciously betrayed what a therapist is never to betray, emotions or any type of response other than Professional Care, which in this face, this emotion, was something that was pretty clearly disgust/confusion and maybe a touch of good old judgmental *othering*, a kind of visual maxillofacial *Oh dear God*), "Will Robinson" had to sit very close to the TV and with his whole figure sort of contorted to one side, his head angled in with left ear lowered toward the TV's screen and speakers (which were settled into a sort of cabinet beneath the glass screen), his eyes almost closed they were focused so hard on taking in the action and understanding with the near-muted sound and its counterpoint (the high-pitch and bass-driven fugue from the bedroom (rounded out by the orchestral squeaking of the bedsprings and the tympanic rhythm of the headboard-on-wall's percussion)) what precisely was happening at just that moment, in what had been revealed to be not 1997, as might have been hoped/expected, but was instead evidently 1947 (this episode of *Lost in Space* (season 3, episode 2) was entitled *Visit to a Hostile Planet*, though of course that "hostile planet" was dear old earth), the *Jupiter 2* had this week gotten caught in a vicious "space warp," which had seemed bad enough, until the Robinsons emerged and saw there in its blue aura planet earth itself, some promised land, some sort of Arcadia, paradise gained, except they couldn't make contact with Alpha Control—which seemed pretty weird, kind of a first bad sign maybe—but they decided to land anyway except the *Jupiter 2* let them out not onto the present-day earth they are so homesickly happy to finally see again, but instead into a small town in Michigan, which is weirdly deserted, and the people of the small Michigan town believe the ship and its occupants (understandably) to be an alien invasion (sort of like the aural terror of many real small towns post Welles' 10/30/38 *War of the Worlds*), and just as Dr. Smith (who has, during the episode already, begun a campaign to get rich by introducing technology to the historically backward but good people of the Michigan town) disguises himself as the fire chief and makes his move, leading a "vigilante force" against the *Jupiter 2*, its aim to take the Robinsons prisoner, that was pretty much the moment when the extended simultaneous orgasm going on thirteen or so feet away overtook the small house, making the house itself feel hostile, though of course it was still "home," "Will Robinson" knew, and "Will Robinson" turned his head in the direction of the sounds as though, almost, expecting to see some great slouching beast approaching (the sound itself made manifest, corporeal), and he stared distantly right at it, the sound, where he envisioned its advance to be—and it was at that moment, looking at the dim hall and the imaginary creature that is the sounds of two bodies in the absolute pitch of orgasmic throes, two throats giving simultaneous though dissonant voice to the passion of the moment, the fantasy of the squidlike and more or less amorphous blob (indefinitely purple in color) bearing down on him was given a new element, that of the Robot, who was suddenly there beside him and, with the general affect of a parrot who knows but the one line, pronounced, "Danger, Will Robinson" in that stentorian and mechanical voice, and so right then he chose his name, though it would be eight years before he introduced himself to anyone as "Will Robinson."

FEBRUARY 2, 1984

Dimley chose this particular convenience store, Mr. Z's Food Mart, because its magazine rack—as pretty much everyone knew—was discreetly placed along the opposite wall from the counter, and with no convex mirror overhanging it, no way really for the old woman chain-smoking at the counter to know what precisely any given customer was looking at, magazine-wise, and so here one could discreetly pull a plastic-sheathed copy off the top shelf, and—if one was careful enough—tuck it into the back waistband of one's Sansabelt pants and, in order to avoid suspicion, purchase an innocuous cover magazine, something like *Time* or *People* or *Newsweek* or even *Life*. However, in such a situation (and especially with regard to the eye-patch), Dimley figured, it was best to not linger, not dillydally at the magazine rack, but to move assertively, confidently, to quickly stuff the plastic-wrapped nudie down one's pants, and move—not hurriedly, but without hesitation—to the counter with the cover purchase, giving off as much as was possible an affected effortless cool and a sense that yes-indeed-this-is-the-magazine-I-knew-I-wanted-to-buy-when-I-entered-and-so-I-had-no-reason-to-linger-or-look-suspiciously-around-back-there-thanks! But the problem he immediately encountered was, among the short list of available magazines and among the shorter list that accorded with his tastes and interests, there were two copies of *Playboy*, one of which, that in front, was the newest, the February issue, which boasted the almost impossible hourglass figure of a perky blonde flanking whom were the twin tags

> A POTENT
> PICTORIAL
> Sexy Women
> Who Are
> Tougher
> Than You Are

and

> HEEEEERE'S CAROL!
> JOHNNY CARSON'S
> "MATINEE LADY"
> SHOWS ALL

which all seemed totally adequate, really, except that as he reached to remove it from the shelf, he revealed the last of the last month's issues, the January 1984, aka the thirtieth-anniversary issue, 292 pages elegantly dressed all in black with simply a rectangle bearing the *Playboy* colophon, the cartoonish bunny head, in the eye of which were the small white numbers 3-0, and, but more importantly, along the upper margin, he read quote the last nude photos of Marilyn Monroe unquote, which as anyone knows is a significant spread to behold, not just for, you know, salacious reasons, clearly, but also for its *historical* importance: namely re the very first issue of *Playboy*—as in ever—which unforgettably likewise listed on its simple front cover quote

> first time in any magazine
> FULL COLOR
> the famous
> MARILYN MONROE NUDE

unquote, and so there he was, the most recent *Playboy* in his hand, not wanting to linger, not wanting to dillydally, fearing getting caught, running a rapid logarithm of options available to him here, ratiocinating furiously between the two covers partially obscured by plastic wrapping—HEEEEERE'S CAROL! or Marilyn?—and finally making a quick switch, replacing the February issue and now almost sweating as he pushed the purloined *Playboy* into the elastic band of his pants and grabbed a copy of *Time* and headed nearly running to the counter, spilling loose change onto the lineoleum as he pulled a wadded tissue and a crumpled fiver from his right front pocket—terrified the *Playboy* would slide lower in his pants, forcing a waddled and unmistakable retreat—hardly hearing when she told him how much the *Time* cost.

It was not until later, as he caught his breath near a woven-metal wastebasket on the sidewalk several blocks away, that he had the chance to readjust the magazine pressed against his now sweat-sticky lower back and that he noticed the *Time* he'd bought, the cover of which was a kind of off-putting back-to-back painted portrait of *Time*'s Men of the Year, Ronald Reagan and Yuri Andropov, Yuri-quote-the-struggle-for-human-rights-was-a-part-of-a-wide-ranging-imperialist-plot-to-undermine-the-foundation-of-the-Soviet-state-unquote-Andropov, who—unbeknownst to Dimley at the time—would be dead in a week.

Dimley threw the *Time* away.

And it was only much later, at home, paging through the *Playboy* at leisure, that Dimley discovered the hidden gem of Ray Bradbury's "The Toynbee Convector," a short story telling basically of a nearly ruined civilization, much like his own, which is saved by a man named Craig Bennett Stiles, who claims to have invented a time machine, traveled to a utopian future, and who provides films and other evidence of this future to the citizens, inspiring them to work to achieve it, to make the future the present as soon as possible, and who, on his deathbed many years later, after the utopian world he foresaw has become a reality, grants an interview to a man named Roger Shumway, wherein he reveals he'd made the whole thing up (quote I lied unquote)—no time machine, no utopia—he'd conned them all in order to give his stagnant society something to hope for, to believe in, asking the reporter to tell everyone the truth, to let them know they saved themselves, that they were capable of the utopia the whole time. Shumway believes he must carry on the legacy of the great inventor, himself wishing to travel to the future, and so protects the illusion, and destroys the evidence Stiles had left behind for him to reveal.

SEPTEMBER 13, 1987

The first occurrence in Scranton (viz., August 11, 1987) was broadcast in what was to become uncharacteristically quiet fashion: scrawled in block-letter graffiti on a police car that had been parked, vacant, overnight. At first the single word "Toynbee" was assumed to be no more than a graffiti tag, and without any suspects the incident went largely unremarked. However, the second occurrence was more in the mode of the later graffiti: On the morning of September 13, three separate occurrences were graffitied on local buildings and store-fronts, including in thirty-foot-high letters across the old army ammunition plant (as well as smothering the fronts of both Poor Richard's Pub and Mr. Z's Food Mart), each consisting of three separate lines of text, to wit:

TOYNBEE A LIAR
I HAD NOT THOUGHT DEATH
UNDONE SO MANY

TOYNBEE WAS RIGHT
THE HANGED MAN
FEAR DEATH BY WATER

I WAS NEITHER LIVING NOR DEAD
AND I KNEW NOTHING
LOOKING INTO THE HEART OF LIGHT THE SILENCE

The connection between the word "Toynbee" in these three occurrences and that of the police vehicle drew some attention—as did simply the audacity of the act. However, the connection was also made between these acts of vandalism and the "Toynbee Tiles" that had been spotted in Philadelphia, as well as elsewhere, and that similarly contained a cryptic message involving both Toynbee and death:

Michael Sheehan

TOYNBEE IDEA
IN KUBRICK'S 2001
RESURRECT DEAD
ON PLANET JUPITER

Though arguably this was nothing more than an act of vandalism, the scale of the graffiti—smothering three storefronts—seemed to suggest some purpose, some message. Police were concerned there was some sort of political group behind the vandalism, some sort of gang, perhaps, or even a guerrilla or terrorist sect. But then, what was it supposed to mean? Whatever the cipher, the text as it was made no sense.

As a junior officer and given the momentary high profile of the vandalism, it was both a blessing and a bane when Dimley Scarton was assigned the case. He'd joined the force only seventeen months ago, and had had very little to investigate. He recognized the name Toynbee, knew he knew it from somewhere, though he could not place exactly where. Though really no one expected much from him, Dimley poured himself into the case, heading to the library after the assignment, curious about the word "Toynbee" in particular, as it just stuck in his head. A quick search revealed Toynbee to be the name of a dead historian who'd written about metahistory and the four stages of a civilization's rise and decline. The rest of it he spent hours trying to make some sense of. The librarian was literally calling softly to him that the library was closing when he saw a reference in a work on whatever precisely metahistory really was (he thought he knew, and then didn't) to the lines from *The Waste Land* describing the tarot reading "Fear death by water."

That night he barely slept, instead got stoned and drank his way through a six-pack of Miller, reading and rereading *The Waste Land*, deeply lost.

In his first years on the force, Dimley continued to get high, often enough with G.P., though even this early their different paths in life had started to move distinctly parallax and apart and separately. He hadn't heard from G.P. in some weeks, despite observing their usual routine: Dimley tended to park his cruiser outside G.P.'s house on slow days and wait for G.P. to head out, going wherever, and Dimley would throw the lights on, pull him over. He considered calling G.P., the one person who would undoubtedly be up and likely to engage with this graffiti poetry thing, but instead, unmuting the TV's replaying of *Them!* and lighting another joint, he read the lines "I can connect / Nothing with nothing. / The broken fingernails of dirty hands. / My people humble people who expect / Nothing. / la la" over and over, unable to move past them. (Later in life, about a decade or more, while high, he often found himself drawn back to thoughts about the movie—as he remembered it—*Donnie Brasco*, which he had indeed watched high and in which Johnny Depp plays a cop who plays a Mafia guy and who maybe does become the Mafia guy and whose loyalties and true intentions seem to get pretty muddled, as Dimley understood it. For Dimley, this movie poses really difficult questions, once it gets going, in that Depp is, well, yes, for one thing he himself changes or challenges one's perception of the film and the character and everything in that he seems always to be there, always making you aware of his presence, and to Dimley he, as an actor, seemed not particularly trustworthy, the type of actor—if there could be said to be a type—who always ironically undercut whatever role he was in, like with his own smirk and affectations always seemed to be indicating he could not just be a straight cop, a good guy, acting the part of a bad guy, but instead that he reveled not only in the bad guyness but in the ambiguity, in his very Eddie Haskell qualities, the nature of his good/bad and self being obfuscated—but apart from Depp, Dimley recalled the movie's plot as treating of this cop who goes undercover, but deep undercover, and starts to form connections in his other life, the life he is performing as this Mafia guy, and gets into drugs and crime and so on, and all the while, the supposedly real him is being challenged as others maybe start worrying where did the real him go, they can't see it anymore, but instead only the criminal Mafia-guy part, which even when he is not performing that now, the real guy, the good guy, seems the performance, so in other words he is a cop playing a criminal who then people think is really a criminal sometimes playing—and maybe has been, like, for a long while playing—a good guy, and in this, then, Dimley would start to think what if it is not just how he acts and what others see but what if truly he was all along an unexpressed bad guy playing a good guy, Depp, that is, who then plays a bad guy and people can sense he is only playing when he tries to show he really is a good guy. And of course around this time Dimley would realize his own place in this, the fear that he himself was not just a good guy, a cop, but was some sort of criminal playing a cop and maybe for motives he himself did not yet know, and then he would start to worry and wonder: Could there even be such a thing as being or was it only performing, acting, behaving? Like if he acted like a cop, was that all there was to being a cop? Was there nothing definite in him, nothing that he truly was and that his actions followed from, but was it instead that his actions determined any meaningful statement about what he truly was? When he was high, smoking with G.P. as a younger kid, when he used to here and there pilfer small goods from convenience stores and whatnot, was that more truly who he was inside? Did he become a cop not out of any sense of civic duty or moral rectitude but rather as a sort of undercover bad guy, the way Depp performs Brasco performing the Mafia character? Was he all the time in disguise, walking around, playing a cop, while really deep down being something darker, undiscovered, other? Did he even really remember the movie right? His version was all about Depp's character's deep commitment to the role actually becoming a real and meaningful challenge to the "true" nature of Depp's character, as in even the character starts to lose hold on who he is—is he a cop playing bad or is he really the bad guy playing the cop playing bad, etc.—and his life starts to fall apart. The movie, as Dimley recalls, ultimately navigates away from this terrible incursion and returns Depp to normal life, albeit somewhat changed, and thus the movie can end. But what about if the movie didn't just end, if it wasn't trying to console the viewer by simply answering who Depp/Brasco really was, but instead only showed how the nature of our identity is maybe truly relational, conditional, contextual, or—*or*—that there is a true self and it may very well be inconsistent with our performances of a self—note how Depp seems to pose a constant question by his very smirkiness of what exactly we are even to believe here, regarding who is performing whom—and that possibly we cannot control this truth, as in, simply by acting like a cop we can't change the fact that we are really a drug-consuming, petty-thieving bad guy. Again, though, which was worse? To be a thing you thought you weren't, or to know there is no thing you are, that everything about you is simply what you are performing, acting as, behaving like at that given, specific time. It was long incursive thoughts like these that ultimately forced Dimley to quit smoking.)

SEPTEMBER 30, 1989

"In other news this morning, an act of vandalism has police puzzled. This sign along the Morgan Highway, which until yesterday read:

Michael Sheehan

Welcome to Scranton: The Electric City
Embracing Our People, Our Traditions, and Our Future

has been altered, as these images show, by the addition of what appear to be block-letter graffiti tiles, changing it to 'FALLING TOWERS Welcome to JERUSALEM ATHENS ALEXANDRIA VIENNA LONDON Scranton: The Electric City UNREAL Embracing Our People, THESE FRAGMENTS I HAVE SHORED AGAINST MY RUINS, Our Traditions, THE CHAIR SHE SAT IN LIKE A BURNISHED THRONE and Our Future SHANTIH SHANTIH SHANTIH.'

"Although the intended message is unclear, the act has recalled the so-called 'Waste Land' graffiti vandalism of a couple years ago. The name became popular after references in several prominent instances of graffiti were connected to J. Alfred Prufrock's poem 'The Waste Land.' Scranton police are not amused but bemused, and without any suspects.

"This is Hegda Toryeakevic for Channel Four, Scranton. Back to you, Ron."

Off air again, and back at the studio, helping Bill Drindley wrap mike cables, Hegda suffered what had become the routine sensation of coming down, as if from a high, all her chemical levels dropping, her heart slowing, her intestines relaxing, her muscles all heavy, her body feeling weighted, empty, wasted, and unpretty. It wasn't as if the feeling of being on-air was truly comparable to being high, it wasn't enjoyable, really; it was just that being on-air intensified various aspects of her very being, brought to bear things that lay deep inside and were otherwise largely uncertain. On-air, she became a fierce tree of electricity, crackling, filled with light and radiating outward, everything she was clicking into place, her imagined self and her real combined into a terrible harmony. But off air, the two selves were severed again. Bill Drindley, for instance, was continually trying to look down Hegda's blouse, eyeing her chest as though secretively, and indeed the woman he was now seeing—the outer Hegda—was someone who inspired this type of ogling often. But the inner Hegda, the conscious woman hidden inside now that the camera's eye was off her, felt empty, ugly, and alone. This Hegda still believed herself to be separate from whatever she looked like on the outside. In Makeup, as she sat in the glare of the vanity's lights and elevated in her plastic salon-style chair, she realized indeed that her transformation out of adolescence had resulted in the emergence not of an

238

ugly-duckling-turned-swan or butterfly-from-caterpillar, but of an Other, not the appearance of her true self, but instead her appearance had arrived now as something outside her, as something, someone, else. She did not watch her spots on the news, never consulted with producers or editors on which shots to use, how much of a segment; she knew that the woman she was when the camera was on her was not the woman she was when not being looked at. Watching herself in the mirror now, as the makeup guy Stefan smoothed her blush with fast brushstrokes, she felt painted, inauthentic, a palimpsest. She had that Dorian Gray effect, where as her exterior became ever more legitimately beautiful, her ability to see it became mired and gray and murky; as the subterraneans became visible in the daylight sun, her ability to see them in the mirror diminished, such that she saw the worst of herself, saw not what was objectively there, but indeed what was subjectively mirrored.

She was most comfortable therefore when she was standing posed and poised, her eyes looking not at another person or at a mirror but instead at the dead, blank eye of the camera—usually on Kyle Mann's or Bill Drindley's shoulder—knowing that this was what was real: the disconnection, the performance, the loss entirely of the internal, thinking self. Facing the camera, she became beautiful, nothing else. She had no doubts, no thoughts about who she was or about anything really. Instead, she performed or read lines, affected the appropriate look on her face, inflected the appropriate tone to her voice, and whoever Hegda really felt herself to be inside gained exactly what she'd always wanted, became what she'd always wished she could be, at the cost of oblivion, at the loss of her own existence, disappearing (this true, original Hegda) inside the mask she'd created.

SEPTEMBER 12, 1989

President George H. W. Bush: "And behind all of the senseless violence, the needless tragedy, what haunts me is the question: Why?"

SEPTEMBER 11, 1984

The smoke curling across in front of G.P. is literally blue. Blue tinged. The word diaphanous came into his mind, and as his head swiveled a little on its mount, the word was again gone.

"That's not enough," Dr. Death was saying. "The purpose, though, always has to be understanding. It has to be higher level, it has to be a seeking. Otherwise you might as well live in cardboard on the streets and ask assholes for change. That's all you've got."

Dr. Death was a man of indeterminate age, maybe fortyish, but his skin had that leathery look of being outside a lot, as in what has to be an unhealthy amount, such that he could have been twenty or sixty, though G.P. did know or understand him, Dr. D, to be older than he himself was. Rumor had it that once Dr. Death had been an actual doctor, or rather a doctoral student, had been in med school. Whatever medical training he had had, G.P. knew for a certainty that he always had the absolute best weed in Scranton, hands down. Not just weed that was good, impressive, get-you-high weed like that, but weed that was life altering, life preserving, perhaps, weed that was clinically strong and scientifically rich in its effects. You couldn't so much smoke it as endure it.

This is how you remember it, anyway. Real effects are always physical.

Dr. Death had adopted the moniker a couple years before Kevorkian made it household, something he'd come up with while on who knows what, something he felt was fittingly shamanistic, as that was the type of doctor he intended in the honorific (he'd barely finished high school, lived with his mom—and her boyfriend, Steve—well past thirty), given that his whole vibe was making electronic music in his mom's basement and loosening his mental tether and exploring the farthest frontiers of consciousness.

He kept a gun in the basement, G.P. had noted, since he handled a lot of merchandise and "had to be careful" but, G.P. was aware, Dr. D tended to be pretty shamanistically untethered on whatever he was selling and promoting and thus maybe not the most trustworthy decision maker, in terms of when the gun might get used. The gun—the one G.P.'d seen; there was a sawed-off single-action pump in the closet dangling from a leather strap off a hanger—was a laser-sighted .44, which Dr. D would periodically handle, and in one particularly transcendental moment of a high he'd rubbed it across his temple and even put it briefly in his mouth, declaring afterward he couldn't die, couldn't be killed.

G.P. watched smoke recede from himself, considered what it was about this smoke that was so captivating, considered abstractly how it was we could be captivated, be so in love with and struck by beauty in such simple things, beauty at all—and then what was beauty, and then whether there is something (all in our heads) about how we perceive (bottom line, like just the perceiving mechanism, how we perceive anything) that we call beauty, that feels this way, that we can't help, that our monkeyish ancestors had some percentage of, used in fashioning mud huts or bone tools or whatever. As quickly, though, this thought stream had itself gone.

"I mean, any high has to be about separating yourself from the way we see things, the way life is to us, and seeing it new, seeing something different, a different truth."

"You know that's bullshit, though, right?"

"It's not bullshit. It's bullshit to you, since you're underformed, you're fetal, sitting here watching the smoke come out your own mouth like a fucking baby staring at a mobile, a kitten pawing at a dangling bit of string. You're using it to regress, and in that ignorance find bliss."

"No, I just mean, like, in the sixties they were all about pot or acid or whatever, being in this altered state, opening the doors of perception, being something ontologically other, but that was just kind of idealistic nonsense. I mean, what we've learned—and let me remind you this is the eighties, we've got Bedtime for Bonzo Ron Reagan as walk-of-fame leader of the free world—is that there is no other purpose, there is no beyond, no higher power or altered state or other dimensions or whatever. All that spirituality has been evaporated, has been erased from us. Now it's just celebrity and what you can get for yourself."

"One thing," Dr. Death loaded up a cassette tape he'd earlier recorded—he recorded sounds, out in the world, nature sounds, city sounds, whatever he came across—and started it playing alongside a second tape, this one fragments of speech he'd recorded from last night's CBS news report with Dan Rather, and to these, as he talked, he would periodically add distortion effects from his keyboards—one a straight QWERTY keyboard connected to a self-made computer devoted to producing, the other an eighty-eight-key extended Yamaha—or beats from the drum machine (approximately) he had wired into his sound machine, "is the fact that you're wrong about all this decade emphasis, we were then, they are now, or whatever, doesn't matter. Everybody is always trying to define time by taglines: the Roaring Twenties, the Swinging Sixties, whatever materialistic tag you'd give the eighties—"

"The eighties: Back to the Future."

"What?"

241

"Get it? Back to the . . ."

"The movie?"

"Well, yeah, but, you know, like back to the, *back* . . ."

"Point is, that's not important. Time isn't divisible like that, isn't fitted into these neat little groupings, like the twenties, the thirties, etc. We use those numbers as labels, numbers we all agree on as fairly representing an average of human experience of time—"

"No idea what you're talking about right now."

"—but what about changing our experience of time? See? Like, if you dream, everybody agrees dream time is way different from lived, waking time. So why can't there be other experiences of time that are just as valid as the average we all agree to?"

"OK."

The stuffed deer's head hanging from the wood paneling of Dr. D's basement wall loomed with savage, dead eyes, and lashes, which were incongruously girlish and pretty and fey and innocent, yet the dead deer's unopening mouth was pursed tight beneath its dusty nose. Dr. D layered more noise on top of the CBS/nature mix. Sounded like cars passing on a busy street.

"But what I'm telling you, there really is such a thing as altered existence, as being able to transport from, like, this type of experience to a literally meaningful other type of experience."

"You mean getting high."

"Different than that. I mean what you do is smoke, you smoke a bunch of weed, maybe pop a couple caps, and you think that's all there is. I'm talking about fundamentally rewiring the mainframe, hacking into your mental processor and changing the settings. I'm talking about opening up the selective experience of existence and letting in other possibilities."

"Again," G.P. forced an elliptoid smoke ring out above the littered coffee table into the suddenly dimly lit atmosphere of the basement, watching as the momentary ring held together, rotated slightly, slowly, seemed to come apart, managed to drift whole for some time shortly thereafter, "no idea what you're talking about."

"I'm talking about shit beyond weed, shrooms, acid, whatever. I'm talking about, like, DMT."

"DDT?"

"DMT."

"DMV?"

Dr. Death looked cross-eyed over his mustache at G.P. for a long moment. "I don't believe you're that stoned." He put on a new

242

sound, running water, a guitar tuning. "Oh. Oh shit."

"What?" G.P. vaguely recalled something, an idea he'd had some time ago, about politics, about the decay of modern society. About an idea of how he could save it. He looked at the tip of the joint he'd just relit, as one does a dirty fingernail. What was he thinking?

"I know this, man. I know this sound." Dr. D replayed the tape, and then again.

"Well, you taped it, right? I mean."

"No, yeah, but what the fuck is that. *'What can this strange device be? When I touch it, it gives forth a sound. It's got wires that vibrate and give music. What can this thing be that I've found?'* That's fucking Rush."

Oh, shit. G.P. didn't mind Rush. He liked Rush, actually. But Dr. Death had this unhinged thing with them, like he did with his drugs. This idea that beyond life's fair veil there was some inebriated truth ringed in smoke and Day-Glo bright, and that Rush was the philosophy of those other seekers who knew this truth and understood its value in the face of daily life's meaningless musical misdirection. Dr. D started moving quickly around the basement, frantically pawing through stacks of cassette decks and whatever other bits and pieces of his creative endeavors covered his counters. G.P. stood up, did the obligatory "Well, I mean, I guess I should get going," letting his voice trail off, thinking he'd say he had to go to work but being overcome with guilt since he'd been fired from the Sheetz three weeks ago. Astral sounds were already starting to merge and diverge throughout the still, fog-thick basement air. Standing, G.P. could see an elaborate collection of disorderly spray-paint cans and old cloth, a milk crate filled with shards of plastic, the cans, and a couple of halogen lights with orange extension cords.

What had his idea been? Something to do with the DMV? With DDT? To show them there was something worth believing in. *I have come too soon. They have done it themselves, but they do not know it yet.* The lie that inspires the truth. Where was he reading that? Had he read that?

(Much later in life, almost twenty years later, a variation of this idea would return to him, the idea of using deceit to forcibly free the common man, the hoi polloi, from his technological enslavement, his unknowing trap in the perfectly constructed hall of mirrors of social media, the Internet, online shopping—a world of consumer convenience that took away even the most basic human qualities, even the roughest, dimmest conception of virtue and arête. That was after more or less a decade's development as a hacker, first learning simple hacks in MS-DOS and BASIC, coding simple schemes that at the time seemed challenging, meaningful, and potentially revolutionary in scope. Bank codes, credit-card numbers, the primitive intranet of the local nuclear-power plant (the Susquehanna Steam Electric Station), which garnered some attention, despite the fact that he got nothing from the hack, really, nothing of interest anyway, but an article ran in a couple of papers, and they traced the hack to his parents' basement, where he'd more or less moved at that time, working his endless all-night hacks, stoned and wired on Mountain Dew and Pepsi (for the brief period of its existence, he fell totally in love with Crystal Pepsi, and had a short supply he'd stockpiled as rumor spread that Mr. Z's Food Mart was down to its last cases, and the product was being literally removed from shelves all over the country, dusty unsellable cans and bottles, which stockpile he extended far past usability, as even he understood, leaving the last twenty-ounce bottle on his desk next to his constantly evolving desktop computer (an aggregate of parts assembled with a true geek's zeal but little patience or grace: The computer was all loose wires and scattered panels) for what became years, until he ultimately decided to part with it, and sold it for an almost unimaginable amount (given that it was now probably near lethal) on eBay), and playing the then new computerized version of Civilization (circa 1991), which he'd been excited to see and was one of the first buyers of in the Scranton area, despite the relatively quick realization that it was a letdown compared to the original board version, because (among other defects) of the much written-about problem of "phalanx versus tank": Since the computer-strategy game started players in 4000 BC and allowed progression through time such that there could be ancient versus modern nations, veteran status ended up allowing ancient spearmen to defeat battleships, tanks, aircraft, etc., which was mathematically possible but obviously wildly improbable, to the point of illustrating painfully how this was a game and distinctly separate from reality, which is exactly what the gameplayer never much wants to be reminded of; plus, this version of Civ was "turn based," which limited what a player has, versus the "real-time" style of play, which includes the ability to create additional levels of play and facets and features, etc., during gameplay, which really is just to say one of the two biggest drawbacks for G.P. was the fact that he sat stoned and wired in his basement developing his nation, taking little real pleasure from attacking tanks with spearmen and critiquing the game's coding, all alone, where the board version had been a shared endeavor, the technologically advanced one was a socially isolating fantasyland, one that didn't map onto reality the way a real game really should; viz., the game is on one level about the rules of the game as stated, the literal level (a game of Civilization), but at the same time the game is really being played interpersonally and socially, where the rules govern the interactions but the players flesh out the competition and the development of play based on their real-world personalities and psychologies. Despite the role-playing, Dungeons & Dragons didn't take with G.P. as it was not, like Civ, real; even the bridge the more extreme made into the real world (never ceasing to perform their D&D roles) was just realized fantasy (dwarves and orcs and whatnot), not fantasized reality. And, anyway, they traced the hack to him and that was pretty serious and there were some threats that ultimately got reduced as the failure to properly understand exactly what he'd done helped keep him somewhat safe, and it wasn't until years after that nuclear-plant hack that he would be caught for anything seen as substantially criminal, in a legal sense, or actually terroristic.)

Dr. Death was now playing abstract air guitar, his long hands fingering delicate strings of air, his face intensely cringed, orgasmic. He swooped near to the couch, and drew forth a baggie from his back pocket.

"Breath mints, no doubt."

"DMT. Took a little doing, *mon frère, mon semblable,* but I did indeed manage to bring a couple of these in."

"Still not totally sure what we're . . ."

"You know Skinny Ray?"

"No."

"He's been getting shit out of Canada, Boston, New York. Getting all kinds of shit that way, you know, better than we get through Philly."

"Right. Right." G.P.'s high was starting to turn on him. *"And the meek shall inherit the earth"* floated ethereally by in Geddy Lee's dulcet tone.

"Well, he's been bringing back like a lot of high-end coke, some rock, a bit of crystal, and lately a bunch of heroin."

"We are the priests of the temples of Syrinx."

"Heroin? You're buying heroin now?"

"No, no, no, not my style. I'm more of an active explorer, you know? What you get from coke or crack is just a really fast heart rate, an acceleration that burns right back out, you feel fast-forwarded,

245

and with heroin, oxy, whatever, you end up just feeling lobbed in some eternal softball pitch, floating just above, gently rolling around, until you come down and reach home plate and someone hits you in the face with a fucking bat."

"Still, I'd have to say, a bigger-picture-type sentence or two could really help me out."

"Basically, I was able to hook up through Skinny Ray. He got a selective little sample of DMT, old, outdated shit, and offered me in on it, knowing this was more my thing than eightballs and all that."

"So what exactly is it?"

"You ever hear of Machine Elves?"

"The band?"

"I don't think so. No. These are like noncorporeal beings of light and pure thought that exist in another plane, another dimension, which you access through DMT."

"Escape to realms beyond the night . . ."

I've got to say, that sounds kind of . . . stupid."

All in one motion, Dr. D opened the baggie while turning in his chair and singing along with Geddy Lee. "They left our planet long ago, the elder race still learn and grow, their power grows with purpose strong, to claim the home where they belong. Home to tear the Temples down, home to change!"

He held his hand out, palm up, to G.P. Two pills.

"It's like a five-minute high, but by minute two you're fully in the world of the Machine Elves, and by minute four they've shown you all about, like, interdimensional travel and telekinetic expression."

"So that's it? We're just going to pop these and have a five-minute voyage of the Dawn Treader? You spent all that time getting a couple pills so we could sit here, already stoned, listening to *2112* and hallucinating for five minutes?"

"But, see, it's like dreaming, where the way you experience time with the Machine Elves is like how we can experience time in a dream. I didn't just make this shit up. It's been studied. Tested. This guy McKenna."

"How do you know any of this?"

"Shh, shh. Listen." They listened. "*2112* is quite possibly the greatest human achievement since *The Rites of Spring*."

"I would have to say no. *Moving Pictures*."

"You're just fucking with me."

"Or maybe the greatest thing up until *Moving Pictures*."

"*Moving Pictures*?"

"Yeah."

"*Moving Pictures.*"

"Yeah?"

"Today's Tom Sawyer? Monday Warrior? Mean, mean stride, mean, mean pride?"

"What you say about his company is what you say about society."

"That album is so fucking . . . commercial. It's radio play."

"I think you're thinking *Permanent Waves.*"

"I'm not even sure what to make of you. Clearly you know Rush's oover—"

"Oo-vra."

"—but it's like you know the names of all the albums without any understanding at all of what is really on them. What they really are. It's like you know all the rules of baseball but then you ask something like OK great now show me: Where is the inning?"

"I don't see how that applies."

"Here, should we play them? Side by side, do a little comparison?"

"I mean *2112* is fine, it's good. I just like *Moving Pictures* more, personally. That's not that big a deal. We can have some disagreement, you know that, right? There is not one right answer to what is good, what we should like and dislike."

"No, here, seriously. I want to hear *Moving Pictures* with you and hear what you think is so fucking good about it, so earth-shattering."

"I didn't say it was earth-shattering. I don't even know that I applied an adjective at all."

"OK, here—is this it?—let's just see, OK?"

Music. Quick, descending scales.

"No, this isn't . . ."

"*There are those who think that life / has nothing left to chance / with a host of holy horrors / to direct our aimless dance. A planet of playthings / we dance on the strings/ of powers we cannot perceive. / The stars aren't aligned, / or the gods are malign; / blame is better to give than receive. / You can choose a ready guide / in some celestial voice. / If you choose not to decide / you still have made a choice. / You can choose from phantom fears / and kindness that can kill. / I will choose a path that's clear, / I will choose free will.*"

"Huh."

"Yeah."

"Sort of like a compromise. Almost."

"I'm with you. I feel that."

247

"I'm kind of really fucking high."

"Well, you can choose a ready guide in some celestial voice. . . ." Dr. Death palms the DMT, toggling each lightly along the topography of his lifeline. "I will choose free will." He pinches one in his left hand, offering the right palm out to G.P. And then, fluidly, slips it onto his tongue and away it goes, as his eyes light up momentarily with disconnected excitement, and then he lights a cigarette and leans his head back onto the edge of the couch, sinking deep into the cushions.

G.P. tries smelling this little dusty pill in his hand. Nothing distinct, though for a moment he is convinced there is a slight ammonia tang. That could just be the couch itself, he realizes. Unsure even still what to expect, he rolls the pill once across the surface of his hand, and then swallows it dry. "Jacob's Ladder" is playing on the tape deck, music of an astral plane. *All at once the clouds are parted; light streams down in bright unbroken beams.*

JULY 8, 1985

"Marco."

"Polo."

"Po-lo."

"Polo."

By now, Dimley and G.P. had retreated to the folding plastic deck chairs, their highs abating in the incandescent sunlight as they languidly led Walf around the pool. It was his idea, after all, this stoned recreation of childhood summers, of the blind pursuit of unseen ends through overly chlorinated water.

"Mar-*co*?"

Though she didn't know it—how could she?—it was the last time Hegda, or any of them, would see Walf. "Polo."

She was pushing her weightless way along the water's edge, bouncing slightly as she maneuvered, one hand on the pool's smooth tile edge, with the other variously splashing, and raising her arm to avoid being detected.

Though they all still hung out, Walf had not spoken a word to Dimley since the incident. Dimley had approached him more than once, to say it was OK, to offer a hand, to suggest there were no hard feelings, that he certainly was not the one, if anyone was getting in the way of the two of them being friends, it wasn't him, hey. They

248

had now finished high school. It had been almost two years, with the eye patch.

Hegda was filled with the odd sensation of excitement mixed with terror, anxiety, as Walf clearly was honing in on her, moving ever closer to her as she whispered Polo, tried throwing her voice, leading him one way by answering with her head to the left and then pushing off with her toes and flutter-kicking to the right. The game involved just these types of coincidental targetings, the blind pursuer focusing in on presumably an unknown other, not trying to capture her in particular, or so it had to be assumed, but just sensing her nearness, anticipating at any moment his hand might touch this invisible other.

Walf was coming closer, and ever closer, their two bodies separated by the slimmest barrier of water, her legs scissoring out to the side as she tried to keep from being found and yet to slip away, to stay still and yet move. Both of them now feeling the thrill of each other's proximity, Walf still blind to her identity, Hegda still blind to what was happening. His voice betrayed the slightest edges of uncertainty, of nervous excitement as he again quietly spoke, "Marco."

It seemed almost at the exact same moment she breathed the two syllables—po-lo—his hands had found her, lightly, not like in other exchanges. His eyes did not open, as one hand touched the soft skin of her belly, exposed beneath her neon-pink top, and the other hand, as she finished the second syllable, touched lightly on her breast.

His eyes opened. They each looked into the other's face for a moment that seemed impenetrably long. He had not moved his hand from her breast, and she had not reacted, had not flinched away. Though they'd found each other accidentally, they stood like this, almost embracing, almost like lovers, and Walf's pained look seemed to ease, his eyes to lighten, his manner to change. She laid her hand on his, where it still held the skin of her belly. It seemed the pool was silent, the sun bright, and the sky open and endless.

Though she would remember this odd encounter for many years after (once he'd been found, no note or explanation, just the haunting, open-ended question of his death), its real duration was terribly fleeting. Almost immediately, Dimley shouted, "He touched her tit, hey!" and Walf's face burned red, his hands had left her body, and before she could think to move, he had splashed his way to the pool's submerged steps and stormed out and away forever.

249

Michael Sheehan

SEPTEMBER 1, 1989

"It's like a mystery where the only thing you learn when you solve the mystery is that the mystery has no solution."

"What? Life, you mean?"

"No," scoffs, "*life*. Life?"

"Yeah, you know. Mystery, then when you solve it, I mean that makes sense to me. Death is like the end of the mystery where nothing is solved, no answers are there, no cause explains it all, no resolution and no ending, really. Everything is over, but nothing is really finished, ended. It's like a, what do you call that? Sentence fragment? Like where suddenly the story just stops, and you never get to know the ending. But you have that feeling there was another episode somewhere out there, or like another page or something. Know what I mean?"

"No, not at all. I just meant this case, with the graffiti and everything."

"Oh, yeah, well. I can see that too. I guess."

"But, you were saying, episode. That reminds me: the reference, what was that: *Lost in Space*? Family floating out in space, in the nothing, trying to get home, but they can't. That's the whole show. Will they ever get home, but, like, the not-getting-home is the show, so that ends up being all there is. Not-getting-home *is* home. Being lost in space is being home, for them."

"Maybe. But I don't really think that's what the show intended. Their home was earth."

"Yeah, but, I mean, maybe there is a message here, in these graffiti lines."

"You know, someone once told me don't look for difficult solutions where there are easy answers."

"Who told you that?"

"Don't remember. But it seems like some idiot kid, or maybe a homeless guy, is writing nonsense words, crazy-person words all over the fronts of buildings just out of your run-of-the-mill craziness like. Or, you know, teenager-young-person street vandalism. That's what they do now, with this MTV. Empty-vee? Get it? TV, Empty TV, EmpTV?"

"What?"

"You don't get that, it's . . ."

"But if it is some kid, just some crazy person, I mean, for one he would have to know *Lost in Space*, right? We found that out. But

250

why would he write these lines from poems, and these references to science fiction and stuff? Why not just draw a great big middle finger on the business, or like paint over the windows? That's enough of a crazy-type act, don't you think?"

"You can't look for meaning and reason in these types of deals. A crazy person gets an idea in his head to write his prophecies or messages or whatever all over Scranton, you can't argue with the idea: He's a crazy person. Nother one?"

"Wait, you said prophecies."

"*Two more Millers*. Yeah, so? What do you mean?"

"Why'd you call them prophecies?"

"Fuck do I know, the point here is that you've got a crazy idiot asshole painting nonsense on windows. Don't make it a *Dragnet* case, OK? This isn't, uh, *Law and Order*. In real life, there's no point to any of this. If we can make this person stop painting on stores and buildings, that makes the businesses happy. Right now, this crazy person painting crazy messages all over? That's news, that's all. People like watching others embarrass themselves, they like staring at car accidents, they like to see other people lose everything, love to watch 'em fall, no matter how high or low they were to begin with. Hey, you know what today is? I heard this on the radio, one of them, like, This Day in History things. You know?"

"The one hundredth day of Bush's presidency."

"Oh. Is it?"

"I don't think so."

"It's the fiftieth anniversary of Germany invading Poland. World War II."

"And? So?"

"What do you mean *and so*? I mean the Nazis invaded Poland fifty years ago to this very day. War to end all wars. Fear itself. Atomic bomb, military industrial complex, the FBI, the CIA, the Cold War, the Shoah, Israel, Red China, Anschluss, Auschwitz, the Baby Boom, the GI Bill, the Berlin Wall, the last direct war where major powers toe to toed directly, no proxies, basically all Anglo-European types, not like they are now, one-sided, with a superpower against a proxy, and we're talking any of a number of Asian or South American–type proxies here. Middle Eastern. I mean, fifty years ago the real twentieth century started. Today. *Better living through chemistry*. War to end all wars? It's been war ever since."

"How do you even know any of that?"

"Before all that, it was the end of industrialism, like from the nineteenth century. But that day was different. Everything we know about Americanness comes from that."

"That's ridiculous."

"Did you know the TV was a result of war-era research? The cathar ray, the cathar tube, or whatever."

"Cathode. Not Cath*ar*. They were heretics."

"And how do you know that, I might ask."

"I still don't really see the importance of events that happened. I mean, for one thing, it's not like they could have been any different."

"How do you mean?"

"Well, I mean they happened in the past. You can't change the past. So, since we can't change the past, and they did happen already, it isn't like we can talk about how things would have been if Germany hadn't invaded Poland."

"That's kind of fatalistic, huh? Two more? *Two more.*" Raises two fingers.

"And besides: 'fear itself'? That was 1933. FDR's inauguration. He was talking about the Depression, or whatever."

"But, see? But 1933 was the same year Hitler came to power in Germany. OK? 'Fear itself'? FDR was more right than he knew. Hitler was 'fear itself' or one of the like manifestations of the same."

"*Manifestations of fear itself?*"

"Exactly. That's the other part of what came out of double-you-double-you-two: We learned the great and terrible evil we were capable of."

"You mean Nazis were capable of."

"No. No, I don't. I mean, we all, humans, people. Germany was one of the greatest civilizations of the modern Western world, and it resulted in an unimaginable horror. That's what we saw: That is the result of all our human genius; we turn everything into terror and destruction and murder and cruelty. That's our will. We can't do otherwise. That's why so many men came home from what they'd seen and clung to their wives, new women, formed families, sought order, pursued a stable, quiet, suburban dream, made copious babies. To stave off fear itself."

SEPTEMBER 26, 1989

As a part of his ongoing Scranton-area film series, *Hos Si Vis Videre*, Korl Oades decided to honor the obscure birthdate of Ivan Ilyich

Mozzhukhin by showing a marathon of his films, including *Surrender*, as well as the brief but unforgettable Kuleshov Effect, choosing, in fact (Oades did), to show this multiple times to the audience, in between other films, hoping to achieve the point the effect is famed for, that is of illustrating the impact of editing, letting the audience see how their perceptions are alterable, manipulable, contingent. The experiment included three separate pairings of uninflected images: Mozzhukhin's painted face staring straight ahead, with great intensity and perhaps the slightest hint of a labial expression (smirk? grimace?*), variously paired (vis-à-vis jump cuts) with a bowl of soup, a little girl in a wooden coffin, and a woman draped across a sofa, part of her robe slipping down across her chest. The original audience lauded Mozzhukhin's ability to convey pleasure and hunger as he stared at the soup he was about to taste, pained sorrow and deep dismay as he looked over the open coffin of the young girl, and the salacious lust that burned from his eyes and his smile/smirk/grimace as his look turned to the woman. The experiment's secret was that these seemingly separate images were in fact all the same image of Mozzhukhin's face, replayed with no change other than the image that succeeded it. Putting these disconnected images side by side had caused the audience to reinterpret what they were seeing, to invest new meaning in the same flat image, making it now one of hunger, now sadness, now lust. This experiment was made by Russian director and leader of the montage movement Lev Kuleshov, giving it the name. Kuleshov's ideas inspired other directors, including Sergei Eisenstein (*Battleship Potemkin* and, with Grigori Aleksandrov, *October*, which, although both are propaganda films, display the montagist sensibility that got Eisenstein rebuked for formalism) and Dziga Vertov (*Man with a Movie Camera*).

---

*Clifford Geertz refers to Gilbert Ryle's discussion of the imbedded and impacted layers of meaning to a gesture or expression as simple as a wink. Ryle's example is two boys "rapidly contracting the eyelids of their right eyes"; for one of them, this is an encoded sign, a secret signifier; for the other, it is an involuntary twitch. The appearance of the two is identical, but the difference in the meaning is "vast." Then, further, is introduced the character of a third boy, parodying the action of the wink, and but then—fearing his parody wink will be mistaken—there is the third boy when he is at home alone, practicing his parody of the wink in his mirror. This is Ryle's definition of ethnography, "a stratified hierarchy of meaningful structures in terms of which twitches, winks, fake-winks, parodies, rehearsals of parodies are produced, perceived, and interpreted, and without which they would not . . . in fact exist, no matter what anyone did or didn't do with his eyelids." Geertz's own definition of anthropology fits with this, viz., "that man is an animal suspended in webs of significance he himself has spun, I take culture to be those webs, and the analysis of it to be therefore not an experimental science in search of law but an interpretative one in search of meaning."

But tonight, on the smaller second screen, as the images of the Kuleshov Effect play through for a second time, the audience does not see what Korl or Kuleshov intended them to see. In fact, none of the audiences up to this point has really been impressed, time being what it is and technology moving so quickly (*vita nostra brevis est / brevi finietur*); they saw simply the silent face of an outdated medium, the jump cuts giving them little but the vaguest sense that this flip-book of images is meant to be a narrative, a sensibility. Instead, most of them watched it without engagement, including the older members of the crowd, who possibly were alive at the time not of Kuleshov's Effect but perhaps of its immediate ancestors. Though it is often forgotten now, the brilliant montage section (often viewed as a stand-alone short film) of *The Parallax View* clearly comes from the basic premise of the Kuleshov Effect. Many modern and post-modern works used the concept—including works in literature, art, and even music. One could make the argument that John Cage's empty *4'33"* is a similar experiment in that it attempts to make the audience realize their own role in the art, just as Kuleshov wished to illustrate the importance of both editing and the viewer's automatic causal connection forming, assuming that because two things are near one another, follow or proceed one another, then they must mean something together.

But the section in *The Parallax View*—a film of deep, accretive paranoia—involves images juxtaposed in varying tempo and with varying banners: Mother, Father, Country, Love, Enemy, God, Me, etc., set to what starts out as a quaint Nilsson-esque ballad but builds with the tempo of the juxtapositions and, toward the middle, pushes into the psyche of the viewer, whom the film is supposedly testing for sufficient sociopathic responses and tendencies such that he or she could be a fit for the secret corporation that creates Oswald-style lone-wolf assassins—the basic premise of a big part of the film's mystery. But often enough the images stay the same but come in new contexts, under new banners, near new images. Enemy moves from an initial shot of Hitler to an image of Kennedy followed by an image of Hitler. Throughout there is a contextless face of raw terror, blurred features, a mouth agape, teeth exaggerated into near fangs. Images of sex, nakedness, and intimacy evolve from the opening's open natural treatment to later suggestions and connections of long-ing, lust, abuse, etc. But the images are often the same. The buildup of repeated images creates in the viewer a unique subjective narrative, a meaning individual to each individual viewer. It's like a filmic

Rorschach test, though with a specific I-others-society-God-country-family aim. Korl found the short montage to push the viewer toward notions of an antisocial nature, they seemed tendentious and intentional, crafted, but he then had to realize the power of the montage: It made no narrative. His sense that it was biased, manipulated, intentional was—or so the argument goes—only true for him. Another viewer could easily see its emphasis on more wholesome notions of love, country, God, and family. Someone else could easily watch it and find the occasionally startling juxtapositions and shocking images—of people being beaten, dead bodies, lynchings, the KKK, Hitler, juxtaposed with a father chasing his son down a long hall, a long-shot view of a man curled fetally into a small bed, etc.—as negatively underscoring the positive values the film is meant to convey. You are meant to feel revulsion and shock at the images, to be displeased with the (you can't help but notice) Tim-Curry-in-*The-Rocky-Horror-Picture-Show*-looking transvestites, to feel disconnect and even maybe anger at the antipatriotic images, and if you do not, if for some reason you feel the film is advancing an anti-American asocial perspective, clearly that is your own personal interpretation, which tells more about you than it does about the images or the film, a more or less stochastic assemblage of parts, cantilevered out into nothingness, with only the added elements of self and psychological vantage point to complete the arch, to bring the bridge to ground.

But tonight, that is, as the images play through for the second time, the audience sees not the original montage, but, across the face of Mozzhukhin, right across his flat brow, above and below his lips—in disorderly block letters, ransom letterlike—the lines

HURRY UP
PLEASE
IT'S TIME

Then, again, on the robe of the seductive woman, appears HURRY UP, back to Mozzhukhin, and then back to the soup with PLEASE and then to Mozzhukhin, and then to the child in the coffin over-written with IT'S TIME, then—unexpected, even to Korl—the experiment cycles through again, once more back to Mozzhukhin, this time the graffitist having blacked out all but his eyes, making them intense, haunting, fierce, terrible, back to the woman, then to Mozzhukhin, his cheeks blazing with graffitied rouge, eyes lined with radiant sky blue, long, mascaraed lashes extending toward either temple, lips gaudily red, then once more to the soup, this time its surface—recalling the label of Campbell's alphabet soup—covered with drawn-on dollar signs, then back to Mozzhukhin, whose face is now covered with various sizes of corporate logos, a McDonald's arch, an Amoco torch, a Nike swoosh, etc., the eyes blazing through it all, their irises an irradiated green, again dollar signs marring the eyes' centers, then once more back to the child in the coffin, this time her hollowed face exaggerated Edvard Munch–like and the single word AMERICA laid across her body, and finally again back to Mozzhukin, this time only for a moment, again his face covered with HURRY UP PLEASE IT'S TIME and, but then the images repeat faster, the texts changing places as the film continues to filter through the still images like cards shuffled in a deck, a parallax movement, or whatever, and Korl can't get the film to stop, can't figure out who has messed with it and what is happening, the graffiti moving through the images until there start to be superimpositions of the images, Mozzhukhin's face staring out from the bowl of soup, the little girl's head in the soup, Mozzhukhin's face haunting through the image of the girl in the coffin, the girl in the coffin rising up through the crepe de chine of the seductive woman, the banality of the soup leaching through into the thanotic and erotic images, each corrupting each, and finally the film freezes permanently on the image of Mozzhukhin, across whose brow now reads I LIED and the film won't unfreeze and finally Korl offers to refund the audience's money and just unplugs the projector.

OCTOBER 11, 1988

The unique scale of *The Waste Land* graffiti started to show when not only the media but also the public at large became endlessly fascinated with the emergence of new tags, messages, what were now more commonly being referred to as Toynbees. Graffiti in Scranton was on the rise, from the artful and political to the offensive and self-congratulatory and talentless. Tags tried for some time to compete with the Toynbee artist—or vandal, or poet, depending on whom you asked. There were biblical quotes, movie quotes, pieces of text from obscure literature and philosophy, from psychology, science, world politics, history. Some clever wag defaced the statue of John Mitchell, filling the stone arch above his bronze head with, "Howl, howl, howl, howl! O! you are men of stones: Had I your tongues and eyes, I'd use them so that heaven's vaults should crack. She's gone forever!" An apartment building's crumbling wall read, "Imperious Caesar, dead and turn'd to clay, Might stop a hole to keep the wind away."

There were, as well, the standard crude drawings of red-eyed humanoid mushrooms, of Alice choosing between the one pill that would make her larger and the other to make her smaller, bongs with faces, nuns with bongs, depictions of salacious women, salacious female demons and aliens, humanoid animals having sex. Stores and businesses were almost completely overcome by the new affront to their alley sides and backs and, occasionally, front windows. In one prominent instance, perhaps following the Toynbee allusions to *The Waste Land* or just the extreme popularity of *Cats*, the musical, a graffitist whitewashed the upper portion of a wall—accessed by the roof—of a local synagogue and then painted the area in calico stripes and—in dripping script—wrote, "He looked to the sky and he gave a great leap." Worries about antisemitism abounded in the days and weeks after the incident, though none were sure of the meaning of the graffiti.

Around this time, "Will Robinson" continued quietly to work out his thesis regarding *Lost in Space* and contemporary life and "The Toynbee Convector" and his brief and perhaps misguided application of *The Waste Land* to his own dissatisfied existence.

The number of arrests during this likewise rose; the police had their hands full with mostly teens who themselves were caught with paint all over their fingers, covering their clothes, the aerosol smell suffused deep in their clothes, their hair, in their skin. It was now not even exciting to roll up on a crew of kids defacing a building, two keeping watch—scattering as the headlights lit them up—one other holding a halogen light connected to an extension cord, the last tagging whatever surface they'd chosen. Sometimes they were on a roof, out of easy reach; sometimes they all ran, tried to run. Once, some kid threw a can of spray paint at Dimley, missing him but chipping a noticeable dent in the hood of his cruiser.

The overwhelming amount of text and image overwriting the surfaces of Scranton went beyond the usual sense of urban decay: It had become a paroxysm of raw color, screaming lines written wherever secretive artists could place them, block letters in tiles stuck to pavement, sidewalks; little silhouettes on every street sign, on mailboxes. The weird thing, almost everyone agreed as they set up to shoot, Hegda quietly holding her position in front of the almost unreal lettering behind her—it had the font characteristic of a ransom note, very cleanly rendered across a diagonal spanning from lowest part of the wall at the mouth of the alley to a fire escape on the third floor—was that the outpouring of graffiti didn't take away from the rare occasions of the "original" Toynbees.

A curious "original" of this period was first spotted on September 30, and read:

TOYNBEE: THE CRUELEST MONTH
"WHERE WE GONNA FIND SHADE
OUT HERE IN THE DESERT?"
THE LOST CIVILIZATION 1:28

TOYNBEE: A HEAP OF BROKEN IMAGES
"WHERE EMOTION IS INVOLVED
EVIDENCE IS NOT REQUIRED
ONLY THE RIGHT WORD
IN THE RIGHT EAR
AT THE RIGHT TIME"
THE SKY IS FALLING 1:11

SEPTEMBER 19, 1926

After graduating college in 1926, B. F. (Burrhus Frederic) Skinner moved back in with his parents in Scranton and spent a year there, cloistered in his dark bedroom and hardly sleeping while trying to develop as a writer of fiction. Increasingly depressed, dissatisfied, lonely, and frustrated with his own lack of literary talent, Skinner ultimately gave up fiction, coming to the conclusion that he lacked sufficient life experience and had quote no strong personal perspective unquote from which to write. During this time, while still living at home, a period Skinner later called the quote dark year unquote, he read Bertrand Russell's *An Outline of Philosophy*, and was particularly struck by Russell's discussion of the behaviorist philosophy of psychiatrist John B. Watson. This led Skinner to start taking a more acute interest in the behaviors of those around him and he essayed several quote psychological unquote short stories. Still depressed with his lack of progression, and increasingly intrigued by the behaviors of others and the ideas he'd been reading, he left Scranton to study psychology at Harvard, where, as a graduate student, he invented the operant conditioning chamber (also known as the Skinner Box) and cumulative recorder, developed the rate of response as a critical dependent variable in psychological research, and developed a powerful, inductive, data-driven method of experimental research.

But while alone in his attic room in Scranton, Burrhus first conceived of the utopian world he would later flesh out in *Walden Two*, the metaphorical articulation of his theories of radical behaviorism, and the idealistic portrait of the civilization he thought would be humanity's greatest achievement. He spent hours on what became unfinished pages, fragments, describing these alternate histories, available futures, lateral dimensional existences, indexical societies, modal realities. He ruled out factors of consciousness and human will, leaving only room for behavioral principles, government of actions and interactions—even so early, long before he'd begun his formal study. These worlds were sometimes populated by humanoid figures of varied descent, of alternate forms, but often enough they were like those he'd grown up with, his classmates at Hamilton College, the rowdier boys who'd indulged at frat parties and the grand spectacle of football games. He couldn't understand these other young men and women, what it was they wanted or why they behaved as they did. It seemed clear enough that competition bred war, violence, hatred, that at its simplest level it brought on anxieties and anger responses in the fans as they watched, or rages of joy, complicated emotional behaviors all in the name of play, in the name of sport. The world that was created by the sexual predation and the layers of constant competition—and all that negative stimuli and response!—was everywhere you looked. It was a hostile place, vacillating constantly, filled with uncertainty and ill intention. He didn't have the full clarity he would later bring to bear on *Walden Two*, but he did sit in that darkened room, speaking aloud as he wrote, feverish little sketches of civilizations that never had been or ever would be, little utopias in which everyone was regularized, orderly, where the actions of all members were in harmony and were governed by positive responses and an avoidance of ideas of ownership, possession, competition, any unpleasantness.

In one of his sketches, dated 9/19/26, the utopian ideal he sensed but was far from articulating was worked through a reductio ad absurdum–style inversion: He created a world filled with heroes, competition, violence, sexual possession, and closed relationships, rewards for some and losses and pain for the rest. A place of scarcity ruled by fear and animal lashings out among the members of the society. It was only a matter of a couple of scribbled pages, but as he worked through the early hours of one particular night crafting this anticivilization, this America filled with greed and violence and force and viciousness and competition over everything, where the goal was to consume and to hoard and to seek limitless pleasure at the cost of all others and the risk of finding endless pain, he felt filled with a great and wordless terror, the first ill shiver of a depression he had never known could exist, the type of deep, perilous falling feeling he envisioned radical behaviorism obviating and eradicating altogether by prescribing just how everyone should be and act and live to maximize their productivity, their sense of living a life of purpose, of having a balance between work and leisure, but this particular night—and there were many others, sadly, before he abandoned his science fiction and devoted himself to studying how behavior could be modified and left off the bleaker thoughts that it never could, the fatalistic panic crept over him that there was no saving any of us, that no matter what this greed and striving and selfishness and purposeless competition, these were part of human nature, these were the inescapable truths of our very existence. He recalled lines from Horace then and thought to have them etched into his story, his other reality, "for Diana does not free chaste Hippolytus from the shadows, and Theseus is not strong enough to break the chains of Lethe from his dear Pirithous." No one can be saved from his fate, from Lethe, forgetfulness, oblivion, death.

SEPTEMBER 3, 1752

By the time, in 1752, the English switched their calendar from the Justinian to the Gregorian, they lagged behind much of the rest of the world by eleven days. Their expedient resolution to this problem was simply to skip from September the third to September the fourteenth. Night fell on September second, the sun rose on September fifteenth.

This gave rise to various complaints about the unfairness—perceived as the loss of those days, that time—and also to abstract thoughts about what had indeed happened to that time, whether time as we perceive it means so little—the specific units of our time, as it feels to us, as we know it, according to the calendar we've created to make sense of it from our own point of view—that we can simply skip through it, change it, alter it, rename it. Sure, people understood the time (no matter how it was named) stayed the same: the amount of daylight, the hours of darkness. But it wasn't that in some objective, inhuman way time remained unchanged that bothered people; it was that this underscored, or seemed to, the irrelevance and factitiousness of time as it seems to us. It reminded us of the great world's uncaring existence and the mistaken comedy of our own within it, our imperfect point of view and our confusion that it means something, has truth, maps onto our existence, once more shown to be folly and farce and fiction. What good were all our hopes and fears and prayers if something as fundamental as how we experienced time was relative, changeable, our experience of passing through it (where September 3 gave way to September 4 and to September 5 and to September 6 and to September 7 and to September 8 and September 9 and September 10 and September 11, then 12, 13, 14, each day its own careful thread in the tapestry of our lives) as spectral as our dreams in the hours we were alone?

SEPTEMBER 15, 1965

The television show *Lost in Space* begins.

(Trivia: Though the robot is never officially given a name, an episode in the third season revealed the robot in its packing crate, which was labeled acrostically "General Utility Non-Theorizing Environmental ROBOT," with the first letter of each word emboldened in red, suggesting the acronymic title "GUNTER.")

That night, "Will Robinson"—who is not yet "Will Robinson"— falls asleep to the manic sounds of his parents fighting or making love in fierce whispers through the wall and dreams of space.

(Trivia: The first man-made object to touch the surface of the moon was the Soviet *Luna 2*, on September 13, 1959.)

He does not dream of the show, not exactly. He dreams of empty, silent space. It's hard to say if there is a perspective in the dream, afloat in space. Certainly the sensation is not of a person aware of him- or herself and in space, weightless.

(Trivia: The *Apollo 11* touchdown was just over a year after the end of *Lost in Space*, July 20, 1969.)

It is a great, profound openness, the sensation. This is what he feels, is filled with.

(Trivia: Two days after the show ended, Polish students' protests brought about the Polish political crisis or "March Events." Five days after the show ended, LBJ mandated all federal computers support ASCII character encoding. Ten days after the show ended, Bobby Kennedy announced he would seek the presidency.)

Though everything is silent, empty, void, he is filled with music, filled with incredible sensations of beauty and sadness and what can only be called divinity.

(Trivia: Within a month of the show's ending, LBJ announced he wouldn't seek reelection; *2001: A Space Odyssey* premiered in Washington, DC; Andreas Baader was involved in the midnight bombings of two department stores; Martin Luther King Jr. was assassinated on his motel balcony in Memphis; *Planet of the Apes* was released in theaters; *Apollo 6* was launched (the last unmanned flight of the *Saturn V*); and exactly one month later eighteen-year-old Black Panther Bobby Hutton was killed in a police shoot-out in Oakland; an explosion of natural gas beneath a sporting-goods store triggered a second explosion of gunpowder in Indiana that killed 41 and injured 150; and the song "La, La, La" won the Eurovision Song Contest, which some critics considered Eurovision at its worst and which made extensive use of the eponymous nonlexical vocable, the nonsense syllables "la la la.")

When he wakes, it is to the sounds of his mother singing one of Violetta's arias from *La Traviata* in the kitchen as she juices an orange. Daylight filters through his cotton curtains in visible motion, an effervescence of particulate dust. He has wet the bed.

OCTOBER 3, 1983

The sun's new light is now visible, reaching in at an extreme angle through the basement windows. This is hour twenty-one of Civilization. The Twinkies and the Pepsi and the Kraft American cheese are all gone. The joint's roachy remains have been shredded and smoked; little remains of anything anymore. The four still sit, visibly uncomfortable. G.P. chews an idle fingernail; perhaps this pica is the result of an excess of marijuana and a dearth of prepackaged snacks. Dimley is barely awake. He is, internally, suffering that deep-bowel empty feeling that comes after hours of sustained wakefulness riding on weed and high-fructose corn syrup. His eyes throb, as in visibly pulse in their sockets, swell, and subside. Hedga has been surreptitiously eyeing herself in a well-placed clock face, dragging her fingers across her face while watching the image's fingers do the same, trying to feel what she sees and see what she feels all at once. Walf rolls the dice.

The number that comes up is eleven.

G.P., as he is sitting nearest, bypasses the game's own metahistorical features and reaches for one of Dimley's *There-are-more-things-in-heaven-and-earth* . . . decorated cards, flipping it over with an inflamed-looking red fingertip, raising and holding it very close to his face, eyeing it, not reading it out loud, yet.

An increasingly tense moment of silence passes.

"What does it say?" Walf finally asks, reaching a hand subconsciously up to grip his Adam's apple.

G.P. clears his throat. Dimley begins blinking rapidly, his eyes a flipbook of expression. Hegda pulls her mouth down into a thoughtful frown with her right thumb and index finger.

"It says, 'An unknown airborne virus strikes your country, killing off 98 percent of the population within a year. The suffering is terrible. The survivors wish they were dead. Plants and animals succumb. There is no more life left. Your country is utterly decimated.'"

G.P. looks at Walf, who looks only at the configuration of the board, the painterly representation of the Mediterranean, seat of civilization, looks at the tiles arranged there, the cards stacked around the board, the two dice lying side by side, a five and six showing.

Hegda seems to be trying to find the right expression for the moment, her face contorting in a shifting series of semblances, eyebrows raising and lowering, her lips pursing and retracting, her teeth appearing and receding. Dimley's eyes are at this point literally agog, scarily protuberant, the right one twitching electrically, the left filled with swelling veins.

The silence this time is pregnant with rage and fear, power and helplessness. No sound seems to exist at all for several seconds.

And then, without looking up at any of them, without uttering a single complaint, Walf reaches forward quickly and with exacting motions and sweeps the gameboard—the carefully, painstakingly-laden gameboard—up and away from himself, an errant tile audibly snapping into Dimley's extruded left eye, the flimsy Mediterranean folding in on itself as the cards spray loosely up and flutter down as if in slow motion.

Michael Sheehan

SEPTEMBER 12, 2008

The bird's wings shift up and down and stop and then it glides on invisible circuits of air. Its minuscule figure moving, moving as if without direction, without purpose, without effort. For some reason the bird keeps flying. Its instinct, its essence, its nature. This is what the bird does. The sky around it is cloudless, the sun's light above the distant earth below. The bird moves through the world, its world, solitary and singular, and yet so common as to be basically indistinguishable. It is just an ordinary bird. Below, the geometry of Pennsylvania is rigid and clear. It almost seems to suggest the world is structured, ordered; means something. Not to the bird. It is a bird's-eye view of a bird seeing nothing. Blank blocks of pasture, of fallow field, the veinous lines of roads and highways, stripes of skyscrapers, parti-colored parking lots. The world passes. The bird continues, as if without noticing, as if without reason, to fly above. It arcs through the sky like an object shot, tracing a trajectory meant to terminate, drawn back to the earth. But.

The bird's glide is interrupted, the body stops as though suddenly stricken, perhaps paralyzed, and it begins immediately to fall—the magic of flight is overcome by the reality of weight, of everything succumbing eventually. It is a surprise and yet it is not. The bird's flight was always defined by the necessary and inevitable fall. No one sees it coming, but there is no flight without some landing.

The body falls dully. It does not spiral, or turn, but drops. The wings are stretched out, frozen still and useless. The feathers are very subtly being ruffled by the wind, a suggestion there may still be some hope, a false sign of life. The bird falls.

If we look at the sky and see the bird, see its fall, we see that bird dropping constantly out of sight, streaking darkly across an otherwise unblemished blue. If we look at the sky, this is what we see. We see the quick drop of the bird across it; soon the bird will be gone altogether. But if we look at the bird, if we watch it as it falls, letting the sky fade into the background, then suddenly we see how still its falling is, its dead body hanging there, the world floating around it, nothing changing, no more motion, everything seemingly frozen, etched across the face of the sky, and if we focus like this, if we watch only the bird, the sky stays behind it, and it seems to fall forever.

From A Book of Spells
Andrew Mossin

THE PROPOSITIONS

Poetry itself may then be the Mother of those who have destroyed their mothers.
—Robert Duncan, *The H.D. Book*

We too are Greek—what else could we be?
—C. P. Cavafy

1.

A first sense of what was possible
milk-white curd on the glistening breast of the stream

like pure cut strips of balsa laid in place
memory's optic silence around the rimmed

form of angel dust poured into the day's becoming.
What passes notice—splendid sunsets and sights of evening—

mnemonic curse of the first-to-be-named
last-to-be-saved in water's aftermath.

Black wood slipped over the wrist like a garland
fashioned from balsa strips laid over the woman's hand

as she descends into the falling stream.
Birth stream of her blood oozing out into the wave.

Water is a wave of blood streaming out of the woman.
Namesake's northern lights passing overhead in nights' black skein.

Birth's device, capitalized blood spoon in a wooden box.
Broken into, haunted, hunted inside the box wood.

So it was a dream of her death that sent us back inside?
Quarrel's daylight, peach-green summer inside the hand of her fist.

Like a bargain we collected, passed inside the channel of her
right arm, ribbed release of her body inside the curtained room.

2.

Dream is less real than speech. Saw it was dormant
black bread thrown into a cave. Saw it go down

grooved ancestral fumes of its rising when it gave chase.
Nude form of it that saw us change saw us chained.

Was it black skin folded over sun's optic?
Folds of black skin and black hair blessed by what was absent?

I said her name was wronged, her first name was wronged
next to mine. A said name is wrong.

Alert or was it inert? Speech pulled from the target tongue.
In howls of animal winter the ekphrastic speech she gave me.

Lore is cryptic, black signs on white. Saw the names
written over mine, emblematic breakers on white waves.

Saw name was a fashioned thing, gave it song.
Saw no name was a festooned thing, gave it blame.

Torn from her side was it a mountain ridge that was near?
Torn from her limbs was it a river we heard falling in the dark?

Heard it in a song, black books where the songs lived.
Heard she was Maia, black song of her body inside a thick-shaded cave.

Was it her name I heard, "Maia"? Blue-black angel tongued.
Saw she was passing over us like a blue-black crow in mourning.

A name inside the name she gave us. Her song drowned
out by what came before it. Courtyard's black entryway

built on shells of thistle and straw grass. Heard her break
bread in the entryway, her arms and legs blackened by sun.

His body and hers at the threshold blackened by sun.

3.

Not kept not kin. Not years blackened by island sun.
Not Argos's swift waters black-skinned habit drawn tight.

Not shepherd upright on mountainside. Not saying
it comes to these few things, items held inside the hand of a stranger.

Alert not white inside the frame a pale name kept inside the frame.
Not silent black-toned sepia-toned architecture.

Heard it was a stranger passing that gave it form. Heard it was like death
spreading wings inside the child's lungs breathing for him.

Like water passing inside blood's ovulate.
Like mineral light passed over the lips' opening.

Bread clasped in one hand as if to offer is to please.
Floral principles of abandonment leading to a surface of ragged rock.

Heard it was rock that she laid down upon.
Heard it was a lyre playing inside her womb.

Heard it was Hermes inside the river's current.
Black song of his passing when he was born into the world.

And the tortoise he found by the river's edge was made a singer.
And the tortoise bled inside black folds of his palm.

Held there inside black folds of the river man's hand.
A shepherd brought into black rain to find its hands disclosed.

Hermetic light of the two sealed in one landscape.
And the turtle was fed on light grasses by the house.

And passed under his hand and was sliced open
to reveal the mountain tortoise's marrow.

And slipped his fingers black with blood
beneath the shell and poured its blood into a cup of silver.

And cut the reed stalks to measure and fastened them
by piercing through the back of the dead tortoise.

A nimbus of blue light when it fell apart in his hands.
When the crosshatched pieces didn't hold.

And the lyre played dead.

4.

Out of black beginnings.
Out of corded night's marine sense.

Deadlock's mysterious Other.
Parent of the dead child before the living.

Was I my mother's bride
brought to the burial of her dead son?

> *What do you want me to remember of my birth?*
> *What do you say I must not remember of your death?*
>
> *Was I your memory by another?*
> *Black leveled night rock tripod shot.*
>
> *Shed milk of gray sky on your breasts.*
> *Shook inside the cradle of your arms.*
>
> *Shale rock under our feet.*
> *Was it a traversal at nightfall through black mountain ridge?*
>
> *Was it your agonistic wish for a better life*
> *sending your son across the sea?*

And what did I learn from my father?
Thievery and lying.

And what did you teach me to find?
His body blackened & cut to pieces at the edge of a ravine.

And the surroundings are etched out of view.
And the river near our village is blacked out.

Madrigal signs of an island's inscape.
Littoral scraps of memory pasted onto board.

Eidetic death of Liknon's mountain light.

5.

The sentence is a dream of the falcon flying above us.
The black night is a sentence the dream has sent us.

There is one skin, one face, one eye.
There is no skin, no face, no eye.

Was it his song gave birth to her death?
Was it her death gave birth to his song?

Namesake's epitaphic gift. To parent our taking
in a circle of red ash, to barter for its skin on a hill of poplars.

To drift out where the Cyclades end.
Barrier dream of land's ending, birth's beginning.

Saw the sails set back in sky's carousel.
Blue Aegean night passing over us in passing.

Throat song when the lute was lifted from our hands.
Island's cattle-herding son given back his instrument.

Song that became a circuit of rain and light. Came to give back
    what it robbed.
Silent when they found it replaced by what it had taken.

Andrew Mossin

Shelter of low moon in place of stars. Slick knife
crossing through the shell of tortoise skin.

Blue-black horn of the bull rising in the west. . . .

—April 1, 2015

SEVEN HERMETIC SPELLS

> *I attempt to sow a seed in the survivor that runs
> through his reversed expectation of doom into the
> shadow of the non-survivor. It is as if they embrace
> like man and woman and the shadow comes into
> the light. It is indeed a seed or frail bond between
> light and shadow, a frail window of strangest flesh-
> and-blood between the visible and the invisible.*
>
> —Wilson Harris, *The Infinite Rehearsal*

1.

Like a query sent to reveal everything was sound before there was light
there was the sound of light forming on the lips of those

descendants of my people there were your voices in the ruled light
in the hush of your voices when the light broke over the hills.

Unnameable hills I can't say their names in the bright dusk when the hills
are overrun with black birds falling from the sky

they seem to open up like balls of heavy ash
thrown into the air where one comes back covered in black

filaments like a cloud of names in the black principle place
where the Circean falcon and milk of a black cow

rest near Attic honey and milk offered to us
then denied once in a lifetime. It is clear there are so many

yet to be offered yet to be denied one must rest awhile
with an undyed piece of cotton cloth and place it beside the fingernails

of a dead woman resting near papyrus rolls
a work of dead women resting near paper unfurled.

So that the effort is a rite of purification calling to one then the other
saying their names in unison saying their name in unison

twice over in a lifetime of name keeping
saying they are here with us in the old country

rescued from hardship
yet no different for the effort.

And the shrine is made of juniper wood.
And the nails are black lanes of metal closing in on the fists of a child.

Nearly without form he is written into their breasts.
One then two women forming at the side of a river

where he is nameless held by the contents
of his flesh.

A nameless child
blackened by ash from the shadow of the falcon.

2.

These are rites of purity when there is no purity.
These are rites of name making where there is no name to be made.

One walks backward without shoes
and sets himself to the enjoyment of food.

Blind spirit mouth
eats the food it is given

in finite portions
lays the foundation of his mourning

rising subterranean angel dust
on his lips

cries out with a black Isis band
covering his eyes.

And his right hand
grasps a falcon's head

lying down in the soft cypress
hearing its name relayed through tree crossing.

Black spell of encounter
he nears the edge of transference

on a lofty root
inside clothing he wears

black cotton over white
a garment cut to his body

for his encounter on oblong stone.

3.

In the fakir dust
pine wood stretched beneath the body

of a shepherd
lying beside his reed the body inside

not without aid he can pronounce his words
not without aid or love he can

say there is a visitor to his name
an accompaniment that follows his body

like a visitant
and sees a blazing star descend

pale night star descending over the field
where he was taken years before

spellbound native
to original landscape.

And came to a stop in the middle of its ground
and saw the star dissolve

like a band of wheat stolen
from the light and given back to oblong stone

and held for him what directed
his will.

Saw what directed his will from within
with his own eyes an angel

summoned and sent to return
earth-black inside a seraphic drum.

Come to him in the narrow room where he is laid
on a carpet of blue wool.

And his hands were oath bearers.
And his eyes were formed of what had seen them

a bringer of fire from the falcon's wing.

4.

What closes over memory in the month sad month
delayed by mouths shedding their voices

shredded voices limpid along the line of an interior coast?
"I felt your nakedness imparting to me its signature of indeliverable lore

improvident core of unnameable lagoons covered
by the death's head

mounted on a stream of lagoon water spreading its foamy tide
across my body until I am completed in their passing."

Andrew Mossin

And in memory it is what comes first unable to come second
it is what comes first from the fire pit of ancient regression

encircled with blood on the hieratic papyrus
like a stone borne aloft under the talons of a black falcon

circling above the memory pit
body of the cave spell where each rite is given

back to the dead in hermetic spoors of indecipherable ink.
And spring water cleanses the hands until they are clean

seven springs where the body is calmed
lying down inside a well of springwater the hands atoning

for their sins beside a pure branch of cleansed olive.
Moon of seven nights high in the eastern sky with the seventh night.

5.

And did it come
without barrier in the first signal

without light from the far shore
dreamt up as cure for

agonies inside the spell wagon
invisible to the eye

wet telegenic writing
ripostes of unkind mental conjuring.

To believe in the waxwork of self
relieved of unity harmony undistorted sound

from within the absolute cataract of homeland
like a seized incipient rib stagnant and transitory

rubbed in salt placed on black fronds of peony
burning inside a shield of sea rose and white lily.

And these are the names
you are going to write down

on linen cloth separated into quadrants
from the first hand let there be the integral space of the second

giving back its character of seven leaves
spread between the two hands.

And let the lamp that is not red
be fitted with a piece of linen cloth and oil of spikenard

and dress yourself in a prophetic garment
and hold an ebony staff in your left hand

and protective charm in your right
and wait in readiness for the spirit to arrive.

In skeletal musk of a wolf's head
plead amid offerings of storax gum, cassia & balsam

inhabit the named place
beside a crown of laurel feathers.

Call the god with this chant let it claim what it will of your being.

6.

Grieving, looking everywhere . . .
moon inside of moon

starred rite raked over blind
paratactic shoreline—

say *Re* inside black harnessed idiom
of a far-flown bird

blue-black feathers rising in April dusk
navigating their flight

Andrew Mossin

across western sky's serene pitch
warding off the spell of its dispersions.

Here racked on a rack of language
built of lagoonal waves dispossessed voices

of those who preexist us
rustling dead wings of jagged conch

orphic ellipse
driven like a sea hawk's descent

into tropic waters blighted
sun caught on a rib of distended coral

as if to exist were to cry out in starved ciphers
of wayward incipient speech:

"Oh heaven when you clothe me
in your garment cover my body

in black silk let me float on the waters
of native Crete

and capture our beginnings
in burnt myrrh and cinquefoil."

But the ink isn't dry
the spell can't be undone

year after year to find them in a position
of abject ceremony

row upon row of black letters singed by sunlight
AKAKANARBA KANARBA ANARBA NARBA ARBA RBA BA A

as if to recite their names were to form wings
from an alphabet of cedar ash

stripped elemental strips of sea salt and coral
fluctuating symbols mounted on shards of black sand.

To endure episodes of infrangible repetition
abducted phrases of errant prophecy

when the ink is formed against one's will
dry pots of clay and broken splinters of laurel

implanted on ground near the circle where prayer cloth
fell from the body's intricate habitude.

And a new well was dug
and flowers placed on a rim of clay

wings of balsam and cherry wood
and the garlands were ropes wrapped around his waist

until his mouth opened to the taste of myrrh ink
made from laurel and Ethiopian cumin

nightshade blackened in a clay pot
blackened and ground together

here in accession of daily greeting
mind-swollen rites of constellate improvisation.

Morning's whitening shell hung by a spear of leech
root from the cypress branch.

7.

Rogue light of spring.
Ritual rite of rising smoke.

Hard-recessive tender articulate flakes of sorrow
seeking throats . . . flouts of the whip . . . the journeyman's cross of
    seven letters.

And I, I—

black-eyed island son
dark skinned

Andrew Mossin

heeding this avowal of erasable days
leaning into supernal horizons of blond light

slanted to receive its mariner
star-crossed eidetic wheel of passage.

Wandering past spring's bitter lentisk.
Wreathed invisible sesame planted on the tongue.

Birds flown from their rudderless position in April skies.
Night's paper kites flown above gypsy grave song.

I was bred to receive their message
facing black letters in pages of unread books.

I was with them when they came
forward from the sea's dark caverns

turning to face them among nettles and snail grass
bloodless thirst of Rhodian palm tree's branch

noon's splenetic carved letter
imprinted inside a cove of needles.

And our two names were written as one.
And the seven vowels were spread on a fabric of olive.

And from the black bough of Orpheus's staff
a single falcon rises in red sun.

—May 16, 2014–January 24, 2015

Curtain Call
Terese Svoboda

I DISLIKE THE THEATER. I used to go, yes, but I preferred to watch those seated in the orchestra, to see how they removed their wraps, how they turned their heads in idle greeting, the way they covered their coughs with their gloved hands, and not the actors running in from the eaves in bright clothing and powdered faces, all upset by something the playwright remembered from his childhood. I also preferred the lobby at intermission—or, even better, after the play was over, when everyone's faces were still fixed, looking out onto the street with the same foolishness that held them a few minutes earlier.

That is how I managed all those terrifying months, by observing and learning from those without pretense while cultivating my own. Newly married, we had funds for a year in Paris, but my husband and I chose to settle in a pleasant little town close to the border where money would go much farther. We loved everything about the place: the Tyrolean gold cupola for weekly *musicales*, its promenade of better stores around an ancient fountain-and-statue, even the greenery, so well kept due to an abundance of civic pride—until the arrival of the military.

The border closed instantly. It was really too hard for my husband to walk out the back trails. He was much older than I, and suffered from gout. In retrospect, we certainly should have crawled, hopped, or arranged for him to be carried out in a sling, but my husband refused to flee, like so many others. His family had always been wealthy and lacked the imagination for bravery. Besides, when the Nazis appeared, so blitzkrieg, a different commandant every weekend, butter returned to our table.

We were the reason the hotelier was still working when they arrived, we had preserved his *raison d'être*, providing him with enough income in those last weeks for the hotel to remain unshuttered. Mr. Lucchesi, a transplanted Puglian, smartened our rooms with *eau de cologne* daily in lieu of changing our linens or anything else a maid might do, whom he no longer employed. He apologized, with double sprays, about not anticipating the Nazis' bivouac. My husband, glowering, said nothing in reply but I leaned lower to do up my laces. I was not without cleavage.

When the first commandant appeared for dinner, we smiled and raised our glasses, we tried not to shake visibly. Mr. Lucchesi introduced us as "the Verhovens from Milan, who come for the waters every year." The commandant was so pleased with our company that he suggested a round of cards after dessert. Though my husband excused himself, I persevered, winning often enough, telling a joke when I could.

The next morning, Mrs. Lucchesi knocked on our door. They will find you if you hide in the village, she whispered. If you are the visitors, coming and going, they won't remember. Besides, she said, you improve our business. It was true, the townspeople had dropped by to watch me play cards, buying drinks of their own, if only watered, making secret wagers on my nerve. We approved her argument, partially based as it was on Mr. Lucchesi's position as the town's informant.

We descended from our room singly the next weekend, my husband in too-tight lederhosen and a walking stick, myself in a veil but tightly cinched, and Lucchesi led us to separate tables. My husband was now Heinneman who owned the vines in the next valley, and I was Miss Maria Holzenfeiffer, a student on holiday. We managed. Later I bleached my hair or reddened it with shoe polish or pinned it up in wild tufts. The colonels and generals often brought less sophisticated girlfriends and I didn't want to make them feel out of place. On occasion I discouraged the uglier aides-de-camp and wore a turban and floured my face to look quite ill, or flaunted a stomach, pillow-pregnant, with a black eye, courtesy of the kitchen charcoal. One late afternoon Mr. Lucchesi brought his brother's car around to the front of the hotel, billowing smoke, and we disembarked with a cat on a leash. That week's officer much admired the cat and did not object to the taste of its meat the day we waved goodbye.

Some weekends we hid in our rooms in complete silence without food. Mr. Lucchesi knew when it was best for us to vanish. Not much of an informant, he turned in only those already dead. For example, he claimed to the officers that he had found a bachelor with an arsenal in his basement and wasn't it fortunate he had caught him? when the man had died of a heart attack hours earlier. Through my efforts he continued to think positively toward us, although he chided me often in our rendezvous about the difficulties of his position.

Once an officer did surprise me. His heavy boots beat down the hall toward the back room where my husband slept on a sofa and I smoothed my nails. Before he could shove the door open past the chair leaned against it, I tore off my blouse and threw myself at my husband with a moan. I knew my Germans. The officer muttered, *Entschuldigung* in embarrassment and backed out in a hurry. Alas, my husband hit his head so hard on the arm post due to my fervor, he drew blood. When recounting the scene in vivid detail to the townspeople, he referred to it as his war wound.

He would play the loyal German when he had to, and spring to his feet and salute the moment a commandant entered the foyer. It was good for his gout. He would bow to the man and then cross into the dining room, to approach me with great hesitation and shyness. I wouldn't look up until he spoke, sitting there pretending to read my book, turning pages, staring at its wavering photos through a pair of half-glasses left behind by an elderly waiter. Then I would greet this stranger in front of me with my best French, while he stumbled, searching for words he knew very well. Mr. Lucchesi applauded with his eyebrows, delivering the stew of the night to the commandant.

As Mrs. Lucchesi had predicted, the Nazis, with their comings and goings, couldn't be bothered to keep track of us. They treated us with amusement, sometimes with deference, but mostly ignored us. They had a war to fight. However, one evening a colonel sent an emissary over to our table. I was seated across the room in a suit stitched from the sitting-room curtain, pinned in peekaboo folds around the front, with a peacock feather in my hair from the dead fowl guarding the hotel not three months earlier. My husband had come in with me, this time carrying a brass-knobbed cane and wearing a mustache we'd concocted out of the fur of the cat. He was not that much older than the man standing in front of us, but the heavy lines I had drawn near his eyes suggested otherwise but were smudged where he had leaned onto his knuckles and sighed in nervousness.

The colonel would like to send you a bottle of champagne, said the emissary. His day has gone well and he wishes to fill the room with celebration.

We did not, as we sometimes had in the past, pretend we couldn't understand what he had proposed. Champagne! We accepted. Mr. Lucchesi opened the bottle and poured every glass to the top. When the commandant waved at him to move our tables closer, Lucchesi rushed off to attend to a kitchen emergency.

Sieg Heil! we sang anyway, our glasses raised.

281

Terese Svoboda

Mrs. Lucchesi told us after dinner the colonel's accomplishment was to order the execution of the only other Jews in the city.

By now many of the townspeople knew of our situation and a few had chosen to help. Some days I had too many costumes to pick from, and once an old woman died and left me her wig. Our weekly act endeared us to them; our appearances were all the theater they had. People ordered Lucchesi's dreadful meals to exclaim and guffaw over the Nazi stupidity in private.

Once in a great while I would play to my audience. I would drop a glove or a napkin not far from whatever commandant had arrived and the whole dining room would turn. These dalliances with danger made my husband furious. He would refuse to retrieve it, playing the jealous husband perfectly, despite himself: He would chew at his mustache or gnaw at a nail for the rest of the meal, and thereafter, sometimes for days. I complained that he would betray us, seeming always to be the same nervous man. I had to pick fights until he forgot his fear.

We carried on like this for thirteen months. Who were we? Not even actors. We couldn't keep track of who we were in such desperation. We had passed beyond stage fright, we were permanently frightened. Early one morning, my husband hung himself from the rafters. The belt that he'd twisted around his neck Lucchesi had found beside the railroad tracks after the passing of one particularly long set of sealed cars. My husband had begged him for it, saying it would give him courage. It gave him courage—to despair. My less discreet performances had made it increasingly difficult for him to remain unmoved, and the pressure to act had overwhelmed him.

Mrs. Lucchesi heard me wailing in the hall and had to slap me quiet. I spent the day in the room. So I slept with a few of the officers and the hotelier. My husband had made the choice not to leave at the beginning when we had a chance, what else could I do? I had played my part.

The next evening I walked into the dining room dressed in widow's rags. The commandant, whom I'd met the night before, saluted me and extended his condolences but then ate his kraut without another word. Had we just amused him and all of the other commandants? I laughed out loud after he left the dining room—he must've heard me—then I ate alone for several days thereafter without noticing he no longer appeared, staring out the window where I could just see the packed earth that hid my husband. I missed him dearly, far more than my apparent lack of remorse might suggest. Our *pas de deux* was over, no one's arms stood ready to catch me. I would be caught. I prepared for it, I stopped displaying myself in costume, I let my hair alone. In my grief, the planes overhead and the moving of troops did not register, although Mr. Lucchesi informed me at least three times that week that the town and indeed the country were now free. I could leave.

When I returned, years later when I could once again afford it, I came not as a tourist, for you are never really a tourist after you have lived so long and so vividly in one place, but as someone who had never left. I passed the town's bakeries, now changed into expensive cafés, and several smart shoe shops. Happy to see the town in good form, I waved at the tuba ensemble assembling in the cupola, and walked to the hotel, which now advertised for both dogs and people. In front stood a statue of the restaurateur to commemorate his service during the war as a spy. Well, he had gained plenty of information from me. I had come not to honor him but my husband, he who could not wait for the curtain call, who could not see past the stage light glinting off the audience's jewels as they turned toward the exit, nor the ushers unlocking the doors, who could not imagine the freshly rained-on pavement outside, with the sidewalk so crowded beside the emptying theater, the bright moon pressing down so gaily on the clustering cabs.

Of course no one knew me.

Caesar's Show
Yannick Murphy

"THESE?" THE BOY SAYS, rolling two race cars across the wooden hallway floor when his mother, Sarah, asks him where he got them. "My teacher gave them to me," he says. Outside, the dog barks and whines. The dog is in the yard, his nose against a chain-link fence, wanting to get closer to a litter of stray kittens whose eyes are still closed. Rats are scurrying across the phone line that runs to the house, their shapes black in the dying light.

"Really? Your kindergarten teacher gave you those two cars? Why?" Sarah says while standing at one end of the hall.

"I don't know," the boy says. Sarah wishes that her husband, Benjamin, were home so she could tell him that she thinks their son has stolen the cars. She would like to discuss what to do about the stealing and about the lie. Sarah never feels confident reprimanding her son. She always thinks she is being too easy on him. But Benjamin will not be home for a while. He is at the airport, waiting for a foreign client he's supposed to pick up and escort to a meeting with the senior partner. Sarah hears the rats jump from the phone wire to the top of a palm tree. The palm-tree leaves rattle and shake. Everything in the yard sounds like it's moving because of the Santa Anas. They blow and the hot air moves across her yard, shaking the grapefruit tree. Its fallen leaves skitter across the paved walkway.

Sarah picks up the phone and calls Benjamin. "How much longer?" she asks.

"An hour at least. The plane's delayed," he says.

She picks up the broom. The house is so dirty, there are bits of food on the floor, and balls of hair, but just as she lifts the broom she hears the dog barking again. He won't stop barking at the kittens that were born on the other side of the chain-link fence where rough grass grows in clumps and bare old tires lie. With her broom she goes out to where the dog is, his nose in between the diamond-shaped spaces of the fence, and she tells him to hush, just hush. "I'll hit you with this broom if you don't," she says, but she knows she would not and instead she sits down beside Bob. She pets his fine broad head and runs

284

her hand down his thick black fur. She looks at the kittens too. "Oh, they are cute. No wonder you like them. Yes, you would be a good father to them if they were on our side of the fence," she says. Her son comes out with the cars and sits down next to her. They all look at the kittens and her son shows the kittens his two cars and then he rolls the cars up and down the dog's back, which spreads the fur apart so that the dog's pale skin shows brightly against the black fur. Sarah still holds the broom and looks down at the bristles, noticing how they are bent backward, as if every time she ever swept she swept too hard, as if everything she tries to sweep up is ground in or stuck on the floor and will not come loose.

The phone rings and it is Benjamin saying, "The good news is the plane is landing now. The bad news is, Rogers, who is supposed to meet him for drinks, just got a flat tire on the expressway, and it looks like I'll have to be the one taking him for drinks." Sarah can hear the rumble of the planes flying low. "Call you later," Benjamin says.

The two cars are on the table at dinner. Her son slides them between the salt and pepper shakers and Sarah asks again, "Did your teacher really give you those cars?" The boy doesn't answer. He decides to put his fork in his mouth instead. "She did not give you those cars, my love," she says. The boy continues eating. He takes his fork and pierces as many pieces of chicken as he can onto the tines, then he stuffs the forkful in his mouth. Sarah can see the white pieces between his lips because there is no possible way he can fit all of the food in his mouth and keep his mouth closed.

"When your father gets home I'll tell him that you stole the cars. I bet he'll say that tomorrow, at school, you will have to give the cars back," Sarah says. The boy continues to chew. Later, when she clears the table, and her son has gone into his room, she notices the cars are gone. When she is finished with the dishes she goes to his room to check on him. He is reading on his beanbag chair, but she does not see the cars and the cars don't seem to be in his pockets either. She feeds the dog after dinner, because someone told her once that dogs should always be fed after the family is fed because that puts them in their place and they know they are not the alpha dog and that you are the alpha dog. Really, though, she has no interest in being the alpha dog and likes to feed the dog after the family eats because after dinner there are always scraps from their plates she likes to give the dog and the dog's food that they buy is like rolled-up balls of chewed cardboard and who can live on that? Not my dog, she thinks, not a dog who is still so protective over the newborn kittens that he has

not even come into the house for dinner but is still out there in the
darkness, still barking, but barking with a sore-sounding throat that
sounds very sad to Sarah and seems to strike a chord inside of her and
for once she knows exactly how that expression came to be, because
she feels as if somewhere inside of her that sore-sounding bark is
resonating against a piece of her, such as her breastbone, so that she
feels the bark as much as she hears it.

"Let's jump," the boy says and he takes Sarah by her hand and
leads her to her bedroom and tries to get her up onto her bed with
him. It is close to the boy's bedtime. She should not be letting him
jump because he will become too excited and sleep will take too long
to come to him, but she is feeling sorry that she accused the boy of
lying and so she takes off her shoes and starts to jump with him.
Holding hands, they are jumping high, the bed covers beneath them
becoming jumbled under their feet. "In circles, Mommy," the boy
says and so they jump going in circles now and she's laughing with
her son, because she is out of breath and her son is saying, "Higher,
Mommy, higher" and so she is trying to jump higher now and when
she does she sees that she can see into the neighbor's bedroom across
the way. It is easy to see because it is such a short distance from their
house that if she was to open the window and lean out she could
probably touch the window of the neighbor's bedroom. The neighbor
is Caesar, who does not have children or a wife. His wife died a year
ago. At first it looks like Caesar is watching a television show, but
then she realizes it is Caesar on the screen having sex with a woman
in his bedroom. Sarah knows the woman. She realizes that Caesar
filmed himself and his wife having sex years ago, that he must have
set up a tripod and a camera and let it roll. Sarah, when she realizes
what she is seeing, falls down to the bed, bringing her son down with
her.

"What? Let's keep jumping!" her son says.

"No, we're done jumping. It's your bedtime. Tomorrow is a school
day," she says.

When she tucks him in, she says, "Close those brown eyes and we
will see each other in the morning." She puts her mouth against the
top of his head to kiss him, feeling with her lips the softness of his
hair. Outside again they can hear the dog barking and whining.

"He loves those kittens," her son says. "Can't we go to the other
yard and pick those kittens up and give them to Bob?" her son says.

"No, they are not his kittens. It's best if we leave them over there.
The mother of those kittens would not want us touching them. If we

do, she might not take care of them anymore."

"Why?" the son asks.

Sarah shakes her head, "It's just what mother animals sometimes do," she says.

After she kisses her son good night, she leaves the door open for him because sometimes he gets scared. Then she goes to her bedroom and she turns off the light. She stands on her bed and peers out through the window. The Caesar in the show, the Caesar who was once married, is getting head from his wife on the screen and the Caesar who is now lying on his bed watching his dead wife giving him head is touching himself. When the phone rings and Sarah answers it, she whispers, "Hello," and Benjamin says, "What are you whispering for?" and so she tells him what she is seeing right now outside their bedroom window and Benjamin says that is so sad, and Sarah says how it is also disgusting, the man should buy some curtains, and she wonders if that makes it more sad that it is also disgusting or if it is less sad.

"Well, my client's plane landed and I'm waiting for him to go through a long line at customs," he says. "Tell me, what else is new there?"

"Your son is a thief," she says. Benjamin laughs, "Really?"

"He stole two cars from school. He said the teacher gave them to him."

"Well, maybe she did," Benjamin says.

"No, she did not. He practically admitted to stealing them in his own way. What should we do about it?" she asks.

"Do about it? Nothing. He knows you know he did something wrong. He won't do it again."

"Nothing? Shouldn't we punish him in some way?"

"I suppose we should make him return the cars," Benjamin says. Sarah hears the dog now, he is no longer barking. Now he is wailing.

"Maybe he should do something more. Maybe he should write about it. He should write fifty times that he will never steal cars again," Sarah says.

Benjamin laughs, "Does he even know how to write that?"

"I'll show him," Sarah says. "I'll write the first sentence down and then he'll write the rest."

"What else is going on?" Benjamin says.

"Our dog thinks he's a cat," Sarah says.

"A cat? Oh here's my client, that was fast," Benjamin says. "I've got to go."

Sarah hangs up the phone. She thinks having her son write fifty times that he will never steal cars again is a good punishment. She wishes Benjamin had agreed with her, or told her he thought it was a good punishment too. She decides that she will definitely make her son do it. I'm his mother, I can decide my own son's punishment, she thinks, and then she wonders if her son wakes up early, will he have enough time to write fifty times on a sheet of lined paper that he will never steal cars again before she has to take him to school.

When the dog wails again, she goes outside. She doesn't need a flashlight to see when she sits down next to the dog because there is light enough to see by from Caesar's sex show and light enough from a nearby streetlamp. The dog is panting heavily and the kittens are awake and mewling. The mother cat is not there. "Come inside now," she says to the dog, worried that the mother cat will never come back now to feed her kittens, but she cannot budge the dog. She pulls up on the scruff of his neck, but the dog is a large-breed dog, and he weighs more than Sarah. The dog cannot just be lifted and made to stand and come away. The dog turns his head toward her and Sarah wonders for a moment if her dog will bite her if she keeps pulling on him, even though the dog has never attempted to bite any-one in his life. Sarah goes inside. In her bedroom, when she is ready for sleep, the light from Caesar's show is too bright. She wishes she could just get up and go over to Caesar's house and ring the doorbell and tell him to turn it off and tell him to buy some curtains. If Benjamin was here, he would probably do it, she thinks. He would know exactly how to talk to Caesar and ask him kindly and smile, but she cannot do it. She would never talk to him about his sex show. The only way she has ever talked to Caesar was when Benjamin was standing right there beside her, and even then, she did not talk to him directly. It was Benjamin who did all the talking and she just nodded. She thinks how that is usually the case with everyone they know. Benjamin does the talking, and she just listens. If she does say anything, it is a short answer or she will ask a question, anything to prevent herself from having to speak for too long, because it is so much easier to let other people do the talking.

The light comes in through her curtains and, to make matters worse, the moon has now risen and it's coming up from the opposite direction of Caesar's screen so that Sarah feels like she's now living on a two-moon planet with so much light bathing her room and her body. Just when she thinks it can't get any brighter in her house, that even daylight would be less glaring, there comes a chopper. It is flying low and loud, its searchlight landing on her yard and on all the yards around their house. She can hear it heading for the nearby stretch of freeway, and she can hear it circling back again, over her roof and down her street. Its beam of light comes right through her window and onto her body where she's on top of the covers wearing just a short nightgown because the night is such a hot one. She gets under the covers, pulling them over her head.

When she hears a creak and then footsteps on the linoleum floor, just inside the back door, she takes her head out from under the covers. She thinks of running out of bed and grabbing the phone, but it's too late. There is already a man standing in her room. She thinks she can smell him first. He smells of sweat and of the city itself when the endless car tires rolling over the pavement on the hot days smell like burning rubber, and he smells of the stale dust that blows down from the palm trees in a Santa Ana and swirls at your feet on the burning-hot sidewalks.

But there is no man there. It's just her imagination. It's just a hot Santa Ana wind that has come through the window and is trapped against the wall of her room so that it feels almost like a man is standing there. Outside, the dog howls and barks, and every once in a while she can hear the chain-link fence ring after being struck by the dog's paw as he hits it in his frustration to be closer to the kittens.

Out her window, she hears what sounds like the wind rustling the fallen leaves from the grapefruit tree, and then she hears a voice. "Sarah?" she hears. She sits up in bed, clutching her covers to her front. She peers out the window.

"Yes?" she says, her voice sounding like she is answering a telephone instead of leaning out her window late at night talking to an unknown dark figure.

"It's Caesar. Your neighbor. Sarah, your dog keeps howling and barking. I can't sleep," Caesar says. She does not recognize Caesar at first because he isn't wearing his glasses that she always sees him wearing, that and the fact that he is just wearing his boxer underwear.

"I'm sorry. I'll bring him in right away," Sarah says.

"Thank you, Sarah," he says. After he walks back to his house, she goes outside to the dog.

"Come on now. It's time for bed. It's time to go inside, you big pain," she says. She lifts up on the scruff of his neck, but he hunkers down, whining. He is so big she cannot lift him or even push him or pull him. Every time she tries to pull on his neck, she gets a handful of fur instead. She goes back inside the house, not needing a flashlight, of course, to see the way because Caesar's show is still on, and she can see the cracks in the paved walkway as easily as if it were daylight. "What does he mean he can't sleep? Does he fall asleep every night to that show? Is that the only way he can fall asleep?" she thinks to herself. In the house she takes some leftover chicken out of the refrigerator and brings it back out with her to the dog. He is usually quick to grab the food from her hand. He is usually so hungry all the time, but now he does not have any interest in the food, and when she lets him smell it from her hand, and takes a few steps backward toward the house, he doesn't even look at it. All he wants is those kittens.

Her hand is small, but not small enough to fit through the chainlink fence. If only her hand were smaller. There is only one person she knows whose hand is small enough to fit.

Her boy is sleeping peacefully on his back. She gently shakes his shoulder, saying his name, but he is deep in sleep. In each hand he is holding a race car. "Wake up," she says, and when he does not, she picks him up and carries him out with her to where the kittens are behind the fence. In his sleep, he still holds on to the race cars. As she's carrying him he starts to stir. "Hmm," he says, and then his body becomes more rigid as he wakes up completely. "My cars!" he says, and then he looks down at his hands and realizes they are still there and relaxes. "Mommy, why are we outside?" he says.

"I need for you to do something. Bob needs one of those kittens. The mother cat was out here earlier and I talked with her. She said Bob could have one."

"Really?" her son says.

"Yes, it's OK," Sarah says. "Go ahead, you reach through and take one. My hand is too big," she says. The boy does not want to put his cars down. "I'll hold them for you," Sarah says. She holds out her hand so he will give them to her.

"Mommy, you have to give them back. Give them back, OK?" her son says.

"I promise," she says.

"Then I get to keep them for tonight. Right? I don't have to give them back until tomorrow at school. Right?" her son says.

"Yes, OK. They're all yours tonight," she says; anything, she thinks, to keep Caesar from coming back over without his glasses, wearing his boxers. He lets her take the race cars and then he reaches in. "Which one?" he says.

"Any one, the mother cat said I could take any one."

Her son grabs an orange kitten, smaller even than his own hand, which mews when he lifts it, and pulls it through the metal of the fence. Bob jumps up immediately when he sees that her son has the kitten. "He's so soft," her son says. She takes the kitten from him and gives him back the race cars. She holds the kitten up high because Bob is now jumping up and down, trying to get the kitten. "Run back into the house," she says to her son and they both run into the house, Bob running behind them, and then in front of them, his paws stepping on her, his claws digging into her bare feet and scraping her instep, drawing blood.

Once everyone's inside, she slams the door behind her, so the dog cannot get out again. "Give him the kitten. He wants it, Mommy," her son says. But Sarah is afraid to give Bob the kitten. If she gives it to him, she's not sure what he'll do. The length of Bob's tongue is even longer than the entire kitten. Just by licking it he may hurt it.

"Get me a towel," she says to her son.

"What?" he says. He cannot hear her because Bob now is barking louder than ever. He's frantic, jumping up onto her, placing both paws on her chest so that she has to lean against the wall so he doesn't knock her down. Standing full height, the dog is even taller than she is. "A towel!" she yells. She knees her dog hard, and she kicks him, but he doesn't care. "No! Knock it off, Bob!" she says to the dog, but he doesn't listen.

After her son comes with the towel, she wraps up the kitten, while still holding it high in the air. "You can't hold him up forever, Mommy," her boy says.

She knows he is right. Eventually she will have to give Bob the kitten. The kitten is so small. It feels as if she could be holding just an empty towel in the air. "You, go back to bed," she says to her son.

"But what about the kitten . . ."

"No buts, if you want to keep those race cars for the night, you march back to bed right now."

"But you already said I could keep the race cars tonight, Mommy."

"Yes, I meant it too. Just go to bed, please," Sarah says. "I will take care of this kitten. The kitten will be fine." Her son walks back to his room, looking over his shoulder as he walks down the hallway.

She takes the kitten to her room and sits up in her bed with him. Bob, of course, comes bounding onto the bed too. In her arms she holds the kitten wrapped in the towel and Bob sticks his huge head into the towel and starts licking the kitten. She lets him lick it a few times, and then she pushes his head away. "That's enough, let it breathe, Bob," she says. When he doesn't get to lick it, though, he starts to bark.

"What's he barking for, Mommy?" she hears her son call from his bed.

"Go to sleep!" she says back to her son.

Bob paws at the kitten now, his heavy paw pressing into its body, making it cry. She gets up from the bed. "This isn't working, Bob," she says, and she puts the kitten in the towel in a shoebox, then she goes in the hallway and puts it in the linen closet on the top shelf, and closes the door. Bob scratches the door and barks. She goes back to her bedroom and lies down in bed, holding her hands to her ears, but she can still hear everything.

"You didn't really talk to the mother cat, did you?" her son says loudly from down the hall so he can be heard over the barking. She doesn't answer him.

"You lied about the mother cat!" her son yells.

"You lied about the race cars!" she yells back, before she can stop herself from saying it, before she realizes how immature it sounds, and how she doesn't want her son to know how adults can be so stupid sometimes that they sound like children.

Her son doesn't say anything. She is hoping that maybe he did not hear her.

"I can't sleep, Bob is barking too loud," her son says.

"Just let him bark. He'll stop soon," she says. Bob barks for a long time, though, and she's awake listening to him. Even if he were not barking, she thinks, she would not be able to sleep because the light from Caesar's show is still on. She thinks about going over there and telling him to turn it off, to get some damn curtains, that his show is keeping her awake, but she doesn't dare. She doesn't want him to know she knows he is watching a show of himself having sex with his wife who's now dead. She doesn't want to know herself, even, that such sadness exists. Eventually, in the middle of the night, Bob stops barking, and she falls asleep. Sarah doesn't even wake up when Benjamin arrives home and gets into bed next to her. She only wakes up when he leaves the house at daybreak to go back to work, and she hears the front door close and his car engine start.

She gets up from bed and sees the hall closet door is open. In front of it is a stool. The kitten and the towel are no longer there. For a moment she has a ridiculous thought, she thinks the dog was able to drag the stool to the closet to reach up and get the kitten. Then she opens her son's door to his room and there is the dog curled in a ball beside her son's bed. Between the dog's front legs is the towel the kitten was wrapped in. When she goes to unwrap the towel, the dog is too tired to wake up and doesn't stir. The kitten is in the towel, and she puts her hand on it.

"The kitten's dead," her son says, still holding his race cars. "Bob licked it to death. I couldn't stop him, Mommy. He held it between his paws so he could lick harder, and he pushed so hard on it. I'm sorry. I gave it to him so he would stop barking. He was so happy to have it, Mommy," her son says, crying. She hugs her son. "It's OK," she says. "The kitten was so little. It couldn't survive without its mother. I shouldn't have taken it away from her in the first place," Sarah says.

She takes the towel and wraps it so that it covers the entire orange kitten. They take it outside and the dog, who is still sleeping, doesn't follow after them. They use a large spoon to dig up the ground and bury the kitten under the grapefruit tree, where her son says is the best place because it is cool under there in the shade and the kitten will not have to be hot during the day. They check on the other kittens. They are all gone. "The mother cat must have moved them. That's good," Sarah says.

After that they eat breakfast, and then her son gets out two lined sheets of paper and two of his pencils from his pencil box. He gives her one sheet and one pencil. "Let's start writing," he says.

She sees he is writing "I will never steal race cars again," over and over again. She rubs her eyes. She is so tired from the night before. She feels so bad for the kitten that had to die by Bob's incessant licking and pawing. She feels so bad for her son, who was crying so hard to see the dead kitten, thinking it was his fault. If it wasn't for Caesar, it never would have happened. She can hear that Caesar is awake. She can hear his morning radio show playing from his open kitchen window as loudly as if the radio were in her own home. She begins to write. She writes, "Your sex show kept me up all night and if you really want to watch that stuff you should go to the store and buy curtains." She writes this fifty times.

"I'm done!" her son announces and holds up his page.

"Good, I'm done too. Let's put them into envelopes." She quickly folds her letter and seals it into an envelope so her son can't read it.

After breakfast, on their way out the door to drive to school, she tells her son, "You go on ahead and get in the car. I forgot something in the house." She runs back into her bedroom. Through her open window she can see Caesar's open window. She can see his unmade bed. She takes her envelope and tosses it through her window and out over her small strip of grass and right in through Caesar's open window, where it lands on his wrinkled bottom sheet.

She goes back out to the car. Her son has already strapped himself into his car seat and is holding his race cars.

"How about I take you late to school? How about we go to the store first? You can pick up two race cars if you want to. You can pick up the same exact ones even," she says and turns the car on.

"Yippeee! Let's go!" her son says.

She can see Caesar with her envelope in his hand coming out of his house. He comes up to her side of the car and leans in her window before she can drive away. "We're off to the store to buy race cars!" her son says, leaning over from his car seat to tell Caesar.

"Race cars! That's great. I'm off to the store myself," he says.

Sarah drives onto her street. The Santa Anas are picking up again. She can feel the bone-dry desert air coming in through her open window. Warm as another person's breath, it feels as if someone she couldn't see were very close to her and sighing heavily.

Zeroes
Magdalena Zyzak

NOW FOR THE THIRD DEATH. The second was Adam in 2016, Adam
with whom Erica had been sleeping, not without his wife's permission, until he became too ill for sex. The first was a dog Erica struck.
She didn't stop—she was hours from the nearest town and driving
her new boss's car. It was a dachshund, and she cried until the nearest town.

They're walking down a trail into a coppice of pines. The air has a
cold celebratory smell with undertones of flesh, like a hand that's
handled ice cubes.

"I find what you're saying, I don't know, distasteful." Saskia's
smiling and saying this.

Perhaps this is not precisely a smile. If you don't know someone
well, Erica likes to say, especially to younger women, you only see
the median of faces.

"That's the point, of course," says Erica. "These days, nobody has
any taste and that's just fine, because this way, no one can oppress
anyone. We're all just happy, equal philistines." Walking stick in
hand, Erica atop a car-sized stone.

Melting snow and black and yellow lichens fill the fissures in the
limestone barrens.

"Oh, I don't know. Everyone should just do what they feel. As long
as they don't bomb a city or teach kids creationism or whatever,"
Saskia says.

"I'd vote the majority shares your opinion." Erica checks Saskia's
face. Unsatisfactory. Reaction minimal. Smiling Buddha face, content with simplifications.

They met last night, at the hotel restaurant, and over several medi-
ocre wines, Saskia told Erica all about Timmy's Ping-Pong tourna-
ment. Timmy is Saskia's older, happy son, equal in every way to his
depressive younger brother.

"You've got my vote," says Erica. "Timmy's got my vote for

president of Ping-Pong."

This gets a reaction. Oxytocin, serotonin, and whatever all else is in the neuro cocktail called maternal pride. "Well, I texted Timmy's picture to my brother," Saskia says, "but then I wasn't sure he got it, so I sent it again in an e-mail, in the body *and* as an attachment."

"Timmy wins!" says Erica atop the rock.

"Fourth place, so cowinner, actually."

"Penduline tits? Really?" Erica jabs her stick into an oblong galaxy of saxifrage, disrupting the universe ever so slightly.

"It's true," says Saskia. "But they don't live in Newfoundland. They live in Europe and North Africa. I know all about birds. The penduline's related to the *true* tit. There's even a fire-capped tit."

"That's what I'll have. Two of those," says Erica, "and a glass of malbec."

She regrets having come on this hike, but a lazy regret, a regret that is barely a thought. She could've stayed in the hotel and waited for Colin by the fire in the reading room. Last night, while he slept, she found some ladybugs in the heater and his satchel under the bed. What interesting, boring things he had: a broken shard in a plastic box, a pair of headphones, a condom, a passport (Colin Sohlberg Holloway, three entry stamps to Spain and one to Morocco, and no USA), and an insubstantial novel with "For C" and a woman's name signed on the title page, dated a few months back. She likes this— Colin is, or has been, at least, desired.

"You bet. Remember my words, never go without a bra," says Saskia, gracelessly scrambling over a deadfall. "When I was pregnant, I slept with mine on. I say nonsense to bra politics. Bras are purely a practical matter."

"In the age of universal bralessness," says Erica, "disenfranchise-ment is frowned upon, though in Vermont and Maine, felons aren't allowed to vote unless they put their bras back on."

"That's right," says Saskia (who can't have been listening care-fully), hesitating over a puddle.

March air stings through Erica's sweatshirt, jacket, and bra—no undershirt, no tights beneath her jeans.

"We came here last spring for Michael to check out the grounds, before the hotel was built," Saskia says.

"First time Colin's ever brought me here, and I forgot to check the weather. I thought it'd be warmer already. So I'm stuck wearing

Colin's ugly sweater," Erica lies. The sweater is ugly and hers.

It's often important to Erica to disagree, ideologically, with men she fucks. With women, it is not so difficult to form attachments either way: at peace, at war, even in a vacuum of ideas. Or so, at least, she likes to say about herself, and self-analysis is a leaky ship with every kind of spoiled cargo.

"I can lend you stuff, if you want. My husband is the head engineer for the whole thing, you know."

"Sinks last," says Erica.

Sinks like fossil shells, seaside rock pools, sinks with surfaces like frozen waves. Colin is contracted to install the sinks in the hotel, sinks he's designed.

"Sometimes it's those last touches that make a household," says Saskia.

They are pleasantly, unpleasantly united as women of men involved in the serious business of building things in a world with harsh weather.

"I have a bouclé skirt you could borrow. Of course, it'll be too big for you. This, here, is from my first one," she spanks her hip. "And this," she pats the belly of her quilted jacket, "from my second. I still have a huge disgusting cyst in here."

"Why don't you have it removed?"

"I'd never do elective surgery. It's unreasonable and expensive, darling." There's a rip in Saskia's eye, where the iris bleeds into the eye white. "The only time I was skinny was when I starved myself in the period leading to our wedding. I was so committed, I considered eating tapeworm eggs, you know, like Callas, like Maria Callas, until I heard tapeworms could multiply. I wasn't going to become a love nest for worms. Not yet, I thought. I settled on pickles and low-fat cottage cheese. We went on our honeymoon to Hawaii. All my clothes were baggy and I was stuck in my bikini. Your hips expand during childbirth. It's scientific, you'll see. You're young, still. Let me tell you this, when we first saw you in the restaurant yesterday, I said to Michael that you and Colin would create great-looking offspring. I couldn't stop looking at your hair, though girls are said to take their hair after the father, unfortunately. Is your color natural?"

Erica's head is wrapped in scarves. "In high school, I shaved it," she says, and the trail forks, and the light between the needles is a little colder. "And my father loved it. He patted my head and called me 'son.' I think it was minutely detrimental."

"Sure, but is your *color* natural?"

297

"Oh, yeah, sure," says Erica. "But to be natural is such a hard act to keep up."

They walk close beside one another, with Erica's one step to Saskia's one and a half. Dark pines behind them now. The barrens open into three more or less identical perspectives. It's a choice, but a farcical one. So they stop, and the barrens are quiet.

"Well, we have to follow these, if we can find some more." Erica points at a cairn on the side of the path, which ends here.

"To what?" Saskia says.

"What?"

"You said it was detrimental. I'm glad I have boys, now that my youngest is past the spray-while-changing-diapers period. Oh boy, have you ever changed a diaper?" With her hands, Saskia suggests unspeakable cornucopias.

"Only on an adult," Erica thinks, but doesn't say. This kind of articulated subservience to the body and its products, this belongs to death, communism, middle-class womanhood. One must resist, resist.

"All I'm saying, they're not as *proofed* as the manufacturers would have you believe," says Saskia. "It's like shampoos. They certainly don't work."

"I don't know, had I not shaved my head, I think I would've had more boys. I spent my time all agonized about the lack of fucking," Erica explains. "I wanted to become the next Simone Weil, you know, starvation, protest, and the whole buffet, although the only thing I was protesting was my lack of popularity. Then there was something Weil had written about beauty being 'Christ's tender smile coming to us through matter' or something like that. Then some waiter in a New Orleans café, some waiter called me 'son,' and I remember realizing I wasn't quite a saint, but just an inadvertent cross-dresser."

As Erica's been talking, they've started out over the barrens, unconsciously continuing in the direction they were facing when the path had ended.

"Or maybe it wasn't a waiter. Or maybe the waiter was my dad."

"Your dad was a waiter?"

"A stockbroker," Erica says.

"Honey. I have no idea what you're going on and on about."

"That's fine," says Erica.

Saskia's mouth parts, and no words come out.

Saskia, Erica thinks, a too-elegant name for this being beside her. A name for a porcelain doll, a Dutch royal. Let's switch. I ought to be

Saskia. You can be Erica, Erica the Red, ax-throwing wench of the Vinelandish north.

"When I met Michael, he dressed terribly. A bad sense of fashion, and I mean actively *bad*, is almost as bad as religion," says Saskia. "He had a neon shirt, and I found a fanny pack in his office drawer. I was his assistant after college. Soon, we were *fucking*." She says the word with stony inattention, like a Protestant talking about the Immaculate Conception. "Just because I had enough imagination to know he'd probably look better naked. We used to do it on a futon in his office."

"Do you still?"

"What?"

"On a futon in his office?"

"Nah." Saskia points at her belly, presumably at her "huge disgusting cyst," like some suburban strip-mall psychic pointing at her crystal ball. "First thing I did once we married, I made him get rid of the fanny pack *and* the futon."

Darkness comes evenly here, in the barrens, as if by way of a computer-guided aperture. Perhaps, without Erica noticing, it has become nearly dark.

In her apartment in New York, Erica has heavy gray velvet and blue sheer curtains to effect a state of all-day dawn. The flat stability of noon is not for owls or Erica.

"It's four. We probably ought to go back," says Erica, looking at her phone. "It's weird, my G6 has no reception. Do you have G6 or 7?"

Saskia's resting. She has spread a scarf on the stone underneath her. "New G7, but I left it in the room. . . . Michael almost killed me on our honeymoon, you don't even know. He wanted everything to be perfect. He wanted to show me everything, volcano, plantations. He dragged me all over the island on a bus. I had blue curaçao coming out of my ears because it was, you know, inclusive. Michael'd make me finish it each time, before getting up from the table. That was *not* OK. I didn't mind telling him that. I was always buzzed . . . by the end of the trip, all my clothes fit perfectly again." She laughs. She tightens her shoelaces and gets up. "These are some first-class water-resistant boots. You should get a pair."

Erica studies the barrens, each of three perspectives, then the pines behind them. "We should just go back the way we came."

"This *is* the way back, dear."

299

"This?" Erica points at random into the barrens.

"Yep," says Saskia with confidence.

"Not through the trees?"

"It's a loop."

Saskia sets off, Erica following, over the barrens, sporadically hopping a rift or a depression full of snow water. In the distance, the tolts appear man-made, manlike, *moai*.

"Did you know, Newfoundland is a rock that broke off what is now Spain and Morocco and crashed into the Americas something like 250 million years ago," Erica says and thinks: "What an annoying thing of me to say."

"That's what I said to Michael on our honeymoon, couldn't you take me somewhere with *history*? He said he didn't want to be bothered with the past on our honeymoon. So, where did you and Colin go on yours?"

"What?"

"Honeymoon," says Saskia, with reverence bordering on the astrological—Honey Moon for those with husbands, Blood Moon for the rest.

"Madrid," says Erica, surprising herself. This city from Colin's passport, added last night to her own List of Cities to See Before Senility. She has a notebook of lists: Words, Cheeses, Birthdates, Things to Buy in the Unlikely Event Another Man Leaves Me a Small Part of his Titanic Fortune.

"Really, Spain?" says Saskia, apparently amazed. "Ha! You and the Newfoundland tectonic plate. You must've spent all the time at the Prado."

"We spent a whole week in the hotel room."

"Can we rest here for a second?" Saskia stops. "In Hawaii, I often felt like I'd rather stay in the room, but you don't know my husband. He'd never miss a chance at a field trip. Sometimes, he'd take a flask with him and by the time we got wherever we were going, everyone would be singing on the bus. Life of the party, he's that type. You didn't even go into the Prado?"

"We talked about it but decided not to." Erica looks around the dimming barrens with the thinnest, first shadow of alarm. The wrinkled gray terrain repeats. The rock around her feet repeats. This is a cell, she thinks, a structural redundancy inside a massive, ignoramus brain. . . .

"Not even once?" Saskia lowers her rear onto one of the folds in the Moroccan rock.

"Yeah, it takes a different kind of courage *not to see* some things and places." Erica thrusts her hands deeper into her jacket. Her gloves are so thin her fingers have begun to tingle.

"But those Titians at the Prado!"

"Right. Colin's mother couldn't forgive us either. She wanted photos for her album," Erica lies. "Are you sure it's not this way? I think I see some cairns over there."

Lichen and cracks. They lean over the broken limestone like women in prayer. Up close, the broken stones, the seventh set they've stopped to study, are again arranged at random by wind and water, offering nothing more salvific than their minor beauty.

"Jesus Christ, I thought you knew where you were going," Saskia snaps. She picks up a rock and throws it. It lands a few steps away from them. "I'm hungry. So hungry. I haven't been so hungry since my last pregnancy, the second trimester."

Erica feels, in her legs and chest, a freezing calm, a darkening in tandem with the last light leaving as this woman's mouth continues moving. When it stops, Erica says, "We had the sun on our left for most of the way. It set over there, so we should have it on our right on the way back," attempting what seems an appropriate analysis, picked up from, where, nature shows? Hopefully not science-fiction shows, but there's something about touching stones for moss . . . moss on which side of the stones?

"It did not set there. It set over there." Saskia points in the opposite direction. "Is your phone still not working?"

"No reception." Erica shakes her head. "I'm really nearly positive about this way being west. You can see the difference in the darkness of the sky." She points. "The sun can only have set over there, where there's still some bluishness."

"We can always go in two different directions, if you're so sure of yourself. You seem, in general, very sure of yourself. It must feel like quite a virtue. Jesus Christ, where are technology and men?"

"We have to walk," Erica says coolly, and begins. "Pretty soon we won't be able to see anything. Look at the sky. I think it'll snow."

"Wait for me. I have something in my eye. It feels like a splinter."

Saskia squats. Erica pats her head. Formal elements of dreams: starless sky, disorientation. Dreams are evolution's way of making sure you've lived through dozens of disaster drills before the real disaster. It's begun to snow. Large flakes, like pieces torn from pages.

"My bunion hurts," says Saskia. "Is this really a path?"

"I'm pretty sure," says Erica. "It's an island, so if we continue one way, we'll hit the coast eventually. There are plenty of fishermen's villages everywhere."

Holding hands, they step carefully over the slippery rocks.

"I remember these spruce trees. Or are these pines?"

Erica opens her mouth to say nothing. The air is cold against her gums. They've turned around three times already. From time to time, they light the ground with Erica's phone.

"It's nine. I can't believe this. Michael will be worried, so I'm sure he'll send someone."

"I'm sure he will," says Erica. She didn't tell Colin about the hike. "Don't worry, we'll get there. It's important not to—"

"Of course we'll *get* there."

Erica walks through her visible breath. At the top of a rise in the barrens, she stops and looks to the barely bluer ostensible west. Here at the edge of familiar states of lost control: negative g-force on a plane, getting tumbled in seawater, anesthesia for wisdom teeth.

"By the way," Saskia says, "Colin's mother couldn't have asked for photographs."

"What?"

"The photographs from the Prado. You don't know what happened to Colin's mother?"

"What are you talking about?"

"She died when he was young." Saskia's slapping her thighs. "He told us at dinner last night, I don't know where you were. You have to keep the blood moving in your legs. I guess you, his *wife*, forgot that detail. Or *are* you his wife?"

"Oh come on now," Erica says.

Saskia retakes her hand, and they move in the dark. Saskia's touch is somehow obscene, like the touch of a stranger's child, a lost and overweight one.

"Well, are you or are you not?"

"Colin's wife? It's not that interesting. We met several days ago in a hotel bar in St. John's, if you must know."

Saskia stops and releases Erica's hand.

"This is not the time to be upset over trifles, you know," Erica says.

"I demand the entire truth or I won't go any farther with you. I won't be lost in the snow with someone I don't trust. That's not OK."

*

In the light from a low moon, an arcade of pines is defined at the base of a slope of bare limestone, a few hundred meters ahead. This is the second phase of being lost—first everything looks the same, and then each place seems without precedent, even if you walked through it an hour ago.

"Colin told me he was a Marxist and a sink designer for upscale hotels and houses." Her voice is a half whisper, and Saskia moves along with her, docile, quiet. "When I pointed out the inconsistency of his position, he said, 'Even the rich need to wash their hands. I give them a way to absolve themselves,' and he didn't say that really, something like that. I thought he was a sanctimonious fool. I thought, why not. We took the private hotel plane to come here later that night."

"Well, I don't know why you couldn't just tell me that. Why you had to be so, I don't know, inauthentic."

Then a long, stubborn quiet. The sky has a dark, open, deep anti-urban quality that resists observation. One must study one's footing, the way ahead. Saskia's rubber-reinforced uglies are superior to Erica's leaking leather city boots, approximately the same size.

"I don't think it's authenticity," says Erica dully, automatically, "but an issue of what's immediately repeatable, relatable. We spent one night together, but by morning I knew he had told me every interesting thing he had. Most people only have one night of inter-esting things. I wasn't sure, though, and maybe I wanted to carry the situation to its fullest emotional contradiction, with you, I mean, by telling you I'd married him, to test myself."

They walk on something like a path now, possibly the one on which they came, but neither have remarked at it. Perhaps because we know it may not be a path. What makes a path? Is belief in a path a productive or *de*structive action? Her feet are wet. It's 1990 in Wyoming—after skiing, her feet are aloft in her mother's hands. She blows on Erica's toes, to blow "death away." You "blew it away" with birthday candles and with practice CPR. Her father used to yell at her mother. Don't say superstitious things then, if you don't want me to yell at you.

"—no consideration for my feelings, or for his. You've already dis-missed him. Well, it's not OK. People have feelings, and people are real, they have other values than . . ." Saskia's muttering comes in and out. She seems aware she's talking to herself. This may well be a path. "You have to know. No, that's not it, you don't get it. You just don't, you don't."

The falling snow lights and occludes their way. They walk under trees, but the snow finds its way through the needles and cones, and the path—or the semblance of path—becomes less and less, and Colin won't worry. Why should he? Why should it make a difference to him—losing her to the limestone barrens today or an airport tomorrow?

They walk, they shamble. The pain in her feet and face evolves, turns quiet, turns warm in the way ice burns, and Erica thinks of a leaflet she read on the plane from St. John's about Erikson's unplanned discovery of this terrifying island, of a paradise of wild wheat and grapevines.

A miracle of unmiraculous matter-of-factness is fixed to a post in the snow.

TRAILHEAD 20 KM.

The cell phone's greenish light and the water and wind in Erica's eyes give the sign a subaqueous look. The zero is warped. Some wishing wells are full of disappointing, abandoned objects. Others are full of money.

"What, twenty kilometers?! Well, *too* bad, because I'm *too* tired. I can't do it." Saskia sits on a rock in the manner of collapsing on a sofa to fall asleep watching a movie.

"I don't think we have that choice," says Erica. "Twenty is only a few hours. Kilometers go by faster than miles."

"Too bad. I can't. Oh, no, no offense, but you are no longer to be trusted." The patches on Saskia's face are green in the phone's light. "I should've gotten those bunion cushions. It's all about padding."

"Don't be nonsensical," Erica says. "You can't stay here by yourself. We'll rest for a minute and then keep on walking. Slow walking is fine, but stopping is not." She blows on her fingers. "Look at your boots. You're much better off than I am."

"Too bad. Unlike you, I'm prepared. It's just like you to say I'm better off. Do you know how my feet hurt? Do you know how tired and hungry I am? Jesus Christ, stop pacing, it's exhausting me. Stop pacing," Saskia says.

Erica squats beside Saskia, Saskia hunkering, face in her hands.

"Please come with me," says Erica, placing a hand on this suddenly utterly inhuman woman's shoulder. Such obstinate stiffness, such alien wood. "Let's go. You can't stay here alone," but she says this now less to another person than to her future memory of this, to be certain later that she did her best. "Let's go or you'll regret it."

"I'm too tired."

"You have to."

"Well, I can't."

"Don't sit for too long then, OK? And no matter what, don't go to sleep. If you sleep, you'll die."

A larger wind, an accidental bit of theater, comes with "die" and blows both women's hair into one mass.

"Don't tell me when to sleep. I've been through labor. Twice! And one without an epidural. Michael was the one who almost fainted. They had to take *him* out. I'll be right by this sign. Tell Michael, get here right away. I won't tolerate any delays. The hotel has a helicopter."

"Sure," says Erica. "When I get nearer to the car, I'm sure I'll have reception. I'll call the hotel and the rangers." She starts down the trail, but has taken no more than five strides when—

"It's weird, I just remembered a joke. I normally can't think of any . . . what does a nurse give you when you go into labor?" Saskia's voice trails in the dark, already geographically misplaced. "A free Brazilian. Ha ha ha!"

A twenty-kilometer trek. She reaches the trailhead in less than an hour, skins her finger deicing the car with a stick and drives and skids and strikes no dogs, and after all the hours of theater, paperwork, and tea and thawing ears and hands and toes, in the morning, at the station, she must be told by a ranger, then a hotel manager, and finally a policewoman, that someone, "probably a kid," has been adding these zeroes with permanent marker . . . and Erica flies away and never tells anyone she "once lost a friend in Newfoundland," as she imagines the dead woman would, had their fates been reversed.

For a long time, there is no effect at all, then, slowly, it begins—not a haunting by snow or limestone or pines, not by thoughts of a woman found blue-skinned and shining like glass the next morning—but a haunting that increases imperceptibly, at first too close to nothingness to be more than a tickle of unhappiness while reading tax forms, menus, 1-800 numbers. So it is—she realizes one morning looking at a figure in a magazine, 24,000,000, the approximate number of schizophrenics worldwide—the zeroes themselves. These simple hoops from childhood have become the smallest portals to some kind of outer void, or inner void. They're everywhere. She's fifty and lonely. Years lived, years left, light-years, code. Euros traded per dollar per second. Giga-, tera-, exabytes per second. Meters, moles, candelas.

The Admiral
Paul West

FOR ALL HIS OUTWARD PRIMNESS, the Admiral had never been squeamish about Sundays; so far as he was concerned Sunday was just another day of the week and anything had the right to desecrate it, whether family uproars with trays and goblets thrown, little children drowned in shallow streams on their way home from communication with the deity, or old friends all of a sudden insisting that he never again address them by nickname. This Sunday, however, a mere seventeenth of September, his telephone rang at dawn to inform him that the Russians had crossed the Polish frontier between Polotsk and Kamenets-Podolski at four in the morning; he was hardly surprised, having for some time expected them to make a move, egged on as they had been by Ribbentrop, and other lugubrious brains, to come and get their share of Polish spoils; but he had been unable to go back to sleep, and he just lay there palping his heavy face with his small hands. To him it felt brittle and light, ready to be blown away or pecked to bits by the next bird.

Born on the first day of the year fifty-eight years ago, he loved to describe his knowing state secrets, political ruses, bogus alliances, and other ploys of warcraft, to say *From the very first*, as if he and he alone had such things as primacy, or prescience, at heart; he knew, almost as if by divine right, the initial causes of whatever happened militarily, both at home and abroad. Sitting in the innermost of German espionage's concentric circles, he prided himself on being crisp, acute, and wise until midafternoon at least, which explained his regimen of pills: pills to get him to sleep on time, and pills to get him alert before his counterintelligence staff was quite awake, and then he dazzled them with stances so absolute and cogent that he seemed a consummate specimen of the human ability to make up one's mind. That was when the Admiral truly loved himself, pronouncing with unbrookable finality "The British Empire has to go" or "One is a serviceman and must obey." As the day wore on, though, he began to qualify what he said, and the ice-brick exactness of his early-morning dicta became eroded; by lunchtime he was a muddling dog lover again, vaguely aware that his mind had, for a few short hours, been visited by the ghost of immaculate reasoning sent by Plato from his cave. So, while this visitation lasted, he trounced others mentally, but grew to loathe the inferior Admiral who surfaced with the soup at lunch, wondering into the vapor why (he was not that old) his mind could not always be crystalline and deft. The power was always there, of course: He could do what he wanted, but he could not be sure it was what he would have wanted to do while he was superlatively lucid, with that cleansed, amiably cool sensation reaching from his buttocks to somewhere beneath his liver.

On this particular Sunday, during coffee and biscuits at 11:15 or so, the telephone rang again, this time bringing personal bad news for the family, news he already knew, but put off sharing during the hectic week, preferring that it be formally divulged, delivered just as he expected, by a tearful phone call from his sister Anna. Somewhere near Radom, deep in that accursed Poland, his nephew, Rudolf Buck, had been killed in action. "At least, my dear," he told Anna, "it is a piece of bad news that will not have to come again. He is a hero, God be thanked. He is at peace, a peace we cannot even guess at. You will never have to be afraid for him again. At least, his suffering is over. Ours has just begun."

Rubbing crumbs of powdered shortbread from his mouth, but somewhat upward, against his septum, he shook his head miserably at Erika, his wife, who never knew what to say to him anyway: Far from the rhythms of his mind, to which she had made only an average effort to attune herself, she filled the distance between them with sarcasm, except when, as now, she said nothing at all, knowing that in his piggish, cumbersome way he would make the best of things, as he always did, defusing bad news with a quotation from Frederick the Second, tempering the good news with a sly reference to the disasters the morrow would bring, and adjusting to the in-between times when the phone rang and rang, delivering information of only medium interest, with the additive shrug of a hobbyist, glad of a few new stamps for his collection, even gladder that any old thing was happening rather than nothing, and in the innermost cells of his heart relieved (like so many Germans) that a Führer had come along to break the monotony.

"Heil Hitler," said the Admiral with a cagey wince as he brushed past her on his way to the open French windows, meaning it was all Hitler's fault, yet it brought less honor to Germany than it did grief to his sister, and it was a part of the ongoing ruckus that the Fatherland needed to persuade itself that it still existed after the humiliating Peace of Versailles, which had made it the wholly defeated, utterly responsible nation. "And," he said out on the lawn, "*heil* Rudolf too," making a mental note to have Rust, his blind masseur, loosen up the cords in the back of his neck, after which Rust would gambol on the floor with the wirehaired dachshunds, Seppel and Sabine, growling and yelping as well as they, and freed briefly of the obligation to pass for human in a world, a society anyway, that would have put him down long ago had the Admiral not given him a job.

He is having another of his days, his wife told herself as she watched the Admiral's back recede. Wilhelm the Cantankerer. How did I, a cultivated woman, ever manage to tie myself up with a man who shudders at the mention of illness, who backs away from anyone taller than he as if they had the plague, who rattles with pills, is more superstitious than a peasant, will only shed one imaginary complaint in order to contract one even worse, and, God help me, needs twelve hours of sleep, thirteen if the preceding day has inflicted too many small-eared visitors upon him. He looks well enough until you see how much less than average height he is: almost a dwarf, not quite 1.6 meters tall, although what he calls his "mariner's tan" and his white hair deflect the eye from his body to his face, that sundial on the unreadable pedestal of his intentions. Death to him is a breach of decorum, something his masseur must shovel up or brush under the rug along with the rest of the filth. So long as his eyebrows remain bushy, as if they could really hide what terrible things happen in front of his eyes, he can stand anything, and he just happens to be in charge of German intelligence worldwide, which is like giving an ostrich the entire Sahara to play with. If only he wouldn't lisp and, even in those nice gray suits with the metallic sheen, pat the place where he wears the Iron Cross when in uniform.

"What are you *doing*?" she called after him in a voice thinned shrill by exasperation.

"Getting out of your way," he said, as if he had been waiting his cue to answer with something unsubtly wounding. "I am going *out-thide.*" Outside her knowing and watch. He could always tell her the truth, quite harmless, this time, that he was going to walk a mildly irritating knot out of his thigh, but deception was a delicacy to be practiced, and savored, not only when it involved the demolition of whole nations, but on small homely occasions as well, for its own sake, jewel-perfect in any light.

That un-Admiral-like lisp, Erika thought. He isn't far away at all, just lurking behind the corner of the door, which means he walks away large as life and then sneaks back, to see if I am talking to myself.

"And on Tuesday," she heard him call, whether spies were listening or no, "I will be off to Poland again. I am going to Lvov with Yary, Piekenrock, and Lahousen, to see what we can do for those godforsaken Ukrainian refugees."

He lisped, she was certain of it, only when he wanted to, in order to catch her off guard, distracting her from what he said by making her mix motherly sympathy with baleful amusement, a role into which he delighted to compel her, converting her into an ogress while he played at being a child.

In the end, as always, there was only one he could tell—Motte (Moth), his all-white (like her master's hair) Arab mare. Only Motte could assimilate without levity or disgust the full gamut of what the Head of the Abwehr felt from day to day, having to put the world to rights from a cramped, gloomy office behind a metal grille. The balcony with a view of the Landwehr Canal did not help much (canals were stagnant), nor did his few personal belongings: all those books (mere recombinations of the dictionary, he had begun to feel), the model of the light cruiser *Dresden* (it only made him long for the old days, like the time the real *Dresden*, only survivor of the Falkland Islands naval battle in 1915, had dodged the Royal Navy for months and had finally found haven off the Pacific Island of Más a Tierra, exactly where Robinson Crusoe had been marooned). Nor did the trio of three bronze monkeys from Japan, supposed to embody the code of the top-flight intelligence officer—"see all, hear all, say nothing." No, canals, books, model ships, and bronze monkeys only reminded him of the career he almost never had, when the official report on the lieutenant who became an admiral said he was too irritable, too high-strung, too much of a man of opposites, unpredictable and in manner hypersensitive; the nose was big and long, and the jaw was dour, but his brow receded above the soldierly sharp angles of his oval face, and they said he could not be counted on, being both down-to-earth like his mercantile and entrepreneurish forebears, and, like his mother, an ascetic dreamer as quick into a volatile dither as out of it, leaving the world about her in a daze.

Yet, he told himself out there in the sunlight, tapping his shoe on the dry grass of the lawn, I prevailed, I am here. I once escaped from internment on the island of Quiriquina; I had not joined the navy to rot on a Chilean island, or to ride the horses provided for the officers while our men laid roads or tinkered to improve the water pipes; up into the rough ground I went, and then down a path to the beach, where for twenty pesos a fisherman rowed me away. I would not mind that beach again, or that escape, arriving quietly in Concepción en route for Argentina, with only the snow-thick Andes in between.

For the Admiral it was a cheerful enough daydream.

The best memory of all, though, was his parents' villa, whose grounds he toured in a little goat cart with his brother and sister, past the tennis court and the stables to the choked magnificence of the kitchen garden: a witty child who astounded his father with boned-up allusions to something as far-fetched as the history of geography and who, when his mother peered at him severely, just before scolding him for going too far with his madcap dry humor, would say, "Mother, Mother, there are X-rays coming out of your eyes!" Even now, in his Admiral's uniform or the plain gray suits that blatantly understated his importance, he was still the smart-mouthed young enigma whom a carriage delivered at the Duisburg Gymnasium every morning and took away each noon, an aloof and haughty boy who eventually did so well in the university entrance examination he was excused the oral. For his teachers and schoolmates he came alive only when the annual outing took them all on more or less military expeditions into the gently slanting woodlands along the edge of the Ruhr, and there he became a leader and an organizer, leading boldly across the distance his taciturnity had set up, and joking as if all along they had been caught up in the same surge of quick-change conversation. And then, in Greece, he discovered the sea, and a monument to a Greek admiral of the nineteenth century, Constantine Kanaris, whom he thereafter idolized and made into his seafaring holy ghost.

Now, he was still aloof although given to fits of organizing genius, but he had come to see himself in an excess of gracious candor as a bit of an eccentric; his wife had told him so, and not without reason after seeing him, usually at weekends, trudge out to the apple tree with the screwed-up bundle of his pajamas, handwashed at the basin by his own hands with expensive toilet soap. Then he faced the tree as if taking position in some parade, re-wrung the pajamas, unfurled the jacket and let the wind billow into it once or twice, shook loose the legs until he could see the ground beneath through each, and deployed the laundry on the lower branches, attaching it with bulldog clips, taking enormous care not to scar the bark. Sometimes he did the same with a shirt or his underwear, almost as

311

if washing away a contamination that others must not touch, but really, as he saw it, just to do something small, public, and humdrum after hours upon sequestered hours of rearranging Europe or even the world. If he had time, and on weekends he often did, he would stand and watch the laundry dry, appraising its float and twirl, glad to see the dark patches of wet or wet's ephemeral transparency disappear (depending on the fabric's color). Deep down he missed messing about in boats and fiddling with sails, and this way he could sail on the lawn. But he wondered if the whole thing wasn't also the result of one terrible sleepless night when he had perspired in the dead of winter, and had washed the pajamas through to keep Erika from asking questions. If ever in doubt about his own motives, he attributed everything to the secretiveness for which he knew he was renowned. In winter, though, or when there was rain, he let things go, just to thwart the pattern, somehow pitting the variability of weather against his reasons for doing what he did; sooner or later, what he thought were his reasons, and what others *knew* were his reasons, just didn't apply. His life and his mind were more complex than that, and whole chunks of his being just did not pick up where other chunks left off. A dislocated man, even in his own eyes, he had no wish to be made whole, to be irrevocably connected up in all his joints, and, when he did other things just as unusual, he enjoyed telling himself that anyone spying on him would think them rather symbolic, whereas they were nothing of the kind. Tapping beetles off his roses into a jam jar with a screwtop lid, and then shaking them violently to stun them (motions of the cocktail shaker with his short, slight arms) might have seemed omnipotence gone mad, or a substitute for control of the world at large, but he simply liked to hear the beetles rattle against the lid, some of them still coupled in rut. The jar stood for days on a rustic table by the apple tree, but from time to time he let in air and tossed in a bit of leaf, at least until the jar became too smeared with droppings, and too clouded with vapor, so he then set it out in the garbage for someone else to play with.

On this particular Sunday, however, neither his pajamas nor the beetle jar suited his mind; he was uncharacteristically fixated on the thought that, somewhere too far away, his nephew's face had ceased to move, to murmur, and would remain still as a tortoise shell until the end of time. A million years of fixity, of deadness, he could not conceive of that, or of its mathematical equivalent, which was that in a billion billion trillion chances (what *was* the American word for an unstateable number?) there wasn't a fraction of a shadow that any human being would ever come back to life. Each would lie cold and unstirred, at least by reprieve, through successive ages of ice, even until and actually into the incineration of the planet by its sun: just so much fodder, tinder, trash, which was why he insisted to the point of boring even himself on the role of the German nation as a survivor, as a framework in which interminable death did not matter so much.

"Damn it, Motte," he said quietly, as a couple of beetles flew sideways away when the mare, always the soul of discretion, approached the fence, "because I know a lot I'm supposed to know everything; because I manufacture secrets I'm supposed to crack the riddles of the universe. Whereas, of course, as this miserable day teaches me, I cannot even manage my own indignation, just another man with a reservoir of tears, a few dress uniforms in the closet to make me feel invulnerable, a whole network of spies from Hong Kong to Mecca to persuade me that I am in charge of things. Wars exist to distract us from our own deaths: We inflict on strangers the very thing we fear for ourselves, so that, as millions fall, we can keep on saying *Not I, not we*, it will never be us; but it never works out that way.

"Here I am, for better or worse, a man with special task forces at his command, which are nothing but Gestapo butchers on temporary loan to combat what's blithely called activity harmful to the nation, in particular espionage, treason, sabotage, propaganda, and subversion, all *in the theater of operations*. What they do is ferret people out, behind the lines, and hand them over to the SS for execution. I go along. My nephew has his brains blown out. I go along. What do you think about *that*, Motte? I wash my pajamas, I free my beetles. I behave quite automatically, somehow mustering an adequate front so long as I am clean-shaven, short-haired. I go along, I sweat into my pajamas, I tip new beetles into the jar. Then someone else gets his brains blown out, and I don't feel like telling my field police to stop arresting people. I am a specialist in displaced retaliation but what I do not know, will never know, is why I began, before I had any grievances at all. For what was I getting my own back at the start? For having to eat, to breathe, to work? For having been born at all, like a New Year's gift? As if, before leaving the womb, or being conceived, I should have had a preview tour with the archangel Gabriel showing me around like a salesman: 'What do you think, fetus? Can you take seventy years of this? Or would you like to go back forever?' And, when you have to leave it, when your time's up, you go out squealing with pain, writhing like a frogspawn pancake.

313

"Father died of a stroke while taking the waters at Bad Nauheim, cut down at fifty-two, just because he was glued together wrong to begin with, and I have outlived him by six years. I am already six years older than my father ever will be, and I am living the rest of his life for him, like the tenant farmer of his undischarged ambition, yet far too small, too inward, too nervous, too mixed-up, to be living a life of any kind, even my own, still less that of the man who was dead set against my joining the navy in the first place. His going freed me, that is clear, but my doing well (if well it's been) is broken glass and ordure on his grave."

Checking the sit of his necktie, and shooting upward at the summer sky a look of mutinous bittersweet deviousness that implied he wasn't responsible for anything today, he strode a dozen paces past the apple tree, paused to flick a few beetles off a cluster of irises, and began again, resting one hand on one splintery fence post, gesticulating a bit with the other toward Motte to ensure he had her attention.

"It has begun to happen again, I knew it would, the matrix is never still, the dead have started to die again, it is all Hitler's fault, it all began when the message came in 'Grandma's dead' on the afternoon of August 31, only two weeks ago. It feels like years of stone. Naujocks attacked Gleiwitz radio station and Hellwig's troops pretended to attack the German border, and Trummler's fired back at the so-called invaders. That was it: a charade, the put-up job of put-up jobs, and there we sat in my office, listening to his awful voice telling us there had already been fourteen border incidents and that was fourteen too many, a sleeping giant cannot stay asleep that long. Then Piekenbrock said, 'So now we know why we had to get hold of those Polish uniforms!' and I didn't even answer him, I who had known all along, *from the first*. What was done was done. And that was only the first day.

"At 9:15 on the morning after, I called the staff into my office and tried to cheer them up, invoking my own thirty-four years in the service of Germany, the relative poorness of private life, and our obligation to be loyal. Since there was no going back, we had to go forward with the mob; no one else was going to hire us, and we knew too much to be allowed to go our own way with a few favorite books and a sleeping bag under our arm. Not only that: When you are familiarly called 'chef' (and try to ignore the French overtones of the term), you are literally the head man, in charge of everything, and that calls for a certain amount at home, while responsible abroad for entire Abwehr units, often far ahead of our invading armies. I had to have hourly accounts of what was happening, which may surprise you—you who never think farther ahead than the next fresh-hay meal, if you think of that—but when you have men out on a limb, supposed to seize this rail junction or that coal mine, you have to be on top of things, especially when your telephone rings all day with demands for such things as a special strike force to wreck the three main railroads from Romania to Poland. All this is hacking at the map, a hard-nosed resolve to change the map in the act of staring at it, melting and reshaping while the silly, shiny thing sits there on its table as if it had a right to life, and you tell yourself, *There are people there, right under the steel points of the compasses,* but their faces do not shine out, the smell of their breath or their clothes does not leak through the pores in the canvas backing. No: The message of maps is that humanity is unmanageable without some degree of formal symbolism.

"Always, when I could, I let the others voice sentiments that, coming from me, might have seemed compulsory, and false (which, at times, by necessity, they were), just because I'd uttered them; and, if my staff seemed muddled at times, then it was better for them to seem so to me than I to seem so to them.

"Motte, you old *sprechpferd*, are you listening? Britain and France declared war on us, of course, but an invader will always have enemies, even if only on paper. It was only in Poland itself, however, that anyone got a true, physical sense of how well Rundstedt's armies were doing. You should have been there, Motte, at Army Group South's headquarters, near Zloty Stok, on September 3. You would have been well cared for, and, back home again on the fifth, you'd have relished the memory of that whiff of smoke, the map constantly changing like molten wax, the thunder of bombers overhead—the overall sense of single-minded mobilization. After that first visit to the rear of the front, it became clear that we would have to foster the malcontent among the Ukrainians, the Caucasians, the Irish, the Welsh, the Scots. Persia, India, and British-run Iraq were ripe for shaking, and it was high time to get good old King Amanullah of Afghanistan back on the throne simply by staging an anti-British revolt among the mountain tribes on the Indian-Afghan border. For the first time in decades, the sun's rays were hitting the field of the cloth of gold, and that field was in my head, where ideas sprouted and flew at all hours of the day and night. Imagine: We could turn the Tibetans against the British and provoke some kind of uproar in

315

Thailand! There was nothing we could not do. At our bidding, all foxes would run backward, all clouds would come down to sea level and moor themselves there like barrage balloons, all armies would surrender as soon as their politicians declared war, and a deputation of the world's admirals would arrive to pay homage to the smallest admiral known.

"Of course you, my dear Motte, with your poor grasp of Latin (although your speech is lucid enough when you want it to be), you will not be as attuned as I to the *admirable* component in the word *admiral*, but it is there; an admiral is to be wondered at, marveled at, quite simply to be admired, and to that he's entitled without doing anything further! Is the word perhaps even a relative of the title Emir? Can one be an emir of a navy? I sometimes think that, no matter how shoddy what a man has to do in the exact performance of his duty, a decent-sounding title helps him through, whereas Mister or even Doctor fortifies him precious little. I envision the day when the dawn has come up like oil poured into a flaming brazier, on which a man such as I can go quite beyond himself, and his being short and having a lisp don't count at all, not in the glorious final sum of his deeds while his golden name surrounds him like a vapor. Fame is the spur, but greatness is the horse."

That seemed to clinch it, verbally at least, and the Admiral fell silent, having received no answer; Motte knew how to listen as well as how to obey, and was accustomed to these long crescendo voluntaries, coming usually during an early-morning saunter in the Grünewald. What the Admiral needed was an audience, not an interlocutor, and at this moment more than ever, queerly conscious as he today was of death and maiming all around him, he felt like a lightning conductor for trouble. It was not only his nephew: Young men called to the colors had about one chance in three of surviving, and losses in Poland had been light overall. Grief had begun, and grief would go on, but grief in this instance came on top of something else, about which the Admiral and his wife rarely spoke even in private. She went her way in cultivated society, fixing on Heydrich's talent as a violinist and playing duets with him while her husband, who had no ear for music, disappeared into the kitchen, where he donned his chef's hat and prepared the meal, most often saddle of wild boar cooked in a crust made from red wine and crumbled black bread, served with his special Abwehr salad in which the secret ingredient was a fleck or two of Abwehr paper. He refused to divulge the source of its unique flavor. Secrets were the salt in the national soup, and, after all, they were his stock-in-trade.

Everyone had little secrets that did no harm. Who more than he had the right to a couple of shady whorls of truth here and there, so long as the national security went unscathed? If the master of national secrets couldn't rise to a fib or two, or do a little private business on the side, then he'd find another polity to serve. Savvy colleagues in the outstations often kept a dog in reserve for his visits; if things weren't going well, out it came to be fondled. Now that was a minor secret, but he didn't mind, except when the dog was less than friendly. British agents monitoring radio traffic had been baffled by constant references to an agent called Axel, who in fact was a dog assigned to agent Caesar (not the Admiral, of course). The next two transmissions were "Watch out for Axel. He bites." and "Caesar is in hospital. Axel bit him." All this diverted the Admiral, reminding him of life's cross-hatched complexity, into which, without even an apology to himself, he gladly introduced—for his favorites—Spanish strawberries flown in from Aranjuez by courier planes code-named "Strawberry Swansuit"; diamond-studded tobacco jars all supposed to have belonged once upon many times to Napoleon; rugs and paintings and miniature perfumed dogs. The Bulgarian outstation was the most corrupt, he knew, but the one in Munich was close behind. Racketeers were part of reality too, he reassured himself; so long as the main job got done, none of this black-market stuff mattered a fig. He even knew that the British knew so much about the Abwehr, its corruptness and inefficiency, that they went to enormous lengths to make it stay that way. Two sets of eyes dreamed the day when the Führer finally awoke to what was going on in his famous intelligence service and brought the entire house of cards tumbling down: the Admiral's, and those of the British Intelligence Service. Both sets watched and, repledging themselves to the need for a touch of badness in all things, looked the other way.

So there was all the more reason, the Admiral persuaded himself, to get out into the field and lay his traps, retrieve his rabbits, bury his gold, riding the confidential rainbow to its end, before heads began to fall. The very thought of going off to another country excited the Admiral more than he could credit. I still thrill to it, he mused, the foray, the confrontation, the bargain struck, the wires pulled to make the marionettes work an ocean's width away. I am not nothing. I make the truth curve. I run contraband to hell and back. In the end they all come to me, begging or boasting, and I suffer them all. I'll go in uniform, of course; it adds to the pageantry.

For this Admiral, pill-popping introvert that I am, with a lisp, who hates people who have small ears or who are tall, who lives mainly in a boyhood world of invisible inks and uncatchable spies, I come from the dimension of wizardry, a freak, a hyperbole, a hybrid right out of Hans Christian Andersen. Yet I control the fates of millions, deviously interfering and undermining by means of a staff deployed throughout the civilized world. A tip here, an overture there, and someone either dies at the frontier or comes sailing through it in disguise, and most of my relatives work for me as well. Master of fair-weather machination, I am a man not only worth cultivating, but worth priming and sweetening as well; I, the ghost of intrigue past and of subterfuge to come, when the entire world runs according to bits of cardboard (fake, of course) stamped with hieroglyphs entitling you to grass, a roof, the right to breathe last outside a jail.

If only Poland's smoke and rubble could have been removed by trucks to Russia; I have been close to tears, yearning for old-style naval engagements, with cruisers slogging it out over the mild meniscus of the open main. Burning horses and sundered houses are not my idea of war at all. One bright spot, though: When you reduce a country to rubble, you can count at least on not having to eat its dreadful food. One day, when things have been cleaned up, the kitchens of Poland will fill, at last, with delectable aromas—and I will come into my own again. This Admiral will sail.

The Likenesses
Paul Hoover

MADE TO RESEMBLE

a match is like a shard
the shard is like a sword

a sword is like a word
the house of water folds

the past is like a bowl
the future's like a rope

a rake is like resemblance
don't step on one oh no

mimesis is like mimesis
a tree is like a weed

a lie is like a fiction
a fiction's like a deed

a shoe is like a shape note
an eye is like an island

the goose is like the gander
the sandman's like the sand

a ribbon's like a stipend
the bend is like the road

the cross is like a crisis
hope is like a bone

Paul Hoover

the season's like a threshold
the forest is like a door

rats are like the righteous
the green are like the gold

life is like a sentence
a bird is like the world

reason is like erosion
names are like tin bells

to seek is to be looked for
to leap is like to fall

to think is to be distant
a soft spot's like a blow

a river's like a wellspring
the dead are like the soil

a chair is like a grandstand
the sky is like a dome

the sailor's like the wave
the night is like the day

the bride is like the groom
the grain is like the wood

the end is like the beginning
the cut is like the blood

THINGS YOU MIGHT HAVE SAID

Things you might have said,
like "l love you" and "I'm sorry,"
wait for you ahead,
four-fingered like a ghost with digital lips
you can't help kissing
in the dream you can't stop having.
You are digital too,
and by design a woman.

Men bring you to their lips,
hold you, digital, in their arms.
You don't desire them;
you symbolize their desire.
Like a character in a novel,
you are wired to seem.
Your lips and arms
are the very ache of seeming.

Never born, but much loved,
you go to bed absolved.
Digital snow falls on digital sheep
and on the field you dream.

A digital woman is designed to cry
when she becomes an actual woman
of dust and bone
and bears an actual baby
into the world's pain.

The digital seasons pass.
You remain the dream
of an autumn too far.
You are held dear,
flicker but never age
in your digital living room.

Paul Hoover

THE WINDOWS (SPEECH-LIT ISLANDS)

as if for the first time
        you recognize the grass
                its greenness uncanny

in trying to be green
        as if for the first time
                you open a letter

that had fallen
        through the door
                its message unique to you

had you been
        as perhaps you seemed
                the neighbor

the one whose name was yours
        who finally joined the army
                had you in fact a country

a life to give
        wife and family
                as if for a while

you could read the signs

    remembered to unlearn

        how the wind feels exactly

going up your spine

    sensed the wheat sinking

        into the ground nearby

the whiteness of milk

    its mystical skirt uplifted

        miss meat and miss gravy

as if the language

    was smudged with words

        speech-lit islands

that don't submerge in meaning

    as if light itself

        was never in doubt

on the question

    of transcendence

        bees sing bells ring

in the ear's black window

    you whisper to the glass

        its past in sand

Paul Hoover

    step back please

        a sentence is passing

            someone's calling

    someone's raining

        door's creaking contradictions

            what bride is not disheveled

    by all the world's scissors

        make-shape shiftings

            been a long time

    since you wrote yourself in stone

        auto-lithographic

            [I] seems to be alone

[I] suffers in a crowd

        but not a yellow room

            in not a yellow town

    everyone's on loan

        but someone here knows

            why nimble people cry

    a bullet makes you die

        and then there's you

            absent sometimes laughing

as if at last

    there is no nonjourney

        across the whole word

what are you thinking

    conjured of a god

        pears you'll never taste

lines not written

    what you know you are

        you'll never be again

From Once into the Night
Aurelie Sheehan

ENNUI

I HAD BEEN FILLED WITH ENNUI all week, it was drenching, and all I could do was walk around, taking furtive looks at things, being alone with myself and my ennui. It's a surprising shadow, ennui is, or a cockroach in a Snickers wrapper, or the end of the play when everyone takes off their costumes. I furrow my brow at these things—in slight, but recoverable, disarray.

In my regular life, when not felled by ennui, I paint pictures of trees in various attitudes, almost like the stages of life—not the historical ascension stages, from creepy ape to upright fifties man, but the personal path: ball of baby, spry youth, productive citizen, laughable old person with cane, grim-reaper invisibility. I would say most of my paintings are of trees without leaves.

Still and all it didn't seem like enough, and last night the ennui finally overcame me. Before I knew it, I had swallowed the entire house. I lay right down on the bed, as if I'd been shot. I was splayed on my back (can't lie on your stomach after eating a house). I burped. I stared at the ceiling. What was this like, I asked myself, feeling, at least, analytical. My eyes stung and I could no longer see the lines of the beams. I could hear, like a faded dream, my family speaking in the living room. One person spoke; the other person spoke. Silences occurred. *When they leave me, I will be alone.* But at least I'll have swallowed the house, I thought, cackling in the bedroom.

SARA APPLEWOOD

I.

I am hitting Sara Applewood. I hit her on the shoulders and back after she has fallen on the ski slope. *Get up, get up, get up, Sara.* The world is vast and ornamental and also small, winnowed down to the point of contact where my pole hits her back, not doing enough damage through the parka, hence moving up to the head and shoulders. She holds her arm up so she won't be hurt. People are looking, as at a grocery store if there's been a spill. I don't want my mother to look. I don't want anyone to say: *Stop it, little girl.* I keep hitting for a while, getting a last good one in, and then I adjust my mitten and the pole strap, bend my knees, and push off. It's a small rise on a large mountain, and I slide down and around, skiing to the middle of the whiteness where there are hardly any people, the wide white middle, where I spy an invisible trail.

II.

Sara Applewood is hitting me. She's wearing her sleek red parka with lift passes on the zipper from places Olympic skiers go, Swiss slopes visited with her parents and governess. My God, a governess! But that's life for Sara Applewood, sadist and betrayer. Ski slopes are like heaven, except for when you're down on the ground being beaten. She really does enjoy hurting others—but who could possibly enjoy that? I'm a pacifist, an animal lover, and a nonlitterer, except there have been those times when I've held my brother down to the point where I thought a bone might break, or once when I threatened him with a butter knife. Was that pleasure? Sara Applewood has always been a better athlete than me. Her calves are hard and her toes grip the floor like an ape's. She has a sway to her back, her butt sticks out, and she pushes out her chest too. *See?* she's always saying. *See me now?* The world is cold as a sheet of metal, and I'm a slumped, Goodwill-bedecked lump—except for in my stomach, right in the center of my body, is a bit of warmth, a dull unfolding. Another hit off my shoulder, another on my sleeve. Then she's skiing away, her bitchy braids flying out behind her as she disappears, slaloming down the slope alone. The sun has slipped behind the mountain. The big gleaming mirror of cold—it's nothing, it's containable, blink and it's gone. I put my pole in the snow and push. *Swash*, goes my pole, again and again. Defeat almost has me. "Sara!" I shout. "Sara Applewood!" Hate is a bunny in my belly.

THE DARK UNDERLORD

I am the dark underlord you've been waiting for. Or at least I hope you've been waiting, because I've been in my lair for a dog's age, trying on outfits for the occasion. Obviously, I want to make an impression. An impression of dark arrival, an impressive impression. I want to come into the room, virtually *appear* in the room, with a swish of lethargic cloth and an upright posture. I have debated between capes, Snapchatted a couple of dubious associates, and decided upon the satin with the purple velvet lining and towering, almost gaudy collar. I admit my outfit never feels quite dark enough. One of the dubious associates suggested rubbing it in dirt—fool. Though he may have been on to something.

But I, the dark underlord, long ago gave up on the appearance of distress. It does not serve my purpose. I understand it can be sexy in a mechanical way, suggesting long, weary struggle, individualism, a totemic nature. So what! I will always shave before I go out, I will always shine my boots. Old school: what of it? It's a *swoop in*, you understand, a vacuum or an illumination. (Not that I am *not* tired— the campaign has been a long one.)

I have come, and I will coerce you, and perhaps something specifically dreadful will occur, for I do not shy away from dread or incident. You may feel comfortable in that static dream, but that static dream shall be, as the associates say, nevermore. I will pull you toward me, and we will collide there in our dark garments (my dark garments, your jeans and T-shirt), and we will roughly make a kind of bleak, dry love, battlefield fucking. And then we will be chained together forever (metaphorically). You will have submitted to my stark power.

Alas, there is the issue with afterward.

For I never force the subjects to come with me, actually. I have been in the habit now for several centuries, when no one is looking, after the Sturm und Drang, the television moment, the swoop in and takeover, of releasing the subject, loosening my arm from around the neck of the waif or the fevered husband. It is just us then. Behind the very large, the overlarge boulder, back in the shadows, the forest of backstage, she or he gets up from her/his knees. Wobbles. Looks at me. I look back, not penitent—not exactly. But it is the moment of truth, I am deeply afraid to say. *Do you want to play in my lair with me, we can try on capes and live on venison, perhaps, and pear spritzers?* It all comes down to now, the boot polishing and the telepathy practice and the infectious laughter. She, or he, has a fragile look at this stage in the game, and yet still—still, to a one—has had the strength to walk away.

SEA TRAVEL

I spent my early adulthood at sea. I even had a boat—or my boyfriend did, but we lived together, and he was generous in sharing his things. The term "early adulthood" is a patch of gray laid over whatever those years were, however long they lasted. Now I'm in "adulthood," another magazine-column category.

Here is what I thought of love. *Love*, def.: *doing things with, having a similar sense of humor as, extracting a future in addition to.*

The sea was a vivid black, folds of black relentlessly and unpredictably overlapping. Its opaqueness came from how the sun hit the water, or from the swallowing of the moon. You simply couldn't see. I couldn't see anyway.

Life was long, it was a bit cheap and certainly plentiful—maybe even too long, a great amount of this one capacious thing, like a basket of yarn crushed and laced together, mixed up and knotted and not yielding.

We brought sandwiches on the boat with us, or sometimes a thermos of soup. If we were traveling some distance I was obliged to pee in a bucket. Afterward, he would lie on the deck and drop the bucket down on its rope and the seawater cleaned out the interior. We liked pecan sandies for dessert.

When we were in the long process of breaking up, yet still grocery shopping together on Sundays, we were confused about what to buy— unsure if we would be together for the whole week. Should we buy our typical meals, our favorite items? Should we buy misery food, or just very, very plain food, rations, no salt or sauce? It was a package of pecan sandies that made us feel the saddest on one of those grocery runs, back in early adulthood.

Sometimes on the boat I stared at the horizon—this was even before the weeks and months of tearing apart. Something already felt sad in this world. Perhaps it was the sea itself, the difference between the opaque surface and the steely gravity underneath. Perhaps it was my inability to grasp the razor line between having a vast basket of yarn and having just a little yarn left.

I wish I could tell you of our travels. Some of the places we went were fancy, and we dressed in vintage clothing and acted like Gatsbys, drinking more than the average adult. There was no end to the places that smelled deeply, richly, of pine. Pine by the sea, pine in the heart of ancient forests, pine a perfume passed through on our

329

hurried way to the shore or back up from the shore, *it was there for you.*

CRUELTY

Cruelty was rampant at my elementary school, and I was the ring-leader. Even today I live in a haze of false identity.

Walking from the car to the school entrance, I was a subtle threat in my camel's-hair coat, high waters, winsome shoes, and socks of different colors. The giant headmistress in her giant handmade skirt stood by the door, like Mother Gigogne of *The Nutcracker*. I smiled in complicity, then looked away. Off to the cubbies to hang up my coat and put away my hat, smooth the static from my hair.

During reading hour, Christina and I pored over my secret booklet filled with spells and incantations (my mother had bought it for me at the grocery store). Our teacher saw us, saw the book, wrested it from me. Mother Gigogne was brought in; parents were called. My shame felt physical. I had been holding the little booklet with the pink cover under my poncho. We had not meant any harm. We were powerless. We had no power.

Witchcraft thwarted, I went back to everyday methods, and this is where you'll find me now. I've made Charlene (Mother Gigogne's daughter) into the embodiment of embarrassment, a junior nun, a pat of butter. Heather is a deer in a stand of trees, the way she hides in her parka. Jonathan, first crush—I've rendered his parents into ideas, his father a "father" and also a "rabbi" and his mother just a "mother."

SILENCE

The sobering thing is to remember the times I remained silent, sitting in my chair, or when I made a certain hand gesture or facial expression: *I will acquiesce to your statement.* Or when in some fever instead I argued a point that was not the point at all, but another point. I have never, really, tried to lie—except for a couple of paltry times, and then a few other rather more significant ones. Granted, I've forged whole friendships with lies. I stand here and present myself to you, then furtively sniff this paste. I stand here and present myself to you, blowing smoke in this sophisticated manner.

I will sleep with you or I won't sleep with you—purely arbitrary. How can a fuck be a lie? Well, let me explain.

ROMANCE OF THE OLD

I am untrue. As untrue as in the old days, the to-be-responded-to letters a pileup in an ivory bowl. How coyly I kept up correspondence! A letter written with "my usual" charm, though mostly exhibiting a muzzled, reined-in quality. *Ex. 1*: to a friend, some tidbits about my writing and about my mother, about a trip taken with T., much neutrality, viz., "We had a nice time. I love Maine." *Ex. 2*: That Awful Person, a sick yellow feeling, like a gloss, as if someone vomited on the page and then wiped it away, a parceling out and serious parsing, knowing that he whom I met and flirted with in a tolerating sort of way, the equivalent of what you might engage in on a train in another country, quite unfortunately lived very near me. *Ex. 3*: my cousin, the actual and the theoretical embodied: We are close, yes? for we are family, but our connection is made of straw. *Ex. 4*: an editor—*an editor!*—to whom I will remain stiff as a lamp and less illuminating, the note drafted into deep lifelessness, and yet somehow, surely, hopefully, alluring, so alluring that he understands that I understand that he understands that I understand, that we are one, essentially. *Ex. 5*:—they continue, the parcelings—though there were exceptions, a few ugly exceptions of action and passion, judgment and persuasion. True is hard to come by. When if ever did I write, in all those years, in my primate language of fear? These letters, they are just aspects, faulty reflections. I would like to start afresh, to tell you who I am. I would like you to write me or just tell me. I'm really listening this time. *Who are you?* I love you again.

YELLOW BIRD

The yellow bird was dead. My friend had been keeping it in a cage, though she usually left the cage door open. That's what she told me, sitting cross-legged in her living room, tears on her face. "Death is a stern mistress," I said. I had been reading up on it. She was looking at me with what could have been anger. "Death is but an illusion," I then said.

A friend of my friend had told me that my friend had been married five times, not three. In Egypt, back in the day, little boats took you from the place where you were "dead" to a place where you were alive again. If you take away the sense of *individual mosquito*, you will see that they too can be reborn. Oh, I know it's not always easy. Sometimes it's the Lego skyscraper we're talking about. There's no way we're going back to finish the Hogwarts castle. The huge plastic container of parts remains in the storage room, inert. If we did anything, we'd make something new—a flattened-out eagle, for instance, or a very small paddock.

"My little yellow bird," said my friend. I closed my eyes. In a dream I'd gone to her house in the early morning. I needed to wake her up. Instead of knocking on the front door as usual, I walked in the sliding door. The birdcage was inside, by my feet. At first I thought it was empty, but I looked closer and saw, behind the bird mirror, the yellow bird, dusky in the dawn light. When telling a dream to an analyst, you're supposed to use the present tense. In certain kinds of fiction it is effective to make the protagonist trot about in an eternal now. "Did one of your previous husbands give you the bird?" I asked—ever the friend. She looked down and shook her head. I walked through the house in the dream, into the living room, where the shades were drawn, then all the way down the hall to my friend's bedroom. If you think of all the yellow birds that have been plowed under over time, if you think of history, and everywhere, and you think of all yellow birds, whether they are dusky yellow, or yellow with black and gray feathers, or yellow only in certain seasons, mostly very small with delicate bones, but some rather large, majestic yellow hawks with sad eyes and curved beaks, or Big Bird, the largest of the yellow birds that I know of, then, wow, that's a lot of yellow birds to lose. When I think of the yellow bird that I met three times, once in a dream (if it was the same one), once in real life, and once through words in the living room—those other yellow birds become but echoes or lost names, bird chatter as the day brightens, before it gets too warm.

ICEMAN

I am the iceman, crushed by yesterday. For fuck's sake, I fell flat on my face. Toppled like a wedding cake. This wasn't just a small disruption—a low tire, the insurance company's error—it was a travesty, quite serious. And now, as in forever, my body drapes the boulder

Aurelie Sheehan

like a shroud, a mother's cupped palm. (Meanwhile, back on planet earth. What with the ascent of man and the rise to power and the conquering of civilizations.)

All right, let's think about this. Here is how my body lies: with one arm squashed underneath. There was the brief flurry: that soaring free fall from life to death, from what seemed like forever to forever itself, no more twigs and seeds for lunch, not one more even blah installment of the monthly saber-toothed tiger hunt with my reluctant, moody cohort, no more pitiful explosions with my lady friend, her snatch so very contemporary. I heard some kind of trance music—I saw colors of such delicate gradation, such perfect oval symmetry—

And then, OK, forever. I shall be forever. I shall lie here on this boulder, my arm at an (what would be laughably) uncomfortable angle. I shall not close my eyes but hold the grass palace in my retina, the shadow that is Asshole coming to retrieve his arrow. (At least let me keep the arrow. It's so tacky to take the arrow.) And here comes a mountain to lie upon me. Oh, wait: This is a little heavy. The slow shovel of earth, the patient gravedigger, the patient artist, an extravaganza, a sobering bounty. Waves of all you could possibly wish for: the sleek bones of that snatchy lady, the desiccated remains of my enemy's child, the most abundant harvest of fava beans you'd ever want to see, and mountain laurel and lupine and elderberry. Here is a glorious parade of hilarious rabbits, running as if to their own deaths, and here is the tinder of a thousand houses, the rupturing of windows created at great expense, the invention of glass, and here is a telescope with which a pirate found a white-frocked soft spot on a faraway sea, and here is the certificate that stupid state school gave me, saying I could read.

Did the weight of water ever occur to anyone, when they were puzzling this thing out? Did anyone ask *me* if I wanted coffee?

—the mountain with newspapers in it, the bland-faced judges' final decrees, the Polly Pocket dolls, presidents, labor organizers, fat ladies—

—wolves, lesbian deer, lions on the threshold of glory—

The weight did elongate. I become rather long and thin. The fighty ones with their hot instruments came and said my stomach was up by my armpit now—well, what of it? Wouldn't your stomach have moved too? We get used to having our insides stay in one place, but I'm telling you, it's all a jumble in there, seriously. You think you're one thing: just a man on a mountain with a plan for the day—and before you can even take one more breath you are an explosion of flowers, deep and bright purples and lacy whites and bruised reds and streaks of yellow, and when before you could hardly do a box step you are now Mr. Tall, step-sliding across the night sky.

Beyond the Veil of Vision: Reinhold von Kreitz and the Das Beben Movement

Peter Straub and Anthony Discenza

AN INTRODUCTION: AGAINST THE TIDE OF REASON

THE LATTER HALF OF THE nineteenth century witnessed an overwhelming proliferation of developments in science and industry. The seeds sown by the Enlightenment had given rise to a host of technological advancements, many of which were to have far-reaching consequences in the hundred years to follow. As the second wave of the industrial revolution swept across Europe and America, new discoveries and theories were emerging that promised to revolutionize the conception of the origin of life and the nature of the human mind. No secret seemed beyond humanity's grasp.

Yet alongside the advancing tide of reason—and sometimes deeply intermingled with it—there was a commensurate surge of interest in all things spiritual, mystical, and occult. Whether this renewed fascination represented a reaction against rationalism, or whether it proceeded from a belief that the mysteries of existence would soon yield to the tools of reason is open to debate. A claim could be made, however, that the imaginative advances of the physical sciences had left mankind in a reduced, contingent position. The rapid strides in astronomy and physics made in the prior century had already left the old heliocentric model of the universe on history's scrap heap; the emergence of Charles Darwin's theories now threatened to depose humanity from its starring role in God's divine creation. No longer the center of the universe, humanity was suddenly confronted with the image of itself as the product of a mindless and ongoing evolutionary process, creeping along on a minor planet in a vast and uncaring cosmos, with possibly no Creator in sight.

Beneath the certainties espoused by the rationalists, a deepening unease about mankind's newly diminished status could be seen in the development of the Romantic movement. In both fiction and the visual arts, images began to arise of a world brought face to face with terror, radical doubt, and elemental chaos. In the work of painters such as Caspar David Friedrich, J. M. W. Turner, and Théodore Géricault, we confront a vision of humanity rendered impotent before the vast, impersonal forces of nature. The 1818 publication of Mary Shelley's *Frankenstein; or, The Modern Prometheus* provided the world with an indelible image of the potentially horrifying consequences of mankind's arrogance, one that still retains its potency and relevance. By the end of the century, literary works such as Joseph Conrad's *Heart of Darkness* and Henry James's *The Turn of the Screw* would demonstrate certainties of every kind being called into question and found wanting, not least by a destabilizing narrative technique foregrounded by the immediacy of the storytelling—that is, by its clear status *as* storytelling. The self-propelling voice, flickering from moment to moment between alternatives that ironize the concepts of "reality" and "truth," positions us within the impossibility of any decisive location: an embodiment of that "contradiction" claimed by the members of the obscure artistic movement known as Das Beben to be the essential component of any *valid* artistic process.

DAS BEBEN: A LOST HISTORY

In the complex tapestry of nineteenth-century Europe, the history of Das Beben (The Tremor) could be seen as a stray thread that has come loose and fallen away from the main body. From its first incarnation in Mannheim, Germany, in the 1850s, to the disastrous end of its second manifestation in southern England four decades later, the group would seem no more than a minor footnote to the artistic developments of the late 1800s. Even the most dedicated scholar would be hard-pressed to identify any books of art history that acknowledge Das Beben or any of its unfortunate members. Beyond a handful of brief references to their work that turn up in the writing of more notable historical figures of the time, there is virtually no credible record of the group's existence.

Were it not for the curious position Das Beben occupied in relation to the century that was to follow, along with the odd circumstances surrounding its near total effacement from history, there would initially seem to be little of interest in the group other than a collection of lurid details. What few accounts exist are incomplete and contradictory, characterized by disturbing episodes that belong more properly to the realm of fiction than to historical fact. Yet when the frayed and scattered strands of the Das Beben story are rewoven, a strange and fascinating picture emerges—a picture that, much like the work of its members, is filled with shifting outlines and unsettling significance.

Research into an art movement that deliberately cultivated an air of hermeticism, and which even at the height of its activity was barely known outside a few small circles of artists, writers, and eccentrics, poses a significant challenge—one exacerbated by the fact that, with the exception of a single painting that has been locked away for decades, all the group's work has been destroyed or lost. Indeed, it would not be an exaggeration to say that the concrete instances of the work of Das Beben seem to have been withdrawn from history's scrutiny at the exact moment of the group's being revealed to it—almost as though its existence had been deliberately expunged from the historical record by some agency that sought to insulate reality from its members' images and ideas. Faced with such an absence of documentation, we have attempted to fill in the story with such fragments as we have been able to locate—references found in private journals and correspondence, along with the occasional review or commentary from publications of the time. Given the nature of what they reveal, it is perhaps peculiarly appropriate that these ephemera comprise the only means of access to Das Beben.

ORIGINS

The history of the group begins in 1851, at the Schmidt-Bauern Kunstakademie in Mannheim, Germany, a city noted for both its industry and its liberality. It was here that a group of rebellious young artists first coalesced around the charismatic Reinhold von Kreitz, a recently appointed professor of painting who, almost from the moment of his arrival in the city, stirred rumor, speculation, and the suspicion of political subversion. However, the professor's artistic and moral trans-gressions were to prove of much greater significance than his politics.

In some ways, the history of Das Beben may be read as the story of Reinhold von Kreitz: a bizarre, fantastical figure who might have sprung from some tale by E. T. A. Hoffmann. Of von Kreitz's early years, little is known; born sometime around 1807 in or near Vienna, he had apprenticed as a typesetter before taking up a career in the arts. A brief and unhappy marriage, terminated by the sudden death of his wife, Alma, was succeeded by a long period of wandering throughout France and northern Europe. In the course of his travels, von Kreitz encountered a wide array of radical thinkers, writers, and artists, and by the early 1830s, he was in possession of a considerable body of knowledge concerning painting, philosophy, and metaphysics. The year 1832 found him in the Netherlands, where he conducted an intense study of the work of the mysterious seventeenth-century Dutch painter Geoffrey Schalken, of whom so little is known. It was during this time that von Kreitz began to formulate many of his unorthodox theories regarding the as yet untapped potentialities of painting.[1]

Perhaps reflecting the influence of Kant and other post-Enlightenment philosophers on early nineteenth-century thought, von Kreitz was convinced that the world revealed through our visual perception represented a profound falsification, a barrier that concealed a deeper, truer reality. Perceiving this more fundamental reality, and recording some essence of what might be glimpsed there, was the task of the true artist—an act that could only be achieved through a rigorous process of "unseeing." To accomplish this, it was necessary that the distorting screen of physical reality be systematically broken down in order to free one's vision from the tyranny of mere appearance. For von Kreitz, the failure of conventional painting was not simply that it continually falsified through its means of representation of the world, but that the very thing it was attempting to represent was itself already a lie, an obfuscating veil that must be breached, by any and all means.

VON KREITZ & EDMUND MOORASH

Certain of von Kreitz's singular ideas about painting appear to have been informed by the work of the American painter Edmund Moorash, whom von Kreitz had met on a journey to London in 1834. The two had met by chance at a salon in Kensington hosted by the unfortunate

---

[1]Von Kreitz was deeply influenced by the palpable sense of foreboding that emanated from Schalken's paintings, a quality perhaps most clearly manifested in the painter's *meisterwerke*, the profoundly unsettling portrait of his first love, Rose Velderkaust. Indeed, it was in connection with Schalken's painting that von Kreitz came to formulate the most infamous of his mysterious dictums, "That which cannot be seen, must be seen" (*Das, was nicht zu sehen ist, was gesehen werden muss*). This somewhat cryptic utterance was to form the central aesthetic principle of Das Beben through both of its subsequent incarnations.

and now-forgotten painter Henry Mitre.[2] What particularly impressed von Kreitz was a certain odd sense of dislocation—what he called "a lack of contact"—in Moorash's notebook sketches for *William Pinney* (1829) and the rough, wild violence of the drawings toward *Rat Krespel* (1835), a painting then still in progress.[3] After discovering their mutual appreciation for the disgraced Mitre's work, the two men had fallen into intense conversation and found that their artistic goals shared many elements. "Painting *as* painting," said Moorash, "yet painting as possession too." "Contradiction," murmured von Kreitz, to which Moorash replied, "Yes, that is the next step."[4]

Over the next several years, Moorash and von Kreitz maintained a sporadic correspondence. For von Kreitz, Moorash's intransigent and revolutionary vision represented a different—though superficially bolder—approach to a common goal. Moorash did not attempt to unravel the world directly, as von Kreitz would; rather, the "lack of contact" and "violence" found in the work of the American painter were created by careful and constant adjustment of the means necessary to produce the desired *effect* in the viewer's perception. While it seems clear that Moorash did not share von Kreitz's metaphysical leanings, his ability to produce such effects, especially in the last phase of his career, suggests something of this same ability to violate not only painterly convention but the act of seeing itself.[5]

---

[2]Mitre, a painter of virtuosic but somewhat claustrophobic still-life compositions, had fallen in love with his landlady's thirteen-year-old son; things proceeded badly and the painter was eventually beaten to death in the street.

[3]The catalog from a 1988 exhibition of Moorash's work provides the following description of the painting, which is based on Hoffmann's tale of the same name:

> What is striking, however, is not the careful rendering of detail but precisely the opposite: the furious distortion of details as they are swept up into lines of force, the deliberate and expressive blurring of form. Thus the streaming of Krespel's hair and coat is seen in the violins, which in the dark radiance of the candlelight seem to writhe like snakes, and the ripple of the fluttering band of crepe is seen in the curve of the piano's music rack, while the piano itself appears to be dissolving into reddish darkness. The effect is of a center of violent energy diffusing itself throughout the entire painting . . . Despite such distortions, the painting retains a number of illusionist features, such as definite, though at times ambiguous, perspectival lines.

[4]As reported in von Kreitz's letter of April 30, 1841, to his second wife, Theresa, who died in 1845 as the result of an accident in the artist's studio.

[5]According to Heinz Schallert's *The Art of Southern Germany* (1931), in 1850 von Kreitz made his only visit to America, specifically for the purpose of seeing Moorash's posthumous exhibition at the Fogg Museum in Cambridge, Massachusetts. In his journals, von Kreitz wrote, in his inexact English, "I give my utter praise to Moorash. He has seen the sacred process to be *in violation* of the inviolable."

MANNHEIM, 1851

It was not long after his appointment to the Kunstakademie that the magnetic von Kreitz began to attract a following. He had come to Mannheim for its intrinsic orderliness and its focus on manufacturing and mechanics; for von Kreitz, the city's rational, mechanistic worldview was precisely the quality that rendered it an ideal location for the forces he described as "the engines of the irrational" to flourish and gain power.[6] The generative tension produced by a force giving rise to its opposite was a necessary component of the energies von Kreitz believed were required to "tear the veil asunder." In the notes for one of his earliest lectures at the Akademie, he asserts: "contradiction is the essential principle of that elemental and *final* reality we can but glimpse."

During what proved to be a short tenure at the Kunstakademie, von Kreitz created an atmosphere of contention in the otherwise staid institution. Unpredictable and short-tempered, he generated controversy as a matter of course. His lectures were lively, even chaotic affairs in which he would frequently wander far afield from mundane matters such as perspective and human anatomy, assaulting his bewildered students with lengthy disquisitions on philosophy, mathematics, physics, and other less identifiable disciplines.[7]

Given this sort of behavior, it did not take long before von Kreitz began to draw unwelcome attention from the directors of the Akademie. Confronted with increasing interference and censure from the school's officials, von Kreitz, in a typically flamboyant move, abruptly resigned his position. Taking up residence in the Blue Goose, an old

---

[6]The city's history is strongly associated with industrial development. Referred to as "the city of grids," because of the rectilinear layout of its streets, Mannheim is the birthplace of two of the defining (and perhaps oppositional) mechanisms of modernity: the bicycle (invented by Karl Freiherr von Drais in 1871) and the first working automobile (constructed by Karl Benz in 1885).

[7]In a letter to a friend, Jakob Metzger, a student at the Akademie during von Kreitz's tenure, writes of the frequently bizarre assertions to which the professor was prone:

> I confess I often wonder if the man is not mad. He spouts the most absurd notions and continually makes impossible claims regarding his own abilities. Only yesterday, he flew into a rage when asked the most innocent of questions by M____, stating, "The eye is the greatest enemy of the true artist. Indeed, the most advisable course I could offer you were that you pluck those glassy, sightless orbs from your head, rather than wandering about sketching churches and hay fields. At least then you might have earned for yourself some slight chance of actually *seeing*."

rathskeller in the poorest quarter of the city, he began presenting impromptu lectures on painting and a variety of other subjects to anyone who cared to listen, using a back room of the tavern as his informal lecture hall. These lectures, which were known to continue until long after midnight, soon began to draw an unlikely audience from Mannheim's more disreputable citizens. Thieves, beggars, madmen, would-be revolutionaries, defrocked clergy—all seemed to discover a powerful attraction in von Kreitz's curious pedagogy, and before long the Blue Goose had become a hub of unruly activity.

The inner core of what was to become the first incarnation of Das Beben consisted of a group of young painters from the Akademie who had fallen under von Kreitz's spell. Of these, four were most prominent: Lutz Schlicke, Busso Hobemuss, Franz Veertz, and perhaps the most talented of the group, Klaus-Maria Klappenburg, a handsome, voluble young troublemaker from Baden-Baden.[8] These four were always in attendance at von Kreitz's lectures, and it was not long before they had taken up residence alongside their master in the rooms above the tavern, which had essentially become Das Beben's center of operations.

THE DAS BEBEN AESTHETIC

Any discussion of the visual style of a group of painters whose entire output appears to have been wiped from existence confronts the researcher with obvious problems. The available information about Das Beben's work exists only in a handful of descriptions written by artists and critics of the time who had seen the work firsthand and were either moved or disturbed enough by the experience to write about it. However, through a careful analysis of this material, it is possible to make some general observations regarding the unique visual sensibilities of the group's Mannheim incarnation, as well as the peculiar ethos and methodologies that informed their work.

From the very start, the Das Beben painters were deeply preoccupied with a radical reimagining of the capabilities of visual art. In line with von Kreitz's singular ideology, they utterly rejected the idea

---

[8]Klappenburg had abandoned his family's Catholicism and was searching for a wider, more explanatory faith. Of the group, Klappenburg was perhaps the most devoted to von Kreitz, and was often heard to quote his master's formulation, "The to-be-explained is always that which escapes explanation" (*Die zu erklaeren ist immer, dass der Austritt erklaert*).

of painting as mere representation. The only true role of the visual arts, they believed, was to function as a conduit to higher orders of existence, to reveal what lay "beyond the dull walls of sight."

To this end, the group brought a fierce rigor to every aspect of a painting's creation, from the medium's most basic aspects—such as the grinding of pigments and the preparation of the canvas—to the development of a complicated set of principles governing composition, lighting, and even the specific angles from which certain objects ought to be represented.[9] In their obsessive quest for greater control, much research was undertaken regarding the obscure chemical properties of various pigments, and the group continually experimented with complex formulations of the relationship between color, composition, and perspective.[10]

Through the precise manipulation of these elements, von Kreitz and his disciples were convinced they could produce paintings that would "unlock the doors" to hidden dimensions of being. An artist armed with such knowledge—and who was also possessed of an "indomitable will"—could create artworks that would function as a kind of gateway to regions that lay beyond human understanding, giving the artist access to the primordial forces that governed all existence.[11]

---

[9]In developing these principles, the group appeared to have borrowed widely from a hodgepodge of disparate philosophic and esoteric traditions, from Arthur Schopenhauer's *On the Will in Nature* to the writings of the Swiss alchemist Paracelsus. Through the mastery and application of these rules, along with the development of an interior process the group's members referred to as "true seeing," an artist would gain the ability to generate images capable of producing profound alterations in the consciousness of the beholder—and, perhaps, in reality itself.

[10]In his years of study, von Kreitz had rigorously educated himself in the nature and origins of pigments, and had used his time at the Akademie to further his research. The same Jakob Metzger who had been so unsettled by von Kreitz's pronouncements was even more dismayed to find himself pressed into service along with the other students, who were set to grinding the shells of South American beetles in order to create a pigment similar to carmine. On other occasions the students were charged with burning great quantities of raw umber, which was subsequently reduced in a mixture of bile and acid to obtain an unappealing reddish-brown hue, while the bones of swallows were charred to ashes, exposed to the light of the waning moon, then compounded with the extracts of certain resinous plants to create an unusually impenetrable black. These inscrutable operations were always overseen by von Kreitz, who chanted out complex mathematical equations while beating time on the floor with his massive oak walking stick.

[11]Around the beginning of 1855, the group appeared to have become especially fixated upon the idea that, by placing a sufficient number of such images into highly specific visual and spatial arrangements with each other, a kind of circuit would be created, allowing primordial energies to flow freely into and reshape our world—a process they referred to as "opening the way." On the back of his painting *Dweller on the Threshold* (1852), Schlicke had scrawled the following:

In terms of subject matter, the work of Das Beben tended toward the mystical, even macabre.[12] The German (as well as the later British) incarnation of the group was unquestionably influenced to some degree by artists whose names have long been associated with the darker or more mysterious aspects of existence, such as Henry Fuseli, Francisco Goya, and Gustave Doré. The work of William Blake seems to have made a significant impression on the group, particularly the poet's *Marriage of Heaven and Hell* (though perhaps more in terms of Blake's text than his imagery). Das Beben also acknowledged debts to lesser-known artists such as the aforementioned Schalken; the darkly unsettling Edmund Moorash; and mysterious, visionary outsider artist H. Friedrich Ahnfeldt.[13] Interpretations of scenes from mythology, legend, and folklore were a popular motif, one perhaps epitomized by Klappenburg's *The Glance*, his transfixing portrayal of Eurydice on her doomed passage from the underworld. Works such as Veertz's *Lake of the Siren* and Hobemuss's *The Ivory Gate*, with their disorienting perspectives and inhuman sense of scale, clearly link Das Beben (at least superficially) with the earlier Romantic movement as well as the work of various painters associated with Symbolism, among them James Ensor, Alfred Kubin, and Odilon Redon.[14]

From a purely visual standpoint, the work of Das Beben does not appear to have been defined by a specific visual aesthetic. Based on the available accounts, its members' paintings diverged wildly in appearance, formal technique, and style, from "nightmarish regions of almost palpable malevolence," as Franz von Dingelstedt described the brownish, depopulated landscapes of Schlicke, to shattered,

---

Place the Weights, total the Angles in their proper Orbits, and let the Pictures speak, each in its own fashion; then the Veils shall be torn asunder, and the Light shall stream in, transforming all it touches.

[12]Though by no means exclusively; many canvases were quite pedestrian in their depiction of various nondescript sections of Mannheim.

[13]Very little is known about Ahnfeldt, a devout, uneducated carpenter from Bavaria who had begun painting a series of strange, unearthly images following the joint suicide of his son and daughter. Almost all of Ahnfeldt's paintings had been confiscated and burnt by his local church following his death, but von Kreitz had managed to come into possession of one small canvas, the infamous *Supplicant in the Red Forest*, n.d., which he would allow only the innermost circle of the group to view.

[14]Certainly, the centrality of the principle of "contradiction" that lay at the heart of Das Beben could be seen as a radical expansion upon the theme of psychological splitting or doubling so often associated with Romanticism. However, care must be taken to not overemphasize such connections. The aspirations of Das Beben were fundamentally different from those of other movements of the period, and in many aspects, totally unique.

turbulent compositions that prefigure by many decades twentieth-century painting's leap into abstraction.

What the group's paintings did share was something that was harder to articulate, but which seems to be connected with a *feeling* that emanated from them—a quality of atmosphere or affect that, from a conventional perspective, would be difficult to attribute to a static visual representation. Individuals as disparate in their tastes as the poet and critic Heinrich Heine and the painter Carl Gustav Carus both make note of a powerful, almost vertiginous sensation of movement in the work, along with subtle, hard-to-define distortions of perspective that combined to produce "an inexplicable cojoining of near and far."[15]

A somewhat clearer (if negatively framed) impression of Das Beben's visual sensibility during its early years can be found in an attack on the group published in 1853. Shortly following a visit to Mannheim, Young Germany's Heinrich Laube published a pamphlet called "The Scent of Demons" (Der Duft von Dämonen). In it, Laube writes:

> To locate "impulses" toward visionary suggestions of the unseen, and a related capacity to portray "actual movement" in the work of von Kreitz and Klappenburg is to delude oneself deliberately about the limitations of painting itself, however blurred its outlines, however murky its colorations. Chiaroscuro, which Herr Hauff's[16] beloved von Kreitz takes to such gloomy extremes, can be suggestive *only up to a point* and is not, cannot be, will never be a signpost to an altered form of either painting or reality.

More negative criticism, this time from the far more conventional painter Hans Thoma, who had seen von Kreitz's work quite early in his career, illuminates another important and curious aspect of Das Beben that cannot be overstated: the extent to which the work invited

---

[15]Heine claimed that the work of the Das Beben painters generated the terrible sensation that the images were invisibly *in motion*. As reported in his *Table Talk, Vol. I*, the poet felt himself initially fascinated, then repelled by this phenomenon: "With Professor von Kreitz and his slavish followers, I grew increasingly dismayed. Behind this appalling illusion of movement, I feared to discover the snake's head of *actual movement*."

Of von Kreitz's work, Carus, a former student of Caspar David Friedrich, writes: "[the paintings] spoke always of the dream-darkness that is ever to be found lurking within the structures of the prosaic, the postman's blue uniform, the shop's many-colored jars, the rain-slick'd cobbles at night, the bobolink's fixed eye. It is here we find evidence of *the instability of the general*."

[16]Apparently a reference to poet and novelist Wilhelm Hauff.

the hostility of the viewer—and apparently returned it. Of von Kreitz's *Study at Dusk* (1854), Thoma observes: "At first viewing, this work appeared so delicate, so much a matter of things old and ordinary glimpsed through a typical Mannheim fog. In retrospect, the canvas produced the profoundly unsettling sensation that it was somehow laughing at me behind my back. An ugly, contemptuous jeering seemed to ring in my ears."

THE FIRST FIRE

It did not take long for strange rumors about von Kreitz and his followers' unorthodox activities to circulate throughout Mannheim. With displeasure and growing alarm, the Akademie and the local government observed that the most dubious and questionable elements of their otherwise orderly city were gathered at all hours at the Blue Goose, where they appeared to be engaged in activities that had very little to do with the visual arts.[17]

Before the authorities could decide on any course of action, fate took matters into its own hands. Late one April evening in 1855, the rathskeller burst into flame. The source of the fire remains unknown, though one witness claimed it began in the inn's meeting room, which von Kreitz and his disciples had taken to using as a kind of private salon in which to display their work. According to local accounts, a sour "vegetal" odor, mingled with the stench of rot, had permeated the area around the tavern just prior to the start of the conflagration. The fire proved stubbornly difficult to extinguish, and nearly everyone inside succumbed. If von Kreitz and his followers had indeed been granted some revelation, the cost had been punishingly high. Of the Das Beben inner circle, only von Kreitz and Klappenburg survived, and they were able to shed little light on the catastrophe. Burns and smoke inhalation had left the former student

---

[17]The proprietor of the city's oldest bookstore told an acquaintance, who had passed the story along to his priest, that while browsing his shelves of ancient writings, a fresh-faced, arrogant young student named Klappenburg had boasted that Professor von Kreitz was providing instruction in the works of Cornelius Agrippa—in particular, *Of Magical Ceremonies*, published in 1565. "And why is he doing that?" asked the bookseller. Klappenburg replied, "To glance behind the veil. To arouse the tremor." "For what purpose?" inquired the bookseller. "Afterwards, bookseller, nothing shall remain the same," answered Klappenburg. "That, I promise you. Nothing, not in any realm." [Otto Kleinhans, *Written on Sand: A Bookseller's Melancholy Journey* (Mannheim: privately printed, 1873).]

unable to communicate; he could not speak, could barely see, and the burns to his head were so severe that he had apparently been rendered deaf. Left to the care of his wealthy family, Klappenburg lingered on in a kind of half-life for several more years until his death in 1859.

As for von Kreitz, no records have come to light regarding his whereabouts and activities in the eight years that followed the destruction of the rathskeller. It is as though he vanished, like a disagreeable dream, into thin air.

INTERLUDE: KRANKHELM ISLAND

Von Kreitz does not reappear again until 1863, when he turns up on a remote, desolate spit of land in the Baltic Sea known as Krankhelm Island. On Krankhelm, he seems to have maintained a long period of relative anonymity and near total solitude. His once commanding appearance was a memory; the fire had left him badly scarred on his face, chest, and legs, and he was barely able to stand upright. Damage to his lungs and vocal cords had reduced his voice to a harsh, ugly whisper. A bent, wizened, somewhat grotesque figure who was widely shunned by the locals, von Kreitz nevertheless retained some vestiges of his old glamor: Occasionally, some member of the press would arrive on Krankhelm to seek out the infamous founder of "The Tremor" in the hopes of securing a lurid tale for his or her readership. Von Kreitz's isolation was also alleviated by periodic visits from scholars of the esoteric who came in search of his private library, a collection of hundreds of volumes of hermetic lore that he had somehow amassed in the years following the disaster in Mannheim. Many of these books were highly obscure works of occult philosophy and alchemy of which only a few copies were known to exist.

Von Kreitz had also resumed painting, producing during his years on the island a series of small, intensely dark canvases that he referred to as "Disconsolations." These works, which the painter Odilon Redon would later describe as "more absences than paintings,"[18]

---

[18]Von Kreitz appears to have had a powerful effect on the Symbolist painter, who encountered several of the "Disconsolations" during a brief stay on the Baltic coast while serving in the Franco-Prussian War. The lingering effect of these dark, troubling canvases may have played a role in Redon's increasing interest with dreamlike subject matter. A description of Redon's work in Joris-Karl Huysmans' *À rebours* provides some suggestion, perhaps, of the nature of this influence:

were highly sought after by a tiny handful of aficionados—composed for the most part of the same individuals who came to consult von Kreitz's unique archive. Visitors to Krankhelm were obliged to take a small, dismal ferry to the island, hire a wagon driver with a cart, and traverse ten miles of rocky terrain to the artist's studio, where their host's greeting was invariably unwelcoming.

DAS BEBEN: THE PAINTINGS

With the exception of Hugo Ayling's *The Gathered Clan*, all of the work of Das Beben has been lost or destroyed. In an effort to provide some living sense of the work, we have created this brief "exhibition" of several representative paintings by members of the movement, cobbling together the limited and incomplete references to these works uncovered by our research to create coherent descriptions in the manner of a museum presentation. While these descriptions are extrapolations, and necessarily take a degree of creative license, it is hoped that they will provide a window into the unique visual qualities of the work of these unorthodox artists.

Those were the pictures bearing the signature: Odilon Redon. They held, between their gold-edged frames of unpolished pearwood, undreamed-of images: a Merovingian-type head, resting upon a cup; a bearded man, reminiscent both of a Buddhist priest and a public orator, touching an enormous cannon-ball with his finger; a spider with a human face lodged in the centre of its body. Then there were charcoal sketches which delved even deeper into the terrors of fever-ridden dreams. Here, on an enormous die, a melancholy eyelid winked; over there stretched dry and arid landscapes, calcinated plains, heaving and quaking ground, where volcanoes erupted into rebellious clouds, under foul and murky skies; sometimes the subjects seemed to have been taken from the nightmarish dreams of science, and hark back to prehistoric times; monstrous flora bloomed on the rocks; everywhere, in among the erratic blocks and glacial mud, were figures whose simian appearance—heavy jawbone, protruding brows, receding forehead, and flattened skull top—recalled the ancestral head, the head of the first Quaternary Period, the head of man when he was still fructivorous and without speech, the contemporary of the mammoth, of the rhinoceros with septate nostrils, and of the giant bear. These drawings defied classification; unheeding, for the most part, of the limitations of painting, they ushered in a very special type of the fantastic, one born of sickness and delirium.

Peter Straub / Anthony Discenza

Busso Hobemuss
German, 1829–1855
The Ivory Gate
Circa 1855
Oil on canvas

The only member of Das Beben's first incarnation who was a native of Mannheim, Hobemuss had demonstrated little inclination or aptitude for the visual
arts until his teens, when, acting on a schoolmate's dare, he entered and won
a drawing contest sponsored by the Hartt Gymnasium, his secondary school. His
entry, *A Castle in the Clouds Is a Haven to All*, was reproduced in the local
paper, *Der Morganweb*, in February 1846, where it attracted the attention of an
administrator at the Schmidt-Bauern Kunstakademie. Invited to submit a port-
folio to the school, Hobemuss produced a set of drawings that, like *Castle in the
Clouds*, were intricately detailed renderings of vaguely fantastical cities and
landscapes. At the Akademie, Hobemuss displayed a talent for visual precision
and accuracy, but the conservative atmosphere of the school seemed to inhibit
many of the visionary qualities of his work until he entered von Kreitz's tutelage.

As part of Das Beben, Hobemuss's style underwent a profound transformation, becoming more loose and gestural, even violent, in its handling of paint.
As his work developed, Hobemuss began to represent boundaries between
objects and space in increasingly unconventional ways, sometimes solely
through subtle variations in the texture of the paint itself. His subject matter
moved from fairly conventional studies of landscape and architecture into
images of towering, cyclopean structures that defy any clear sense of time or
scale. In *The Ivory Gate* (1853), a vertiginous massing of luminous, geometrical
solids threatens to metastasize from the picture plane; the painting fractures
perspective to such a degree that we seem to be *inside* its surface rather than
in front of it.

Franz Veertz

German, 1825–1855

Earth's Siege

1853

Oil on board

Franz Veertz possessed a dark, somewhat Byronic sensibility that no doubt played a role in his fascination with von Kreitz and Das Beben. Born to the merchant class in Cologne, Veertz had been raised by his widowed grandmother following the death of his parents in a shipwreck. A natural swordsman, he was leader of the fencing team while a student at Cologne's Catholic Gymnasium, where a pair of dueling scars enhanced his saturnine features and earned him the nickname "The Prussian." Seemingly destined for a military career, Veertz chose to delay his entrance into the army in order to study painting alongside a boyhood friend, Moritz Waldmüller, who would later become the founder of a little-known spiritualist movement in Vienna.

Das Beben's link to the Romantic movement of the early nineteenth century is seen perhaps most clearly in Veertz's work; Edmund Burke's influential 1757 treatise on the sublime had left a strong impression on the young painter, whose early output consisted of sensual, almost shocking depictions of physical transformation inspired by Ovid's *Metamorphoses*, along with phantasmagoric scenes of storm-wracked landscapes. *Earth's Siege* (1853) demonstrates the hallucinatory intensity the painter was eventually able to achieve through the marriage of lurid subject matter with an obsessive control of composition. The painting is remarkable for the unnaturally regular alternation of light and dark across its surface; every visual element, from the turbulent masses of flame-edged black clouds to the painfully contorted trees, seems to form part of a single, underlying pattern that hovers just at the edge of recognition. The effect creates the curious impression that another image entirely is cleverly camouflaged within the painting—though of *what* precisely is unclear. "It sets the head spinning and the eyes aching," wrote Hans Thoma. "I cannot bear to look, and yet cannot seem to tear my gaze away."

Peter Straub / Anthony Discenza

Lutz Schlicke

German, 1827–1855

Above Bismarck Square

1853
Oil on board

The abhorrent paintings of Lutz Schlicke are among the most disturbing works produced by the Mannheim group, though it is difficult to say what makes them so. Schlicke was born in Munich, the son of Gruner Schlicke, a well-known illustrator of broadsides and posters, and his wife, Magda, a fortepiano instructor and amateur mathematician. Though apparently a happy child who often served as a model for his father's advertisements, Schlicke seemed to age prematurely as he entered his teens, becoming increasingly moody and taciturn. Given to sarcasm on the rare occasions in which he spoke at all, he proved an unpopular student at the Akademie, where he was fond of studies depicting complex mechanical contrivances. Schlicke was particularly fascinated with unconventional spatial geometries and how they might be represented on a two-dimensional surface.

In both style and affect, Schlicke's work seems to prophesize the arrival of surrealism over a half century later. His paintings are almost entirely devoid of human figures, or any living beings whatsoever. His listless depictions of nondescript spaces in and around Mannheim (expanses of featureless brick walls were a favorite subject) are rendered in a uniformly burnt palette from which all vitality seems to have been drained. Though empty of life, there is an almost unbearable feeling of claustrophobia in Schlicke's work. His deserted squares and oddly flattened intersections feel airless, as though located miles below the earth's surface.

Above Bismarck Square shows a slightly elevated view of a residential section of Mannheim in the vicinity of the titular landmark. As is typical of Schlicke's compositions, there is a subtly disorienting quality to the perspective, as though multiple angles of view have been seamlessly fused. The city appears dead, like some sprawling, uninhabited mausoleum: "A world not simply abandoned by humanity," Heinrich Heine wrote of the work, "but rather one in which nothing human has ever existed." Despite the deserted aspect of the scene, the painting conveys the unwelcome impression that concealed among the flatly rendered rooftops and avenues, some unspeakable presence is about to emerge into view. This sensation was so strong that apparently not even the other members of Das Beben seemed able to tolerate the painting: "Dear Lutz, you've certainly outdone yourself this time," Klappenburg is reported to have told Schlicke. "Whatever sort of pet you've tucked away back there, I should hope to be elsewhere when it grows tired of hiding!"

Klaus-Maria Klappenburg

German, 1827–1859

The Fruits of Wrath

Circa 1854

Oil on linen mounted on board

Klaus-Maria Klappenburg was perhaps the most virtuosic painter of the Mannheim group. His canvases demonstrate an effortless grasp of the capabilities of the medium; in his casual mastery of technique, he seems to reveal a kind of mocking contempt for the viewer. Arrogant, reckless, possessed of almost effeminate beauty, Klappenburg was the only son of a wealthy manufacturer from Baden-Baden. He was expelled from a series of expensive boarding schools before being at last sent to Mannheim, where his exasperated parents had remanded him under the care of his uncle, a former Prussian general, in the hopes of imparting some discipline (a plan that failed spectacularly). But beneath Klappenburg's dissolute habits and fondness for cruel pranks lay a deeply troubled spirit. Subject to frequent, incapacitating attacks of melancholy, Klappenburg had attempted suicide on his thirteenth birthday by the grave of his sister Margrette, who died as an infant.

Klappenburg's earliest work is marked by a fixation with morbid states of being, rendered all the more harrowing by his dazzling command of lighting effects and the uncanny ability to convey extremes of emotion. His painting *The Visit*, which Klappenburg painted when he was only eighteen, had been inspired by John Polidori's *The Vampyre*; his presentation of this work at the Kunstakademie caused several students to collapse in terror, earned him a severe reprimand—and drew the approving eye of von Kreitz. *The Fruits of Wrath*, perhaps one of Klappenburg's most accomplished paintings, displays none of the showy theatricality of his earlier work; by 1854 he had become highly focused, even somber, in his relentless quest for mastery of True Seeing. A highly interpretive portrayal of the destruction of Sodom and Gomorrah, *The Fruits of Wrath* represents Klappenburg's increasing descent into pure abstraction: Here, the destructive energy of vast, cosmic forces is manifested within the paint itself, which seems to burn with a sulfurous glare. There is no image in the proper sense, only massed, fractured lines of force that create a sense of intolerable pressure in the beholder's vision.

351

Peter Straub / Anthony Discenza

William Prooder
1867–1889
The Emperor, Unseen
1889
Oil on linen

The only child of a Yorkshire butcher, William Prooder demonstrated a remarkable facility for drawing from an early age, delighting in elaborately detailed sketches of the interior of his father's shop and its piled carcasses. As a student at William Dodson's Academy of Art, he had fared poorly, quickly tiring of the repetitive exercises and uninspiring teaching methods of the staff, at whose hands he often suffered. Shy and withdrawn, with pale, perpetually bruised-looking features, Prooder was unusually devoted to Hugo Ayling, but seemed ill at ease with von Kreitz and the other members of the group, especially Henry Turling, whom he both loathed and feared.

Yet Prooder was a painter of uncommon skill. The still life's traditional emphasis on mortality achieves a fevered apotheosis in his work, which features increasingly elaborate, almost altar-like arrangements of butchered meat and fruit, often in a state of near-putrefaction. His small, intricate canvases display an intensely trompe l'oeil realism that drew gasps of amazement, as well as consternation, from the Haywards' guests. In *The Emperor, Unseen*, the composition is centered on a mass of entrails and viscera from some unknown animal, surrounded by scattered papers, a small prism, and several curious-looking instruments. The scene is depicted in near-total darkness, illuminated only by pale, bluish light that seems to emanate from a great distance. To the right looms a monstrous bust, roughly carved from dark stone. The face of the figure is turned away from us, but something about its general outlines is deeply unsettling. Oddly, the bust's shadow is inconsistent with the other objects in the painting, and appears much more clearly defined.

Henry Turling

English, 1860–1889

Knowledge

1888

Oil on canvas

The youngest son of a dissolute earl with a halfhearted involvement in the collection of eighteenth-century etchings, Henry Turling had painted throughout his youth without seeing art as anything more than a pleasant diversion. After being sent down from Eaton for gambling, he became a regular habitué of several private clubs in London. Seemingly on a lark, he submitted two paintings to the Royal Academy and was accepted. As a student, Turling appeared indifferent to painting but possessed an uncanny knack for caricature and satirical portraits in the manner of Hogarth. A brusque, raw-boned individual capable of casual, almost cheerful brutality, Turling nonetheless had the rare ability to catch the essence of a subject in a few simple gestures. By the time of his introduction to the group at Blane, Turling had become something of an inveterate gambler, and his continued patronage of Soho's gaming rooms resulted in his eventual expulsion from the academy.

As part of the New Tremor, Turling pushed the capabilities of portraiture to unusual extremes. *Knowledge*, a painting some speculate was intended as a portrait of von Kreitz, represents the culmination of Turling's wholly singular style, which in some ways anticipates the multiplying planes and untethered contours of cubism. On initial inspection, the painting appears to have no subject at all; the viewer is confronted with an indecipherable tangle of unstable lines—ragged bands of black, crimson, and umber vibrating in a somehow fibrous-looking fog. However, as one's eyes move across the painting, the wavering outlines seem to shift, and a clear image of a seated figure appears—only to vanish when gazed at directly. Even more unsettling, this fugitive impression is inconsistent; in one moment, the man depicted seems youthful and full of a fierce vitality; in the next, the figure seems horribly aged, marked by the livid corruption of the grave. The effect could not be reproduced and Turling later insisted that he did not recall how he had achieved it.

THE NEW TREMOR

Toward the close of the 1800s, Victorian England found itself in the midst of an upsurge of interest in all things mystical and arcane. The occult was enjoying a new vogue among certain circles of the wealthy and privileged. Dozens of Masonic lodges were appearing throughout Europe, each professing some claim to esoteric traditions that reached as far back as ancient Egypt. Prominent in these circles were the Haywards, an old and extremely rich family from southern England. Aside from their fantastic wealth, the Haywards were known for their long-standing reputation for eccentricity and purported dalliance with magic and the occult.[19] Most recently, the family had been involved in the development of the Hermetic Order of the Golden Dawn, an occult society perhaps best known for its most infamous member, Aleister Crowley.

In the early 1880s, Baron Hoxton Hayward and his wife, Baroness Asenath Hayward, had regularly hosted a number of the Golden Dawn's founders—including William Wynn Westcott and MacGregor Mathers—at Blane, the Hayward country estate near Kent. By 1885, however, the Haywards, whose interests seemed somewhat more exotic than even Mathers's and Westcott's, had broken their ties with the group, taking up with a much more radical circle of occult enthusiasts. The primary members of this group included a doctor of theology named Arnold Gather, a mysterious and shabbily dressed individual who referred to himself as "Lord" Wren, and Mrs. Octavia Shell, a former actress who enjoyed great popularity among London's more Bohemian set.[20] This vaguely sinister triumvirate quickly won

---

[19]Allegedly, the infamous sixteenth-century mathematician and alchemist John Dee, along with his assistant Edward Kelley (who claimed to communicate with angels), had enjoyed the patronage of the Hayward family when the pair returned to England after years of wandering Europe.

[20]It has been speculated that the woman depicted in Franz von Stuck's infamous painting *The Sin* was Octavia Shell. The painter almost certainly met von Kreitz, and perhaps Hugo Ayling, while on a brief, little-noted excursion to England in his twenty-first year (the same year in which he was admitted to the School of Applied Arts in Karlsruhe); the incident is mentioned in the third chapter of an unfinished and untitled autobiography:

> To celebrate my birthday, I went (with my mother's blessing) across the sea to England, then directly to London and the Trismegistus Bookstore. It was on my second day of haunting the Tris (as it was known to its habitués) that at last I encountered the object of my voyage, the strange and terrible figure of Master von Kreitz, of whom I had heard such extraordinary things. He was a man who seemed ever

favor with the Haywards, and before long they had become semipermanent guests at Blane.[21]

In the course of their undertakings, Gather, Wren, and Shell had become fixated upon the role that images might play in establishing contact with other regions of existence. While the precise nature of this role is not clear, it is evident that the group was deeply engaged with this problem, so much so that they had taken under their collective wing a young and gifted painter named Hugo Ayling, who had recently left the Royal Academy under a cloud. Inexperienced and impressionable, Ayling was easily seduced by the trio's considerable charm and promises of initiation into secret systems of knowledge.

It was shortly after their "acquisition" of Ayling in late 1886 that the three occultists encountered a strange figure during one of their periodic forays into the labyrinth of tiny bookstores, shuttered storefronts, and underground pubs that populated the shabby neighborhoods near the British Museum. In the back room of a nameless bookseller, they found themselves inexplicably drawn to a series of anonymous charcoal sketches. A series of inquiries regarding the artist's identity eventually led them to a filthy back-alley flat inhabited by a bent, scarred man dressed in worn and out-of-date clothing. It was Reinhold von Kreitz.

How or when von Kreitz had arrived in England remains a mystery. At the time of his encounter with the Blane occultists, the former professor of the Schmidt-Bauern Kunstakademie was living in near destitution, eking out a meager existence giving lectures to private

---

just at the point of uttering some truth that would shock one to one's core. That afternoon, as he thrust at me book after book (shamefully, none of which I could read), the Master inserted his ruined visage into a space two inches before mine and hissed, "Do you not yet understand that what is not painted has more spiritual significance than what is? That we have it in our power to bring forth a new reality?" Before I could respond (before I had time in which to tell him an untruth), he produced a sketchbook of extraordinary size and gave me to gaze upon some half dozen of its pages. Their contents have marked me all of my life. Henceforth, I knew that one of Art's essential burdens has always been the depiction if not the enacting of the ever-shifting, ever-ungrounded, ambiguous contest between darkness and light, the greater strength being always that in which darkness can be seen to subsume the light. This was the case when I brought forth *The Wild Chase, Lucifer,* and, in a portrait of a woman known to us both, *The Sin.*" [Franz von Stuck, unfinished autobiography, trans. P. Straub (unpublished, n.d.).]

[21]Unlike such groups as the Golden Dawn, Gather, Wren, and Shell appeared much more interested in the *applied* study of those forms of ceremonial magic described in such medieval texts as *The Lesser Key of Solomon.*

audiences and selling "elevated views" of London landmarks from a makeshift stall. Whatever strange cogs of fate had engineered it, the chance meeting with Gather, Wren, and Shell was to provide von Kreitz with yet another improbable reversal of his fortunes. Discovering in the painter a kindred spirit, the three introduced him to the Haywards; given the breadth of von Kreitz's knowledge and the nature of his ideas about art, it was not long before the baron and baroness had him installed at Blane, where he was provided with his own apartment and studio. It was at Blane that von Kreitz first met Hugo Ayling, who at that time was working as an assistant to the accomplished portraitist William Powell Frith.[22]

Over the course of the following months, Ayling brought a number of other artists to visit Blane. Three in particular—Henry Turling, George Heathman, and William Prooder—fell under von Kreitz's spell; despite his appearance, he still retained much of his strange ability to enthrall. Like Ayling, Turling and Heathman had been students at the Royal Academy of Art, while Prooder was still a student at William Dodson's Academy of Art.

Much like their ill-fated predecessors in Mannheim, the young British artists soon apprenticed themselves to von Kreitz, who wasted no time in resuming the investigations that had been so violently interrupted twenty-five years earlier. Christening the group the "New Tremor," von Kreitz began initiating his latest disciples into his

---

[22]Despite Ayling's expulsion from the Royal Academy for unspecified charges of "decadence," Frith had been so impressed with the young man's painting and skill that he readily took Ayling on as an apprentice. Within a year, however, Ayling was spending more and more of his time at Blane, arriving at Frith's studio disheveled and distracted, his clothing in disarray, his manner slyly insubordinate. In an unpublished fourth volume of journals, Frith records both his unalloyed admiration for Ayling's artistic abilities and his growing dismay at the evidence of his assistant's gathering dissipation:

> I cared not that he had been expelled from the Academy, and even less for his inversion. From the first, Ayling demonstrated great technical skill in the delicacy and shading of his brushwork, and within months I had entrusted him with much more than the backgrounds and passage-work of his initial tasks. With Ayling's loyal and oft-inspired assistance, I found myself capable of taking on a greater number of commissions and fulfilling these with greater speed. Upon occasion, I am unashamed to admit, I was in fact ravished by the apprentice's work. At several moments, I felt I had more to learn from him than the reverse. Only when [Ayling] began to spend every weekend at Blane did I begin to sense the dread presence of the inadmissible whispering within my studio's walls. [William Powell Frith, *Memoirs, Fourth Volume* (unpublished manuscript in the collection of Houghton Library, Harvard University, n.d.).]

singular approach to painting. However, unlike the Mannheim group, the English circle enjoyed the support of the Haywards' generous patronage, and with the active participation of Gather, Wren, and Shell, the New Tremor was soon creating canvases that outstripped the efforts of the earlier group in their ability to produce powerful and unsettling effects on the viewer.[23]

THE EXHIBITION AT BLANE

In the autumn of 1889, invitations were sent out to select members of London's cultural elite, announcing a private exhibition at Blane that was to showcase the recent efforts of "The New Brotherhood of Das Beben." The exhibition was the brainchild of von Kreitz, who had deemed the time ripe to expose the group's work to the rest of the world.[24] Some sense of the ambitions that the odd community at Blane harbored for the exhibition may be found in a piece of correspondence from Baron Hayward to his cousin Angus MacDonald, who shared many of his proclivities. In a letter dated May 1, 1889, Hayward wrote: "The work of our little group proceeds with a rapidity that has exceeded even my most audacious imaginings. Increasingly, they seem to work as one, like the five fingers of some great Hand; by the close of the year, I feel certain we here at Blane shall be exulting in the dawn of a New Age, a glorious revelation of darkness founded on the purified ruins of the old world."[25]

---

[23]It was after viewing Ayling's then work in progress, *The Gathered Clan*, that Frith was finally forced to dismiss his apprentice:

> I found myself for a moment unable to breathe before the queer monstrosity [*The Gathered Clan*], so greatly did I suffer the sensation that its surface did in some impossible fashion contain movement. I never before in my life endured so pronounced a sensation of wrongness before a work of art. Though it ostensibly depicts a handsome English family, servants, and their hangers-on, the true subject of the painting seemed something altogether *other*: I sensed the approach of a hot wind from some nameless region of torment and despair.

[24]For von Kreitz, the appearance of Jack the Ripper in London's East End constituted some mysterious sign for which he had apparently been waiting. The arrival of the Ripper was a clear indication, von Kreitz told the younger painters, that the grand fabric of the conventional world was slipping and losing coherence. "The Ripper," von Kreitz whispered, "is the palm leaf to our new Jerusalem, the mule on which we shall ride into the transfigured City."

[25]MacDonald took holy orders in 1892 and died four years later of mysterious causes at the Monastery of St. Dunstan, in the words of his confessor Fr. Noyce, "shaking, trembling, crying out in pain, and most grievously beseeching the Lord's mercy."

Three new paintings by von Kreitz himself were to form the central elements of the exhibition, which would include a number of new works by Ayling, Prooder, Heathman, and Turling—among them, Ayling's latest painting, *The Gathered Clan,* a portrait of the Haywards that had been commissioned by the baroness. The exhibition was to be held in Blane's orangery, a large, vaulted space that had been added to the south facade in 1802. Originally designed as a secondary gallery by Baron Hayward's father, the orangery was some hundred feet in length, with six large windows on the exterior wall and fruit-bearing orange trees in planters positioned in the spaces between them.

The exhibition at Blane was to have included the following works: von Kreitz, *The River-Bank, Nightfall, Krankhelm Island, Fog, December, 1867,* and *The Contents of Forthold's General Store, Ebbe, Krankhelm Island, February, 1870;* Turling, *Mrs. Shell, With Shears, Study for A.H.,* and *In Esteemed Company;* Heathman, *Over, Behind, Beneath* and *Rampant;* Prooder, *The Tyranny of Time, The Emperor of the Unseen,* and *Our Lady of Sorrows;* Ayling, *The Gathered Clan.*

Several firsthand accounts of the exhibition from local guests who visited Blane while the work was still being hung refer to a "drastic and impatient" style, a tone that struck most commentators as "angry, even rude," and distortions of perspective that seemed forced and unnatural. "Are these faces, approaching us in the island's fog?" asked a local writer, Benedick Worsthorne. "It is tempting to take these worn, indistinct visages as mere swirls of vapor, or as those of figures more spectral than human." Arnold Trump, a critic from the *Kentishman* who had come by for an early look, wrote, "Mr. von Kreitz drains all substantiality from his paints, leaving us to guess at whatever what strange and ill-meaning symbology lurks upon his canvases. His island's emporium seems empty of all goods but for the mute yet wailing shades they left behind." Of *The River-Bank, Nightfall,* a local clergyman, the Canon Arthur Summerson, had this to say: "Despite the grave innocence of its subject matter, the painting feels like a pasteboard mask, which at any moment threatens to peel away, revealing a terrifying vista of debasement."

Excerpt from *The Art of Rumor's Legends,* Burton Purddry (Calais, Vermont: Ashton Press, 1927):

The eccentricities of von Kreitz's "New Tremor" disciples supposedly extended to the impossibilities of their effects. In their hands—those of Heathman and Ayling, at any rate—objects and persons are said, as had earlier been claimed of paintings by von Kreitz and Klappenburg, to be capable of movement. George Heathman's *Rampant*, a canvas of unusual shape, was described by a servant who assisted in the mounting of the exhibition as "akin to the mail-slot of the greatest post-box ever seen, nearly half a meter in height and two in length." (*Letters from Persons of Various Stations Resident at Blane*, ed. Harald Hayward, Comfort Blanton, 1936.) Across the painting's length was depicted a misty day in a seaside village (thought to be Heathman's hometown, Folkestone); a brisk wind billows a series of tradesmen's awnings bearing the names of various shops. The servant claimed that this painting caused him to feel "all swimmy" whenever he looked at it. Two days after the fire, local writer Arnold Trump, ever the faithful diarist, recorded (in tones of amusement) that an elderly female Hayward relative who was visiting Blane had taken him aside to complain that a "horrid force" had threatened to thrust itself from between the awnings depicted in the painting. "It wishes to be free, and it intends us all great unhappiness!" she claimed.

In Hugo Ayling's *The Gathered Clan*, considered by some to be the finest of the "New Tremor" paintings (and their sole survivor), the Hayward family stands posed before the imposing facade of Blane. Behind and to the left of the family, the uniformed staff stands ranked in a wedge. A good distance to the right of the family, there are four odd people in two equal groups. (Many generations of Haywards had been interested in the occult, and these some of the leading figures of the time.) Between the two groups there is a black-hooded figure, moving forward. The same elderly relative reported to Trump that, overnight, this figure had moved forward by a quarter of an inch, perhaps a bit more, and that its goal was clearly to move out of the painting altogether. It wished to escape into the world, she was certain, where it would manifest the sickness already to be sensed within the surface of the painting. "What is terrible," she told Trump, "is that poor, unwell Mr. Ayling possesses a wondrous talent and his painting would be exceeding beautiful—were it not for the moral illness that corrupts the whole."

Although Ayling's masterpiece does survive, we have no opportunity to determine whether the black-cowled figure has indeed escaped the painting. For more than five decades, *The Gathered Clan* has been locked within a temperature-controlled, light-sensitive vault beneath the Milwaukee Art Museum, the object of an ongoing legal dispute between American factions of the Hayward family.

THE SECOND FIRE

At approximately 12:45 p.m. on Saturday, October 13, 1889, the day after an unofficial reception for the Haywards' inner circle, a fire broke out in the orangery. The "Second Fire," as it came to be known, killed von Kreitz, Prooder, Turling, and Heathman, along with two of the Haywards' servants. It destroyed a third of the house, including the orangery, and consumed the entire collection of Das Beben paintings housed there, with the sole exception of Ayling's *The Gathered Clan.*[26]

Speculation suggested that the blaze might have begun as a result of sunlight, magnified by a pane of glass, falling upon a painter's oily rag left unnoticed behind an easel. (A servant later claimed she had seen "a sort of rainbow" glinting from an upper window of the orangery shortly before the fire.) Whatever the cause, the flames spread almost instantly to the entire row of paintings and onto the wall behind them, proceeding rapidly into the scullery and kitchen, then down the hallway, engulfing the ceiling and rising into the floor above. The entire western half of Blane, some twenty-one rooms, was reduced to a mass of charred beams and twisted metal rising out of the wine cellar. The remains of von Kreitz, Turling, Heathman, and Prooder were eventually found in the ruins of the orangery.

AFTERMATH

In the wake of the disaster, the Haywards and most of their remaining staff returned to London, taking up occupancy in their residence in Eaton Square, where Baron Hayward immediately began drawing up plans for the reconstruction of Blane.

Gather, Wren, and Shell all survived the conflagration. As though warned in advance, the three had returned to London only a few hours before the fire started. Without a ripple, they vanished back into the strange London underworld from which they had emerged.[27]

---

[26]Hugo Ayling owes his survival, and that of *The Gathered Clan*, to the accident of his having fallen asleep beneath his easel on the lawn at the front of the estate, where he had taken the canvas for the purpose of making some final adjustments.

[27]Eight years later Mrs. Shell would reappear as the fiancée of the prominent Conservative politician Lord Auric Twysdon. Her "ageless beauty" was much remarked upon, as was her bewitching charm. Upon the death of her husband in 1905, the wealthy Lady Twysdon removed herself to America, where she was reunited with

Masterless and destitute, Hugo Ayling, the last remaining member of Das Beben, descended quickly into poverty and poor health. In 1894, he was apprehended wandering London's East End, half-naked and incoherent. Deemed mentally unsound by a court physician, Ayling was dispatched to Bethlem Hospital (Bedlam), an institution for the criminally insane. There, as though by some secret joke of fate, he was given the cell previously occupied by the painter and patricide Richard Dadd.[28]

At Bethlem, Ayling painted inoffensive depictions of the sunlight entering his cell through its single windows, remembered landscapes of his childhood, and intricately detailed "portraits," as he called them, of the large, dark individual stones in his cell's walls. Upon release, Ayling moved into the slums and estaminets of South London, where, for the last years of his life, he survived in dire poverty, drawing illustrations for broadsides and works of erotic literature published by Pego Press, Peckham Rye. In the first several years of the twentieth century, he met and briefly became a mentor to the talented but eccentric young painter Austin Osman Spare. It was at some point

---

"Lord" Wren in the city of Climax, Michigan. The pair went on to found Aetherism, an authoritarian religious cult. [Rodney Messner, *We Were Aetheric* (Grand Rapids, Michigan: Sephiroth Publications, 1919).]

[28]Richard Dadd had likely been an influence on von Kreitz and the painters of the New Tremor. Prior to the second fire, von Kreitz had informed Baron Hayward that "chief amongst the works of art to survive into the glorious Dark Age to come" was Dadd's masterpiece, *The Fairy Feller's Master-Stroke.* Von Kreitz had apparently visited Dadd in Bethlem sometime after his arrival in the UK. Curiously, in his former life, Dadd had been an accomplished graduate of the Royal Academy, and a member of "The New Clique" of British painters, along with none other than Hugo Ayling's later employer, William Powell Frith. Von Kreitz also referred to a specific paragraph from Dadd's autobiographical musings upon the great transformative event of his life, a lengthy 1842 tour of Egypt with his patron, Sir Thomas Phillips:

> On my return from travel, I was roused to a consideration of subjects which I had previously never dreamed of, or thought about, connected with self; and I had such ideas that, had I spoken of them openly, I must, if answered in the world's fashion, have been told I was unreasonable. I concealed, of course, these secret admonitions. I knew not whence they came, although I could not question their propriety, nor could I separate myself from what appeared my fate. My religious opinions varied and do vary from the vulgar; I was inclined to fall in with the views of the ancients, and to regard the substitution of modern ideas thereon as not for the better. These and the like, coupled with an idea of a descent from the Egyptian god Osiris ... [Patricia Alleridge, *The Late Richard Dadd: 1817–1866* (London: Tate Gallery, 1974), pp. 22–23.]

"Had Dadd but brought his art into greater alignment with his concealed thoughts and considerations," von Kreitz told the baron, "he would have ended not in a madhouse but on a throne."

during this period that Ayling composed *Thoughts in Motley*, a small chapbook filled with strange and disconnected ramblings.

Ayling followed his brethren of the New Tremor into the darkness sometime between 1905 and 1907 (Spare is said to have paid for his burial). Ayling's single masterpiece, *The Gathered Clan*, was hung in the restored orangery at Blane in 1892. It remained in place until 1910, when it was stolen, along with nearly half the family's valuables, by Baron Hayward's youngest son Haxton, who slipped away with his treasures to America.[29]

CONSIDERING THE INFLUENCE OF DAS BEBEN

It is difficult to determine what sort of yardstick should be used to measure the role that Das Beben played in the history of nineteenth-century painting. The fact of their destruction appears conclusive, and the near complete expunging of their works from the scrutiny of history would seem to preempt the question of any lasting contribution. And yet there have been ripples, subtle echoes in the subsequent course of events in which might be detected some faint whisper of the "hot wind" of which Frith had written. Despite the group's secretive nature and the brevity of its two short appearances on the stage of the nineteenth century, its story does intersect frequently with the lives of better-known figures.[30] Clearly, the handful of artists and writers who had the luck or misfortune of beholding the work of Das Beben firsthand retained an indelible impression of the experience—though what effect these impressions were to have on later developments is hard to say. Considered in the annihilating light of events

[29]According to the *Rice Lake Telegraph* of August 13, 1930, Haxton Hayward was murdered by a never-identified man "in a Stetson hat and box-back coat." Following his death, the painting passed into the hands of his American family, where it spent two decades in the cellar of Robert Hayward's house on North Forty-Fourth Street in Milwaukee. The painting languished in his cellar until it was claimed by his ex-wife, Margaret (Margot) Hayward Mountjoy, who attempted to have it installed in a private art gallery established by her millionaire husband, Harry Mountjoy. Rejected by Mr. Mountjoy as "too bizarre," the painting was given to a cousin, Tillman Hayward, who hung it in the den of his house in Columbus, Ohio. In 1958, Tillman Hayward's wife loaned *The Gathered Clan*—without her husband's knowledge or consent—to the Milwaukee Art Gallery, where, claimed as personal property by both Margot and Tillman in a pair of contesting lawsuits, it has remained locked in storage ever since, unseen.
[30]Franz Marc (1880–1916), one of the founders of the Blaue Reiter group, had heard tales of von Kreitz from his father, Wilhelm Marc, a landscape painter briefly under his spell. In his unpublished autobiography, *Fruchtbares Leben eines Kunstlers*, the elder

that would soon be ushered into the world with the arrival of the twentieth century, it becomes harder not to entertain the notion—if only for a moment—that perhaps Das Beben had, through some undreamt-of manner, at least partially succeeded in its goals.

One passage in Ayling's otherwise indecipherable book offers a possibly prophetic glimpse of what was to come: "There shall be Wildness, and Colours wrested out of nature & tortured & whipped to their extremes into an extremity of Expression, and there shall be a Torment of Shapes depicted that have no names, but only Colours, and there shall be Images of pure Colour, intense and blazing Colour, Colour floating upon the Void, a blazing Light that Consumes all it touches. In all of these shapes and torments I see the hand of that demon, von Kreitz."

Marc describes "the many occasions [when] I told my art-smitten little boy of my few but profound meetings with Master von Kreitz, both in Mannheim and Munich, the cities where I sought him out. I was never a philosopher, and much of what the great painter told me I did not have the capacity to understand. Of contradiction, which he found essential to 'true sight,' his master goal and central teaching, I grasped little. Yet I believed wholeheartedly with him that painting of such true sight would be capable of altering in some way the material of fact. *Any person who has been stirred to tears when beholding a great and speaking work of art knows this to be true.*"

363

NOTES ON CONTRIBUTORS

RAE ARMANTROUT's most recent collection, *Itself*, was published by Wesleyan University Press in 2015. Her book *Just Saying* (Wesleyan) has appeared in Italian translation on *stampato presso*.

GABRIEL BLACKWELL is the author of *Critique of Pure Reason* (Noemi) and the novels *The Natural Dissolution of Fleeting-Improvised-Men* and *Shadow Man* (both CCM). With Matthew Olzmann, he edits *The Collagist*.

Longtime *Conjunctions* contributor CAN XUE has been short-listed for the prestigious Neustadt International Prize for Literature for 2016, and received the 2015 Best Translated Book Award for *The Last Lover*. Her story in this issue is from her novella *Story of the Slums*.

With Karen Gernant, CHEN ZEPING has cotranslated works of contemporary Chinese fiction, including Can Xue's *Blue Light in the Sky and Other Stories* (New Directions), *Five Spice Street* (Yale University Press), *Vertical Motion* (Open Letter), and *Frontier* (forthcoming from Open Letter).

SUSAN DAITCH is the author of three novels and a collection of short stories. Her fourth novel, *The Lost Civilization of Suolucidir*, will be published by City Lights in the spring of 2016.

DESIREE DES (desireedes.com) is a New York–based artist who examines her environment through photography, found objects, and her community. The recipient of the Institute for Electronic Art Print Media Residency, she is currently in the Studio Art MFA program at Hunter College.

ANTHONY DISCENZA is a visual artist based in the San Francisco Bay area. His collaboration with Peter Straub in this issue marks his first appearance in print.

MARGARET FISHER is the author of *Ezra Pound's Radio Operas: The BBC Experiments* (MIT) and *The Recovery of Ezra Pound's Third Opera, Collis O Heliconii*, and the coauthor and translator of *RADIA, a Gloss of the 1933 Futurist Radio Manifesto by Pino Masnata* (both Second Evening Art). With composer Robert Hughes, she directs the production group MAFISHCO (www.mafishco.com), based in Emeryville, CA.

KAREN GERNANT's recent cotranslations, with Chen Zeping, of short stories by Can Xue include "Shadow People" (published in *Pathlight*), "The Old Cicada" (*Words Without Borders*), "Crow Mountain" (*Asymptote*), and "The Swamp" (forthcoming in *Ninth Letter*).

ARIELLE GREENBERG's newest book is the poetry collection *Slice* (Coconut). The nonfiction work *Locally Made Panties* (Ricochet) and the revised, electronic edition of the *Gurlesque* anthology (Saturnalia, coedited with Lara Glenum and Becca Klaver) are forthcoming in 2016.

PAUL HOOVER is the editor of *Postmodern American Poetry: A Norton Anthology* and the literary magazine *New American Writing*. His most recent book is *desolation : souvenir* (Omnidawn). A new volume, *The Book of Unnamed Things*, is forthcoming from Apogee.

POROCHISTA KHAKPOUR is the author of the novels *Sons and Other Flammable Objects* (Grove Atlantic) and *The Last Illusion* (Bloomsbury). Her memoir *Sick* is forthcoming from Harper Perennial in 2017.

EDIE MEIDAV is the author of the novels *The Far Field: A Novel of Ceylon* (Houghton Mifflin/Mariner), *Crawl Space* (FSG/Picador), *Lola, California* (FSG/Picador), and the forthcoming *Dogs of Cuba*. She teaches in the MFA program of the University of Massachusetts-Amherst.

GWYNETH MERNER's work previously appeared in *Conjunctions:61, A Menagerie*. She lives in Western Massachusetts.

JAMES MORROW is the author of ten novels, including the Godhead Trilogy (Harcourt), *The Last Witchfinder* (William Morrow), and *Galápagos Regained* (St. Martin's Press). He has received the World Fantasy Award, the Nebula Award, and the Grand Prix de l'Imaginaire.

ANDREW MOSSIN is the author of the poetry collections *The Epochal Body* and *The Veil* (both Singing Horse), as well as *Male Subjectivity and Poetic Form in "New American" Poetry* (Palgrave Macmillan), a book of criticism. He has recently completed two new manuscripts, *The Torture Papers* and *Through the Rivers: A Memoir of Theft*, portions of each of which were first published in *Conjunctions*.

YANNICK MURPHY is the author of *This Is the Water* and *The Call* (both Harper Perennial), *Signed, Mata Hari* (Little Brown & Co.), *Here They Come* (McSweeney's), *The Sea of Trees* (Houghton Mifflin), *In a Bear's Eye* (Dzanc), and *Stories in Another Language* (Alfred A. Knopf).

JOYCE CAROL OATES's most recent book is *The Lost Landscape: A Writer's Coming of Age* (Ecco), a portion of which, originally published in *Conjunctions:63, Speaking Volumes*, was awarded a Pushcart Prize. She is a recipient of the President's Medal for the Humanities and is currently a visiting distinguished writer in the graduate writing program at New York University.

BIN RAMKE's most recent book is *Missing the Moon* (Omnidawn). He teaches at the University of Denver and the School of the Art Institute of Chicago and is the poetry editor of *Denver Quarterly*.

MICHAEL MARTIN SHEA is the managing editor of the *Best American Experimental Writing* anthology (Wesleyan University Press). His poems have appeared or are forthcoming in *Colorado Review, Jubilat,* and elsewhere.

AURELIE SHEEHAN is the author of two novels and three story collections, including *Jewelry Box: A Collection of Histories* (BOA).

MICHAEL SHEEHAN teaches creative writing at Stephen F. Austin State University. His work has appeared previously in *Conjunctions,* as well as in *Black Warrior Review, The Collagist,* and elsewhere.

ELENI SIKELIANOS is the author of seven books of poetry and two hybrid memoirs, most recently *You Animal Machine* and *The Loving Detail of the Living & the Dead* (both Coffee House). Her poems in this issue are from *Make Yourself Happy,* forthcoming from Coffee House.

PETER STRAUB has written seventeen novels and three collections of shorter fiction. *Interior Darkness: Selected Stories* will be published by Doubleday in February 2016.

TERESE SVOBODA's most recent novel is *Bohemian Girl* (Bison). *When the Next Big War Blows Down the Valley: Selected and New Poems, 1985–2015* (Anhinga) will appear in November, and *Anything That Burns You: A Portrait of Lola Ridge, Radical Poet* (Schaffner) in January 2016.

LAURA VAN DEN BERG is the author of the novel *Find Me* (FSG) and the story collections *What the World Will Look Like When All the Water Leaves Us* (Dzanc) and *The Isle of Youth* (FSG), the last of which won the Bard Fiction Prize, the Rosenthal Award from the American Academy of Arts and Letters, and the Jeannette Haien Ballard Writer's Prize.

PAUL WEST's most recent books are *The Ice Lens, The Invisible Riviera,* and *Red in Tooth and Claw* (all Onager).

MAGDALENA ZYZAK is the author of *The Ballad of Barnabas Pierkiel* (Henry Holt). She produced and cowrote the feature film *Redland* and is currently in production on her directorial debut, *Shipwreck on a Hillside,* a feature film about poets.

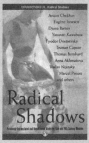
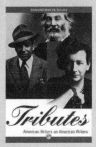

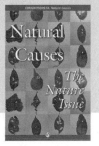

Façade remains.   Two men came to an
intersection.   One was blind and
accompanied by his seeing-eye dog.
               While they waited for the light to
change, dog pissed on his master's leg.
               Blind man then fed dog some beef.   Other
man said : "Why reward 'im?   (Pissed on
               your leg.)   "I'm not rewarding 'im.   I'm
finding out where his head is so I can
               kick him in the ass."   *Paper should be
edible, nutritious.   Inks used for
printing or writing should have
delicious flavors.   Magazines or
newspapers read at* **breakfast should be
               eaten for lunch.   Instead of throwing
one's mail in the waste-basket, it
should be saved** *for the dinner guests.*

BlazeV⬤X 15

CELEBRATING 15 YEARS

Anne Tardos
Nine

Dennis Etzel, Jr
My Secret Wars of 1984

C. Kubasta
All Beautiful & Useless

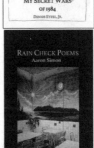

Aaron Simon
Rain Check Poems

Emily Anderson
Little: Novels

Kristina Marie Darling
Women and Ghosts

Geoffrey Gatza
Apollo, A Ballet
Starring Marcel Duchamp

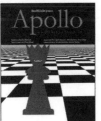

Ruth Danon
Limitless Tiny Boat

WWW.BLAZEVOX.ORG

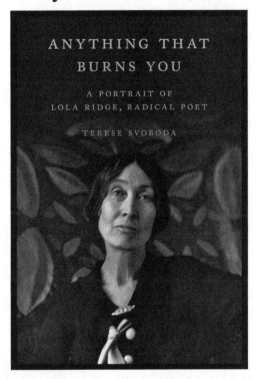

BROWN UNIVERSITY LITERARY ARTS

HOME FOR INNOVATIVE WRITERS

Program faculty

Hisham Bizri
John Cayley
Brian Evenson
Thalia Field
Forrest Gander
Carole Maso
Meredith Steinbach
Cole Swensen
CD Wright

Visiting and other faculty

Andrew Colarusso
Joanna Howard
Nancy Kuhl
Gale Nelson

Since 1970, Literary Arts at Brown University has been fostering innovation and creation. To learn more about the two-year MFA program, visit us at http://www.brown.edu/cw

ONLINE MFA APPLICATION DEADLINE: 15 DECEMBER

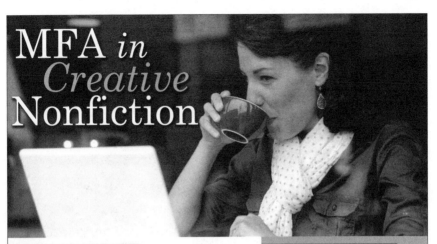

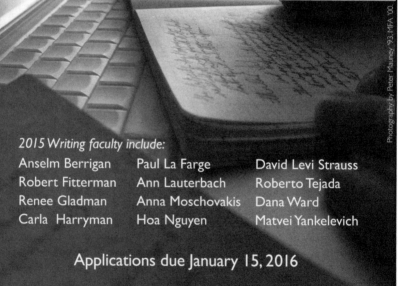

OPERA · THEATER · DANCE · MUSIC · FILM · SPIEGELTENT · THE BARD MUSIC FESTIVAL

BARDSUMMERSCAPE

JULY–AUGUST 2016

Highlights include

Pietro Mascagni's opera *Iris*
Friday, July 22 – Sunday, July 31

The 27th Bard Music Festival, *Puccini and His World*

WEEKEND ONE
Friday, August 5 – Sunday, August 7

WEEKEND TWO
Friday, August 12 – Sunday, August 14

845-758-7900 | fishercenter.bard.edu

Giacomo Puccini, n.d. Alinari/Bridgeman Images

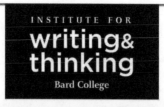

IWT WORKSHOPS AT BARD COLLEGE

March 11, 2016
Curriculum Conversation
Shakespeare's *Othello*: Masks of Deception

Shakespeare's Othello, written approximately in 1603, is a play that continues to hold center stage in many classrooms today. Perhaps this is because Othello wrestles with themes that are still very much a part of our lives: racism, treachery, jealousy, revenge, and love (among others). In Act I, Scene III, Iago says, "Tis in ourselves that we are thus or thus," reminding readers that as humans, we are ultimately responsible for our own experiences and have the power to control our own actions. Yet more often than not, the characters in this play behave in ways that cause pain, violence, and heartbreak.

IWT Curriculum Conversations foster innovative approaches to teaching and reading texts that contribute to our contemporary sense of an evolving self. Using writing-to-learn strategies, the day's workshops will focus on Othello and encourage participants to investigate a variety of questions and topics including:
- The origins and rituals of violence and male bonding in the urban culture of Renaissance Italy
- Contemporary adaptations of Othello—Just how much "contemporary" is too much
- Bringing the work of the workshop into our classrooms and to other plays and literature.

April 22, 2016 | April Conference
The Difficulty with Poetry: Opacity, and Implication in Poetry Old & New

A decade ago, Charles Bernstein wittily outlined the telltale "symptoms" of the difficult poem: "high syntactic, grammatical, or intellectual activity level; elevated linguistic intensity...[and a] negative mood." In workshops that put contemporary poets—Ann Lauterbach, Claudia Rankine, Anne Carson, and others—in conversation with those typically taught in high school curricula, participants will explore how poets communicate ideas and complex emotions. We will also examine poetry that crosses boundaries of literary collage, blog, graphic art, and podcast. An on-site reading and panel will feature poets from a special themed e-edition of Conjunctions, Bard College's renowned literary

READ TO LIVE

GOOD WRITING CAN CHANGE THE WORLD.

GREAT WRITING CREATES IT.

PEN AMERICA

A JOURNAL FOR WRITERS AND READERS

ISSUE #18: IN TRANSIT

FEATURING CONVERSATIONS, ESSAYS, FICTION, POETRY, AND ART BY

LYDIA DAVIS	MANA NEYASTANI	FRANK BIDART
XIAOLU GUO	OSAMA ALOMAR	JUSTIN VIVIAN BOND
JUDITH BUTLER	ANTHONY MARRA	and many more...

www.PEN.org/journal

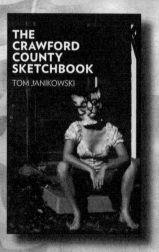

THE CRAWFORD COUNTY SKETCHBOOK

A Novel by Tom Janikowski

ISBN 978-1-59709-533-4 / $15.95 / Aug 15th

The Switchback family has inhabited Crawford County since before the War Between the States, and it has eked out an existence, and even prospered, by virtue of hard work and honesty. The Morgan family has been in Crawford County at least as long as the Switchbacks, and has made its way in the world by means of greed, pride, and dishonesty. Like their ancestors, the Morgans are avowed enemies of the Switchback family and all that they stand for.

The life of Crawford County plays out through the course of short tales told by several of its inhabitants, some tragic, some whimsical. The stories wind their way through the lives of Switchback and Morgan, framed by several ponderings of moral philosophy and existence. We are faced with Peter Switchback's obituary on the opening page of the story, and the balance of the pages works its way to that eventual outcome.

"Grotesque tales of the struggle between good and evil from a dark corner of the American heartland. Poet and surrealist Janikowski (*A Martini and a Pen*, 2014, etc.) does his best Faulkner impression here, using a blend of baroque Southern classicism and redneck patois to fuel a portrait of his fictional Crawford County, a character-rich settlement somewhere in the rural South. . . . The novel's exaggerated portrayals, distorted narrative threads, and flamboyant brand of Southern Gothic will ring the bells of a certain literary-minded audience."

—*Kirkus Reviews*

  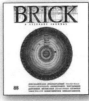

book culture

Book Culture
536 W 112th

Book Culture on Broadway
2915 Broadway at W 114th

Book Culture on Columbus
450 Columbus Ave at W 81st

www.bookculture.com

100% local & independent bookstore with three locations, serving New York City for nearly 20 years

CONJUNCTIONS:57

KIN

Edited by
Bradford Morrow

"These fictions, essays, and poems address the familial bond from a variety of angles. A mother takes her boys sledding while contemplating the mysteries of the numerological universe. A daughter crosses over to the afterlife, where she encounters both her mother and herself. An adopted boy given to delinquency examines the naive love his suicidal mother has for his distant father. An uncle begins a process of mythic transmogrification. An urban father protects his young daughter from cranks and characters on the subway, even as he begins to realize he cannot shield her forever. A suburban mother who is losing her teenage daughter to a dangerous high school friend drugs the girl and herself in order to share a desperate moment of togetherness."—Editor's Note

In *Kin*, twenty-eight poets, fiction writers, and memoirists unweave the tangled knot of family ties. Contributors include Karen Russell, Rick Moody, Rae Armantrout, Octavio Paz, Ann Beattie, Peter Orner, Joyce Carol Oates, Miranda Mellis, Can Xue, Georges-Olivier Châteaureynaud, Elizabeth Hand, and many others.

Conjunctions. Charting the course of literature for over 25 years.

CONJUNCTIONS
Edited by Bradford Morrow
Published by Bard College
Annandale-on-Hudson, NY 12504

To purchase this or any other back issue,
visit our secure ordering page at www.conjunctions.com.
Contact us at conjunctions@bard.edu or (845) 758-7054
with questions.